Praise for *A Most Unfortune*

"While the author drops in a couple of shocking moments in the story's latter half, he skilfully retains a slow burn all the way until the smashing conclusion… An exceptional, edgy tale with convincing plot turns and a well-incorporated wartime setting." – *Kirkus Reviews*.

Other novels by Ed Crutchley

The Black Carriage
Bad Days in Broadacre
Hummingbird
Procession
Iliba Unravels

A Most Unfortunate Affair

Ed Crutchley

Summary

The arrival of Captain Quinn, an inexperienced and reckless intelligence officer, disrupts the delicate equilibrium of a WW1 battalion in northern France. He and Captain Michael 'Moose' Cody, one of the company commanders, discover themselves rivals in both their professional and personal lives. As their intensifying feud stumbles towards an inextricable ending, which one of them will survive?

The Author

Ed Crutchley was born in Cambridge, England, in 1950. He has worked for over forty years in manufacturing, mostly in France and the United States, where he managed factories, worked in innovation, and was a consultant. His non-fiction includes a book about patents, of which he has several himself, and his grandfather's diaries from 1930s Australia. His novels, six so far, revolve around escapades with streaks of surrealism. He is married, has one son, and lives with his wife in Kent, England.

Dedication

To Eugenie and James

Author's Note

This story is entirely fictional. Any similarities between the characters portrayed and people living, or dead, are unintended.

1

The 10th (Service) Battalion's new intelligence officer, the young, tall and square-jawed Captain Quinn, had nothing for the brigadier's visit scheduled for that afternoon. Woken up far too early by the nightly ammunition cart, and recovering from yet another meandering nightmare, he saw the world as moribund.

He panicked. He couldn't get back to sleep. Ever since his arrival at the front, his daily reports to the colonel had been little more than blank sheets of paper. Patience had already been wearing thin. The brigadier's visit would be the last straw. Quinn had to conjure up something to keep his job.

He had a tent to himself. He had been sleeping fully clothed, leg wraps and all, to be on the alert. It was once again raining outside, and now the merciless pounding on the canvas prevented him from concentrating.

He got up and poked his head out into the dark November night. The torrential rain soaked his blond hair. He saw the lights remained extinguished in the headquarters cabin just opposite, and in the tents of the other officers and mess nearby. Even if he had wanted someone to talk to, the colonel, major, and four company commanders had left for brigade.

He went back to his table and lit the oil lamp. He had books and one or two magazines. Perhaps he could try to read. He looked up at the overhead canvas being pummelled. What on God's earth had he done to land up in such a cursed place?

He had a problem to resolve. He decided he had to be on the move. Putting on his Burberry and waders, grabbing his helmet and periscope, and storing away his precious hip flask, he set out for the firing line for an early pre-dawn inspection.

He headed for the only tree in the neighbourhood, long become leafless, marking the way to the trenches. He thought how stupid it was to have left such a target standing. Rainwater was noisily cascading through its vacated branches, flooding the ground below.

He realised he had forgotten his map. He turned to go back until he remembered regulations against taking such documents into the trenches. Puddles all along his way were merging, disguising lethal potholes galore.

He passed the ammunition pile that had just been replenished with fresh crates. It was protected by a tied-down tarpaulin gathering water. He doubted that anything untoward would break out under such appalling conditions. The meeting of his fellow officers at brigade had to be just to keep them all busy.

The trenches were nearing. He felt different each time he approached, more alert, more feral. He duly adopted his dislikable swagger that a year of intense military training had failed to suppress. It would help condition his mind. He would go hunting for the propitious opportunity he so desperately needed.

He descended below level into the abject rat-infested labyrinth of filth and debris presently being drenched yet again. At least it was getting a dousing. As he swaggered through the hellish network of communication trenches, some on which the wattle was disintegrating in front of walls slowly being washed away, he remembered by instinct each of the twists and turns that he had negotiated in the dark dozens of times already. He felt reassured. This had become his lair, his fusty paradise, his den of turpitude. Careless construction meant that in places, waterfalls were pouring over both sides of the trench.

He passed the silent shadows of men in capes reluctantly emerging from their funk holes, rifle breeches protected from the mud with canvas, bayonets permanently fixed, as was the rule. Out of sheer boredom, a few men were preparing for the upcoming stand to and inspection by their NCOs, but it would be awhile yet. Others were stealing a quick wash and shave with the remaining time available, helping themselves to the nearest water barrel before it emptied. No-one, it seemed, had thought of harvesting the rain.

With no faces to recognise, or signposts that could be read, he felt like one of the rats that followed everyone around for chocolate. He brushed one of the hanging sack cloths that served for rubbish. They were always torn and overflowing. How men loved the squalor. It seemed to satisfy their basic instincts. It certainly did his.

To those who bothered to look up and notice, Quinn cut a lonely figure. In that respect, he was far from alone. All around him reigned an air of depressed resignation, peevish men struggling to recognise themselves, let alone each other, as alive, exhausted and on edge from lack of sleep, unable to pray for the end of their seventy-two-hour tour in the three-hundred-yard line held by the battalion. This was not the way to conduct a war.

And events had yet to begin. Things were about to get worse with daylight. The approaching sunrise, desecrated by inundation, would herald yet another day of work-party drudgery. There would be the draining and revetting of waterlogged trenches for the umpteenth time, the caved-in walls to resuscitate. There would also be the ratting, chasing and beating to death any of the bastards that hadn't already been drowned or entrapped by falls. Much as it appealed to certain instincts, it was not what anyone had enlisted for.

"Ducking weather!" Quinn heard as he passed unrecognised.

"I doubt it," he said.

Mercifully, he was only a commander for that night. None of this appalling mess was his problem. His sole concern was reading the real enemy, presently entrenched not even two hundred yards away, and no doubt identically challenged. And that swung back to his problem. There would be nothing to report. It would be yet another day of trying to survive the *intemperies* as the locals so aptly called them. The rain put paid to the use of gas, and the nefarious effects of any explosive bombs, shells, or mortars would be severely dampened by the waterlogged ground. And if the enemy ever dared to cross the channel of mud that separated the opposing lines, he would be slowed down enough to be picked off at will. The war was on hold.

He swaggered along all the same. He thought of trench warfare of the past, mostly in much warmer places. With trench foot finally defeated, perhaps even this was better than pestilence, scorpions and drought elsewhere. He wondered how he would look back at it in later life. He thought of his father, condemned to having to keep talking about his past experiences just to stay sane.

Where the duckboard ran out, he found himself humiliatingly knee-deep in mud. No-one looked up. He would make a fool of himself all alone, just as everyone from orderly to general did every day. In this quagmire men were together but alone, surrounded by indifference worthy of Piccadilly Circus, a distant oasis, so oddly the object of so much reminiscence. At least it was still dark. At least there could still be dreams.

His horribly slow progress only served to remind him of the lonely purgatory in which he had found himself. It had been two weeks already, ages on a front where bodies were counted dozens of times faster than days. He had been told that it had been Brigadier Lightfoot himself who had imposed him on the battalion. He had followed an intermediate corporal, who had followed the ineffective Major Hickman. He had yet to make an impression on the fastidious Colonel Wilkes, not to mention the four company commanders who stolidly kept their distance.

The timing of his arrival had been inopportune. The spell of weather-enforced inactivity had contrasted with the Indian summer of bloodshed that had eclipsed just before his arrival. Despite the mousetrap remaining sprung, each of the enemy's presumed mortar positions pinpointed and assigned a code word for waiting artillery, there had been nothing to report for days, not a whimper, not even a single sighting of movement in the hostile trench so dangerously close. The rain had pervaded. Not even the absence of wire entanglements in so many key places, nor, for that matter, the lack of the brigadier's favourite v-shaped ditches, wire-filled and artillery-proof, had shown signs of enticing a hostile advance. There had not been as much as a whisper from the listening posts, no hint of mine work that might send the battalion sky high and land it homogenised, assigned to history.

The unrequested respite, the enforced calm in hostilities, had only encouraged paranoia, including Quinn's own. Everyone had waited for an unpleasant surprise in order to blame the new boy. Quinn was in danger of being written down for good.

"Good morning, Captain!" came a Glaswegian accent.

Quinn recognised the voice of one of his snipers headed for the rear, no doubt to the latrines. He scowled. He wondered yet again why the man hadn't signed up with one of the regiments where people might have understood him. It was bad enough interpreting voices from Kent and Dorset.

"Nothing happening, I suppose?" he called back in his polished accent, hoping to comprehend the answer.

The man only shook his head and struggled on in the dark. Quinn wondered why he had chosen to waste his time. Everyone and everything had ganged up against him. He was at a metaphorical dead end, hemmed in and castrated. The infernal rain and mud had to be telling him something. Had he been a religious man, like most of the battalion, he would have suspected the message to desist. His father had always insisted that problems made people happy. It had become his turn. He had to find a way to take his predicament to the enemy.

There was a timely flash and roll of thunder. Quinn had an epiphany as he kept glancing back to follow the shadow of the Scotsman disappear. Out of despair had arrived salvation. The way forward was to make something happen, test the enemy, force events himself, do his pitiful masters' jobs for them.

"Precisely because I have nothing must mean something," he concluded to himself as he prepared to move on.

Resuming his increasingly difficult swagger, six muddy feet below ground, Quinn strained to lift his pace. So did the rain, but it no longer mattered. It was time for change. Inspired after the brief encounter with his sniper, he too would leave the load of yesterday behind. He had become sanguine. Now he would make history.

Passing alleys leading off to bombing posts and a covered dressing station, Quinn finally reached the fire trench. Its occupants were maintaining the obligatory silence. Leaning against the side, he pulled each leg out of the liquid mud in order to advance, straining to maintain his air of confidence. It was almost two feet deep. Yet if anyone had cared or been able to study the expression on his face in those very first traces of daylight, they would have detected its gradual brightening. Quinn was headed for the only friends he had.

He wasn't there yet. The Lewis gun post took no notice as both men tried to decipher shadows through their respective loopholes, an exercise that had long rendered them ineffective. Beyond the next traverse was the shallow sap leading to a listening post. Quinn waited there for a few seconds, but nothing seemed to happen, and the sentry confirmed it with a shrug. He moved on. A mortar team, lodged in a recess further along, stood with their backs to the wall, eagerly keeping an eye out for iron rations in the downpour, the first of their four-thousand-calorie-a-day regime that would mark the end of the stand to. They would have to wait for quite a while yet.

There was another turn in the crenulated trench. Quinn was at last gazing at the only place where he would be welcomed, his goal, the fire steps occupied by his snipers, his motley bunch of precision killers, delighted to find themselves so coddled at last. These were men to whom he didn't have to prove himself. They were aliens to him, and yet they praised the ground he stood on. In their presence, he metamorphosed in turn, revealing a quite particular gift of leadership unseen by anyone else.

The snipers constituted Quinn's first command. By order of the brigadier there were many fewer under him than was normally the case, only a dozen, so that the team could remain flexible and efficient. Each of the company commanders had kept their own, a situation that both they and the brigadier preferred.

As soon as he had arrived, Quinn had started to work on his team, locking out the colonel who had taken up the habit of spending his spare hours alongside them bagging trophies. The men, who had already been taciturn by nature, had been nurtured in no time at all.

Quinn had convinced them how much they were special, why they should behave differently, how they were a skilled band among very ordinary men, masons of their art. From the very first day, he had encouraged them to be distant and mysterious, to feel elite, to live and breathe the furtive role that they had been assigned to. The snipers had responded as he intended. They became in thrall of him. They stuck together more than ever. They walked around camp and along trenches with mean stares directed towards anyone who looked in their direction. They emphasised their difference, shunning any reaching out, flaunting their skills. They even started to swagger like their master. And the entire 10th Battalion had begun to notice.

"Morning, Captain," the first of the snipers whispered, a cockney this one, looking away from his rifle periscope as much to alert his colleagues as to show respect.

"Anything to report, Schemensky?"

The gaunt man in the ghillie suit swung around.

"Not a *wurst!*" he mouthed as he held out an arm to help him out of the mud.

Quinn hauled himself up beside the man with a prominently pointed chin who had boasted a brace two weeks before. He raised his periscope over the parapet to see for himself and waved it about. The enemy would at least take note. His crew, meanwhile, continued to do what they had already been doing for hours, exhausting themselves by peering through their line of loopholes into the emptiness beyond, at last beginning to receive its first dose of daylight. Objects were taking full shape.

Steadying himself on the elbow rest, Quinn scanned several times from left to right and back again. The tree stumps, that moments ago had been shadowy adversaries, were becoming tree stumps again. The football goal posts that bizarrely stood there on their own had re-become goal posts. No-one was out there after all.

Alive, that is. That thought reminded Quinn of the man who had preceded him, a mere corporal, the appointee of the reluctant colonel already under pressure. He had achieved nothing more than a death that would forever make his descendants proud. The reality was that his rotting corpse was lying somewhere out there, blown to smithereens, and no doubt repeatedly desecrated by stray fire ever since. As far as the battalion was concerned, the pathetic man had become one more forgotten part of its history, yet another wasted life. And unforgivably, the condemned corporal had left his snipers as meek as mice. Quinn would never allow himself such a legacy. One way or another, he would leave a fingerprint on events to come, make his team feared and formidable. Most of all, he would better by far his infernal father's over-recounted exploits from just over a decade and a half before.

Quinn looked up at the sky and squinted in the rain. He pictured his emaciated old man, the enfeebled sun-drenched general, creams, lotions and medicines having become his favoured company. He would bark away, exploiting his deafness to pretend he couldn't hear, as he lay in bed in his woolly hat and thick socks, his stomach filled to the brim with cheese to get to sleep, which he never could, the same thing he tried every night. How Quinn detested the bully. How his atrophied state sickened him. He didn't believe a smidgeon of his stories about South Africa. It was not where Quinn ever wanted to be. And with what he presently had in mind, the result of an unassailable determination, the surrounding scene presented his very first opportunity to prove himself better. He kept his calm. He said nothing. He continued to scan patiently, left to right, right to left, and left to right again.

He wondered if rats crossed the lines. Birds certainly did. Their cacophony had already begun.

He snapped to his senses. There was once again absolutely nothing useful to see. Supposing the enemy wasn't there, after all? Supposing they had got wind of the upcoming attack being dreamed up at brigade, and made a tactical withdrawal? Was the battalion staring blindly at a golden opportunity? It certainly seemed so.

He reflected on the overall situation. The trench formation was as it had been for a month. The maps hadn't needed retouching, even by hand. The battalion had been sent up to the same *wurstless* scene so many times already. Front-line duty had become perilously routine and eventless. All men thought of, while they manned the firing line at night, was food, the end of their two-hour watch and unmolested sleep to follow it, any morning off because of night duty, and the pleasure of a midnight march back to camp after a dangerous relief. Where were the warriors in them? What had happened to their hunger for glory?

Quinn had yet to experience his baptism of fire. The loss of his predecessor, three weeks before, had accompanied the last action of any note. The weather had turned. A trickle of conscripts had replaced a mere third of the casualties. The occasional humourless exchanges of fire that followed had ceased altogether. The boredom had accentuated the antagonism Quinn encountered as the bearer of no news. He had grown to hate the deployment every seventy-two hours, during which he found himself increasingly ostracised, the fate of an empty-handed messenger. All that remained was the pleasure of joining his tiny band of front-line men three or four times a day. They had become his life, his only refuge.

Quinn continued to scan silently alongside his men. He too had memorised every square foot, every feature within sight, the rocks, the stumps, the shell holes, the lifeless traces of the enemy line, the anonymous cadavers in front of it. It was all a question of potential, a built-up energy waiting to be freed. He thought about the powerful battalion entrenched behind him, its rock-hard men, equipment and arms, and of what it might be capable.

Why was nothing happening? All the commanders could do was talk, plan, and debate things that might never happen, just like right then at brigade. The colonel should have long ago ordered more patrols, tempted the enemy to show himself and his own potential. The brigadier should have insisted. Quinn had already hinted as much, many times. The battalion was on the back foot, sclerotic, wasted, scandalously steeped in torpor, reduced to only thinking of its survival, of sitting out its war.

There wasn't a moment to lose. He knew it. The men had become so bored that they had resorted to *n'importe quoi*. A few of them had spent most of the day before perfecting handmade rakes in order to compete pulling in a severed hand with a ring on it, a prize washed by the rain that had glittered during the rare bouts of sunshine. Underemployed battle-hardened men were well on the road to becoming a danger unto themselves, their minds descending into a spiral of self-destruction. If the enemy ever took the initiative, the battalion could pay dearly.

Quinn pulled away and looked down the line, all the way to the next turn. Silence except for the rain. Right now, he had a rare opportunity to do something. He stood poised. The seedy clique around him took notice.

2

It was an ominous situation. Because of the absence of Captain Cody, the inexperienced Captain Quinn had been put in temporary charge of the hundred and fifty men of C Company manning the front line. He had conducted his very first company meeting just after dusk and thought it had gone well. And because of the exceptional absence of the colonel, major, and three other commanders, Quinn had by default become the senior officer present. Whether the colonel had intended it, that gave him lien over what remained of the battalion.

Quinn had already grown disdain for Colonel Wilkes. His unhealthy-looking red face, raspy voice and tendency to rush around nervously, were not the hallmarks of a good leader. He reminded him too much of his father, impetuous, too ready to give an order, especially one Quinn often regarded as poorly thought-through.

He recalled the colonel's parting instructions to avoid initiative at all costs, stay put, hunker down and repel if necessary. Any distress flares, he had asserted, would be seen from brigade. But the brigade was miles away. This was an exceptional opportunity, one that Quinn could never have expected. With his superior intelligence, he would exploit it to the full.

He braced himself to bite the hand that fed him, show it a lesson and give the battalion a success at last. He climbed down into the mud and swaggered back to the junction with the communication trench, Devil's Corner, as it was called.

"Corporal Jones! A patrol if you please!"

The sound of his voice raised more than a few eyebrows. No-one ever called out in the firing line unless there was an attack.

The tall, serious, and assiduous Jones, a welder in civilian life, had to be nearby. A deeply religious man and as respectful of authority, he would be more compliant than his platoon leader further down the line. Confronted with an instruction to mobilise, he would never stand on ceremony or insist that his men be endlessly pre-tasked. Obedience was in his blood.

Bodies, supposedly at the ready, came to life. Everyone already had their boots on, as was the rule. Their heads were covered in cap comforters under their helmets. Putting their box respirators and helmets aside, they pulled the comforters over their faces and reached for their rifles and usual accessories. They lowered themselves into the deep mud and dragged themselves through it towards Quinn. Sure enough, the tall Jones appeared among them, somehow managing the hard work more effectively than his men. Despite being annoyed by the interruption as he was about to inspect their rifles and gas masks, he said nothing.

"Fancy a stroll, Jones? As you are?"

Jones understood what that meant. He would have preferred a clear order in normal English, but from such an obviously inexperienced toff that was a tall order. He began to make a gesture in the sense that perhaps he should inform Lieutenant Piggot but realised the futility of it in time. After telling his men to help themselves to bombs and rifle grenades, the crates of which had been aligned opposite the fire step, he followed Quinn back to the snipers and beckoned his men to close in behind him. One by one, they hauled each other up to the ledge for the impromptu jump off.

Jones had done this hundreds of times before. He was one of the battalion's most successful patrol leaders, and his men proven grenadiers. It gave him pride. It also meant that he perpetually found himself one of the first called, which wasn't always fair.

But Jones was hesitant. Nowadays, patrols only went out after cautious preparation. There were carefully developed rules to follow, a chain of command to respect, hours or even days of cogitation and endlessly revised objectives, aerial photographs and latest reports to study, crawling suits and bandoliers to distribute and don. For a start, waders were left back in the trench. There was no spare flare gun to hand, no Lewis gunner to accompany them, or wire cutters. They had not agreed on a password with the sentries or removed their badges and discs. This didn't look right at all, but the captain's orders had to be obeyed without quibble.

The rain had subsided into an intermittent, wind-swept drizzle. Quinn organised runners in each direction to warn the lookouts, but that was all. Leaving his precious snipers in place, even though they were best disguised for infiltration, he drew his revolver and climbed over first, right away feeling the cold on his chest that had just been dampened by the side of the trench.

Before they followed, Jones ordered his men to put a round in their barrels and engage their safeties. After putting on their gloves, they went over, at once regretting the motherly security that their trench had offered them.

Quinn, buttoning up his coat, led the party of ten out into the drenched no-man's-land, zig-zagging through the entanglements in front of them, and skirting any shell holes in order to make progress. They kept low so as not to be visible to the machine gun post over the rise in the woods to their right. Jones, slightly ahead of his men, kept looking left and right. He repeatedly motioned to his men to spread themselves out a little more. They glanced down into the large crater to their left, where most believed Quinn's predecessor, or what was left of him, lay. Jones swore he spotted a severed leg in the mud, but it could have been anything. He made a quick sign of the cross all the same.

One by one, they returned their heads forwards. The gusts of wind spared them an eerie silence and kept them company. Quinn began inching ahead and had to be caught up. Jones reckoned they had already advanced all of thirty yards. It was a miracle that they had still not been spotted in the growing light. About now, it would become certain.

Quinn pushed forwards. It became even more of a struggle to keep up with him. His followers feared that they might have ventured too far. Out of instinct, each of them prayed as they sallied forwards. They prayed not have to join the fate of so many of their comrades. They prayed that the trench ahead had been abandoned, left as a gift of glory.

Still nothing happened as they continued to advance. It became as if they had crossed a danger zone and safely emerged the other side. The crippling apprehension fell away. Even Jones changed his mind and felt revitalised. He admired the tall and bareheaded young man boldly leading them in his waders. The boredom of the preceding days had evaporated. This was looking like a clever gamble. Perhaps the captain wasn't such an idiot after all.

The danger zone merged into a dreamland. With every cautious yard, their options seemed to multiply, and so did their confidence. They hoped to become heroes. The trench might be occupied after all. It might yield the odd sentry. They might keep him alive. And even if there was no-one, there would surely be something to discover, papers or identifying items missed by the enemy in the dark. Whatever happened would be good for them. It had been miraculously ordained. To a man, they felt as dangerously over-confident as their ad hoc leader.

They were a third of the way across. They had become bunched together in their false hope. They crouched even closer to the muddy ground and set about exploiting the shell holes for cover, sprinting as much as they could from one to the next as they advanced, lifting their boots by the toes to minimise the sound of clicking mud.

The hard rain resumed. The cold made up for their exertion. The ever-increasing daylight seemed to rescue them from the unknown, make them feel reassured, even at home.

Tac tac tac tac!

It startled every one of them. Their hopes were dashed, their dreams abruptly curtailed. The sound of the machine gun and its tiny missiles beat the splashing rain to win their attention. They collectively dived into the nearest hole, a large one, and waited, heads kept well below level, safely shielded from the stream of rounds passing over their heads.

After a couple of minutes, Quinn daringly looked over the side. His blond hair was soon targeted. The whisker-trimmers ricocheted off the shattered rocks around him. He had second thoughts about what he had instigated. The single machine gun was the equivalent of scores of rifles. The increasing daylight rendered his venture impossible. He cursed himself for not having done his very first outing hours before. He told himself that he would never make the same mistake twice.

Despite the setback, Quinn recovered his determination. They had carried plenty of rifle grenades and cartridges with them. At least they could pound the trench ahead to provoke a reaction. Quinn ordered them into three teams and to splay their aim to cover as wide a front as possible. There was enough stable debris lower down in the crater to support the guns.

They set up and opened fire. The grenades shot upwards. Quinn daringly raised his blond head once again, this time from a different position. It was better than a periscope. The rounds landed too far.

"Ten degrees upwards!" he shouted as he ducked again.

The men steadying the rifles adjusted accordingly as best they could. The second volley was close but a little short.

"Three degrees back!"

In two cases, they appeared on target. Quinn ordered them to hold their angle and fire at will. There were now two men steadying each rifle. Jones, meanwhile, rounded up all their Mills bombs just in case of an enemy rush. He lined them up for easy reach.

Tac tac tac tac!

Then there was silence except for the rain. Everyone prayed the machine gun had overheated. Quinn hoped they were standing up to pee on it and would be picked off by his snipers. They waited. Nothing happened.

Quinn looked towards the rise over on their left, appearing higher than he had imagined. If the enemy had a machine gun or snipers there too, they would find themselves in deadly enfilade.

They had exhausted the grenades. They had to pull back. After checking for one last time that the trench in front wasn't stirring, Quinn ordered his men to collect their bombs and take it in turns to withdraw to the first crater behind.

Tac tac tac tac!

The machine gun had been waiting. The first man up was hit in the ankle. He fell onto the edge of the crater and received several more rounds higher up his torso. Jones struggled over and pulled him back in, but he was already dead. He turned him over. His face and front had been blighted by exit wounds. At least the shredded uniform had held him together.

Quinn cursed himself for not organising artillery, his second mistake. But then brigade would have refused the mission. Mercifully, the enemy trench still hadn't opened fire. Mercifully, the ridge to the left remained quiet. Twenty yards backwards, that's all they needed, twenty yards for which Quinn had failed to get permission. Twenty yards that could get him into a serious pickle.

But he wasn't defeated yet. He still felt elated.

Jones had thought of the hill to the left as well. He shouted they had to hurry. Even if there wasn't a second machine gun, sniper, or fire from the trench, there would be artillery further back. It would be horrific. Shell fire was always worst.

He looked over in Quinn's direction. The captain seemed to enjoy himself. Jones repeated his warning. Quinn ignored him. He was convinced that the battalion would have raised the alarm by now. In a matter of seconds, they would see artillery coming to the rescue, obliterating the machine gun altogether, and to their left for good measure. Jones knew better, as did his men. They had seen it too often. Reaction was always slow. Orders took time when nothing had been planned and shared in advance. Men hesitated. Questions had to come first.

Out of frustration, one man ran up the side of the crater and over the top. The machine gun started up again but missed. Seeing his chance, a second man did the same and took a round below the knee, but kept going. As far as anyone could tell, they had both made it to the next hole. No-one called out to check. Quinn didn't raise his head.

The rest of them got up in unison and followed, frantically scrambling over, Quinn to their rear. The machine gun opened up again. Quinn heard one cry after the other. One man screamed in pain. There was nothing anyone could do.

From their second crater, they heard rifle and Lewis gun fire break out from their line. At last! But there was still no artillery. Even the Stokes stayed quiet. Someone could at least have sent smoke.

Tac tac tac tac!

Only Quinn and one other made it back. The others had succumbed to the infernal rain of bullets that had chased them all the way back. One had even cried out when he had accidentally touched one of the red-hot rounds that had gone through him and been stopped by a rock.

Men in the fire trench helped the two of them down into the mud and escorted them back through the support trenches. They ended up shocked and dazed, alone in the pouring rain, squatting on the mud next to the deserted battalion headquarters.

Quinn yearned to escape back to his tent.

"Did you see the corporal cop it, Captain?" the private asked, his hood now lifted to expose his face.

Quinn said nothing as he struggled to come to terms with what he had instigated. He could be court martialled. He wouldn't stand a chance.

The adrenaline had not subsided. His mind raced for a way out. He needed to frame a story, create a diversion. At least he had taken initiative. He continued to fumble around for a positive angle to place on the disaster.

He thought hard. The enemy trench had never reacted. He could have been right about it being deserted. His discovery would change any plans being cogitated back at brigade. Before they found time to lay into him, he would propose another patrol that night, before the enemy did anything about it, well before his superiors had time to decide his fate. With luck, it would save him.

He thought of the private sitting next to him, the sole survivor of the section. He would end up talking to colleagues. Quinn's name would be blackened in the ranks if he did not set matters right straight away.

"No, I didn't..."

"Hopper," came the prompt.

"But his sacrifice was not for nothing, Hopper," Quinn assured him, just in case. "We did a vital job tonight. You and everyone will be remembered for it."

Hopper looked at him condemningly and then turned away. This was the usual pathetic bumf that came from officers. Everything had to be positive, always positive. Never mind the cost. Never mind that he had lost mates that he had grown up with. His world had emptied.

"I will include mention of your bravery, Hopper," Quinn said.

An orderly emerged from the trenches and spotted them. There was good news from the firing line. Jones had survived and was on his way. He had been hit in the shoulder and leg, but he could still walk.

They both stood up to await Jones' arrival. As Hopper fidgeted, keen to see his corporal again, Quinn felt relieved. It was one disappearance less for the tally against him. Perhaps Jones could somehow share the blame.

They listened to the rain. They heard the distant machine gun start up again. Hadn't it already done enough?

Jones eventually appeared, supported by a colleague. It was clear that they had skipped the dressing station and that he needed attention. Once they had passed the tree, Quinn and Hopper walked up and escorted them to the first aid post nearby.

As the medical officer worked on his wounds, Jones said nothing. He avoided eye contact with Quinn as he looked on with Hopper. The resigned look on his face told all. He would say what Quinn expected, back him to the hilt because he knew his place, and he would make sure that Hopper did the same.

That's how it had to be. But it didn't mean that it would be simple. He also knew how his lieutenant would react, and Captain Cody too once he returned. Jones would be caught in the middle of a firefight between his superiors, and not for the first time.

From his operating table, Jones bitterly watched Captain Quinn head back to his snipers. Officers like this one had no respect, trod all over the other ranks and harboured a destructive rivalry with their colleagues. He waited apprehensively for the arrival of Lieutenant Piggot. Where the hell was he? How he hated them all. Hopefully, the morphine would soon calm him down.

Quinn had only just regained the firing trench when the enemy belatedly showed his wrath. After a succession of parachute flares, somewhat pointless in the growing light, a barrage fell in front of them, dangerously close to the enemy line and slowly moving in their direction, throwing up vast curtains of mud.

Quinn grabbed his helmet that he had left there. There was no way this could come from nearby. He waved for the closest mortar to hold off and sent an orderly along the line to pass the message.

Very soon they were being pounded with a combination of high explosive and woolly bears. Injured survivors were moaning in pain, the firing trench and others behind it being disfigured beyond recognition.

"Flare gun!"

Another shell landed. It fell right on top of the sergeant preparing to send up the SOS. Quinn was bowled over by the blast and almost drowned before Schemensky hurriedly pulled him out.

"I'm alright, Schemensky! I'm alright!"

He soon recovered, got up, spat out mud, and wiped the blood from his face with his sleeve. He reached for the telephone. The line was stone dead. Two shells landed just behind them, spraying them with yet more mud.

The noise was horrendous, even from battalion headquarters at the rear. One sentry counted two hundred rounds, and through his field glasses, spotted a dozen direct hits. A second kept trying to get through to the battalion. It was in vain. It was up to Quinn to order a flare.

There was a pause. Back in the trench, no-one moved. Despite the ringing in their ears, they could hear moans and cries of pain coming from many places further down. They didn't stop. Everyone instinctively reached for their respirators and waited.

There was no gas. Five minutes later, a second barrage descended on the support trenches behind them. Again, more shrill screams and cries for help. A bombing post nearby got a direct hit, exploded in several rapid stages, and mud, debris, and body parts fell all around them.

The barrage seemed to inch away, no doubt obliterating each swathe as it went. It became more selective. After each explosion, they heard men shouting out for each other, asking if they were still alive. Everywhere, there were yet more moans, cries, and screams.

A round landed right on top of the lone tree further back. Only a six-foot splintered stub remained. It must have been hundreds of years old.

The onslaught had finally ceased, and the rain persisted. Word came through to what remained of the front trench that the tree had gone, and that further back, the first aid post had miraculously escaped a dud shell, but a team of pack animals had received a direct hit. Some cobs had been with the battalion since it had come out. Men were reported to have rushed over to put the injured survivors out of their misery. Battalion headquarters had been smashed. Three rifle racks nearby had been destroyed. An ammunition dump further back, together with the run-down barn just next to it, had also received fatal direct hits.

It all became too much for Quinn. The little that had remained of his ego gave way to the surge of bad news. He was in a mind to climb out and get himself slaughtered while the enemy remained angry. One way or another, it would stay with him for the rest of his life.

It was Schemensky who saved him in time. He bent down from his ledge and tapped him on the shoulder. He repeated it several times. Quinn emerged from his daze and responded.

"All 4.2s or more," the sniper said. "Maybe 5.9s. Nothing light at all."

"What?"

Schemensky repeated, mouthing it as he went along in case Quinn had lost his hearing. Quinn understood. He was too new to have been able to tell the difference. He felt rescued from the abyss. None of the shooting had come from the trench opposite or anywhere nearby. It was just as he had first thought. Without bothering to thank Schemensky for his vital information, he turned around and swaggered his way to the rear in the rain. Once again, everyone ignored him. He felt himself revitalised. It had been close.

He encountered Lieutenant Piggot on the way, busy giving orders to a group of men frantically digging out survivors from blown-in trenches. Piggot broke off, harshly looked at Quinn, but walked past him, no doubt convinced that the captain's demise had already been ordained. There was a cheer from where he had just left. A man they had just deemed dead had opened his eyes.

When he finally emerged from the support trench, Quinn encountered scores of men running in all directions. Stretchers were being ferried back to the head of the light railway a quarter of a mile back, the same that Jones had no doubt taken already. NCOs were organising dozens of working parties. Carts, braving the daylight, were arriving with munitions in anticipation of retaliation.

Quinn cynically observed that the battalion seemed to function perfectly well without its top commanders. He saw battalion headquarters was a shambles. The rain was running down its newly slanted roof. To where would he find himself summoned? Perhaps they would drag him directly to brigade.

Lieutenant Piggot turned up, still furious.

"What have you unleashed, Captain?"

"They have no sense of humour," was all that Quinn could say, infuriating Piggot yet more with his arrogant grin.

"At least you could have sent up a rocket, Captain."

"I was out there," Quinn said, as if boasting. "How could I have sent out a rocket I didn't have?"

Piggot walked away, disgusted.

"And anyway, it wasn't coming from their trenches!" Quinn bellowed after him.

With a wry smile, Quinn removed his helmet and held it bundled with his precious periscope under his arm. As rain poured down, and matted his blond hair to his forehead, he looked out for Jones in case he hadn't left after all. But he held back from re-entering the first aid tent. He scanned for Private Hopper, but couldn't spot him either. He so wanted to point out to them that their excursion had been a success, after all.

3

The bombardment had stirred up brigade. The discovery that telephone communications were down precipitated the immediate departure of Colonel Wilkes and his team.

Captain Michael Cody, 'Moose' to his closest, was by far the shortest of the four commanders. Of slighter build as well, his dark and sharp features, heavy eyebrows, and tendency to say little, portrayed a man inclined to be thoughtful and serious. As commander of C Company, presently manning the front trench, he was particularly worried.

"Definitely no SOS flares," had insisted the sentries at the brigade lookout post.

They had also been looking out for other types of visual signal from the battalion but spotted nothing. The brigadier ordered an immediate riposte on the enemy artillery, anyway. From recent aerial observations, they had a reasonably good idea where it had to be.

After dashing for two miles in the pelting rain, with the heavy guns about to open up behind them, the party of six officers and the colonel's orderly realised that all had suddenly gone quiet ahead. They were halfway through an avenue of plane trees, encompassing a straight portion of the road, when they encountered a dispatch rider from battalion.

"Severed cables," the rider announced, shouting to be heard over the noise of the rain and his motorbike. "At least three direct hits."

It wasn't the first time this had occurred, despite the cables being buried six feet under. Before riding on, the messenger told them a little about Quinn. He confirmed it had been Cody's company that had paid the brunt of the price. At least twenty had been killed, many more than that injured, and considerable damage done to both the trenches and rear facilities.

Seated on his horse and making sure once again that the guns ahead were still quiet, Colonel Wilkes was beside himself. A volatile man at the best of times, and apt to create dramas for no reason at all, he took it out on the messenger. Then he looked over at Cody, in his mind his least ambitious commander, a constant observer of life and always totally at home with himself. Cody was ungracefully huddled in the pouring rain with his colleagues in the small mess cart. The colonel wanted to make sure that he had heard it all.

This time, the colonel had good reason to be angry. There were less than two days to go before the attack they had just been planning, and Quinn had disobeyed a direct order. The colonel's theatrics over the affair were also to be expected. It was part of who he was, even in better times. Although he had already served during the Second Boer War, in his early twenties, he took badly to pressure. His permanently red face and balding head gave away what to expect. The various postures of his unhealthy-looking body followed suit. He was a dynamo of discontent. His dislikable style was to pace around impatiently, plotting his next scheme while complaining about everything, leaning over plans and maps and wiping the fallen ash from his permanent cigarette, his raspy voice calling out whatever he saw while his entourage waited for his next broadside. Yet despite what Quinn thought, most of his ideas were credible, and his actions well-decided. It allowed him to keep his job, despite being the very worst man to lead others.

"Where's the patrol report," he barked at the rider.

The guns behind them finally opened up.

"None, sir!" the rider shouted even louder than before.

In the growing din, the rider calmly saluted and took his leave, no doubt expecting to get better treatment at brigade. As the colonel and major parleyed between themselves, Cody and his colleagues set about divvying up the tasks they would have once they got back.

"Who'll deal with the Engineers?" Captain Talbot asked.

Talbot's longer service, good looks, red hair and moustache, and that he commanded A Company, made him their natural leader. Captain Fuller volunteered. Captains Cody and Cragg had most of the men positioned forward and would have plenty of nastier issues to deal with.

Resuming their journey at a slower pace, all six of them went through again what they would each do as soon as they reached the battalion. When the captains discussed the trench work, the colonel didn't intervene. Captains Cody and Talbot glanced at each other to share their relief. The colonel had run a building firm in civilian life and was always expected to say his word, but rarely did. His inexplicable *laissez-faire*, over this and certain other matters, gave his commanders just enough autonomy to hold the battalion together.

The friendly guns kept going and so did the rain. Time was of the essence, they all agreed. They knew too well that the brigadier would never cancel his visit. They would have a mere couple of hours to sort out as much as possible. The breaches in the communications line to brigade had to be repaired right away. Major Hickman would see to that, as well as any damage to headquarters and general facilities. The four commanders had to be ready to itemise the damage to each of their effectives and materiel. Cody would also have to interrogate his survivors, starting with the injured waiting to be evacuated.

"As soon as he's gone, we'll launch the inquiry," announced the colonel.

All four commanders could not help thinking that he had brought it all upon himself. He had placed too much confidence in the pompous and inexperienced new arrival who had so rapidly provoked animosity among his colleagues. A rare blind spot in the colonel's intellect had been exposed. It could see itself exploited as the daily pressures of the front led to uncontrollable animalistic behaviour between his subordinates. Foxhounds would go for the kill. It would be Quinn's turn first.

For the time being, they refrained from hypothesising about the reasons for Quinn's action. It would have been out of order, especially in front of the colonel. The major, who should have done more to prevent the colonel's mistake, asked a couple of questions about Quinn's background.

"Of excellent stock," the colonel assured him. "His father was a general. Second Boer War. He did well."

"Well, that was a fine example!" said Captain Talbot quietly enough so as not to be heard by the colonel. "Perhaps the blackguard made gangsters of his snipers too!"

Cody glanced at his colleague.

"Come on, Talbot! Enough of that!"

Talbot's comment had been out of character. Cody liked and respected his colleague but was prepared to correct him if he thought he had stepped out of line. Officers were expected to remain circumspect, show forbearance, avoid being effusive, always display equanimity.

Talbot had been born in India and had already been serving for six years before the war. He had a propensity for bringing people together and gaining respect. He was calm yet athletic, a quiet hero, and was certainly the cleverest of the four of them. Cody believed he had two weaknesses, though. The first was that his university education all too often led to a theoretical approach to problems which his lieutenants constantly had to rectify, although, as with the colonel, it actually strengthened his unit. The second was more sinister, and the cause of Cody's off-the-cuff challenge. Talbot was known to drop individuals like a ton of bricks if they didn't serve or suit his purpose.

Huddled on their cart and out of hearing, the four of them agreed that at least one of them should have stayed back. It had been a shameful mistake. Quinn had appeared to them a lone wolf from the very start.

"Nothing is going to happen tonight," the colonel had fatally barked after he had been challenged twice.

As they were jolted along, the four captains compared notes.

"So, the colonel badly measured Quinn," Cragg summarised.

"The brigadier will see it that way," assured Talbot.

"Expect harsh words behind closed doors," predicted Cody.

Their thoughts gave them no satisfaction. The humiliated colonel would somehow end up taking it out on his battalion. The four captains would be blamed for not insisting enough, let alone not saying what they had suspected about Quinn. Because of all the flack flying around him, Quinn himself could even end up avoiding a good part of the retribution he deserved, especially the Order of the Bowler Hat, the greatest humiliation of all for a man with ambition.

"Fortunately, his victims will never get to know any of that," cynically said Fuller.

As they resumed their original pace, the rain continued pelting down. The increased jolting and general racket now prevented them from talking between themselves, so Cody reasoned with himself. He dreaded what he was about to discover. There would be yet more lives extinguished or rendered incapacitated because of an own goal that would have to be covered up. Even after over two years in the trenches, he still had difficulty inuring himself to the crushing responsibility and bad conscience stemming from such cockups.

And who had been killed? How many more good men had been incapacitated for good? Whether the colonel ended up taking it out on him, he should have refused to leave. It was his company posted to the firing line that night. While he and his colleagues had been profiting from hot showers and the first change of clothes for two weeks, not to mention the well-equipped brigade mess, C Company was being ripped apart. Any punishment meted out to Quinn would be small change for Cody's personal feeling of guilt.

He thought back to Quinn's arrival two weeks before. It had rapidly upset the delicate balance that had worked for so long. The brigadier himself had often pontificated about how the stability of all kinds of organisations rested on a knife-edge. From the outset, Cody had felt incensed by Quinn's arrogant comportment when he needed the experience of others so much. He recalled how he had reacted, or rather hadn't, to the advice of those around him. The man was a harum-scarum, yet another Woolwich engineer trained to think he knew best, and for whom everything was possible, another product of a rushed dispatch to the front. His lack of manners had added to it all. They had experienced such men before, but Quinn somehow seemed worse, more irretrievably hardened to the core, than any. He had so far endeared himself to not one of his colleagues, in either the battalion, at brigade, or among sister battalions along the front. Only his small team of snipers had welcomed him with open arms.

Quinn had also deserved his unpopularity by encouraging jealousy. One way or another, he had repeatedly touted his better stock and schooling enough to turn everyone off. Appearing, as he did, broad-shouldered, athletic, intelligent, and irritatingly amateurishly enthusiastic about his job, he had overwhelmed his colleagues with his air of superiority.

In a short space of time, the very sound of Quinn's nondescript soft voice had perversely become synonymous with the antagonism he generated and the short shrift he invited. In his self-created world, Quinn had set himself up for a fall, and neither of his superior officers had seen it coming. Cody himself had wanted to say something from the beginning, pass on his first suspicions. What had held him back had been his own stupid, blind respect for the custom that fellow officers were expected to sort out such matters between themselves. The colonel's special character had only rendered matters worse. Cody would have been damned if he had said something, and damned if he hadn't.

Once again, Cody tried to imagine what had led Quinn to carry out what he had. He searched for mitigating circumstances. Too many times he had seen overbearing pressures lead even the best of men to become destructively and immorally creative. Despite all, Quinn's situation had to be understood first.

They hadn't got far to go. Cody thought about his four lieutenants and their expected *sturm und drang* over what had happened. They would be certain to accost him first thing.

At least none of them remotely resembled Quinn. He thought about each of them. Lieutenant Piggot would have been in the front trench. He was a car mechanic by training, but had always said how much he distrusted engineers, which bode badly for Quinn. But then, Piggot also had an attitude towards all types of authority.

"Yes them to death!" was his motto that Cody had once accidentally overheard.

Cody shivered yet again at the thought. But it never detracted from the fact that he always saw and advocated Piggot as the most reliable of his lieutenants.

"You should think of Smalby instead," the colonel was constantly saying.

The colonel had never seen Piggot the same way. In Cody's mind, Lieutenant Smalby came second to Piggot. Smalby was clever and looked up to authority, which had worked with the colonel. His experience as a factory supervisor made him good with men. But he was inclined towards undeclared pet schemes that too often amounted to insubordination. As for Lieutenants Mowforth and Cobbold, they came distant thirds. Piggot and Smalby were the ones to watch for.

Cody wondered how he had survived overseeing such a menagerie. Yet despite the challenges his four lieutenants presented him, he wouldn't exchange them for gold.

They passed a loaded ammunition wagon that must have become paralysed during the night. Its wheel appeared to have been sheared off after sliding into a ditch. Watched by their colleagues, four men were taking care of the repair, slipping all over the place in the mud and becoming soaked in the process.

Captain Fuller recognised them to be from his company.

"What a waste!" he said.

He was sorely tempted to jump off and organise them properly. He would send a sergeant up instead, if one could be spared from the chaos they were about to encounter.

"Everything at once!" grumbled Cody.

As they made their final approach in the rain, they encountered a burying party headed into a nearby field. Then they spotted that their tree had gone. The place seemed strange.

The colonel and major broke off to inspect the remains of headquarters and the damage nearby. Cody and his colleagues drove closer to the trenches. They jumped from their cart next to the reserve trench and dispersed to their respective companies. Aghast at the damage, Cody headed to the firing line before returning to interrogate the injured.

"Captain!"

It was Hardy, his loyal orderly, who was as short as he was. He had just been up front and was headed to recuperate a spare stretcher.

"It's dreadful, Captain."

"Is it true that Captain Quinn started it?"

Cody could speak frankly with Hardy. He knew it wouldn't go anywhere.

"Yes, Captain."

Cody told him to carry on. As he passed one stretcher after the other headed to the rear, he recalled the brigadier's reminder the night before to spread the men out in order to lessen the risks. Cody hated having to be shown the initiative. To make it worse, this time he had been caught out.

"Damn Quinn!" he muttered.

He was appalled by the chaos. All the way up to the front men were still being dug out of collapsed trenches. This was far from a war footing. A little further on he saw that at least the remediation appeared industrious and well organised. C Company had been put out of action but was responding diligently. Thank God the enemy had stopped short in following up.

By the time he had finally struggled through the infernal mud to the front trench, he found it unrecognisable. He spotted Piggot organising stretcher parties and repair teams. With ever-increasing difficulty, he made his way towards him, bracing himself for the verbal onslaught.

Things remained unexpectedly calm. Piggot appeared relieved to see him. He passed command to his sergeant and broke off. He reported twenty-seven dead so far, mostly from C Company, and many more than that injured or missing, perhaps forty. In the original incident that had sparked it off, he said,

Quinn had helped himself to Corporal Jones and his men without advising, but he preferred the captain give his own account as to why.

"At least Jones and Private Hopper made it," he said bitterly, instinctively putting his hand over his brow to deflect the mud being washed down his forehead by the incessant rain.

Cody asked him about his colleagues, Lieutenants Smalby, Cobbold, and Mowforth. Piggot described what each was up to. None of them had been injured. Cody thanked him, asked him to send him Private Hopper, and ordered him to carry on. As he headed back to the rear, he continued to take stock. The damage to his company and its trenches was terrible indeed. He would have to organise new conscripts right away. It was small change to have it confirmed that none of his men had been responsible for what had happened.

He emerged onto flat ground, looking towards the sad remains of the tree as he went past. Just before he entered the first aid tent, he glanced at the trace of the dud shell. It had been close.

Jones was still there. He had been seen to and was lying on a stretcher slightly apart from the others, still waiting for evacuation. He confirmed his lieutenant's version, that Quinn had instigated the patrol on his own, without prompting or explaining his intentions. After describing the meagre preparations, he ran step-by-step through what had happened during the patrol and how it had been solely the machine gun post that had put paid to it. Nothing had come from the enemy trenches while they were out.

Over the dulled noise of the rain splashing on the canvas above them, Jones spoke bitterly about each of his men who had fallen. His unit had been wiped out. He swore that it had been one of the best he had ever commanded. They had got through the horrific campaign that had marked the end of summer, only to experience this.

"A waste if there ever had been, Captain."

Cody looked around. There was a lot of movement around them, but no-one had been listening in. Jones was a strong individual. Cody knew he didn't need any consolation. In fact, he would resent it. He thanked him instead and wished him luck, hoping to see him back soon.

"I'll rebuild your section with the best conscripts," he said. "Who should fill in for you?"

"Private Hopper," Jones said without hesitating. "The Lieutenant already knows."

Cody did the rounds of the other injured before he left, stopping at each stretcher and saying a word of encouragement to those who could still hear. One or two worryingly dared to ask why the whole thing had happened.

Just as he emerged from the tent to face the downpour, Cody found Hopper standing there. They both stepped back inside, and Cody interrogated him as he had Jones. There was nothing new from Hopper's version. It all looked clear. Cody thanked him and left to find the colonel.

The colonel was alone with the major, unable to stand upright to one end of what was left of headquarters. The far side wall had been partially blown-in, leaving that end of the reinforced roof propped only a few feet from the ground. They had dispersed the staff elsewhere and had removed their capes.

Cody suggested they occupy the corrugated elephant shelter next door that had been destined for the trenches, but neither of them were listening. The rain outside had just died down a little. They could at last lower their voices.

"Well?"

Trying not to show any emotion, Cody recounted what he had learned, and that some of the wounded were challenging Quinn's action. All his lieutenants had survived. He reported on the condition of his trenches and thought that with the present effort they could be more or less up to scratch in a few hours. New conscripts should be requisitioned right away, and he needed to shift men around in order to spread experience. The survivor of Jones' section would take it over as soon as new men arrived. He would see to that right away.

"Did you find Quinn, Captain?" the colonel asked.

Cody replied he hadn't seen Quinn. The colonel stormed outside and asked his orderly, who was standing in the drizzle, to go looking for him. He returned inside muttering that he would drum the man out of the army for what he had done.

Relieved that he hadn't yet found himself on the receiving end, Cody almost felt sorry for Quinn, whatever his responsibility. It hadn't been an auspicious beginning to Quinn's career, and the promised reaction to his blunder would only make it worse. It would have been fairer if the colonel had seen fit to wait a day or so before conducting the post-mortem.

Quinn was located and escorted over. Leaving the orderly outside, he entered the hut appearing humbled, the first time Cody had ever witnessed it. As all four awkwardly remained standing inside the shambles, the colonel calmly asked Quinn why he had organised the patrol contrary to orders. Cody saw that he was ready to explode.

"And where's your bloody report!" the colonel said, stepping up the tone.

Quinn's sudden resumption of stature and his subsequent reply turned their expectations upside down. He now showed no remorse, back to his usual self. Awkwardly recovering from bumping his head against the roof, he bent down a little and looked graceful. He condescendingly announced that he had made a vital discovery about the enemy line. He insisted the battalion react while there was time. His 'difficult' outing had been a success.

Cody, as surprised as any, had the impression that Quinn was used to this kind of situation. But he was new to the army. It could only have come from a tyrannical home or schooling, those elements in his life about which he had so often boasted. He studied Quinn's rain-swept face as he spoke, his steadied eyes and curling mouth above his square jaw. Normally he would have despised the man more than ever, but this time something worked against his instinct. He found himself prepared to listen.

Quinn rounded off that he should have been with them at brigade, as if the incident had been their fault.

He had truly tempted the devil.

"I've never seen such gall!" spluttered the colonel, still stunned, once Quinn had been curtly dismissed.

The major and Cody were speechless, too. Bypassing the major, the colonel asked Cody for his opinion. Cody had been dreading being put on the spot. Quinn was a colleague. He had to duck the ball. He replied that if Quinn were to be proven right then there existed mitigating circumstances, despite the terrible cost.

"So you think we should believe him and bring forward the attack?"

The colonel was not taking a word of it.

"I think so, sir," said Cody, trying to appear as convinced as he could.

He wondered if the colonel felt on the defensive. Could the Quinn affair threaten his position? The major nodded to Cody's reply with a shrug, which was noticed by the colonel. This was an awkward situation. Quinn's sort would have to wait, yet battalion would cry for blood.

Cody had wanted the major to say more. He felt agitated by his self-effacing comportment. He resented how he never seemed to play a key role in such discussions. It was no doubt one reason for which the brigadier had taken the intelligence duties away from him in the first place. He was always just standing there, pensively sucking on his pipe, spindly legs akimbo, his thin dark and oiled hair neatly brushed to the back, his handsome but expressionless face constantly taking in all that was being said, his mind no doubt secretly hoping that one of these days the colonel would submit to an infarction.

In one or two obscure ways, the major echoed his superior officer. He had also been a lieutenant during the second Boer War. During his intervening civilian life, he had been an accountant with interests in the stock market, but had never once interested himself in the battalion's finances. It was just like the colonel and the trench building. It was a mystery why.

The colonel was far from finished.

"A successful outing, my arse!" he ranted, theatrically turning back after glancing at the major and getting increasingly worked up. "If the bloody man thinks there's a cockleshell badge on the way, he's got another thought coming!"

His face had now become purple.

"We should show restraint, Colonel," Cody daringly proposed. "For the time being we should actively support him."

The colonel calmed down a bit, his colour changed a shade, he scowled and called for a runner. While they waited, he scribbled a brief message to the brigadier, repeatedly muttering something about how the means did not necessarily justify the end. He had turned on Quinn and was deeply uncomfortable with what his two ad hoc advisors had precipitated. He was proving himself to be the last person in the world to conduct the inquiry over the affair.

One of Captain Fuller's corporals arrived from the cable party. Cody felt relieved by the timely interruption.

"We've found a foreign wire connected to the old telephone line, Colonel."

He did not want to add a layer to the fiasco, but he had no choice. Colonel Wilkes knew what it meant. It had happened before. The enemy had been listening in by induction.

"Keep digging," he said. "Just enough to be certain where it goes, and that it's the only one."

He turned to the others.

"At least we learned something."

The corporal ran off after the major reminded him of the urgency. The colonel wondered aloud how the hell the enemy had managed it this time. He decided he would speak confidentially to the brigadier about it. He would never allow Quinn's folly to take any credit for the discovery.

Cody saw that there was nothing left for him at headquarters. He dropped by his tent to continue to interrogate Hardy, from whom he was bound to get an impartial opinion. Then he would return to what remained of his company.

4

The rain had stopped by the time the staff car drove up, almost precisely at midday. The young driver struggled to double-declutch as he turned off the dirt road into the camp, and the spectacle somewhat calmed the apprehension of those who stood there waiting. Finally, conforming to the rules of caution, the driver drew up well short of headquarters.

Brigadier Lightfoot, a heavy-set man in his mid-thirties, had bulging cheeks and a crop of short, curly black hair. He clumsily climbed out with his briefcase and then reached back inside for his hat. The colonel sank when he saw he had come without his aide-de-camp, a taller man, also with spectacles, who was infinitely more approachable, and always compensated for the brigadier's lack of humour. The colonel possessed a pathological fear of his unpleasant commander and had always done his best to keep his distance.

He hesitatingly approached and saluted him.

Cody had always sympathised with the colonel. The brigadier was indeed a tough case to deal with. One could never detect what he was thinking behind his polished spectacles. He was a political player *par excellence*, ruthless, cynical, and usually unfriendly, who at best could yield a wry smile when it pleased him. His all too rare bouts of humour failed to cut the ice.

"Fill me in, Colonel!" the brigadier said.

He had been forewarned to forget about any inspection. The colonel acquiesced and beckoned the major and Cody to keep him company. Cody couldn't help noticing how much he for once appeared humbled and on his best behaviour. The three of them hurried off to confer inside the ramshackle headquarters and, once installed, the colonel rattled off about Quinn's exploit, the losses of men, and the resulting conclusions. Then he passed the baton to Cody, asking him to add his perspective regarding the damage from the bombardment.

The brigadier listened attentively, occasionally intervening with pointed challenges, his quiet voice and rapid speech reminding them how clever and alert he was. Watching him perform, Cody couldn't for a single moment imagine the unsympathetic brigadier at home with a family. No doubt it was the reason for which he had remained a professional soldier for over twenty years, constantly posted abroad away from his wife and children as much as possible.

"He collects toy cars," the colonel, who usually only talked about work, had once revealed.

It had seemed as incongruous as the comment unexpected. Scalps might have seemed closer to the mark.

The brigade had to act before the enemy. There was no question of waiting until dusk. The decision was made to bring forward the plans they had laid out the night before and attack that afternoon. It would be an exceptional time to do so. Precise orders would be brought over within a couple of hours.

Before the brigadier left to warn the other battalions, he skimmed over the local attack plan one last time. Using a map as his prop, the colonel reminded him about the machine gun post. Any preventive barrage should take care of that known threat and any possible positions up to the left.

The brigadier once again warned them to keep spreading out troops. Cody swore that there had been an instantaneous glance in his direction when he said it. The brigadier seemed to have labelled him as a deviant. It was his style to pick on a different weakness each time he visited.

The session hadn't taken long. They emerged and walked the fifty yards to the car. The brigadier became distracted by the remains of the tree on the way. He studied the splintered stub with some pity.

"They must have been thinking of it for weeks," he said with a wry smile.

The colonel said nothing but made the appropriate face. The tree had become a familiar sight to which his entire battalion had become attached. The enemy's grim sense of humour compared with the brigadier's.

He opened the car door for the brigadier. They needed to be rid of him. The driver started the car.

"By the way, what do you plan to do with Quinn?" the brigadier asked, once again glancing towards the splintered stub before climbing in.

The colonel felt awkward. He realised the position he would put himself in if he spoke his mind. He said he would wait and see after the action.

"Don't wait too long," the brigadier said as he threw his briefcase to the side and settled in. "You shouldn't stand for what he did. This had been a thriving battalion until he turned up."

The colonel said no more. In his mind, either way it went, Quinn would pay for his affront. And, contrary to custom, he was determined to lead the inquiry himself.

As the car drove off, he turned to the major and Cody, still standing beside him.

"What did he mean, this *had been*?"

At half-past two, battalions along a three-mile front stood to. Heavy shelling was to begin at Z hour, designated to be in two hours' time. At Z + 1, they were to expect a creeping barrage to shield their advance. Because of the probability of returning rain, gas would not be used.

At exactly four-thirty, guns that had been moved forward to two miles behind them opened up. Waiting in their trenches, men stuck their fingers in their ears, even though the noise was being dampened by the soft ground. The barrage seemed so intense that it would be a miracle if anyone in front survived.

In Cody's sector, at one point, there occurred a notable surge of pounding much further away, where the machine gun post had been as well as to the left. The surrounding men breathed a sigh of relief as both landscapes were changed forever. Impatiently waiting next to his men, Cody thought of his young wife, Kate, a proficient artist. How she always let off steam when the subject she was painting changed.

At Z + 1, whistles blew. Shells started landing a hundred yards from the enemy trench. Leaving their jerkins behind, waves of men clambered over the parapets into no-man's-land, content to be advancing at last and out of their partially repaired trenches. As they negotiated their way forward, a few crows stubbornly feeding on carrion on the open ground reluctantly scattered.

Cody led the first wave with his depleted company, Hardy by his side with a spare rifle. His barely over a hundred men under four lieutenants remained spread out in front of the entire length of their sector of the firing line, from time to time concentrating as they negotiated shell holes, ditches, and batches of defensive wire. They advanced in tune with the barrage, at twenty-five yards a minute. Shells exploded vertically in front of them. They watched the barrage pulverise the first trench. With no fire as yet coming back at them, and with the artillery for once getting its aim right, it gave them a great feeling of power.

C Company's objective was to take and occupy the first trench. Talbot, following behind with his larger A Company, would leapfrog over them in order to advance on positions further forward. Fuller and Cragg were to remain in reserve, ready to come to the aid of any position in difficulty.

Their bayonets pointed in front of them, C Company criss-crossed the first stretch of no-man's-land, keeping several yards between them once the absence of wire allowed it. The ground was soggy, but it was the shell holes and tree stubs that slowed them down most, forcing them to move sideways as much as forwards. In that respect, the barrage had made things worse.

Lieutenant Mowforth's men arrived at the level of the goalposts, long stripped of their paint by weather and become splattered with mud. One or two men made a point of touching them for luck. Everyone kept advancing. Nothing at all was coming back at them. As they closed in on the objective, Cody ceased to curse about the added obstacles caused by the barrage. Other concerns were about to take over.

When they jumped into the trench, they discovered it emptied. The support team caught up and Cody had Hardy dispatch one pigeon to confirm the gain. He ordered his men to help turn the trench as fast as possible. Since the mopping up team wouldn't be needed for its original purpose, he ordered its men to assist.

"Spread out! Spread out!" he yelled as he hurried along the trench to check that all was well.

He noticed at once how much faster he could move. The enemy seemed to have done a far better job of draining this one. As soon as spades arrived, Lieutenant Smalby's men were detailed to establish precautionary bomb stops. A cheer went up as A Company jumped across them and continued to advance.

Cody had only just got back to his commandeered dugout when the enemy artillery finally opened up. Shells began to rain down right on top of them. Their trench must have been targeted in advance. Attitudes changed. Whatever the sort of the others, C Company had been deliberately singled out.

"Thank God it's spread out!" shouted Lieutenant Cobbold, who was next in the line.

Indeed, the shells were landing haphazardly. They hunkered down with their hands to their ears. Hardy reckoned they were mostly 77- and 105-millimetre shells and no heavier. That put the enemy artillery at a possible two to three miles away, out of sight given the terrain between. The chances were that the position was new.

"Should we advise?" asked Cobbold, whose orderly beside him was busy getting out another pigeon.

Just as he spoke, two friendly planes unexpectedly flew over them. Brigade would soon find out for itself.

The merciless bombardment continued for half-an-hour all the same. The sense of intense oppression grew. Some men screamed. Others were silenced by their comrades as soon as they tried to. Cody wondered how much they could take.

When the respite finally came, Cody hoisted his periscope to spot any sign of A Company ahead. They appeared to have invested a position fifty yards away. He informed everyone around him and asked for them to pass the message on.

Friendly artillery started up once again. Before long, B Company appeared and crossed their line. Captain Fuller stopped for a while. Cody greeted the round boyish face of his colleague. They were both smiling.

"I'll never thank Quinn for this, Moose."

He had been the first to express his dislike of Quinn.

"I've seen boys get blackballed for far less."

Cody didn't reply. He put his arm on his colleague's shoulder in sympathy. He liked Fuller. He had been a science teacher before the war, and it often made some of his ideas a little far-fetched, failing to recognise the limitations of his men whom he was inclined to blame too often when things didn't work out.

"Good job by the artillery," Cody said to change the subject.

Fuller had always openly admitted that he would have preferred joining the artillery. He nodded in agreement and disappeared over the parapet.

Cody walked along the trench once again, leaving Hardy in place. C Company had advanced with Lewis guns, and these were now being reinforced by Vickers and Stokes teams. It was getting dark, and time to organise wiring parties. A large party set about running a buried cable back to brigade, and Cragg's D company came forward to help.

Cragg himself came by. He, too, referred to Quinn.

"What do you think Wilkes will do now, Moose?" he asked.

Cody shrugged. He was getting a little fed up with all the obsession over Quinn, but he had time for Cragg all the same. Out of all his colleagues, the tall Irish-born Cragg was undoubtedly closest. A well-built boxer, he had a clean face, his thin brown hair brushed sideways, and large ears that had earned him the nickname 'Lugs' before he had been promoted. He had been an accountant in civilian life, joining the army two years before the war. Whereas Talbot was the natural leader among the four commanders, Cragg's reassuring voice and common sense, and the ability to delegate, made him the commander most respected by his men.

Hopper, wearing his new corporal's stripes, turned up. He asked permission to head over to the site of the machine gun nest now only a five-minute walk to the right of them.

"Lieutenant Piggot is alright with it, Captain."

Cody, Hopper, and Hardy went up together before it got too dark. They discovered that the position had been so pummelled that there remained little to learn. Hopper picked up what appeared to be the remnant of a stand that might have held the machine gun itself, but they found nothing else until Hardy spotted a shattered helmet quite far away.

They looked back towards the old firing trench below. Cody lent Hopper his field glasses to determine if he could spot anything, as their advance had skirted where the corpses of his comrades lay. It had become too dark, and they decided to return.

"At last they'll get recuperated," Cody remarked.

They settled in with a minimum of sentries, given that A and B Companies were in front. Ahead of them, intermittent firing went on well into the night. Cody waited by his new telephone, convinced he would be ordered to dig a new v-trench. The brigadier's visit had left him as haunted as the poor colonel.

He looked over to where Hardy was sitting next to an oil lamp. As usual, his orderly, who had been a storekeeper in his previous life, rarely sought conversation. With his rifle slung over his shoulder, he would resolutely keep himself awake until his equally taciturn master had fallen asleep, tallying up his list of provisions needs for the officers and NCOs, and making sure from memory that he was one batch ahead on each item.

At daylight, reports drifted back that the new enemy line was proving impenetrable. The chatter from brigade seemed to indicate that it was considering a new line of trenches just forward of where the men ahead were pinned down. So far spared of any further digging or wiring, Cody waited for orders.

Hardy returned with breakfast rations for both of them and opened a tin of bully beef. He already had tea on the boil.

"Since you've nothing better to do, Captain!"

They stayed put all day and until dusk, by which time it was decided to invest fully the new front line and beef up reserve and communication trenches on the nearside. For this, a fresh brigade would take over, and the battalion would pull back to a camp five miles to the rear. When they heard this, the men cheered. They had earned the glory for the advance and avoided the tedium of consolidating the new front.

Shortly before they were due to move out, the colonel came forward with Quinn. Without saying a word, Quinn continued onwards to make sure of his snipers. Hardy escaped out of hearing, intending to check his lists.

"He's off the hook," the colonel confirmed once they were alone. "I wanted to tell you that in person."

He was still agitated all the same. He added Quinn had earned his reprieve from any inquiry, but that the brigadier had insisted that he should never be recognised for the successful advance.

Cody surprised himself by coming to Quinn's defence.

"It's up to us to make amends, sir. For the battalion's sake."

"What!"

"I think the brigadier should reconsider, Colonel."

"I will ensure that he is destroyed forever, Captain," the colonel said. "Success or no success!"

He became distracted by what he could see of the excellent state of the surrounding trench.

"Find out why they have been better than us at this, Captain."

Once again Cody couldn't fathom why, with his supposed professional interest, the colonel hadn't stayed to figure it out for himself. He stood up to watch the colonel leave for the front line. Leaving the trench business aside, he thought about Quinn. He thought about his own reaction towards him. Why come to the defence of such a deeply unpleasant man who had been at fault? For all the horrific occurrences and blunders since the war had begun, Quinn's case was a first of its type.

There was a small amount of time left. Hardy returned and Cody asked him to fetch Lieutenants Piggot and Smalby. After detailing them to examine the trench and make notes, Cody installed himself on an upturned ammunition crate in order to catch up with letters of condolence. Hardy grabbed his rifle and raised himself to the freshly prepared fire step to keep lookout.

Cody started with his seven men who had died during Quinn's escapade. As usual, he dated the letters and gave his address simply as France. He had a list of the men for the spelling of their names and their next of kin. The addresses would be taken care of by brigade.

He had done this countless times before, always in his personal handwriting. Crouched there, modestly shielded from the rain that had just started up again, and under his dim oil lamp, these were hardly appropriate conditions for inspiring what he was about to write.

His letters would be read repeatedly by their recipient's families, and for decades to come. He had to take as much care as he could. He ended up reeling off the same bland message that told nothing of the reality.

> *Please accept my sincere condolences for the loss of your... He was of great value to his company and battalion and shall be missed by all. On the night in question, he bravely went out on patrol when they were surprised by an enemy machine gun post. He fell alongside six of his comrades. Only three survived.*

He paused. He felt dishonest, but such accounts were inevitable and become routine. When they had first arrived, he had planned to visit each of the bereaved after the war, but that had soon become inconceivable. The endless hostilities had long corrupted him like everyone else. Perhaps he no longer deserved his rank.

Lieutenant Cobbold approached, but Hardy, still up on the fire step, waved that his timing was bad. Cobbold quietly retreated.

Cody continued writing.

> *I can assure you that his sacrifice was not in vain. The information the three survivors returned with allowed a vital advance only hours later. Your.... will be remembered for his sacrifice.*

Cody broke off. His mind turned to his mother who had brought himself and his two younger brothers into the world and raised them. He wondered how she would have reacted to such a letter. He thought of his father. He would have encountered so many such letters addressed to his parishioners, and become proficient at consolation, at interpreting what couldn't have been said.

Cody's father had instilled his principles into his sons, a sense of loyalty, a need to watch other people's backs, especially those who had been deemed to have done wrong. Sometimes Cody looked with envy at the more dissolute characters he encountered around him. Proud as he was to be displaying such an oriflamme of decency, he knew all the same that, if he was not careful, he would find himself ostracised as much as someone like Quinn. Friendship and respect could be as fragile as principles, especially in hard times.

5

The morning felt damp, but less cold than the day before. The 10th Battalion was encamped in an area as yet unscathed by war. A rise in the terrain between the camp and the front even reduced the worst of the noise and flashes at night. The battalion had seen worse.

Breakfast was being served. Under a calm grey sky, men were lining up in front of each of the field kitchens and then randomly dispersing into small groups to consume their food. It was an opportunity for quiet bonding, discovering a little more about the lives of colleagues they hadn't necessarily spent time with in the trenches, finding out what happened to so-and-so, and listening to the rumours and small talk that kept the battalion alive. The scene was almost balmy, such an about-turn from the savagery and desolation of the days before. One could be forgiven for believing that such dramatic swings would twist and turn the minds of its participants and leave them numbed. It was likely true.

Cody and his three fellow commanders had walked over from their billets in the nearby village to join in, as was their custom when they weren't encamped with their men. They were sharing a fallen tree at a choice spot one end of a large field that had been left to fallow, next to the camp.

It was an occasion for badinage. The camaraderie between them, as for all ranks, was high. Most of the troops had originated from isolated lives in the country, or small villages, totally unused to sharing danger, miraculous survival, and defying death, let alone the close company of hundreds of others. In a way, it reminded many of them of their school days, before they had had to negotiate the lonely path of fending for themselves in a challenging and disinterested world. The men who were already married often felt the camaraderie more than their colleagues. It was a reminder of the freedom of bachelor days. The experience made them dread the day when it would all end.

All this was despite the colonel. He had little regard for such matters. He seemed to do everything he could to foster alienation in the ranks and between his officers. His commanders thought he believed it created a frame of mind far better suited to conflict.

"For Wilkes, Quinn makes sense!" Talbot had remarked a week after the intelligence officer's arrival.

Thanks to the close-knit unity of the battalion's captains and lieutenants, who successfully fended off the colonel's attempts at disruption, such occasions as the present one became a relief in more sense that one. Instead of idling away their respite time focusing on the negative, instead of harping on about the lousy decisions that got them to where they were, the disasters they had had to face, or the mistakes they could see coming, the vast majority exploited the opportunity for peace of mind.

The previous occupants had, for once, left the camp in a fit state.

"How about starting off with clearing-up parties," Talbot said.

They had all been impressed. It was true that the usually belated remedial action on the final rest day always left something to desire. The battalion had been as culpable as any, and stronger environmental discipline from the start would be good for morale.

"Doesn't quite fit with the way Wilkes sees things," said Fuller.

True or not, it didn't matter. The effective shield put up by the four commanders bound them together and made it such a united battalion.

Cody looked over at Cragg. He was reading again.

"Finished yet?" he asked.

Cragg always took ages, which was odd because at every occasion like this he took advantage. Cody was unlikely to see soon the Conan Doyle that had already been read and battered in the trenches by the others. A few months before, Fuller had jokingly suggested to the colonel that he keep written orders brief for his colleague's sake. Cody was convinced that Cragg had been taking revenge ever since.

The closest town was an hour's ride away, which was far, and they hadn't yet tried it out. Most of it was still standing, and it was reputed to have more than its fair share of distractions. There was bound to be at least one day ahead when they could escape for the sight of a pair of ankles.

"Any volunteers?" asked Talbot, reckoning that he could lay his hands on enough horses.

Horses had become unusually scarce.

He had got out his pocketknife to work on a loose branch, as he always did when the occasion presented itself. Sometimes his constant hacking away drove the others to distraction.

"We'll bring Moose along with us," quipped Fuller, knowing full well that Cody would never engage.

The joke between them was that their friend was an erudite conversationalist. They all looked at Cody, having predicted his reaction.

"Just do the corralling for us," said Talbot.

But they already knew his answer.

"It's all your talk of monasteries and art, Moose," Talbot said. "It gives them such a sense of security."

Cody thought that ridiculous coming from by far the best-looking officer in the battalion, quite capable of selling off his own mother had he wanted to, but he refrained from saying so.

They had only been there a few hours. The relief had taken over four hours in pitch black, the march back to camp less than half that. Once again, leaving the trenches had tested their patience, been like a drawn-out unpleasant detraining or disembarkation, and a thousand times more dangerous. What a joy it had been to land boots on the relatively hard ground of the road that led away from the front.

And once again, how flexible had been the human mind? From the very first hour of its arrival, the battalion had adapted to the environment of peace. At last allowed to smoke, men forgot about the threat of terror of the days before, the constant fear of surprise, the permanent nervous awareness of the nearby enemy and what he might do to them before they were relieved, or how they would be picked off while the relief was underway. They found the time to send one last letter home. The occasion anointed an extraordinary transition between two worlds, one inhuman, unpredictable, and terrifying: the other of peace, normality and freedom. It would be quite a few days yet before the butterflies resumed ahead of a return to the abyss.

On this occasion, there was more than the usual football competition on its way. The four captains began discussing the upcoming divisional horse show and boxing competition, two events that were due to be held next to the camp. Thanks to the brigadier, the battalion's week-long rest period had been fortuitously timed. His magnanimity had been for a reason. The tiny local village had no facilities to speak of other than an *estaminet* so small that it was out of bounds to the troops, and an equally useless shop and a young lady with long blond hair who lived on top of it. Since the shop did its best to refuse custom in order to protect the needs of the villagers, and there was no waterhole, Rapunzel, as she was known, provided the greater service. The stairs leading up to her room were always crowded.

But there was an entire battalion to cater for. Everything possible had to be found elsewhere to dissipate its unspent energy. Boredom and frustration could turn destructive at any moment. What better than to keep the men busy in competition. In fact, it was the only choice.

All that was days away. For the rest of their first day of rest, the men would relax and write letters and queue up for the luxury of hot showers and clean clothes. A round of inoculations for typhoid and paratyphoid had been scheduled for the following morning. The unpleasant after-effects would mean a rare day or two off from the obligatory parades, duties, and training.

"No-one will be fit enough in time," predicted Cody as they continued to down their breakfast.

He was referring to the battalion's showing in the field days to come. He planned to compete in the over fifteen hands class of the horse event and was worried for himself as well. The colonel had begrudgingly promised his mare.

Dismissing his concern, his comrades wished him luck.

"I think she should be reserved for us," Cragg said, putting aside his book.

His mind was elsewhere. He was referring to Rapunzel, whom he constantly thought about, and overlooking the fact that officers could ride further afield for such matters.

The others caught on and laughed. The comely Rapunzel had a gloriously Gallic face that reminded Cragg of a portrait in the National Gallery that he had long taken to. During their last stay at camp, he had recounted how he never missed a chance to see it, and would walk up to it, ignoring hundreds of old masters along the way, as though the subject were a long-lost friend. On one occasion, he had even caught himself greeting her in front of a crowd of silent visitors.

"Moose, you couldn't ask your Kate to come over and render us a service?" said Cragg.

They all laughed, except Cody. What Cragg had meant, because he had suggested it before, was for Cody's wife to paint Rapunzel's portrait for them to keep at the mess.

They talked about the camp. Only a short walk from the village, it consisted mainly of wooden huts, some of them quite leaky. Apart from the sports field it bordered, a mile away was an improvised shooting range which they would use on remaining days. The local villagers could come and watch, quite unlike better-equipped neighbourhoods they had encamped next to, where the flow had been in reverse and visitors forbidden.

But the pretence that it was all going to be only fun for the next few days was a guise, and in reality, they knew it. For the officers and NCOs, the respite from front duties would be replaced by the need to train up a wave of new recruits expected to be bussed in that morning. The battalion had become nearly two hundred men down from anything considered acceptable, and it would take a grand effort. By the end of the week, officers, NCOs, and men, were likely to be keener than ever to get back to the trenches.

Talbot spotted Quinn leaving the breakfast line and heading their way. He put away his knife and briskly got up, and Fuller and Cragg, catching on, prepared to follow suit. Remaining seated, Cody held his arm out and asked them to stay put.

"Please, gentlemen!"

Coming from the man who had taken the lion's share of the losses caused by Quinn, all three of them reluctantly acceded.

"It doesn't pass well," Cody reminded them.

"I can't stand him, Moose," Talbot ranted. "I know his type. If he stays, it will only get worse. If I hear his voice once more…"

"He'll go," assured Cragg.

Quinn arrived before more could be said. He asked if he could join them. Cody gestured for him to share the tree so that they would all face the same way. Quinn chose instead to sit opposite them on the ground. He seemed to have deliberately made himself lower than they were. Cody wondered if this was a sign of contrition. They had spoken little since the incident and there remained much to fathom about his present state of mind.

"They left me out of the despatches."

It was the last thing any of them wanted to hear. Looking harshly at his colleagues so that they would forget about getting up, Cody tried to deflect the conversation.

"Are you competing, Quinn?"

It turned out that no-one had informed Quinn of the competitions. Cody explained the plan for the week. While all were thinking about the irony of the intelligence officer being the last in the know, Quinn let it be known that he needed to lay his hands on a horse. Talbot and Fuller were doing their best to look the other way.

"A horse!" Quinn repeated.

Cody needed to warn him that the last thing he should think of would be to ask either the colonel or major.

"Try the 3rd Battalion."

If anyone had a spare horse, it would be they.

Suddenly, Quinn surprised them all by standing up and making a motion with his fists. It seemed childish.

"I didn't know you boxed, Quinn," mocked Cragg, who was best known for it and planned to compete.

He had instantly relished the opportunity to challenge him in the officers' competition. Cody flinched at the thought of what might happen.

Corporal Hopper came over and interrupted them. Fifty conscripts had arrived earlier than expected and needed taking care of. They were presently at the other end of the camp being organised by NCOs. Hopper walked off. Cody and his three colleagues briskly finished up and went off to do their duty, leaving Quinn sitting there on his own and with their trays to return.

"First choice is mine!" said Cody.

He had Hopper on his mind.

"How I detest that man, Moose!" ranted Cragg, still aggravated by Quinn's intrusion.

They passed a pile of Vermorals stacked on the ground.

"He's a farmer, isn't he?" asked Fuller.

"Isn't it lead arsenate they use on fruit trees?" asked Cragg.

"Must have got in the water there!" said Talbot. "A bit like around here, if you ask me."

"Shut your mouths, all of you!" shouted Cody.

"You should be the last person to defend him, Moose," said Cragg. "Your sanctimonious attitude is getting to me."

This was not a good sign. For the first time, Cody realised relations were becoming strained.

*

By Sunday, three days later, everyone had become fit again. Normal camp life had resumed, this time animated by the buzz around the upcoming events. After the usual platoon drill, there was a church parade followed by a five-mile cross-country run for most of the men, and preliminary show jumping heats for the competitors.

Quinn had managed to get a mount from the Third. He rode over to Cody to show it off.

"We'll be up against each other, Cody."

Cody saw how good the horse and rider looked together, a far cry, he knew, from his own presentation. He asked how Quinn had fared so well at the last minute.

"An acquaintance of my father's. Or rather the son of. Quite by chance. I didn't know."

He dismounted and, still holding the horse's reign, sat down in front of the small wooden trestle table at which Cody was making notes. Cody stopped writing and asked him what his father did.

"He owns an estate. Three thousand acres near the south coast. It came with my mother."

"Do you have siblings?"

"No. A wife, that's all."

Cody tried to imagine Quinn at his large home and estate, his no doubt domineering father and his 'that's-all' wife. He seemed to have everything. No doubt he enjoyed plenty more in life than riding.

Two hours later, Cody didn't even survive the first heat. Quinn won hands down and by late afternoon had ended up one of two chosen to represent brigade in the finals.

"Don't worry, Moose old chap," said Cragg, who had watched and turned up while Hardy was busy unsaddling the colonel's horse. "I'll get him."

At dawn the following day, the battalion held a musketry competition. At least it had replaced the endless drills. The men were divided into officer-led platoons of twenty and marched several miles between sessions on the range. None of the shooting scores turned out to be impressive, but even the platoons with the most newly arrived conscripts kept their timing. Cody feared it might not last that way.

In the afternoon, after a series of relay races, all companies practised an attack on an imaginary strongpoint near a local farm that included bayonet and specialists' training. Cody oversaw a set of trenches over which the men had to jump. Once again, it proved a mixed showing. There were quite a few injuries among the new recruits, especially the shorter ones. Mercifully, neither the colonel nor the major had thought to pass by.

That evening, the colonel turned up to speak to Cody just as he was leaving camp. Cody had left Hardy with the rest of the men. They walked together through the village to their respective billets. The colonel was upset about Quinn's ability to have got hold of a horse, let alone his success in the heats. It all seemed extremely petty to Cody. He now felt surrounded by men incapable of moving on.

"Why, for heaven's sake, couldn't you thrash him?" the colonel asked.

He then mentioned that Quinn had approached him for leave and that, to his subsequent regret, he had instinctively refused. He had finally given way for the end of the week, hoping that it would at least be a chance to try a lieutenant in his place for the return to action.

"I was thinking of Piggot."

Thinking that Piggot's yessing-to-death would keep the colonel at bay, Cody replied he would be an excellent choice, but with so many raw recruits he needed him more than ever. The colonel backed down and said that he would ask one of the other commanders. He thanked him and left.

Reaching his billet, Cody helped himself to the remains of a bottle of *vin ordinaire* he had picked up on the first day. He sat down on the side of his bed and thought about Quinn's situation. He still felt peeved by the colonel and his colleagues. The affair looked as though it would haunt the battalion for a while yet.

Unable to get his thoughts to wonder away from the subject, and short of the book he had been waiting for, he headed back to the mess in camp.

It turned out that Quinn was there and sitting on his own. The place was tiny and resembled an oversized potting shed. Cody felt he had no choice but to join Quinn. He made the point of congratulating him for his riding. Quinn offered him a beer in return.

Cody invited Quinn to talk about himself. What ensued was a long, one-sided conversation that Cody soon regretted having started. He learned that after leaving college, and before joining up, Quinn had been working for his father. The estate primarily comprised arable land, but they also kept livestock and made cheese, and they had horses. He expected to take it over in a few years' time, hopefully sooner.

"Aha!" said Cody, giving away what he had been thinking all along.

In order to explore his other suspicions about Quinn, he enquired about his father. Quinn explained he had been a self-made entrepreneur and local politician and had served in South Africa. The more Quinn talked about his father, reminding him he had risen to general, the more Cody sensed that the father and son relationship explained more than a little. There had to be a significant amount of mental bastinado between the two. He had been on the money from the start.

"And your wife?"

Quinn had been married for two years and admitted that he missed his life as a bachelor. For escape before the war, he had frequently driven to London to enjoy the company of friends and nightlife, and southern France had provided an escape in summer. Money wasn't an issue and escape an obsession.

"You drive?"

"Can't you?"

Cody looked blank.

"For heaven's sake, man!" Quinn said. "How could you survive without a car?"

Cody wanted him to change the subject.

"Or a horse?" Quinn went on.

Getting nowhere with his taunting, Quinn resumed his monologue. At the outbreak of war, he had signed up intending to get a commission in the Royal Engineers. He had wanted to receive training that might help him for later.

He went on for a while about the merits of the Engineers and of the training he got before arriving at the front. He boasted it as a proper education. He talked about some the arguments he had with his father about pontoon construction and the setting up of defences, and the extent to which changes since the turn of the century rendered his father repeatedly wrong.

"What did you think of the trenches we've come from?" Cody asked.

Cody quietly listened to Quinn going on about all he had disapproved of before returning to the subject of the general. He lived in his own world.

Having exhausted accounts of the constant jousting with his father, Quinn talked about his wife. She ran the farm. She had a brother serving in France.

"One of those new field map units. He's a printer of all things."

From Quinn's dismissive references, Cody sensed that there too existed strains. He couldn't quite decipher whether it had to do with his wife herself or his brother-in-law's profession. Perhaps it was both.

As the one-sided conversation advanced, or arguably descended, Quinn's persistent air of superiority got the better of Cody's patience. Cody tried to piece together his latest understanding of the makeup of the dislikable man in front of him. Quinn's rapid signing up at the outbreak of war surely had something to do with his father. His innate arrogance seemed to be borne out of his status and freedom in life and complex relationship at home that created his need to show himself to be better than others.

At no point did Quinn mention his mother, and Cody, already put-off, decided not to open that door. Yet much as Quinn seemed so far from his own type, and altogether tiring, Cody had no intention of distancing himself from his colleague. As long as Quinn was around, he would see their relationship through to the end. It could be no other way.

The following morning, there was a short parade and inspection before the finals of the divisional horse show. From first light, spectators turned up from the other camps and the usual crowd of locals from surrounding villages.

The picturesque Rapunzel appeared mid-morning. She had a throng that hovered around her, mostly from Talbot's company. Each admitting a whiff of envy, Cody and Talbot had a chuckle over it.

Brigadier Lightfoot and his colleagues were joined by the battalion commanders, but the major-general was absent, rumour had it called to Paris to confer with the French and newly arrived Americans over the upcoming campaign.

Quinn, who impressed with his tall, upright stature and impeccable appearance, did remarkably well. He even upset the Third for having beaten them with one of their own mounts and subsequently taunting them over it. He finally came a close second in the overall competition and earned himself plenty of praise from the other battalions.

"Little do they know!" persisted Talbot.

Cody held back saying anything. He had spotted the colonel from afar while the competition had played out. Even at that distance, his mood was clear. For a good while yet, Quinn would be the battalion's cross to bear. It made Cody angry. Whatever he thought about Quinn, he was becoming very annoyed indeed by the prevailing winds. He ran into Hardy while this was still preying on his mind and pulled him aside from checking the stores.

"What are they all saying about Captain Quinn?" he asked.

"Nothing much, Captain," said Hardy. "He's seen as the usual toff, caught up in a fight with his fellow officers for a typical toff's cock-up. No-one really cares. His snipers love him."

Cody knew he would have heard it as it was.

That evening at the mess, Cody made one more appeal to his colleagues. It was in vain. They had evidently conferred beforehand. They unabashedly reminded him how much they detested Quinn. In his noble gesture to bring peace, Cody had found himself isolated. It was ironic that he disliked the fellow himself.

Straight after breakfast the following morning, in his billet for a change, Cody joined Talbot and Fuller at the shooting range. It had become colder and windier, not ideal for accuracy. Fuller's men were coming to the end of their session with disappearing targets while the other companies, waiting to the rear for their turn, were being supervised in dismantling and cleaning their guns. The accuracy of the shooting was not good at all, yet another poor showing by the battalion. Fuller was blaming it on his new conscripts rather than the weather. He looked across to the colonel who was standing on his own, about fifty yards away, busily taking stock.

"What do you think?" he asked.

They were concerned that the colonel would decide that the practising be continued into the afternoon for the worst performing companies. He might order the canteens into the field to minimise the loss of time over lunch.

Forgetting their awkward conversation of the night before, Cody laughed in jest. Despite having received most of the new recruits, he was sure that his men would do better in order to avoid missing the brigade boxing competition that had been scheduled for after lunch. That would give him more supporters for his men who were taking part.

"Wilkes doesn't look in the mood for spoiling our day, Fuller," Talbot observed.

"Got to be the glorious thought of not having Quinn for a week," said Fuller in return.

Word had got around.

"Or Cragg getting a knockout in the first round!" said Talbot.

None of them had noticed that Quinn had crept up and was standing within earshot. Cody belatedly caught on and diligently led him away before anything could happen. Quinn was fuming, but he said nothing. It conditioned him well for combat.

In the end, none of the companies fared particularly well. Robbed of yet another opportunity to decide which of them was in better form for front-line duty, the colonel decided that the rest of the week should be spent on the range, but that no-one would be denied the afternoon event. Everyone assumed it was only because he wanted the battalion to do as well as possible.

"From dawn to dusk!" he angrily said to his four commanders before they broke up for lunch. "Food on site!"

Quinn accompanied Cody over to the field where several boxing rings had been set up, dirty reused tapes spread around corner posts hewed from branches. The canteens were already serving horsemeat and peas again, and men were impatiently lining up, eager to get on with what was to follow.

Cody asked Quinn if he was going to eat just before his fight.

"That food?" Quinn ranted with reason.

Cody saw his colleague doing everything possible to work himself into the rage he needed. Self-imposed starvation no doubt helped. Across the field, he spotted Talbot and Fuller working Cragg up in turn. It promised to be a good match. He only hoped that everyone would approach it professionally, and that it not be seen as a settling of scores or something that would drag on forever afterwards.

The earlier heats were staged between contestants from different battalions. Spectators strolled around choosing the better fights to watch, but in those first stages, partisanship seemed to take precedent over the quality of fighting. With her entourage of Talbot's hangers-on, the glorious Rapunzel appeared to do her best, distracting the battalion's opponents in the ring.

By mid-afternoon, C Company was doing better than most, and several of its combatants ended up contesting each other. The company eventually won the middleweight competition and came second in the catchweight.

With Hardy at his side and doing all the shouting, which was the only time he ever did so, Cody made a point of watching each of the finals and congratulating his participants.

"Well done, Captain!"

It was Major Hickman passing by. He was in a hurry to get to the one ring reserved for the officers' competition.

"Join me, won't you?"

Hardy went off to watch the other fights. Quinn and Cragg were already in the ring, warming up. Cragg was wearing ear protectors for the first time, which Cody thought to be against the rules. They had drawn a large crowd, in part because of both their tall statures, and the expectation that it would be a tough fight.

Standing next to the major, Cody looked around. His three colleagues and the colonel were already there. He knew what was going through their minds, but expected a nasty surprise from Quinn.

As soon as he came out of his corner, Quinn precipitated on his opponent without the usual sparring. Landing a rapid succession of jabs onto Cragg's face and upper body, he looked feral. A violent uppercut to Cragg's jaw made everyone think it would soon be over. Cragg went down on one knee and then recovered. With blood running down the side of one eye, he looked up at his opponent who had dropped his guard and seemed to taunt him. He leapt up and, with a fierce uncharacteristic look in his eyes that no-one recognised, he landed a massive punch in Quinn's left eye. Everyone cheered. Quinn fell to the ground, dazed. The referee counted. Quinn soon got up and repeated the same onslaught as before, only to be landed another well-placed punch in his temple. Quinn stood his ground this time, but he had lost some of his initial verve. He jabbed his opponent but ineffectively, and his dancing around him looked sluggish.

The bell, which was only a metal plate hit with a spoon, signified the end of the round. Cody found himself within hearing distance of Cragg's corner. Over the noise of the crowd, Talbot was going on about Quinn's tiring in the last round.

"Let him do his thing, Lugs. Then go for it!"

The plate-bell went. Sure enough, Quinn came out and repeated his frenzy. Cragg's ploy worked. Quinn's momentary relapse after all his effort was met by a sudden and surprising pounding by an energised opponent. Two hits to the face followed one to the chest, and then one to the side of his head. Quinn ended up on the ground for good.

But the spectacle didn't stop there. Lying on his side, Quinn opened his eyes and then slowly turned to look up at his opponent. Blinking from the mixture of blood and sweat that was invading his eyes, he stared at Cragg for several long seconds and laughed hysterically. It was as if he had enjoyed it.

Spectators were turned off by Quinn's strange behaviour. The beating seemed to have awoken a monster in him. They wondered whether he would get up again.

Still laughing, Quinn tried to force himself up from the ground. He failed and collapsed for good.

Cody was not the only one to have been shocked by Quinn's maniacal comportment, as if he had wanted more. From a distance, he noticed the colonel trying to restrain his glee, unaware of what had followed. Away from them, Lieutenant Piggot was doing the same, as were Captains Talbot and Fuller.

Cody prayed it was all over for good.

6

The distant front was quiet. Activity along the village main street had wound down with the descending dark, and most of the houses had already been shuttered. One might be forgiven for not realising that a camp of several hundred troops was only a brief walk away.

As he headed for his billet, Cody wondered why the locals had the unhealthy habit of closing their bedroom windows at night. And their children seemed to stay up late. Ahead of him, an old woman in a dark shawl was herding two of them through her front door. Cody's three girls would have long been in bed by then.

Further along the street, a short, stubby man in a cloth cap was leading a horse twice his size towards the far end of the village. Their shadows became projected across the street as they passed the tiny village shop that still had its lights on.

Cody tried to predict how matters would turn out for Quinn. Quinn's extraordinary antics at the end of the boxing match would surely have alienated most who had witnessed them and spurned a desire greater than ever to be rid of him for good.

He wondered if Quinn, from his side, would look for revenge. He needed to be discouraged. Prolonging the miserable affair was out of the question. Deciding that he would do his best to calm matters down, Cody made a diversion to the shop before it closed, catching himself stealing a glance towards the unshuttered window above it. He could hear music, sounding like one of the *Nocturnes* that Kate was so good at. The light was on and the curtains drawn, and a shadow crossed the room, but there was no-one to be seen through the windowed door that led to the stairs.

"*Bonjour, mon Capitaine!*"

The shopkeeper was Cody's landlady's brother. Everyone in the village seemed related to each other. Cody had been instantly recognised with deference, but he knew that prising anything decent out of the old man would still be tough. He tested the waters by looking at him sternly in the eyes, but soon found himself distracted by the man's shoddy appearance. His face looked pallid, his withering black hair unkempt. The large bulge in his stomach, his red cheeks and nose, and the deep pockets under his eyes, pointed to decades of wear.

"*Auriez-vous du calva, par hasard?*"

Cody knew too well that he had to be far from the first officer to have posed such a question in vain. Troops had been in the area for years. But in the country responsible for the word *entrepreneur*, such an art had already proved rare for items that mattered.

There was the expected Gallic shrug. Cody noticed the door to the backroom slightly ajar. Through the narrow crack he suspected the hovering eye of the shopkeeper's wife, undoubtedly the puppet master, *l'éminence grise* of the small enterprise. Her reputation preceded her. The major had referred to her as a notorious grimalkin.

Cody sympathetically looked back at the pathetic husband. He had never seen his wife, but by all accounts, she was well-preserved for her age and physically close to their daughter. How he longed to see for himself. It might even better expedite the matter in hand.

"*Combien?*"

The marionette stood there resolute, refusing to budge.

"*Combien?*" Cody repeated, unable to prevent a quick second glance towards the door.

He theatrically got out his wallet, making sure that his wad of one-franc notes could be seen from the backroom as well. The shopkeeper flinched. It was a positive sign, but he didn't follow up by looking back behind him. He tried screwing up his face in a last plea, but Cody stood his ground. Now Cody felt no pity. Formidable businesspeople or not, this man's family had profited for years from the army at its doorstep. His daughter upstairs even boasted a sculpture that could be visited for a fee despite the *entrée libre* sign posted on the front door. The image of her curvaceous body stuck. Cody shuddered when he recalled her lewd manner of suddenly looking back whenever being followed, a bit like a horse.

The shopkeeper disappeared. Cody heard a creaking cupboard door and the sound of bottles gently tapping against each other. Telltale scuffles told him that this was to disguise a ferocious argument being mimed in the backroom. He heard the slapping of hands followed by the sound of a bottle being resolutely slammed onto a wooden surface as if to say, "*C'est celui-là ou rien!*"

Cody lit up as the man reappeared, albeit with a surprisingly small bottle in his hand, his face looking as though he was about to give away the Republic's very last crown jewel. Glancing back, he mumbled an offer so unreasonable that he evidently hoped that Cody had misunderstood it. Cody paid up all the same. How he hated being exploited by the very people his countrymen were sacrificing their lives for. The only harm the British had done to the village was to have confiscated all the pigeons when they had first arrived. But the enemy would have done the same and worse besides.

"*Vous ne diriez rien, mon Capitaine!*" boldly said the shopkeeper, as he closed up for the night behind him.

Cody walked back to his billet marvelling at yet another *commerçant* who decided who his customers would be and ordered them around to boot. He tried to rationalise a nation so rich in history yet impoverished by pessimism, greed, a miserable outlook on life, and rampant jealousies, even at the best of times. Everyone was constantly at each other's throat. His landlady frequently ranted about her brother and his trickeries, and their feud was, among several others, the talk of the village. And yet this was the north of the country, where people were considered the most open and friendly. The only escapee of this quagmire seemed to be his landlady's glamourous niece, who made more money than the rest of the village put together. She never got a single mention.

After a light supper brought up by his landlady, to whom he avoided relating his visit, Cody braced himself for a call on Quinn. His billet was in a taller house closer to camp. Before leaving, Cody packed up his portable gramophone, hoping to calm the atmosphere by reminding them of home. With luck, Quinn would appreciate a bacchanalian evening together.

Cody saw no-one outside now, despite the absence of rain. As he walked down the blackened street, he came to the realisation that he had got to know the ins and outs of people in the village better than he had the man he was about to visit. Characters took days to unravel. Quinn was taking weeks. The locals admittedly helped by being so much keener to go on about people of whom they disapproved.

Cody heard shouting from behind some shutters on the way. Villagers were constantly at war with each other. Even supposed friendships had to be treated warily. He remembered the multiple warnings against using the French *tu*. Would an early familiarity with Quinn breed a contempt he would regret? He would soon find out.

"That was revenge!" bawled Quinn, nursing his black eye and the cuts on his face as he opened up.

He had displayed no sign of welcome to his garret. Towering over his visitor, he ushered Cody in, adding nothing more, and Cody pulled over a second chair to the small table where Quinn had been cleaning his revolver. The room stank of the solvent he had been using, one that Cody didn't recognise at all.

Quinn leaned over to open the shuttered window. Cody looked around at the oppressive wallpaper. It was adorned with dark-brown and ochre flowers, even worse than his own.

"A fair fight and a good one," he eventually replied as he sat down, hoping he had not been too maladroit.

He had decided not to bring up Quinn's curious antics on the ground. He had still not fathomed them out.

"Even the colonel was for the other man," Quinn said.

At least Quinn was opening up. He still appeared to have some fight left in him. He proved it by striding over to a small shaving mirror above the sink and carelessly smashing it with his fist. Cody stood up in alarm, but Quinn didn't seem to have injured himself, perhaps just brought himself bad luck in displaying his juvenile antics.

"You're a terrible looser, Quinn!"

He sat down again, watching to see what Quinn did next.

"I saw how you went into it. The problem was yours."

"Maybe," admitted Quinn, calming down as Cody removed the calva from his coat pocket and slammed it on the table, as he had overheard earlier on.

After walking around at little more on the creaking floor, Quinn sat down. Cody prayed the calva would be worth it. He got up to start up his gramophone, posed by the door. The music was all he had, Beecham's *Die Fledermaus,* in several discs that travelled in a side slot.

"How can you listen to that noise?" Quinn asked before the music had even started.

"More than noise, Quinn. It brings pictures and dreams."

Despite Quinn's sneer, the music immediately calmed the atmosphere. Without thanking him for either gesture, Quinn got up to fetch two bulky glasses that came with his room. Cody poured half-an-inch in each.

They played cards.

"Why are you doing this, Cody?" Quinn asked after a few minutes into the game. "You, more than anyone should be hating me for what I did. You look to be the only colleague who isn't."

This was a far fetch from Quinn's usual arrogance.

"It was an honest mistake," Cody said, looking up at the mirror to check that it still held together.

It had been an egregious lie, but arguably a white one.

"The others will get over it with time."

"But what makes *you* so different?"

Cody replied it wasn't in his nature to bear grudges. The rest of them would get to realise the error of their ways.

"Just avoid being a cad in the meantime," he warned.

Quinn protested. The arrogance reappeared. *He* had shown initiative. In the end, the battalion had come out well.

"Learn to be a team player, Quinn."

Quinn said nothing. He objected to being patronised. Yet for a moment he appeared susceptible to reason, almost as though Cody's impromptu visit and gesture had made their mark. He poured them each a second measure, Cody first, even though he hadn't yet sampled the first one.

Quinn declared he had a week's leave coming and that he would work off his emotions on the estate at home. Cody almost choked. The calva was indeed strong. Quinn didn't react.

"Tell me more about yourself, Cody," Quinn asked.

Surprised by the continuation of Quinn's civility, Cody replied he had married five years before the war, and they had moved to a cottage a brief ride from the south coast. Cody had built much of their furniture himself and Kate had done the decorations and paintings on the walls. They had three daughters, the eldest six and the youngest three.

He described their small village and the surrounding area.

"Too flat for my liking," said Quinn who claimed he knew the region.

Ignoring the bait, Cody looked up and noticed a drawing pinned to the wall. It was of a medium-sized Georgian country house with woods and fields around it.

"Mine," boasted Quinn.

Cody assumed he meant he had done it himself and congratulated him. He talked about Kate. She was much younger than he. She came from a London family of some standing because of her mother's side who owned a printing company. Both her parents and her brother had recently died, and she was presently inheriting everything together with her younger sister whom she rarely saw.

"Printing too, eh?" remarked Quinn.

Cody remembered the brother-in-law.

"And she draws and paints as well," Cody said, glancing up at the wall.

A garrulous conversation ensued. As the level of the potent calva frittered away, so did discretion. Quinn candidly talked about the difficulties he had with his authoritarian father who never approved of anything he did or allowed him the autonomy of decision he desperately strove for. This prompted Cody to admit strains in his own family and the danger of his wife's lure back to London, and the company of other men being only a matter of time. Some of the first signs were already there, he admitted. For one, she had never sent him a parcel or letter during his whole time at the front, only small cards at Christmas and on his birthday.

"I see the change in Kate's painting as time goes by. It's symptomatic. But we never talk about it."

"He used to be a general," Quinn went on, wrapped as ever in his own world.

Cody was relieved. He had already let escape too much about himself.

The second disc stopped playing just as Quinn's wardrobe opened on its own. Quinn got up to close it but not before Cody, also getting up, thought he had glimpsed the lower half of a whip lying propped up against the back. He thought it strange.

Cody decided not to bother with a new disc and let the old one run around. Quinn returned to the table. He had changed. Ignoring the cards still in his hand, he launched himself into a cringing diatribe. It took Cody by complete surprise.

"You are all failures, Cody!"

Quinn had become quite stern. Cody had second thoughts and went over to lift the needle. Perhaps he should have put on more music after all.

"You're all worn out, exhausted," Quinn said. "You don't look for initiative anymore. Any courage you might have had has gone. You represent what the entire army has become. I saw it at Woolwich already, more interest in self-preservation, in maintaining the distinction between ranks, in bureaucracy, than in prosecuting a war."

The calva was already doing the talking. Quinn had become boorish. Cody patiently waited for the attack to peter out. Quinn was proving to be an immature anarchist, a disruptor of everything that went to ensure that the army could stand up to such a potent enemy. He did not know organisation, of well-honed procedures, of respect of others, or for properly organising an initiative. If Quinn had ever seriously listened to his father, he would have learned how incapable the army had been not so long ago. The Boer War had been a narrow scrape.

"You base everything on what has gone before," Quinn ranted on. "You try to leave nothing to chance. That's your weakness. You've become sclerotic!"

Cody yawned, uncharacteristically forgetting to put his hand to his mouth. It only made things worse.

"Cody, even in your own company your ordinary ranks show more initiative than you do! You're holding them back. You're treating them like pawns. And your colleagues the same."

Cody had had enough. Unable to suppress a second yawn, he challenged Quinn to say what he proposed.

"I would get rid of all of you. I would sweep the entire battalion clean and promote all those good and able men waiting in the side-lines. They could prove a thing or two. Anyone can spot their potential. Those men are hungry. They already know what to do. They will make a change."

"You got twenty-seven of them killed, for Christ's sake!" Cody said.

"I wasn't in charge, Cody! I had the stupid colonel telling me what I couldn't do instead of what I could. I could have organised the artillery, for a start."

Then he started ranting about Colonel Wilkes, how he was too focused on exterior matters and not on the basics of command.

"The trenches are always a disgrace! Discipline is atrocious!"

There was a thump from the room below. Quinn ignored it.

"We are all walking around in mud. I would drain it like the enemy. Remember? I would send out snatch parties and put to work whomever they brought back. They could give us fresh ideas, explain why their equipment is so much better."

Quinn's slurred speech had slowed down, and he found his seat again. Cody quietly put down the cards that he had been uselessly holding in his hand. Enough was enough. The idiot would come to his senses in the morning.

Cody discovered himself staggering as he walked the hundred yards up the blackened street to his lodgings. He halted. With the gramophone in his hand, he chanced a look to the end of the street. Rapunzel's light was out. He thought he could just make out the shadows of the sentries posted at each end to make sure than none of the villagers had any idea of sneaking away.

Quinn had thrown up yet more contradictions about himself. How could the scion of a general prove to have been so ill brought up and irresponsible? How on earth could he have qualified from Woolwich with such an attitude?

Cody thought about the drawing on the wall. It was as good as anything Kate had ever done. He thought about the mysterious whip, and Quinn's maniacal laugh on the ground when beaten. He thought about how he had stood up to Colonel Wilkes in a way no-one else would have dared after such a blunder and disobedience of orders. He thought about the lack of apology he or anyone had received. What to make of it all? Quinn was a strange kettle of fish. He wondered if he would turn out to be even more dangerous than he already had.

Cody imagined the snipers emerging from the side-lines to take command of the battalion under Quinn. He dismissed it all and resumed his walk, listening to the faint echo of his steps. Quinn was just callow. He would soon catch up. The battalion was safe.

Back in his billet, Cody thought one last time about their conversation. It was far from his nature to open up, especially about his wife and daughters. He regretted the calva. It had been a mistake. He felt a deep unease, as if he had lost a part of himself. He prayed that Quinn had been drunk enough to forget most of what had been said.

For an instant, he doubted his latest optimism regarding Quinn. Then he remembered the good news. It wasn't such a bad thing that the man would be gone in a few hours. The battalion could move on in peace with itself. Normal relations would be restored, if only for a brief while. Quinn's return in seven days had to be forgotten.

7

Colonel Wilkes convoked his officers for an early morning meeting. Cody struggled to arrive on time. He looked bedraggled as he settled down next to his three fellow commanders. He felt better after discovering that Quinn had already left.

"Been enjoying yourself, Moose!" sarcastically asked Cragg.

Cody wasn't about to tell him why. The subject of Quinn remained best left alone. At present, it was the state of his head that demanded attention. He had often heard it said that alcohol derived from apples was the very worst of all. Some people claimed it decimated populations further west. Right then he felt among them.

The colonel was, for once, relaxed and in a cheerful mood. He came straight to the point. Orders had been received for the battalion to head some thirty miles north to where a fresh campaign had just begun. The battalion should prepare to set out after dusk.

There was a collective sigh of relief. A change of scenery was always welcome, whatever lay ahead, and the sector would be new to them.

Talbot caught on that Quinn had gone.

"With luck, we'll lose him in the process!" he whispered.

The other commanders heard that and chuckled. Cody was feeling far too sorry for himself to carp over it.

The weather closed in just as they moved out. They marched through the quietened village.

"Eyes right!"

One of Talbot's NCOs ordered a salute to an invisible Rapunzel as they passed her shuttered window. There was a loud cheer among the ranks and then, a mere hundred yards further, she and her village became forgotten forever. Minds returned to what lay ahead.

As the snow tumbled down, the open countryside that greeted them had also adopted an eerie quiet. For the men marching in front, the sound of boots landing on the ever-thickening powder was a welcome relief from the constant splashing they had put up with for weeks. For those who followed, even the fresh slush felt pleasantly different. For the time being, the vague thought of new horizons prevailed. No-one tried to look any further towards the realities they would have to face.

The first snowfall of the season heralded fresh challenges. It would provide a welcome change from the mud, but digging in would become much harder, and audible half-a-mile away unless the ground had been softened by burning straw. Explosive shells would turn more lethal, the freezing wintry days and nights in the open interminable. Everyone would be repeatedly condemned to remove their boots to dry and grease their feet against frostbite. If the previous winter was anything to go by, many would end up wrapping their boots with layers of straw. With the arrival of ice, everyone would be already praying for even the wettest of springs. The fact of the matter was that the battalion's life followed an infernal circle. Only change brought relief.

The troops had taken off first, under the command of the usual transport officer seconded from brigade. Cody and his colleagues had decided to march alongside with their orderlies. They were accompanied by what they would need in case of emergency, the Lewis gun limbers and packhorses loaded with light ammunition and, most importantly, tools for digging in.

The transport officer always enjoyed the opportunity to command a tight ship. Profiting from the momentary lapse in discipline provoked by the impromptu salute, one or two of the men broke ranks to make themselves popular.

"Permission to smoke, sir!"

There was no need for a reply. The look on the transport officer's face, had it been visible, would have provided the answer. His silence did the job.

"Permission to sing, sir!"

"Denied!"

The requests were as predictable as the answers. The transport officer was never one for taking chances during a night march, however far they were from the front. He also was of the mind that the enforced restrictions would encourage the battalion to concentrate on marching. The men were glad to be marching all the same, despite the weight of their backpacks, blankets and greatcoats. The small group of NCOs following the column to prevent stragglers had little to do.

The state of the road was so bad, massacred by the endless passages of animals, vehicles, and limbers, that transport in lorries or buses, even had they been available, would have been impossible. On foot, they would stop and rest at least every ten miles, but without provisions. The water carts, not to mention the medical officer's two-wheeled Maltese cart, or the officers' mess cart that could carry anyone in difficulty, would follow half-an-hour behind, far enough to avoid becoming exposed to surprise. Food would be out of the question too. The company cookers, and the yet more cumbersome four-wheeled service wagons, would follow an hour after that.

To compensate their privation, everyone stamped their feet in rhythm as they marched. It provoked a wry grin on the face of the man responsible, but no-one could see it in the dark either, and true enough progress sped up.

"What did they bloody expect?" he bawled to Cody who had moved up beside him.

He was enjoying himself.

After three hours, the snowfall tapered off. A short while later, the clouds cleared enough for the half-moon to allow them to see quite far. It provided a timely distraction. They were crossing a region as yet unaffected by war. The countryside was fairly flat, bare, and white for miles, totally peaceful, and no doubt of particular beauty by day. Under a coating of snow, the fields appeared raw. Trees were still whole, quite different from the arrays of splintered stubs at the front.

"'Beauty saves the world'!" quoted Cody.

He imagined Kate there, huddled in fur, taking it all in while painting. Then he remembered Quinn's drawing on the wall and tried to think of something else. Kate soon faded away as well.

The battalion continued marching in time along the gravelled road that it had entirely to itself as far as the eye could see, albeit with a little less gusto than earlier on. The reassuring sound of the synchronised landing of boots showed that, for the time being at least, they were in charge of their world.

An hour later, the transport officer broke off with two lieutenants who used their lamps to illuminate his map. After the three of them re-joined the column, word spread that they were in sight of where they would stop for the night. The pace picked up as the front of the column left the road and climbed a rise towards woods on a ridge parallel to the right-hand side of the road.

The battalion would encamp in depth in order to resume its march rapidly. The NCOs saw the men bivouacked according to company and platoon to be at the ready. Men who had not been designated for sentry duty disappeared into the wood to smoke and rest until the cookers arrived. The hungriest of them occasionally drifted to the last trees to look out for their approach.

Cody was far from alone in craving for sleep. He found his colleagues at the edge of the wood preparing to bivouac with Hardy and the other orderlies nearby. He disappeared into the wood for one last fill of his pipe and the others joined him. Talbot, who had sat down and was busy carving again, not that he could see much, asked him what he knew of the town they were headed for.

"A cathedral for certain," Cody replied off the cuff, trying to decipher what was in Talbot's hands. "If it's still standing, of course."

The front had been floating around the town for some time, and so there was likely to be a considerable amount of damage.

"There's a canal nearby," recalled Cody. "Presumably we'll see some of that."

It was an understatement. The canal was certain to be of strategic interest in any battle plan. The presence of a built-up area made them hope that there would be less trench work. The last time they had fought anywhere close to a town had been over a year ago.

"Does anyone have any calva?" asked Talbot while he hacked away in the dark.

Cody swore he was looking up at him when he said it.

"Left it in my billet," he said. "How stupid of me!"

He had successfully fended off his colleague. But it made him wonder if he had been spotted near Quinn's billet.

They eventually established their sleeping positions next to the trees and bedded down for the night.

Cody was one of the first to wake up. He felt that he had slept well despite a brief delay thinking about Kate and the girls. It was still dark. He could hear the occasional heavy gun in the distance coming from beyond the wood.

He went in among the trees and used his torch to study his map. They still had quite a way to go. He went back and walked over to the limit of the impromptu camp to gaze at the white blanket that spread to the horizon. Hardy joined him and as usual said nothing. It was all deceptively peaceful, saved beauty indeed, no doubt at the very edge of the civilised world. Cody assumed that after the far-off rise ahead of them they would begin to re-encounter signs of war.

They would be spared the sound of a reveille there. Cody looked around in order to admire the long line of castrametation surrounded by frost. Behind him, men had lazily risen from under their blankets to stamp their feet and rub their hands, and move away to admire the scenery, their breaths travelling for yards. The cookers inside the wood had been primed. The cold that had set in during the night gave way to the rising sun, and the men broke ranks to line up for breakfast.

The sun had a rapid effect. In the time to have a meal and the first smoke of the day, the middle of the road that skirted their position cleared itself enough of snow to show the way forward.

The battalion resumed its march two hours later. The carts and waggons of the second and third echelons once again waited their turn before setting off, remaining isolated in the abandoned field of disturbed snow and debris that everyone ignored.

By early afternoon, across a landscape on which the snow had begun to melt, the front of the column spotted the outline of a village that had evidently been damaged by long-range guns. The remnant of a church spire to one end reminded them more than anything that a war zone was nearing.

The village turned out to be small, and similar to the one they had left, thirty houses either side of a long narrow street quite unsuited to two-way traffic.

"Quick march!" the transport officer boomed as he stood there at the entrance while the troops passed by.

Such a remote place always provided a target for the enemy. The transport officer needed to get the column beyond the far side as soon as possible. As they marched through, men became distracted by the haunting jagged structures that seemed to be resolutely standing up to the low winter sun, the remains of their decorative red brick walls as they always had been. The Beast had left his mark, destroying once again the work of centuries. Men, women, and children stood outside shattered windows and door frames, with nothing to do than watch the long, endless column march past. Occasionally, one or two feebly reached out to brush the arms of the young soldiers, but no-one stopped to acknowledge.

At the far end stood the decapitated spire they had seen from a distance. Beneath it were the remains of the small church rendered unusable. A group of twenty young children had assembled high on the rubble to watch the spectacle they would remember forever. For its part, the battalion would thank God that the place wasn't home.

As the column emerged, it passed a small farmyard that edged the village with half a dozen cows loitering around a milking shed. No-one gave a thought to the opportunity for fresh milk. They had to get away fast.

On the next rise, about a mile ahead, Cody spotted another column headed towards them, returning from the front. It was marching slower than they.

"Prisoners," said Cragg after stopping to peer through his field glasses. "I'd say a good thousand."

Cody soon made out the telltale cavalry escort. The roadway had become just wide enough for the two columns to pass each other. The transport officer passed the word to be respectful, but he hadn't needed to. The men were sufficiently chastened by thought about what was waiting for them further ahead that they took little notice.

The captured officers passed them last, only lightly guarded and looking distinctly haughty and unfriendly. Cody got distracted by their spiked helmets.

"Dread to think what it's like in their ranks, Moose," remarked Talbot.

Several of the officers were carrying their helmets under their arms. Cody noticed that one or two of them had blond hair and tall statures. He wondered how often he would find himself reminded of his battalion's unmissed intelligence officer.

Two hours later, a jagged skyline that spread across much of the horizon came into view, a rude reminder that they were reaching their objective. As they descended towards the town, they listened to the explosions coming from the other side. Their respite was finally over. It had even clouded over and promised bad weather. They were returning to the gates of hell.

Cody was trying to figure out the multiple rows of tree stubs on both sides of the road when a shell exploded on graze fifty yards to their left.

"Look out!"

The column picked up its pace in order to reach the cover of the first houses as soon as possible. A second shell landed on the roadside just in front and sent debris in all directions. Further down the increasingly visible wide street directly ahead of them, two more shells landed in succession on buildings on either side, blasting rubble into the space in-between. Their march into town would be like the ending of the parting of the seas.

"What do you think?" Cody asked Hardy. "The tree stubs, I mean."

Hardy looked back perplexed. It looked as though there had been orchards. They would have been precious.

It rained. Now well into the town and surrounded by taller buildings, or what remained of them, the transport officer stood aside and raised his arm. The long column came to a halt. Cody and his fellow captains walked up to join him just as a billeting guide from brigade arrived with instructions. They were to occupy the buildings around them for the night.

The four captains proceeded to bring forward their companies, finding themselves further to the rear. They ordered them to pick out cellars at will in each of their chosen sectors. As abandoned doors were forced in either side of the street and in the adjacent side streets, the captains went off to investigate a large building nearby for a possible headquarters and billet. Just before a railway line that crossed the road, they fell on the front offices of a disused candle factory. Colonel Wilkes and Major Hickman arrived on horseback and agreed the site ideal.

As dark descended, the cookers turned up and were set up either side of the street. The rain subsided. There was no passing traffic, just the odd civilian braving the promiscuous shelling and totally ignoring the troops.

"No refugees," said Talbot.

"All happened months ago," said the colonel, quoting from his brief.

Attracted by the glow from the cookers, the men quietly re-emerged from their improvised billets and lined up for food. Cody meanwhile rounded up his lieutenants to inspect the billets with torches. The company had kept itself well together, and he congratulated them. It could muster quickly if needed.

As soon as meals had been dispensed, it rained again. Everyone scattered to their cellars. Cody joined his colleagues who were standing around Colonel Wilkes as they collected their supper while getting soaked.

"Expect to move up in the morning, gentlemen," the colonel advised them.

He added he had hoped to have detailed maps for them to go over, but they had been delayed. The front had reportedly been unusually volatile during the previous days.

In the candle factory, Cody and his colleagues had chosen a large room to set up their camp beds. From a tiny hole in the wall that faced the front, Cragg noticed he could see the flashes and went up to watch. During the night, Cody woke up and noticed that the flashes were neatly projected upside down onto the whitewashed wall opposite. In an odd way they made more sense.

They were awoken by noises coming from next door. Cody instinctively looked over to the white wall, but the front had gone quiet. The colonel, who had been sleeping in the next room, had been found by a messenger and stepped in to announce news. The battalion was to stand to and be ready to move out at one hour's notice. Cody and the others called in the orderlies who had been sleeping along the corridor and had them pass the word to their commands.

It had rained and then snowed for most of the night, eventually turning into a light drizzle before daylight. Most of the NCOs and other ranks woke up to find that their makeshift accommodation had kept them dry and provided adequate protection from the icy wind that had crept in during the night.

Donning their capes once more, everyone made their way down the waterlogged streets back to the cookers that had been started up at dawn in what shelter they could find. As men shuffled around, they talked about the night just passed. Several had shared their cellar with families, some with jealously guarded animals. Several men complained of rats, but on the whole their modest accommodation had been welcomed as different.

Nothing happened after that. The rain persisted heavily all morning while everyone waited and became bored. In the candle factory, Talbot went back to his carving while the others read, Cody having cadged a magazine from Fuller.

The far-off guns remained fairly quiet, and no useful news was forthcoming from the front lines. The battalion waited on the frontier of the unknown. At least it remained under cover.

They ended up waiting all day. During the afternoon, the colonel received two more messages leading him to believe that they would be ordered up after dark. The front was reported to be staying put at less than half-an-hour away. He sent a message to brigade asking for his commanders to be allowed to scout the trenches beforehand in order to organise the relief, but no reply came back.

"It'll be chaotic," he said to Cody.

Advance inspections of a position always saved confusion and improved safety. They rarely missed the opportunity to size up what to expect beforehand. By the colonel's comment, Cody understood that C Company would be first to go into the line. Talbot, Fuller and Cragg discretely slapped him on the back.

"I'll expect you to fill us in, Moose!" said Cragg.

The colonel, ignoring it all and frustrated, sent yet another message.

An hour later, there had still been no reply. They imagined a brigade HQ in confusion, unable to focus or properly organise. It was not reassuring.

Soon after dusk, Cody was ordered to move C Company to the old enemy support line at midnight. It was out in the fields at the edge of town. His machine gunners, snipers, and signallers went up ahead. Lieutenant Smalby led them in order to scout the line.

Just before it was time for the main body of C Company to move out, two guides from brigade turned up to lead the way. It was no longer raining. Cody took up the lead with Hardy. Their advance became rendered increasingly difficult by a plethora of disused wire entanglements, debris, and shell holes, but mercifully there was no stench. Bodies appeared to have been replaced by temporary grave markers.

They discovered the trenches in reasonably good condition and well drained, and relieved men who had been there for two days. The relief took a couple of hours. As usual, the necessity for silence meant that there had been no opportunity to learn what to expect from the men they replaced, but Smalby had done a good job beforehand and filled them in.

An hour after they had fully settled in, Talbot turned up with A Company in order to take over trenches a hundred yards ahead. For the time being, Fuller and Cragg were staying put in town.

Once he had satisfactorily tested the telephone to brigade, Cody did the rounds keeping Hardy at his side. He had with him a hand-drawn map that his predecessor had discretely slipped him and which he needed to crosscheck.

The map turned out to be detailed and looked well done. The sentries had been posted where they should have been, clipboards and report sheets for the intelligence officer posted nearby. The officers and NCOs of the watch were also in place where designated. Cody used the opportunity to quiz Smalby a little more. The last two days had been animated, but the trenches themselves left alone. The trench formation, however, had turned out to be not as pleasing as the map, and it was poorly signposted. Wondering why the creator of such a neat map had not thought to improve what existed, Cody prayed they would be allowed enough time to familiarise themselves properly and make improvements before things livened up.

The men settled in for the night, able to get some sleep under their capes. Before settling in himself, Cody wrote up his situation report. He exchanged it when a messenger arrived with the colonel's counterattack plan for their entrenchment. He read the plan only once. He had already seen enough of their position to recommend changes in the morning.

Shortly before the early morning stand to, the enemy opened up with hundreds of tear shells. Strombus horns went off after they landed with their all-too-familiar thuds. Everyone reached for their box respirators, only to discover that the newly arrived drizzle was rendering the gas useless. Explosive shells soon followed, as if to catch them off-guard.

The enemy was enjoying himself. One shell landed directly on top of a trench occupied by Talbot's men on the far left up ahead. Seeing nothing because of the dark, Cody could hear the commotion and screaming as survivors rushed to the rescue. The out-of-sight scene being played out in front of them rendered it even more frightening.

After a while, the enemy redirected his fire further to the east and the two companies finally found themselves left alone. The stretcher parties had to cross overland in order to get to the rear.

Cody was appalled at the inadequate communication trenches. He counted a dozen wounded heading past after the sprint across open ground. Lieutenant Mowforth was next to him.

"If we stay here, we'll need to dig," Cody warned him.

Mowforth agreed. Keeping well below level, they studied the map to see what could be done. A burst of small arms fire started up in front of them. Talbot was taking even more.

The firing repeated itself every half hour all morning. Further away, they heard bursts of light and heavy machine guns and the occasional mortars. Around midday, the far-off noise became almost continuous. Talbot sent a message over, assuring that his company remained fully operational for whenever they might have to move forward. He asked Cody if he had any news of what was happening. To Cody this was no more than gesticulation on behalf of the enemy.

Father Drake, the battalion padre, turned up. He was wearing his familiar goatskin. He had a padded cap, the same as many of the men he visited, in his case covering his bald head. He had made the rounds of the trenches and joined Cody for canned lunch in his dugout after visiting Talbot and administering last rites to two of his men. Cody had Hardy return to fetch the gramophone from the candle factory. He asked the padre what headquarters were saying.

"Brigade is confident they won't try a breach. We have them too well pinned down. The colonel was fine with me coming forward."

So, brigade seemed to be thinking defensively for the time being. It was a relief to know. The gramophone arrived and Cody started it up for his guest while Hardy set about brewing tea. Men nearby profited by listening in.

Father Drake had already been with them for a year, and he and Cody had become good friends, not least because of Cody's Irish name. They endlessly sparred over the padre's Catholicism and open sympathy for Home Rule versus Cody's Protestant upbringing. Drake always kept up a sense of humour, even during the toughest of times. He had laughed heartily when he discovered he had been nicknamed 'Sinn Feiner' for his political beliefs. He told plenty of stories of his time in Ireland, how he had to share diplomatically his custom with the local Protestant and Catholic stores and bars, and how often he had to calm down feuds between families on either side. In the battalion, he had long earned the men's respect for spending so much time in the front lines and always turning up at the right time. His frequent pre-dawn tours coincided with the men waking up, often searching for someone to talk to about their dreadful dreams.

"There are times in the day when I'm needed most," he often said, as if the men's minds went through predictable cycles.

To make conversation, Drake mentioned someone he thought might have been a mutual friend. He did that each time they ran into each other. Cody did not feel up to it.

"I'm sorry, Father. At the moment, I can remember more people who are dead than alive."

"Your soul needs a break, Moose," the padre observed.

Drake intended to talk about the Quinn affair and the damage it had done to morale. He had been on leave and not forgiven himself for not being there sooner afterwards. Every officer had spoken to him about it since except Quinn himself. Now that Quinn had gone, he saw how things had got better.

Cody described his visit to Quinn's billet.

"I can't remember a battalion in such good shape before that," Drake regretted.

Given Quinn's surname, he wondered if he too could claim any ancestry from the old country.

"Or has he too been bastardised by Anglo Saxons?" he asked.

Cody said how much he had felt it was his duty to defend Quinn and try to calm things down. Now he wondered whether he himself was the fool.

"You were right, of course," Drake assured him.

Quinn had, in fact, given the padre a wide berth from the very first day of his arrival. They had rarely spoken. Cody asked what his colleagues were saying.

"I get the brunt of it, Moose," Drake said. "If only the colonel caught wind of some of it."

Cody didn't envy the padre's job one bit, having to listen and console, but never to betray confidences or be able to make decisions.

"How can men so taken up with fighting the enemy ever want to squabble between themselves?" he asked.

"And it's getting worse each year," Drake remarked. "One wonders what it could lead to."

"Russia? The Bolos?"

"Ireland, maybe!"

"And remember that five years ago we even came close to it in England!"

"You think it was that bad, Moose?"

They talked about conflicts of opinion among so-called colleagues. Cody talked about the reported feud between Queen Victoria and Gladstone, the personal animosities during French Revolution and the Consulate and Empire that followed. The same went for the American Revolution. Leaders supposedly on the same side always seemed always to have been constantly metaphorically knifing each other in the back. And in each case, individuals seeking vengeance resorted to any means available, including sneaking outright lies to the press. Supposed heroes like Thomas Jefferson had been prime for that.

"Humankind is indeed a troubled lot, Moose!"

"Well, you're here to make an example, Father," Cody concluded, smiling at his friend.

"I'm afraid that some of the worst instances are in the Church itself."

It reminded Cody of some of his father's ranting and raving over his colleagues and superiors. He mentioned Quinn again. None of it was comforting.

"A most unfortunate affair," admitted the padre as he took off.

"A most unfortunate affair indeed, Father," called out Cody.

Hardy quietly re-joined Cody. Each of them reached for their pipes and sat opposite one another saying nothing.

Feeling refreshed by the padre's visit, Cody decided that one day he would tell Hardy how much he appreciated his orderly's unimposing presence. He never had the slightest idea what was going through Hardy's mind, but he always assumed that they thought alike. It somehow helped him to see reason.

8

Later that afternoon, and considering the calm, brigade summoned all its commanders. It had installed itself opposite the gas works, to the west of where the 10th Battalion had entered town.

Cody decided to take advantage and leave early. He wanted to explore what was left of the town. Placing Lieutenant Piggot in command, and leaving Hardy with him, he said that he expected to be back before dusk.

He took off on foot. The countryside in-between was desolate. Ground everywhere had been extensively churned up by fighting and remained a rugged sea of dark brown interrupted by abandoned trenches. The road, that had once been lined with iron fencing, but most of it destroyed, had been kept clear, and from what had been fields on either side Cody could hear the odd bird, no doubt in search of trees that no longer existed. Further off to his left, he spotted emaciated cattle attempting to graze on nothing at all. Any isolated farm buildings had long been flattened. Some way off to his right, working parties were laying cables.

At the town outskirts, where he had expected signs of activity, it was quite the opposite. No-one appeared to be venturing outside. It became difficult to get bearings. In the chaos brought about by the rubble from damaged buildings, the streets appeared to lead nowhere. Fortunately, the cathedral stood proud in the background.

Climbing over endless obstacles created by weeks of shelling, and avoiding the threatening bundles of barbed wire, Cody made an obvious tourist. He was spotted by a distinguished-looking man in a beret, the first civilian he saw. The man started walking in Cody's direction.

The man, who looked to be in his seventies, wore a dark winter coat and had just emerged from a bar that appeared to be functioning in yet another half-standing building. His white hair was cut short, and his gait gave the impression of him having once served in the military. Waving Cody down as he neared, the man called over, offering to show him around. He energetically led him into the main square and asked him to imagine how it might have appeared before the war.

The square was large. The ground all around them had once been paved but was now torn up and pocketed with shell holes, some of them large enough for several men to hide in. Every building around had been damaged and was enshrouded in rubble. What remained standing was mostly in familiar red brick, here and there interspersed with bricks in darker or lighter colours. Cody's first reaction was to wonder where the children were. This seemed a paradise for adventure.

Everywhere was in terrible disarray. Cody couldn't imagine how much time would be needed to return the town to its original state. He wondered whether the local authorities would profit in order to modernise the rather glum appearance that so much in the region had inherited over time. He knew of the national obsession for tradition. Deciding the look of the resuscitated town would be a battle royal.

They remained in the centre of the square. In his broken French, Cody replied he could indeed imagine how everything had been. To illustrate his point, the man reached for a photograph from his inside pocket.

"*Magnifique, n'est pas?*"

Cody was puzzled why the old man would carry such a valuable photograph on him. He nodded and smiled. The square had certainly been impressive.

"*Ce n'est pas la première fois, je suppose,*" he said, gesturing towards the signs of destruction all around them.

Cody's guide confirmed he had been there in 1870, and still remembered it, but insisted that there had been little physical damage back then, only to morale. He asked Cody again what he thought. The photograph showed an attractive town hall, on the east side, with its date of construction, three hundred years before, boldly engraved in stone above its entrance. It had all been flattened, as if especially targeted. The magnificent early Gothic cathedral, fifty yards behind it, had now become fully exposed for the first time in centuries, also robbed of its closer entourage of smaller buildings. The old man said that there had been a bishop's palace next to it.

Cody examined the cathedral from where they stood. Both of its spires had been damaged at their summits. The flying buttresses appeared undamaged. Some of the large stained-glass windows had been blown-in, but as much as he could tell, the arches and roofs appeared intact.

As they then panned around them, the old man gave a running commentary on each portion in turn of what remained of the fronting buildings, most of which Cody could understand. Most of the other three faces of the square had been a combination of small shops, bars and restaurants, one or two of which were still operating in the segments that still partially stood.

"What's that?"

"*Une salle de cinema!*" came the proud reply.

The half-destroyed building had been too old to have been built for that. Cody became distracted by several old couples slowly rummaging through the ruins nearby. They had just arrived. They all looked dog-tired and needy.

"What's happening over there?"

Down a side street leading off the square, he had spotted people hovering around a large wooden structure that resembled a Greek temple. At least the town appeared to be belatedly coming to life.

"*Le lavoir, Monsieur.*"

They headed towards it. Sure enough, women and young girls were emerging from side streets carrying their washing in baskets to what turned out to be a large, covered rectangular basin, about fifty feet long, that had wide steps leading down to a pool. Others were already in place, kneeling on the steps, frantically scrubbing on the wide stone surface or rinsing in the water. Cody marvelled how life, so difficult to spot at first, persisted in such hopeless circumstances. The old man told him that mercifully the soap factory was still operating. Even the enemy had needed it during their recent occupation.

"*Venez!*"

He led Cody back into the square and across to the cathedral. Out of the blue, a decrepit motor taxi sputtered past them. Cody had been so distracted, it had taken him by complete surprise. It was the first occasion that he had seen a non-military vehicle in town. He couldn't understand how it was able to advance so fast along the rubble-strewn street. The driver looked old and as though he was carrying a cat in his arms. That was especially odd.

"*Le Maire, Monsieur.*"

Cody could just make out that the driver had a customer inside, a dark shadow sitting in the back.

"*Il fait que des allers-retours la journée entière, Monsieur,*" said his guide.

Cody couldn't decide whether he was complaining or expressing admiration for the man who surely had the toughest job around. No doubt he had been in office during the recent occupation and found himself in an impossible situation.

They entered by the principal door, which had been left opened, and Cody removed his cap. He spotted a stunning wheel window high to their right. A priest emerged from the dark inside and greeted them while they adjusted to the light. He was standing next to the entrance to the crypt and Cody wondered if it had served during bombardments. He announced his father was a vicar in a small village back in England.

"*Ou, mon Capitaine?*"

"The Midlands, Father. A village near Nottingham."

The priest, who understood, appeared as friendly as the old man. Cody asked if there was a bishop. Before the priest could reply, the old man intervened. He explained he had been taken away during the occupation and had never returned. He had sheltered some women making accusations against the soldiers. Cody knew what that implied.

"*Outragées, Monsieur,*" the priest said.

Cody had already heard of such stories from other places that the army had recaptured. It had always placed the higher authorities on edge over the behaviour of their own troops. He wondered if they would one day learn how they compared.

"*Il n'y avait pas que cela.*"

He explained that an entire enemy brigade had been encamped just outside town. Cody listened to a long description, most of which he understood, about how troops had smashed up all the machinery they came across and commandeered all the brass and copper they could lay their hands on. Only the soap factory had been left alone. All weaving machines, all privately owned, had been destroyed. To maintain order, they had taken to fining residents twenty marks for the slightest provocation. As the occupation had worn on, individual soldiers had helped themselves to anything they took a liking to, including furniture and paintings from private homes. The officers had forced people of all ages to work out in the fields to feed the troops. And as part of their preparations before pulling out, they had destroyed all the orchards.

"Ah, those stubs," Cody recalled.

The occupier's behaviour had created a massive resentment, the priest said. He ended up by shrugging his shoulders as if to pass it all off and then brought his hands together before gesturing for them to step further inside.

Corporal Hopper appeared at the doorway, forgetting to doff his cap. He greeted the priest and the old man in French. Then he turned to Cody to announce that the meeting at brigade had been brought forward. Cody made his apologies, thanked his hosts, and promised he would return another day. They dispersed just outside, leaving the priest standing there with his hands clasped, Cody and Hopper hurrying off, and the old man scurrying back to his bar in the opposite direction.

"What was that all about, sir?" asked Hopper.

He had overheard an animated conversation before he entered.

"Thank God we'll never get occupied," was all Cody could say.

"Hope you're right, Captain," Hopper said.

He had borrowed a motorbike to find Cody and left it on the far side of the square. Cody hadn't known that he spoke French.

"My mother."

Hopper had kept quiet about having been born in France.

"Could have found myself at Verdun."

Nothing more needed to be said.

Cody found Colonel Wilkes and the others obediently assembled alongside colleagues from the other battalions. Brigadier Lightfoot had already begun his briefing over the front. He was standing in front of a large board which had a hand-drawn sketch of the town and latest lines of trenches beyond it. An orderly was distributing trench maps to everyone present and handed one to Cody as he took his seat. It smelt freshly printed.

Cody could see more than ever how the trenches he and Talbot were presently occupying were so badly laid out. He leaned forward to point it out to Colonel Wilkes sitting just in front of him. The colonel discretely nodded in agreement, trying his best to avoid being noticed by the brigadier.

The brigadier explained that a field printing unit had been used for finalising the production of the maps, a promising new development, he said, given the recent acceleration of events. He then announced that a fresh attack would take place before dawn. The colonel was informed that 10th Battalion should be stood to at four and ready to be called forward at one hour's notice.

The session lasted for thirty minutes more. To finish matters off, they were driven by car to positions being taken up by artillery outside town, further east from where the battalion had entered. The brigadier, who didn't accompany them, had wanted to make a point about the support they would get, and for commanders to make acquaintance with those whom they would call for backup. Along the way, they skirted working parties from other battalions laying new telephone lines intended to go up to the front. Cody realised that the parties he had spotted earlier had to be part of the same effort.

The position, once it appeared before them, was massive. It was the largest any of them had seen for well over a year. Long lines of field guns and howitzers of all calibres were being positioned a couple of hundred yards in front of each other with space between them for staging new and used shells, and clearance to allow wagons and lorries to ferry replenishments. Men were scurrying everywhere to make it happen in time. Artillery horses, their jobs complete, were being led away to graze on straw in the fields behind.

They were greeted by a captain who assured them that everything would be ready before midnight. He repeated the brigadier's earlier warning that the maps were now changing more frequently than ever, and of the importance of referring to the revision date when communicating coordinates.

They were impressed by what they saw. Everything had arrived in the past twenty-four hours. Cody asked the captain if he thought they had yet been spotted. All he got in return was the kind of shrug that made the colonel mutter he had been in France for too long.

"No planes or balloons yet," the captain belatedly announced.

The light had faded by the time the colonel and the team headed back in two cars. The colonel took up Cody's earlier comments regarding the trenches by saying that they would soon become redundant. He added that the absence of reports of aircraft of any sort bode well. It wouldn't have been the first occasion that they hadn't been adequately warned about the enemy's readiness. If the enemy had the gun positions already pinpointed, any action could become rapidly compromised.

They passed railway yards where a small group of well-hidden heavy-calibre howitzers had been installed well ahead of the main artillery. They were already manned and poised at the ready.

They alighted just after that and noticed how much colder it had become. As they began to make their way by foot across the open ground of a small park, there was the occasional flash from the horizon, mostly directed further east. The enemy appeared to be warming up.

The shadow of the cathedral appeared to their right. Cody mentioned he had just visited it and been impressed.

"Too grim for me," said the colonel.

Cody asked him what he meant. The cathedral was tall, spacious and had plenty of light. The colonel growled he preferred the seventeenth century Dutch paintings.

Just as they were about to arrive the other end of the park, a lone shell landed nearby before any of them had time to react. It was a dud. In the commotion, Cody became entangled in some double-edged enemy saw wire and tore his uniform in several places. He swore. The wire lay on top of an embankment protecting a deserted howitzer pointed roughly towards where they had first entered town. Almost invisible in the dark, the gun looked as though it had been spiked.

"Must have taken one hell of a charge," said the major.

The walk from the town felt uncomfortable in the dark, unhelped by the few flashes from the front. Their imagination wandered. Anything or anyone could jump out at them. The six of them spread out just in case.

They were more than happy to call out the password to the sentries when they arrived. Once he reached his trench, Cody asked Hardy to go around warning the men of the earlier than usual stand to. They could expect to jump off any time after that.

At precisely five in the morning, the artillery went into action. The noise from the explosions in front of them was deafening. Mercifully, none of the shells were landing short.

After an hour, it was still the case, and the enemy was still not responding. The battalion received the warning to prepare to move. A counter order followed half-an-hour later and pack mules arrived with rations for the men instead.

Two hours later, a runner brought new orders for action. A flare signalled the jump off. As they climbed over the parapet from the fire steps, C Company discovered a fresh blanket of snow on the ground that seemed to contradict all the heated action they had just been listening to. Along its line, the company emerged onto flat ground and made its way across the trench that had been occupied by A Company. They got right up to the canal. There was now quiet everywhere, and not a sign of Talbot's men.

Suddenly, the enemy went into action. They found themselves pinned down by heavy machine gun fire coming from several positions along the opposite bank, just as low as theirs, as well what seemed to be from their flank on their side.

Cody ordered his men to dig into the hardened ground before it got light, just enough to keep themselves below ground level. Hardy located an abandoned artillery emplacement a little to the rear where the officers could bivouac, and Cody installed his temporary headquarters there.

"Here, Captain!" called Hardy.

He had found a pile of enemy shell cartridges and passed one to Cody. It felt heavy and was about nine inches long. Cody examined the end in the growing light. It had been manufactured the previous October and was sixty-seven per cent copper. It would make a good ashtray and wouldn't require permission to keep.

After a short while, Talbot made a sign that he was just ahead. A Company had dug in seventy yards in front of them. Everyone waited. The hostile machine guns repeated their sweeps every ten minutes. An hour later, in full daylight, a runner confirmed that the enemy that had been directly in front of them had pulled back across the canal during the early part of the night and dug in behind the opposite bank.

"We had fire from this side as well," Cody said, but the messenger knew nothing about that.

No sooner had he spoken than shells pounded positions along the opposite bank. One of the machine guns was silenced halfway through its sweep. Apart from occasional bursts from the remaining machine guns, both companies found themselves being left alone.

For quite a time there seemed to be an inordinate amount of noise coming from the west, their side of the canal.

"That could be from where they were firing at us," said Lieutenant Smalby.

To Cody, it seemed a bit too far off. A report eventually came through confirming that some hostile troops, reported to be part of a Jäger battalion, were successfully holding out on their side of the canal, and had so far held out against repeated attacks. The attacking brigade had taken a considerable beating and its commanding officer injured and captured. A and C Companies were likely be called forward at any moment, and the two companies in reserve ordered to take up their present positions.

As C Company waited for the order to advance, the enemy shelled across the canal. His aim was haphazard and there were few casualties. Cody went around all his positions to make sure they were sufficiently well dispersed.

"How long will we be here for?" Lieutenant Piggot asked when Cody visited him.

"Look, Captain!"

Hardy, just behind, had spotted a kite balloon being raised over the town. "Must be a fine view!"

The advantage didn't last long. Within ten minutes, an enemy plane, the first they had seen there, flew across and shot at the balloon with two short bursts before turning back. As the balloon spectacularly burst into flames, its two occupants jumped out. From their funk holes, C Company cheered as the two parachutes precariously swung from side to side as they descended, overtaken by burning debris on the way.

Everything became quiet again. Cody told his men to keep as low as possible.

It was dusk by the time the battalion was finally called to move. Taking advantage of a sunken road away from the canal line, C and A Companies marched to new positions west and relieved the companies in them. Cragg's and Fuller's companies arrived shortly afterwards, under orders to leapfrog over them to occupy a series of shell holes from where they could employ mortars and rifle grenades.

As soon as Cragg and Fuller opened fire, the enemy viciously retaliated with machine gun fire and bombs. Their positions were soon located by artillery spotters who had accompanied Cragg and Fuller, and several took a volley of direct hits.

While the 10th Battalion's own wounded were being ferried back across their lines, the colonel sent through the order for Cody and Talbot to advance on the enemy firing line as soon as the artillery stopped. Cragg and Fuller were redeployed to cover their flanks.

As soon as they emerged onto open ground, A and C Companies were met with a hail of fire from both sides of the canal. They hunkered down as best they could. The artillery hadn't done enough after all. It looked like a stalemate.

They waited for four hours until Lieutenant Smalby volunteered to make a reconnaissance of the opposing line only fifty yards in front. He discovered that the enemy had pulled back to a trench further back. Lieutenant Mowforth moved forward and followed up with a bombing raid on part of the new firing line and established a block in the trench. The rest of C Company followed up to exploit the gain.

They had been expected. A firefight broke out. They managed all the same to advance twenty yards along both sides of the enemy trench, while A Company split up and went over to assist with an overland attack on both flanks.

The four-pronged attack was enough to destabilise the enemy. Lieutenant Piggot even advanced thirty yards up his side of enemy trench but was badly wounded in a counterattack. It provoked a partial retreat.

Twenty minutes later, Cody met up with Corporal Hopper.

"Piggot's dead," Hopper told him. "Corporal Speight has taken over."

The news shook Cody. But then was not the time to let the loss of his best man sink in. Hardy joined him with the message that the colonel had been injured in the arm and had to be evacuated. The medical officer at his side had been killed outright. Major Hickman had taken over.

C Company stayed put. The close quarters meant that there was no shelling, but rifle and machine gun fire and the occasional bomb proved the enemy remained determined to prevent another initiative.

Cody asked for a body count. He had lost ten dead, including Piggot, and thirty wounded. They would be stuck there for a while. It had become far too dangerous for the stretcher parties to approach.

At daylight, they spotted a second balloon that had been raised during the night. This time, the enemy didn't respond. An hour later, it was reported that some of the hostile troops remaining on their side had retreated during the night. It remained to mop up those that were left. Cody and Talbot were ordered into action and discovered that beyond both stops the enemy had pulled back. They sent a messenger back to battalion headquarters to report the news and ask for the rescue of the injured.

A shrapnel barrage was ordered to cover the ground ahead of them prior to their setting out. Climbing across further abandoned positions, C Company took the right flank, supported by a machine gun section. Lieutenant Cobbold and thirty men took charge of mopping up any trenches they overran. The engineers who accompanied them could soon find out whether the enemy had had the time to prepare booby traps.

After two hours, the entire near bank had been cleared. All remaining pockets of the enemy had been destroyed or taken prisoner. The new front line had been consolidated all along the canal. The enemy had been shut out of the town for good, but it had been a heavy price to pay.

The entire battalion had taken heavy casualties that were slowly evacuated during the day. The surviving men were exhausted, hungry, and thirsty.

Just before midnight, companies from other battalions arrived to replace them. The relief took three hours to complete. Cody received a message confirming they were to pull out from the area altogether. All four companies marched back into town, past the candle factory, to a position on the far edge where lorries were waiting to take them away one company at a time.

After a ten-mile drive, C Company arrived at a new camp, tents this time, where eighty-five new conscripts were already waiting.

Thirty-seven more men arrived during church parades the following morning. Quinn had accompanied them. As soon as Father Drake had finished the accompanying memorial services, Cody greeted Quinn and filled him in with the news. As they talked, Cody noticed how much the other captains and the major were avoiding following suit. He was annoyed by their pettiness and lack of decency. Priorities should have been elsewhere.

Quinn sensed what was happening and looked distinctly uncomfortable. He didn't know what to do.

"We have to put a stop to this," said Cody.

"I'd forgotten it all," admitted Quinn. "I thought things would have changed."

In fact, Cody had been forewarned that it would be no different. The colonel had been going on for days about how he planned to get rid of Quinn as soon as he returned. Brigadier Lightfoot had reportedly wanted that Quinn be kept from the front forever but had failed to follow through with an order. Hardy had mentioned what he was hearing from the other orderlies about what their commanders were saying. None of it was good.

Cody mentioned Lieutenant Piggot's death. Quinn seemed to have ignored altogether what he had said.

"Did you hear me?" Cody asked. "Lieutenant Piggot."

"Why should you want to tell me that?" Quinn said.

Cody couldn't make out how to take such a reaction. Quinn was not about to show any pity for Piggot, nor anyone else, including the injured colonel. Cody was appalled. Quinn's arrival had initiated something terrible, a breakdown of normality between officers, a body of men who had always held the utmost respect for each other, even during the most difficult times. Now they were descending into infighting that would only do harm. It would cause the other ranks to sense the lack of harmony among the officers, which they would be bound to exploit. Cody felt that only he, in the middle of it all, could put an end to it.

*

It turned out that Colonel Wilkes had not been badly wounded after all. He returned only three days later. Refusing to see Quinn, one of the first things he did was to summon Cody.

Observing the colonel's bandages, Cody asked him how he felt. He looked as though he had forced the matter of his return. It was unusual to see that.

"You should take some leave, Captain."

Cody was taken by surprise, followed by suspicion. It had to be his protective stance over Quinn.

For a while, none of this would matter. Cody had been freed for a week. Hardy would spend the time with Cody's stand-in, Lieutenant Smalby, but not before he had handed over an important piece of paper, Cody's dictation of the night-time stories he planned for his daughters.

Cody took to the road straight after dusk, profiting from a staff car that had just delivered a visiting American colonel. It explained why Colonel Wilkes had been so keen to return.

As the car sped away from the camp, Cody reflected about the extent to which all the difficult action the battalion had just lived through had not been complicated by animosities between its officers. He prayed it would prove the same when he returned.

9

The long, uncomfortable, and constantly interrupted train journey from the railhead near the front had numbed Cody into a contented emptiness. Life skated past his eyes as his war-torn mind slowed down. He was free at last. Gone were all the chaotic orders, marches, men, and mud to worry about, and Hardy's provisions lists as well. There would be no more seeing or cheating death. Cody could at last freely close his eyes or look where he wanted, finally abandon having to glance constantly sideways for others, upwards for airplanes or shells, forwards for yellow clouds, downwards for the unexpected cadaver, wire, booby trap, or fractured duckboard, or, for that matter, behind him for the likes of Quinn or the irate colonel.

And in that sudden onslaught of freedom, everything had become about heading for home. At last he could daydream unhindered, dream of precious days with Kate and the girls, waking up each morning in a proper bed, to calm, choice, and the smell and taste of proper food, and everything else that made life worth living.

Finally at sea, the salty sea air provided another purge of Cody's mind as he leaned over the gunwale. He pulled out his pipe, which he filled. The sun was as high as it would go in the cloudless winter sky. In the distance, slipping away, were the peaceful coastal town that enshrouded the busy port, the deserted shoreline either side of it, and the calm rolling, frost-enshrouded countryside behind.

Close by, gulls were majestically swooping over the wake below, and every now and again racing upwards to deck level and higher, unperturbed by the frantic flapping of the friendly flag hoisted at the steamer's stern. The ice-cold turbulent wind whipped Cody's face as, along with the vibration from the engines below, they prevented him from picking up the faint sounds of long-range guns in the distance.

Across the water, a few hundred yards off, the dazzle-camouflaged torpedo destroyer escort, that had waited out at sea, diligently took up the steamer's pace. An airplane with the same mission flew overhead, pulling inwards and then darting away in order to vectorise its greater speed, its occupants' eyes on the lookout for submarines.

Hell had been left behind, but it would only be on the other side, away from the chaos of the south-coast docks and into the countryside beyond, that such reminders of war would disappear for good, as if it all had never been.

Cody turned around to size up each of his fellow passengers. There were about a hundred on deck, most of whom could stand. Nearly all of them were soldiers, several in bandages of one sort or another, and no doubt headed for hospitals or rest homes along the south coast.

He thought of his own men, those lucky enough to have defied unsolicited graves far away from home. They would have followed the same broken route, the interminable waiting on the quay swarming with imported Chinese labourers, waiting for the next steamer to slide into place, followed by the endless disembarkation of fresh conscripts innocently eager to head for the front. They too would have impatiently scurried up the liberated gang plank in time for space on deck. They too would finally have been able to savour the windy calm of the short voyage. In the end, everyone was the same.

A New Zealander army captain wandered over and introduced himself before leaning on the rail beside him. Cody recognised him from the officer's rest house near the docks. He had been vigorously complaining about the seven-and-a-half-franc daily cost of access to the mess, but now seemed to have got over it.

"Henry Plantagenet took a month to get across," he pointed out after Cody had let on about the delay.

He had transferred from Gallipoli over a year before and was keen to talk about it.

"Much more shrapnel over there," he said. "Better than the high explosives, though."

They chatted for a while about the different munitions they had to face in the local trenches. Cody said he had always wanted to see how the enemy launched their aerial torpedoes. He had heard that the tubes they used were narrower than the missile and he couldn't figure out how. His companion remarked that at least it was a munition that one could see coming.

"On leave?" the man asked, offering Cody a light.

"A week if I can get it."

The New Zealander took the unintended hint. He shook Cody's hand again and went below deck, no doubt to find more willing prey.

*

"Daddy! Daddy!"

It was a few short hours later when Mary and Celia excitedly ran out from the front door, forgetting to close it. They had been inside at the window, gazing out, watching the village street where nothing much moved all day.

Noticing a familiar car backed in next to the cottage, Cody paid the cab driver who had brought him all the way out from the station. As the pony and trap sped away, he picked up his bag and gramophone, opened the front gate, and crouched to the ground in order to hug his two daughters. At last they had learned to first put their coats on, sort of.

"Where's Elizabeth?" he asked.

"We saw the white deer again!" Mary announced.

Cody instantly deciphered the invitation to go walking up to the woods where a small herd of deer lived. One of them was albino. It always gave them away, but it hadn't been seen for ages.

The eldest, now six, duly appeared and diligently closed the door behind her. She had become calmer and more thoughtful than her sisters, and right then better protected against the cold. Cody lifted her up and led the three of them around the side of the cottage and into the back garden that had mostly grown vegetables since the effects of war had bitten.

Kate hadn't heard them. She was tending to her goats. They were living where Cody planned a revolving garden house to protect against the cruel wind that either came from behind, or off the flatlands in front. At her side was Deborah Harrington, her vivacious best friend all the way from London.

The taller Kate looked as slim and beautiful as ever, her long dark hair bundled up behind her head, exposing her long neck and sharp features. Cody smiled at Deborah. He had always liked her. She had light brown curly hair, much more rounded shoulders than Kate, and a constantly smiling face. She was always pleasant company and had social tentacles to be admired, yet despite her thriving sense of humour, Cody had always suspected that behind it all she was a disciplinarian towards her more cerebral husband.

Kate caught on and immediately got up. She modestly embraced her shorter husband as the girls danced around the tied-up goats. Kate broke off and ordered them to be careful of the empty vegetable patch nearby.

"You heard about the white deer, darling?"

"So glad to see nothing has happened to you yet, Michael," said Deborah, smiling.

Cody smiled back. She had thin lips and an endearing manner of speaking without seeming to move them. Cody and Kate resumed looking at each other and saying nothing. Deborah took the hint.

"Well, I have to get back," she announced as she brushed past them both. "Just calling in to make sure that your dear wife is holding her head above water, Michael!"

As they all headed for the car, Cody wondered how Deborah got away with driving around for pleasure during such times. Perhaps it was why she had instinctively not parked out on the road. Her father being a judge did not temper her excesses.

"How's David?" Cody asked as he stepped ahead and opened the side gate.

David, a policeman, had turned up just before the war. Their marriage had been a surprise, and he was presently stationed in India. Deborah replied she had just received a letter that gave away nothing, but no-one seemed to shoot at each other where he was.

"You should get yourself posted there, darling."

They arrived at the car. She had driven it open despite the cold.

"You must come over soon," Deborah said as she turned around to embrace them both. "I promise you another concert."

They had been avoiding it. Neither had wanted to let on that their frugal means prevented it, not to mention the matter of looking after the girls.

Deborah climbed in and Cody cranked the car. A scarf tightly wound around her head, Deborah made a right-hand signal as she careered across the empty road, followed by a wave in the air as she sped away. The very last thing she had done was to give a quick glance in Cody's direction. It was her subtle instruction to ensure his guardianship of her best friend, inconsiderate given that it was he who had been preoccupied fighting for his life.

"So, who wants to go to the beach?" Cody asked as they filed inside.

It wouldn't be for a day or so because the deer had to be investigated first, but there were squeals of delight all the same. No-one cared about the probability of a rough oppressive sea and icy winds, if not rain, sleet or snow. The three girls were as hardy as their mother.

In the meantime, there was news to be heard, dinner for Kate to prepare, without meat or fish since it was mid-week, and girls to be calmed down and put to bed, each with their own tailor-made story that had been left in limbo while their father had gone to war. As always, Cody had diligently used part of the journey back to mug up from Hardy's notes where he had left off, and plan each of his enthralling follow-ons.

They each removed their coats and hung them between the kitchen door and stairs, hooks ranged according to height. Kate installed herself in the kitchen from where she could join in the conversation, and Cody lowered his head to enter the equally small adjoining sitting room with the girls.

The news was one-sided. It had always been so, unless Cody had pre-equipped himself with a story from Hardy or himself, one about a horse, or about a general who had fallen into a ditch, or a band that couldn't play in tune. He never referred to the ugly and incomprehensible violence any more than necessary, and then only to Kate. It was already enough for the girls that Kate failed to conceal her discrete daily nervous scan of the newspaper columns. They saw how she appeared to dread the arrival of the postman or the passage of the village policeman or vicar. Beyond that, an invisible wall had been constructed around them. Through mutual consent and understanding, visitors or people they went to see, talked of anything but war, injury or funerals. The actual stories of barbed wire, lice, trench foot, tapeworm, cholera, and typhoid, not to mention the endless and pointless slaughter, the realisation of the futility of life, would be pretended not to exist.

Cody listened as each of the girls talked, and sometimes at the same time, about themselves and their adventures. Elizabeth had school. There was all they had painted or drawn since his last visit, the one-fingered tunes they had learned on the piano that Kate had stripped, decorated and parked in the room next door that doubled as her studio. There were the new friends, mostly creatures great and small. Mary and Celia whispered about the frogs and snails they had caught outside and sometimes sneaked up to their bedroom.

"Anything on the probate?" Cody called out once Celia had finished a drama about a suspected badger that had upset the goats.

"Oh, you need to mend the fence!" called Kate. "It needs new posts, and I can't do that."

"What's a probate?" Celia asked.

Kate's younger brother, whom they had never seen much of, had killed himself in a motorcycle accident in London. She and her younger sister were due to inherit what he had made from selling luxury cars, but there had been no will. The godsend promised to change their lives. Kate had said that she planned to purchase the cottage and buy a Wolseley. After scraping and paying off debts for years, having sold off most of their wedding presents a long time ago, all they had for income was Cody's five pounds a week, most of which got sent directly to Kate, and whatever came from the meagre garden surplus she sold in the village.

"About a month or two, they reckon," Kate called out.

It was being handled in London where he had lived. Cody had never got used to how much Kate, who all her life had been a Londoner, enjoyed being on the impoverished south coast far away from the society she had been used to. She had taken the cottage to be within easy reach whenever Cody came home on leave. Now that money was on the way, Cody wondered for how long such considerations would last.

The girls had sat down on the floor to draw, Elizabeth the seaside and her sisters the deer. Kate had exceptionally treated them to large sheets of cartridge and a set of crayons each. She walked in, pulled off her apron, threw it on the side chair, and sat down opposite to make up for the moment of quiet. The fireplace roared as she spoke, and Cody half listened while he looked at her home-framed watercolours hanging on all four walls. She had never interested herself in her husband's life at the front, even when they were alone. She talked about herself and life in the village. The locals were presently struggling with shortage of labour. The women had had a harder time than ever replacing their men who had avoided the stigma of a reserved occupation. The harvest had been exhausting, and as had become the custom, she and the girls had gone to help.

Kate's conversation touched a nerve, but Cody didn't object. This was small fare, and in a way a relief from the drama he had left. Yet he had resented the fact that life seemed to go on relatively undeterred by the unimaginable goings-on across the Channel. He thought about the relative luxury they were living in when compared with anywhere he had seen in the devastated towns or villages he had just left. His mind was in conflict. The horror had gone on for too long. Unforgivably, he had had dishonourable thoughts about injury allowing him a longer escape, war wounds just enough to be respectable, yet not so bad as to incapacitate for long. Anything to get away from the hell.

Kate stopped talking and returned to the kitchen. Cody got up to take a quick peek at what she was presently working on. Her studio was a mess. Closing the piano lid and picking up whatever the girls had strewn over the floor, he glanced over to the easel. It looked like a mediaeval scene. There were monks holding what looked like sticks in their hands. It was far from her usual subject or style. How odd, he thought.

He noticed a cardboard box on the piano. For curiosity, he took a peek. There were small fresh cakes inside. But Kate disapproved of such things. He returned to the sitting room. From the kitchen, Kate started talking about problems the butcher was having with his wayward daughter. It was the latest village drama. Cody wearied at the triviality of it all, and once again looked for distraction.

Through the window, in which the glass panes had deformed with age, Cody spotted someone out in the road. He got up to look. It was a young man, only just in his teens. He was standing there on the opposite side.

"Who's he?"

Elizabeth, alerted, got up to join him.

"No-one local," called out Kate. "He's been coming maybe once or twice a week."

"And he just stands there?"

Elizabeth nodded.

"He looks over here, Daddy. Every now and again he looks over here. I've seen it."

She had no doubt made faces at him. Cody went into the kitchen and made his way around Kate to fetch his coat. The village had little history of crime, only the occasional drunkenness. This was unusual and suspicious.

"Have you reported him?"

"A thirteen or fourteen-year-old with nothing to do?" Kate asked.

"Never mind his age. He could be a lookout. Are there any tinkers around?"

Kate accused him of exaggerating, muttering about what the war was doing to his mind. Elizabeth re-joined her sisters on the floor as Cody reappeared and opened the front door, which was part of the sitting room. He could have chosen the back to sneak around, but intended a rapid frontal challenge instead.

He dashed out into the road. The youngster had disappeared. Cody came back inside muttering that if the young man ever returned, he would warn the constable.

The next morning, Cody went with his daughters for a walk in the village. It was a rare sunny day, and they encountered several neighbours on the way.

"Restored the will to live, sir!" called out the old village baker who knew them well.

Cody obliged with a laugh. Kate had long written the man off as indolent, and always complained about the quality of the bread he delivered on his bicycle. Cody preferred to allow him space. He had great respect for anyone having to work all hours of the night to be ready first thing in the morning.

Cody was immediately struck by the number of cats and dogs around. It had not been the case the other side, especially during the last two years. Much of the livestock had disappeared from the weekly markets there as well, including rabbits. He had teased the girls about eating rabbits when he came home.

They walked along a road that headed north out of the village. It provided their preferred scenery and the way to the deer. In a field to their right, several sheep stared at them and then looked in the direction they were heading, as if concerned. Cody wondered if they had spotted a vehicle approaching around the bend ahead and corralled the girls to the roadside. It turned out instead that one of the flock had somehow found itself cut off in the field next door. There was nothing he could do except to warn the farmer.

"Will we see the white deer?" Elizabeth asked.

Cody cursed himself for not bringing back his field glasses. As they approached the woods down to their right, he told them to be as quiet as possible. They peered down into the small valley. The white deer was always easy to spot. Sometimes, if they were especially quiet, the herd walked up and crossed the road right in front of them. Today, it seemed, they were up to something else.

After tea, Cody suggested they sing. They settled down in the spare room where Kate took up her usual position at the piano and thumped away. They ran through their usual melodies and the girls made most of the noise.

As Cody sat on a stool behind his daughters, he noticed that Kate's easel had been moved against the wall. The very odd painting had been hidden from view. He asked Kate about the carton on the piano, thinking she might have forgotten it.

"Deborah brought them, Michael. She knows very well I won't allow it."

Finally, Cody and his daughters went to snuggle together on the settee next door as Kate broke into three *Nocturnes* she had been memorising. Cody remembered one tune coming from the room above the shop. It was something he could never talk about.

10

The shaking wouldn't stop. Cody opened his eyes, expecting to be confronted by his orderly's muddy face and chaos. But there was no Hardy. There were no sounds of gas alarms, shells, or gunfire. He could even hear the birds outside. The girls were jumping on the bed. Downstairs, the kettle had just whistled on the hob, and Kate was playing the gramophone. This was the home front instead.

He had been dreaming that the taxi driver with the cat in his arms, and the mayor in the back, had ventured into no-man's-land and were being shot at from both sides. It took time to accept reality. Kate's music reminded him of the open-air concert Deborah had taken them to before the war. Cody had embarrassed himself by applauding the penultimate movement.

He smiled at the girls and rolled over, intent on dreaming of playing the same music in the trenches on his own. The war just wouldn't go away. It was past time to get up.

It was the day for the seaside. All five of them rapidly devoured Kate's light breakfast and got ready for the outing. Elizabeth managed once again to dress herself to the gills in her hat and coat while Cody made a hash of wrapping up her sisters. Kate appeared from upstairs and the first thing she did was to redo her husband's shoddy work without saying a word.

There was a knock at the front door. Elizabeth, who had been impatiently waiting beside it, opened up, expecting it to be their driver. Cody overheard her talking to a man. Something didn't sound right. He walked through to investigate. Standing at the door was none other than the tall figure of Corporal Jones, bandaged and in his uniform.

"Jones!"

"I apologise, Captain."

Cody couldn't help noticing the grave look on Jones' face. He beckoned him in, closed the door, and ushered Elizabeth away before she became too mesmerised by Jones' giant stature and green eyes.

"I only need five minutes of your time, sir."

Jones was far too tall for the room. He had to keep his head bent down, especially to avoid the ancient beam that ran across the centre. Cody heard the trap pull up outside, right on time. He realised Jones must have walked all the way from the station. In his present state, it must have taken at least a couple of hours. He had to have set out well before dawn.

"We'll have more than five minutes, Jones. Have you eaten?"

Jones insisted he was fine, although Cody knew it couldn't be true. He offered him a lift back in the trap and promised they would talk in town over something to eat.

Everyone filed outside and climbed on board, Elizabeth in front as usual. Cody closed the cottage door without locking and joined Jones and the others in the back. The cab driver passed over blankets, and Kate took one for herself and the two girls to share.

The sky was blue again, and it was quite a bit colder than the day before. Jones and Cody said nothing to each other as they took the road to town. After five minutes, they found themselves in flat, open countryside become far more visible since the fall and perennial trimming of the hedgerows. They pulled up to allow a herd of cows cross the road back to their field, and Kate waved to the woman in charge from whom she bought unpasteurised milk. The woman was being helped by two young boys with sticks taller than themselves. While the women exchanged a few words, Cody tried to imagine why a bandaged Jones would have travelled a good thirty miles and walked so far for a conversation of a mere five minutes. He decided it had to do with replacing Piggot. Jones was out of order, and perhaps he should have shown annoyance over his intrusion.

After close to twenty minutes, they arrived in town and made their way directly towards the beach. People were in the streets in large numbers, spilling onto the roadway where there happened to be fewer horses and only the odd motorcar and lorry. The taxi rode right onto the sand for them all to descend. Cody arranged to be recuperated at tea-time and then joined the others to watch the furious waves and children running away from them. It was such a contrast to fighting.

"Gives you a sense of let-down, doesn't it, Captain?"

Cody knew what Jones meant. A short break away from it all was always welcome for a few days. The day it would become permanent would be another matter altogether. Like it or not, the intense excitement of war had become an addiction.

The plan was to walk along the shore to a small village where they would have a soup lunch on the beach, drinking it out of mugs to keep their hands warm. Cody saw Jones was in no fit state to accompany them, and besides, evidently keen to return home. He gestured to Kate to go on ahead and guided Jones to a small café that overlooked the beach from the busy causeway.

The café turned out to be almost empty and out of tea and coffee. They had soup instead and sat at the window to watch Kate and the girls in the distance as they made their way hand in hand along the water's edge.

"Three girls and a lovely wife, Captain," congratulated Jones. "You're very lucky, sir."

Cody asked him about his own family. Jones replied he had two boys.

"As tall as you, I expect."

"Getting there, Captain!"

"I suppose you want to talk about Piggot?"

"No, no!" said Jones, alarmed. "He mustn't know about this, Captain. If it weren't so sensitive, I would have gone to him."

"But you know he was killed?"

Jones hadn't heard. Straight away, he looked shaken. After a minute of silence, he said that Piggot had been a good lieutenant and had deserved better.

"I thought you wanted his place."

Brushing aside any thought of promotion or interfering with his captain's personal time off in order to discuss it, Jones showed he was obviously keen to get to what had been troubling him.

"Captain, I need your complete discretion."

"Discretion?"

Jones leaned forward and lowered his voice despite there being no-one nearby.

"What I have to tell you, Captain, must never come back to me. I only mean well."

Cody couldn't for the life of him imagine what Jones was about to talk about.

"It's about Captain Quinn."

"Ah, Quinn. In that case, go on."

The Quinn affair had conveniently left his mind. What on earth could have driven Jones to come all this way to talk about a subject that he knew would aggravate him?

Jones described a small hamlet three miles from where he lived, further along the coast. Cody wondered where on earth this was going.

"Get on with it, Jones!"

Jones announced that five of the men who had been killed during the Quinn incident came from the hamlet in question.

"Five? The same village?"

Cody recalled what Kate had been saying about the lack of men where they lived. Jones explained that they had signed up during the drive for pals' regiments at the beginning of the war.

"The hamlet wiped out!" Jones said. "All those men were tenant farmers, Captain. It's certain their widows will lose their homes."

He explained that the estate where they had worked had been struggling. The owner now brought in men in reserved occupation to resuscitate his situation, and no-one could really blame him.

Cody said he sympathised with the women.

"And children as well," prompted Jones

It was still a mystery why he was bringing him into this story. There was no risk of the workhouse for the women. They would get small pensions and could go looking for work and accommodation elsewhere. There were towns nearby. Finding employment would be easy for them. And why on earth did this involve Quinn?

"There is nothing someone like me can do about it, Jones," he warned. "You understand that, don't you?"

"Yes, of course, Captain. It's not about your help at all. It's about Captain Quinn's. Did you know that his father's estate is ten miles from there?"

It was news to Cody. He had no idea where Quinn came from, other than somewhere near the south coast.

"The women came to see me," said Jones. "You would understand that, Captain. I was in charge. They wanted to know more about what had happened, more than you could say in your letters."

"Of course."

"I made a terrible mistake, Captain. It must have come out because of what I felt about Captain Quinn."

Cody asked him to explain.

"I told them how the men had died."

"But why shouldn't you, Corporal?"

"It was what followed. I heard about it later."

"What happened, Jones?"

"The widows walked all the way to the Quinn estate to ask for work. It was raining and snowing, and the children were with them. They had heard it was faring well and employed plenty of women. That way, they could stay together."

Cody replied that they had shown good initiative.

"The Captain was home on leave then," Jones said. "They asked to see him. He refused and threatened to report them if they ever came back."

"What!"

Cody had difficulty believing it. If nothing else, Quinn had been offered the chance to redeem himself.

"There must have been a misunderstanding, Jones. He didn't express *any* sympathy or have them interviewed?"

"The only thing they came away with were the threats."

Cody had a hard time with the story. He wondered if the women were playing games. At the very least, Quinn would have been courteous. He thought about the implications of Jones' story. It was bound to do the rounds. It could spell yet more trouble at the battalion, and that was important. He thanked Jones for telling him.

"Fifteen children to support between them!" said Jones.

Cody tried to imagine why Quinn would have behaved so egregiously. It had to be self-preservation. Had the women become employed by him, no doubt their circumstances would eventually have become common knowledge. Quinn had no doubt wanted to hide the incident. It would not be surprising. Anyway, despite his *faux pas*, the women would surely get employment elsewhere.

They stopped talking and looked out to the waves as violent as ever. Cody paid, and they left. Once in the street, he thanked Jones and wished him a speedy recovery, hoping to see him soon back at the front. He escorted him the short distance to the station and offered in vain to pay for his return ticket.

"I ask nothing from you, Captain," Jones repeated. "I just thought you ought to know."

They patiently waited on the platform, saying nothing to each other, Jones wondering if he hadn't gone too far, and Cody, still confused by the troubling news, worried about what might come.

The train finally pulled in and dozens of men, women, and children alighted, some evidently geared up for the beach. Wartime appeared to have rendered the railway as busy as ever, even in winter. Jones hoisted himself up, his injured leg making the manoeuvre difficult. He closed the door and lowered the window. Cody thanked him for coming.

"I didn't see what to do, Captain," said Jones, saluting. "But thank you, sir, for listening to me and for the ride back. I'll see you soon."

As the train pulled away, Jones handed Cody a piece of paper. It was just in time.

"Perhaps you could say something. To Colonel Wilkes, for example."

"Let me see," Cody called out as he waved goodbye.

As he hurried back to catch up with Kate and the girls, Cody realised he had entrapped himself with his last words. Annoyed as he was, he couldn't really blame Jones.

He glanced at the piece of paper still in his hand. It had Jones' and Quinn's addresses written side by side. He looked across the street. A window in the town's department store advertised a revolving garden shelter. He crossed over and went inside, and through to a yard at the back where they had one on display. It was just what he had been thinking of, with three closed sides and completely open at the front, and an adjustable awning at the front. He stepped on the platform and found it sturdier than expected. The floor was sufficiently off the ground to allay the constant fears of flooding that bedevilled his nightmares. This was worth negotiating with Kate.

An assistant came over to join him. Cody recognised him as the young man who had sold him the gramophone. He asked how much it cost.

"Seventeen pounds, sir. Delivered."

It would have to wait.

Following a shortcut to the street down the side of the store, Cody regained his brief journey to the beach. Approaching the water's edge, he followed the line of waves, every now and again unashamedly jumping like a child between rock pools and avoiding water rushing in from his left. The wind was now carrying the surf into his face. He reached down and picked up a wet and sandy crab for the girls, but much as he tried to distract his mind, the image of Quinn refused to go away. He thought about the fifteen fatherless children and their mourning mothers, the disruption caused by the loss of a home and having to split up and move to a strange environment. What if such a thing ever happened to Kate? What if she had nothing coming to her other than his war pension? The women had each other to share their children. Kate had no-one so close.

The girls were running around on the damp sand ahead. Kate, seated on a soft dune further back, was watching them. After donating the crab to Celia, who ran off to wash it, and investigating a large shell that Mary had just discovered, Cody went over to sit next to his wife.

Kate asked what the Jones visit had all been about. Cody's instinct was to say as little as possible, try not to regurgitate his troubles or allow them to weigh on her mind. It would have given her something to get concerned about. She was a born fighter. There had already been the Suffragettes before the war. She would want to fight for the widows, wrap herself into their plight.

As they were walking along, still distracted, he skidded on a smooth piece of rock and fell flat on his back. The girls were ahead and hadn't seen. Kate just stood there. It was quite unlike her. As he struggled back to his feet, Cody's mind was still elsewhere. He imagined five distraught women and their offspring knocking at their door. Then he imagined Kate reaching into her new inheritance to help them, mindless of her own needs. A wind of self-interest had enveloped him. He felt ashamed, but it was reality. In the end, people had to fend for themselves. Kate had uncharacteristically just taught him that lesson.

She asked again why Jones had come.

"Nothing really, darling," he said, hoping she would at last desist. "Concern for some battalion war widows, that's all."

Mercifully, Kate didn't push it any further. Instead, she ran, far enough ahead to beat him to the girls.

*

The rest of the week passed faster than anyone had hoped for. Despite the cold, they went out every day, always with walks long enough to allow them to talk about everything but the war. The pattern was familiar, deserted country lanes and into woods and fields, with the girls every now and again running on ahead to explore while Cody and Kate, lost in their separate worlds, said little to each other. The young man, meanwhile, never returned.

Despite the relative peace and calm, Cody felt he had detected a change in Kate. He couldn't get over how she had just stood there when he had slipped on the rock. At home the next morning, after he had complained about his stiff back as a result, she had gently gone on about how little he helped her, how much he slept or listened to music, how often he paid attention to the girls rather than herself. It was a first. And then there was the strange painting that he daren't ask about. Something had to be afoot.

The affair of Jones' widows never left Cody's mind either. He hated outstanding issues. That same night he had stayed up and written to Jones proposing to visit the women. After tearing the letter up, he had gone upstairs but couldn't sleep for hours. He was caught between fires. He owed Quinn the loyalty of fellow rank.

He had woken up before Kate and crept downstairs to make beef tea, determined to chase the recurring thoughts from his mind with a book. He couldn't get started. He wanted to find out more about his fellow captain. He got out a map from where Kate stored all the guides and brochures that they rarely used. The Quinn estate was a manageable ride from where he would have to embark. Kate didn't need to know that he was scheduled to take a later ferry. It would give him a decent part of the afternoon to sneak a look around.

Elizabeth was the first to appear, in her pyjamas. She snuggled next to her father, and they tried to nod off together. It lasted all of five minutes.

"Daddy, why can't I go back with you?"

None of the girls had ever asked such a thing. It pleased him she wanted to be with him.

"It's not the right time yet, darling," he said.

"Why not?"

"When the war is finished, we'll certainly go together. It's a lovely country."

"But is the war that bad? Don't other children go?"

Cody chuckled.

"I'm afraid not, darling. It's a very sad place at the moment. And where I am, people are hungry, and all the cats, dogs, and deer have gone away."

"Ah," she said, "in that case I'll wait."

Kate came down looking cross. She had evidently hoped for a lie-in with her husband on their penultimate night together.

Her bad mood lasted for the remainder of the day. For lunch, she served beetroot soup, which she knew too well they all hated. Cody hadn't dared say anything, but Celia had.

"Do you hate us, mummy?"

"Why on earth would you think that?" Kate said.

All three girls started crying, almost as if it had been planned beforehand, but Cody knew full well that such tactics were still a few years off. Kate ceded and gave them bread and dripping instead, her husband included. After telling them they would have to do their own washing up, and seeing how much more they enjoyed the food, she deserted them and stormed out into the garden where she promptly got out the tools to repair the fence that Cody had forgotten.

*

The goodbyes late the following morning were as sad as ever, despite the tantrums of the day before. As the taxi pulled away from the furiously waving girls fighting their tears, Cody remembered that his forthcoming absence during Christmas had long become the norm. He had never even had one with Celia. Kate had promised him some new pyjamas, just to have something to place under the imaginary tree. Now that he cheated on their precious time together, he felt ashamed. The ongoing war could yet tear them apart altogether, one such cheat at a time.

It was yet another cloudless day. The deviation from the port took over an hour into a countryside that he had never visited. The railway line followed them all the way. Skirting the Quinn estate took all of twenty minutes. From the road lined by trees and brick walls, Cody saw acres of fields, haystacks, barns, stables, to one end what looked like a set of small industrial buildings, and finally a pretentious-looking Edwardian baroque mansion.

"Looks in fine form!" the trap driver said.

The estate turned out to border quite a large a village. Cody asked the driver to leave him at the only pub and to wait for his return.

"An hour at most," he said.

It had just turned midday, and the only other customers were two old men in breeches and morning coats who gave the impression that their presence was a daily recurrence.

"Morning, Captain!" the landlord cried out.

He was heavily built and had a round face with rosy cheeks and a thick moustache. Cody judged him to have plenty of character.

"You recognise your cuffs, sir," he said, smiling.

"We have one or two here, Captain. They keep me in practice."

Cody ordered a pint and a cheese sandwich and remained at the counter. With nothing else to do, the landlord obliged by making conversation. Cody asked about the estate that he had seen so much of on the way in. The landlord replied that most people in the village had some sort of connection with it. Quite a few of the men had gone off to fight, and their women were standing in for them. The buildings were used for making and packing cheese. Mostly women worked there, as well as in the fields.

"This region is famous for its cheese," boasted the landlord, pointing to the loaded cheeseboard on the counter behind him from which he had just served. "Every village has its own speciality, although there's less of it nowadays, of course."

Cody raised himself on his stool to study the board. It was well over a foot wide. Around its top edge were the names of local village names delicately carved into the surface. The landlord obliged by reading each of them out, explaining that he had been given the board for his wedding a couple of decades before, when he had started up.

"That one is from here," he said, proudly pointing to the last name and then to Cody's sandwich. "From the Quinn farmhouse."

Cody asked if the village got many passers-by, since it was off the main road by several miles.

"Mostly people looking for work, Captain."

At that moment, another officer walked in. He was on his own. He looked young, well under twenty-five.

"Lieutenant Barker!" cried the landlord in the same manner he had greeted Cody.

The light-haired Barker was tall and lanky, wore spectacles and looked studious. He smiled, came up to the bar, and stood to attention. Cody held out his hand and introduced himself, and explained he was passing through on his way to embarkation.

"A bit off the main route if I may say so, sir."

He had a slight stutter.

Cody smiled back without attempting to offer any explanation. He asked Barker where he was serving.

"Also in France, sir. I work in a field survey unit. Printing."

Cody offered to buy Barker a drink, and they went to sit down.

"Four days left!" Barker said with a sigh.

Cody asked if he lived locally. Barker explained his sister had married into the Quinn family who owned the local estate.

That gave Cody the perfect opportunity.

"Not *Captain* Quinn, by any chance?"

"Indeed, Captain. You know him?"

"I serve with him!" Cody said, keeping up the pretension. "I did not know he came from around here."

Barker appeared to fall for it. He explained he had only been in France for a few months and was helping to set up a printing unit. Cody replied he had already encountered one of their maps just before leaving.

"*Modified* maps," Barker corrected. "We only modify maps."

Cody asked about the printing process, and Barker went into a long description of the machines they used in the field, how they compared with facilities at home where he had served his apprenticeship. He explained how they marked up the stones, and how in France they occupied themselves with overprinting existing maps with updates. In recent times, there seemed to be more and more of them.

"You're getting busier, then?" Cody asked.

"Certainly, Captain," Barker stuttered.

Cody wondered how the scion of a wealthy landowning family got to know and marry the sister of a printing apprentice. At one point, Barker referred to his own family, with a hint that they might be well connected too. He gave the impression of being well brought up and polite. With nothing of the air of his brother-in-law, Cody took an immediate liking to him.

Barker announced that he regularly came over when on leave to keep his sister company.

"May I ask what your father did?" Cody asked.

"He still does, Captain. He's a vicar in Southampton."

Cody pointed out the coincidence. Their fathers might well have met. They chatted for half-an-hour about their personal lives and families. Barker talked about his parents-in-law, in particular the old general who had done so well during the last Boer War. It had turned out to be his military swansong, and his wife had died prematurely, soon after his coming home.

"Typhoid."

The general had since become an effective local politician, but his health had recently declined. Barker's sister spent what time she could looking after him.

They talked a little more about mapmaking. Cody mentioned Kate came from a printing family. Barker offered to show Cody his establishment in France. It was an hour or two's journey from where Cody was currently serving. He advised him not to go through official channels, though, as they were more than touchy over security.

"I look forward to it," said Cody. "I have a few ideas."

He asked about the Quinn farm.

"My sister takes care of about a hundred women, depending on the season," Barker said. "Some of them work inside, especially cheese-making. Others out in the fields in season."

"Is there accommodation for them?"

"Oh, yes. The estate owns more than enough properties for that."

Cody saw his chance.

"I know five experienced women looking for work and accommodation. They have children."

"I'm sure she'll be interested," Barker said, without hesitating. "Only this morning she was complaining about shortages. The pay isn't much, though."

"It never is!" said Cody, delighted all the same.

Before he left, Cody headed for the post office to send a telegram to Jones. The women should ask for a Mrs Quinn at the farm, but Jones should make sure that they keep Cody's name out of their story.

As the taxi drove him back to the port, he couldn't help congratulating himself for his effortless progress. Such luck surely meant that his mission had been a worthy one. He thanked God for pubs, the like of which he wouldn't experience again for a while but dream of all too often.

Something troubled him about the conversation he and Barker had just had. Not once had Barker talked about his brother-in-law. It was even more strange given that Cody had said he knew him. He wondered what it implied.

He then returned the begging question. What kind of mind would have refused five desperate women work when the need had been there on the estate's side too? He wondered how the Quinn affair would end up.

Cody got back to the docks in time for the six o'clock. Failing to recognise anyone on board, he avoided the officers' mess and stayed on deck on his own in the dark, ruminating as he peered down to the water once again. The destroyer was out there again, keeping watch, but there was no airplane this time.

Barker had seemed a nice enough fellow. Cody's hunch was that their encounter would remain between them, that he could continue to manoeuvre without risk of becoming exposed. He would visit Barker in France at the earliest opportunity.

He continued to look down at the dark water speeding past as his stomach filled with anguish about returning to the front. Why on earth was life such a menagerie of conflicts? Couldn't relationships remain simpler and calmer? Apart from what might be the first inexplicable uncertainties in his marriage, Kate was becoming a stranger. He wondered if Deborah knew something.

Quinn was destined to become a major preoccupation for a while. Cody had always taught his men to confront realities, to tackle problems head-on. Everything to do with the young intelligence officer looked increasingly complicated. This bull might yet have to be taken by the horns.

11

Battalion headquarters had returned to the old candle factory. As Cody followed the wood-panelled windowless corridor in search of the source of the echoes, he tried to imagine what fresh surprises lay in store. There were always surprises. The worst thing about returning from leave, however short, was the extent to which the world had changed in the meantime, usually for the worse, always unexpectedly.

The corridor was endless. The place must have once thrived. He imagined rows of busy workers in each of the empty rooms he passed. Electric wires had been left dangling from ceilings. Oil lamps placed on the bare concrete every twenty feet lit his way. He went up a flight. It was like a coal mine that headed upwards.

As he closed in on the noise, he reflected on what he had heard from the sentries outside. The front had been quiet the entire week, the battalion replenished with a new medical officer and one hundred and fifty conscripts. First signs were promising.

He found the room at last, one from the end, a stroke of luck because the conversation had momentarily receded. The colonel must have chosen it during one of his whims, no doubt so that his officers would feel estranged and pay extra attention. Despite what Quinn had said, the colonel hated routine.

The very first face Cody spotted was Quinn's. He was sitting next to the colonel, who no longer had his bandages, at a long table facing the small audience of officers and NCOs. Quinn appeared friendly and rehabilitated. Cody tried to acknowledge him with a brief nod, but Quinn was otherwise distracted.

Fetching a chair from the far wall, Cody made a sign to his fellow commanders as he sat down behind them, close to where he had entered. Noticing that everyone had a copy of the 1:10,000 map that was pinned to the colonel's board, Cody got up and helped himself to the top of the pile on a side table. He checked that his copy was the same as that in the hands of the lieutenant sitting next to him. His neighbour was new.

"Finlay," the lieutenant whispered.

As far as Cody could tell, all the other lieutenants were there. He offered his hand to the man who he assumed had replaced Piggot. He had dark hair and a roundish face and appeared to be approaching his thirties.

Colonel Wilkes engaged in pleasantries, congratulating Quinn over something that had happened the day before. Cody surprised himself by feeling ill at ease. Having thought of little but Quinn all the way from England, he was now discovering that the intelligence officer was back on good terms with the colonel. He wondered how it had taken place and what it might lead to.

Quinn was invited to speak. He stood up and asked everyone to study their maps. He announced they incorporated changes imposed by division that he was about to explain.

Cody winced at the thought that division had cooked up anything new. Such occurrences were usually bad news. It had always appeared that any lapse in hostilities yielded opportunities for dangerous ideas, as divisional staff, or staff from brigade for that matter, struggled to justify their existence. Brigadier Lightfoot's v-shaped defensive ditches, five feet deep and nine feet wide and filled with barbed wire, had originally been an idea from division, fine in concept but suicidal to dig right in front of the enemy. More recently, division had insisted on training troops to crawl under a creeping barrage, ignoring the practical problem of how to get everyone to stand up again at the right moment. And then there had been the plan for one of the last actions before Quinn's arrival. C Company had been ordered to rush all the way along an enemy fire trench towards a machine gun post. The enemy hadn't been so good at their trench work that time. So far removed from reality, division hadn't anticipated the knee-deep mud that had fatally slowed everyone down. It had cost so many lives. As far as Cody was concerned, the less division got involved in anything, the better for all.

He glanced over to Talbot and Fuller who were sitting slightly in front of him and to one side. Their cynical eyes met. The colonel noticed and gave all three of them an angry look.

"You will see at the top left of your map," Quinn obliviously went on, "that Conrad trench has been renamed."

Everyone studiously looked down. The lighting was poor, but they had already got used to it.

"From now on, front-line trenches will be remembered according to their coordinates," Quinn said. "As far as our sector is concerned, Conrad becomes I.1.3. Colin trench just below it becomes I.1.2, and so-on."

There were moans from the audience soon suppressed by another angry look from the colonel. Cody felt the same as his colleagues. This was a needless bureaucratic change to a system that had worked perfectly well since the beginning of hostilities. The battalion's trench names in the area all began with the letter C, and the enemy's designated with a W; Whip, Wiggle, Whack and so-on. Everything had been easily memorised. Communications had been clear and unmistakable. The procedure was well embedded and mastered. Why on earth change it?

At last, sensing the atmosphere among his colleagues, Quinn tried to defend the decision. It concerned only front-line trenches, he explained; those which were most likely to find themselves altered.

"I.1.3 will continue to be serviced by Civil and Cream," he went on. "Civil Avenue and Cream Alley."

"What about the enemy lines?" asked Cragg.

"No change. 'Whip' and 'Wiggle' in our present case stay the same."

"But if we need to bring down artillery on them," intervened Cody, "surely the logic follows to change those as well. *Especially* those."

Without even looking at Cody, Quinn argued the move brought precision to a vague system. Cody felt sorry for his having to justify such a useless idea. The best Quinn could do was to argue that it sped up communications with artillery for reasons of avoidance.

"That's how it's going to be, gentlemen," Colonel Wilkes intervened, aggravated by the negative reception. "There will be no further discussion."

As everyone stood up to file out of the room as fast as they could, Cody asked Finlay to wait for him outside and wound his way through in order to make contact with the colonel standing on his own. The keenness of his colleagues to escape forced him to work against the grain. Quinn was among them. He didn't make the slightest sign in his direction.

The colonel asked Cody how his leave had been, and Cody asked about the colonel's arm. They talked about what had happened during the previous week. The colonel made frequent comments that confirmed that his attitude towards Quinn had about turned. His onetime nemesis appeared to have been fully rehabilitated within a few days. Avoiding any comment about this, or the talk they had just listened to, Cody asked when the next relief was due and if any new initiative was being planned.

"The name change idea was Quinn's," Colonel Wilkes offered out of the blue. "He brought it to me, and I passed it on. I didn't think it would fly."

He seemed to be proud of it. Cody was relieved that he hadn't spoken his own mind.

"The day after tomorrow," the colonel belatedly said. "Quinn dealt with the maps."

Cody started for the door. He was certain that the battalion would be saddled with the change of signposts. The colonel called him back. The major had sided up to him.

"By the way, Cody, you still need to look at your trench crowding again. Assert yourself, man!"

It was an untimely reproach, before Cody had even acclimatised, but not untypical of the colonel. It was possible that Finlay, the new arrival, had more to do in that respect.

Cody decided that his very first mission would be to talk to his men to see why the colonel might have come to his conclusion. He recuperated Finlay smoking a pipe in the corridor and they made their way downstairs and off to the deaf and dumb school where the men were billeted.

Finlay looked sturdy and the same height as Cody. He said he was twenty-eight, described working for a local council's garage, and admitted that he was a car fanatic although he hadn't one of his own. In their continuing conversation he appeared mature and well-balanced, with a sense of humour despite what appeared to be a serious outlook on life, but Cody wondered if he might not turn out to be a little too easy-going. He would have to put him to the test.

Once they arrived, Cody summoned the other lieutenants and mentioned the colonel's comments. Finlay offered nothing, but his three colleagues expressed their surprise. The colonel had done the rounds of the fire trench twice a day while they were up front and said nothing. In fact, they had taken great care to be seen to have spread out, and Finlay had been brought in on it from the start.

"Was the brigadier ever with him?" asked Cody, suspecting where it might have come from.

Smalby insisted that he or Major Hickman had always come alone.

"Except for Captain Quinn, of course," corrected Cobbold.

Cody spotted it right away. The winds had indeed turned. He now wondered where they might head.

On his way to his billet, Cody found Hardy. He was glad to see him.

"How was it?" he asked once they were alone.

"Lieutenant Smalby did very well, Captain."

That night, as if the enemy had found out about the absurd renaming and wanted to exploit the confusion, he let loose along the five-hundred-yard front that the other half of the brigade was manning. A bombing raid and two incursions caused multiple casualties. From its vantage point in the deaf and dumb school, C Company watched the flashes from the front and the nearby stream of stretchers being ferried past to the rear.

A few hours later, just after sunrise, their own deployment, anticipated for that night, was called off. Division followed through with instructions that the entire brigade was to move away from the front for the foreseeable future in order to assimilate fully its exceptionally large portion of new recruits. Another brigade would take their place.

At midday, several hours before the expected pull-out, Cody and his colleagues were taken by car to brigade headquarters, now situated in catacombs not far from the cathedral. They were informed that they could expect to remain in the rear for several weeks. The brigade would find itself spread over several miles. Each of the battalions was shown where it would be encamped. Lorries would commence the operation at dusk. The companies presently in the trenches would be relieved during the night in order to follow.

The four commanders returned on foot to the school to wait it out. Just after dark, instructions came to head out to wait for the lorries carrying out the ferrying from the edge of town. Once again, under the orders of the transport officer, the troops marched off. Men started singing as they joined the long queues waiting for the transport to return. This time, the transport officer and his team let them be.

Cody and his colleagues followed with their orderlies in the second echelon. They would ride in the mess cart, about a three-hour journey given the terrain and the state of the road.

A couple of miles outside town, they caught up with a cart carrying Quinn and others from battalion headquarters, including the padre and the new medical officer. Cody couldn't help himself. They were out of hearing. He turned to his colleagues.

"How's our intelligence officer?"

There was no reaction. It was as if the question had been ill-timed or misinterpreted. Cody saw it wise not to pursue the matter again. How the world had changed.

They had been on the road for almost two hours. Lorries were constantly splashing past them in both directions. The troops that overtook them were continuing to sing.

Absorbed in thinking about the upcoming challenges presented by the extra-long respite, Cody and the others refrained from joining the festivities. Each of them was thinking about how to fight off the boredom that was bound to descend on their troops. Once they had become inured to the violent jolting, the four of them discussed plans for training. After a first day of rest, they would create a mock front for assault training in fields next to the camp. New recruits would be ordered to dig trenches in order to toughen them up.

Their conversation was halted by noise and flashes breaking out behind them. They pulled up and climbed out to watch. A massive attack had begun. It could only be the enemy re-crossing the canal. Fuller thought most of the flashes were coming from the eastern side of town. No-one could believe what was happening.

"The balloons and aeroplanes," said Cody. "We would have spotted the preparations this morning."

They had been watching for ten minutes when a staff car emerged from the last bend in the road they had taken. It overtook and came to a halt. Out stepped the colonel who briskly walked towards them. Orders were to turn back.

The transport officer was still in town. Cody offered to continue onwards and organise up ahead. The colonel agreed and told him that the battalion would muster at the near edge of town to wait for orders. After telling them he had already seen to the third transport echelon and troops that had not yet taken the lorries, he joined the others on the cart as it manoeuvred to head back to town.

As they raced to catch up with the lorries, the driver asked Cody whether anything had been expected.

"Not in a million years!"

Cody was very concerned. More than a third of his company had not yet faced live fire.

Three hours before dawn, the battalion found itself at the ready, half-a-mile from the town gates. The transport, other than the munitions waggons, remained halted two miles further back waiting for instructions. The fighting was getting closer by the minute and had resulted in the decision to muster further away than planned. Some troops from the brigade that had been entrenched up to the canal were showing up at the edge of town. The artillery out west had already pulled back during the night and was now situated three miles behind them, poised for a second retreat if necessary.

The battalion slowly moved forward in four echelons according to company, C Company in second place behind D. The men spread outwards across the empty fields to each side of the road. The fury of the hidden fighting ahead of them was getting louder. They were up against an unstoppable force. Every man braced himself for what might become his last day on earth.

As they neared the gates, a succession of three shells landed on the open ground in front of them. D company had taken direct hits. A couple of dozen men lay on the ground, many not moving, others screaming or feebly calling out for help. C Company advanced past them and merged inwards in order to negotiate the street and join any defenders. The way ahead looked very dark indeed, while there were no flashes.

"Where the hell are they?" Hardy asked, as he stuck to Cody's side.

They had expected to encounter an entire brigade on the back foot. Random shooting opened up directly ahead, indicating a resistance being put up near the centre of town. But the scale didn't seem right. Thousands of men were unaccounted for.

By the time they found their way to the limits of the main square, it was clear they were facing the enemy pretty well on their own. Heavy machine gun fire came at them from several directions.

Cody had his men take position behind rubble and in shell holes alongside the scattered troops already in place. He spotted flashes coming from one of the damaged spires of the cathedral. Snipers had gained a lethal advantage that would worsen with daylight. He ordered Hardy to go looking for Quinn and his men. They were the best equipped to deal with the threat.

Everywhere was dark. Cody tried to make sense of what was happening., The enemy seemed to have got as far as the remnants of the town hall and the line of buildings to the right. Most of the square itself was providing a no-man's-land. He ordered a messenger to warn the colonel that any enemy attempt to carry out a flank action should be blocked, or they'd be done for.

There was a sudden explosion about twenty yards to his left. Five minutes later, Lieutenant Mowforth crawled over to report that two of his men had killed themselves preparing a jam-pot bomb.

"They knew what they were doing," he said.

It had to have been a faulty fuse short circuiting. It had happened before.

The shooting subsided. Everyone lay waiting in the dark. To Cody's right, men had made out some sort of flag just in front of them, its short pole inserted into the soft edge of a shell hole. They called out, requesting to retrieve it, but Finlay firmly ordered them to stay put. The enemy resumed firing. When the shooting momentarily subsided again, Cody heard what sounded like a scramble to get to the flag. Finlay was shouting. Just as he was angrily repeating his order to desist, there was an explosion. Two men had disappeared for good.

"It can't have been booby-trapped," called out Mowforth. "Not this close."

A shell landed right in the square and exploded. Rifle fire broke out from both sides. Cody asked a runner to discover out what had happened to the Lewis guns. If the enemy had been bold enough to have crept up so close, anything might be about to happen.

Two more flashes came from the cathedral. Cody thought he felt one round passing right in front of him.

"Where the hell is Quinn?"

The line to the right, closest to where the flag had been, took two direct hits. Everyone listened to the crying from men in pain. A Lewis gun opened up a little further away. Another followed to the left. Cody felt relieved. More men rushed up to the line, ferrying ammunition boxes and bomb crates. One of them was Hardy who came to lie by his side.

"Quinn?" Cody asked.

"No-one knows," Hardy said, shaking his head in the dark. "I even went to Major Hickman, Captain."

There was about an hour left before first light. Cody knew that if they didn't take care of the cathedral beforehand, they wouldn't last long, especially if the enemy hauled rifle grenades or even a machine gun up there.

He went looking for Quinn himself. He crawled back inside what was left of the building they were fronting, past the company that was using the remaining walls to fire from, and along the outer wall on the other side. He stumbled on a body next to the wall. He got out his torch, taking care with its beam. It was the old man who had shown him around. He had been shot in the forehead.

A little further on, he fell on a group of women huddled together, too traumatised to move. A few yards away, he made out his friend the priest. He had women and children around him.

"*Dieu merci vous êtes toujours vivant, Mon Père*," he called out in his broken French.

He asked him why they hadn't escaped. The priest looked upwards towards the spires. Cody became livid. Where the hell was Quinn?

He crawled onwards to seek the colonel whom he thought was further up the street. He soon found him. After making sure that he had already got his warning about the flanks, he reported the snipers. He wisely allowed the colonel to come to his own conclusions regarding Quinn.

It had become light by the time Cody was back with his men. A friendly plane flew over, surprising them all. It dropped a red smoke bomb just beyond the opposite side of the square and the artillery followed up with twenty rounds.

Quinn finally turned up with his men.

"We were over there," he said, pointing to the right, but obviously referring to one of the side streets beyond.

While Quinn and his team caught on to the peril from the spires, and spread out to position themselves to respond, Cody somehow kept his calm.

The stalemate continued for nearly four hours. Friendly planes were by now regularly coming over, but there had been no more artillery fire. Quinn's men struggled to make their mark, but the snipers up in the spire miraculously only cost C Company two more men.

The enemy on the ground repeatedly sent over lethal mortar canisters.

"Those again!" said Mowforth.

They had come across them when they had taken over an enemy trench a year and a half before. The canisters had been small oil drums launched with an electrically fired charge from wooden mortars bound with wire. At least a dozen had landed around them, but miraculously no-one had been hurt.

Colonel Wilkes called for Cody. Once again, he had to make the dangerous twisting route back to headquarters twenty yards behind the square, but this time in full daylight.

"We have an entire brigade arriving before dark," the colonel announced. "One battalion will provide you support in the square. We'll attack the entire enemy line at six, before they attempt any initiative of their own. The planes will keep coming until then. I want you to lead the attack."

Cody returned to his men to spread the word. Quinn was still there. His men had long pinpointed the flashes from the cathedral, but their return shots were still failing to do the job. He declared that he had already been informed of the attack.

"We'll get them beforehand," he said. "They won't have time to replace them."

Cody showed his annoyance, he wanted done with it, but it was untimely to be seen arguing in front of his men. Quinn caught on. Within half-an-hour the spires had gone silent.

Hours passed with everyone staying put. In the descending daylight, Quinn's men did nothing but monitor the spires to make sure that there was no attempt to replace the snipers.

"They'll try it after nightfall," Quinn predicted.

Cody had foreseen that. He assured him he would get there first.

Everyone in the square prepared for the attack. Ammunition, grenades and bombs were brought up, and instructions rigorously shared along the line. In front of them, the cathedral remained quiet, but a distant church bell struck most likely for the last time.

As a new battalion took up position, and men from the other companies prepared to move in to take C Company's place, Cody's four mortar teams let loose, aided by volleys of rifle grenades and Lewis guns spraying in all directions.

There was a sudden explosion from one of the rifle grenade teams twenty yards to Cody's left. It looked as though a Mills grenade had gone off prematurely. A man waved his arm to say that he was alright.

Five minutes later, whistles were blown. Over a hundred men lifted themselves from their makeshift protection and rushed across what remained of the paved ground, past the shell holes and towards the enemy. More than a few fell in the first seconds, but the enemy line turned out to be sufficiently depleted that the mopping up that followed was rapid, without bayonets having to be used. D Company moved up in order to occupy the newly overrun line and Cody shouted to his men to keep advancing. Shots were coming from buildings in front and three more men fell, but within seconds others were tossing grenades through the shattered windows.

Cody had his back to one wall and glanced upwards to the spires.

"Keep watching!" he said to Hardy who was at his side.

He then ordered his men to consolidate their positions beyond the buildings they had just invested. The square had been won. It was now critical to stop the enemy reaching the cathedral. Cody ordered Cobbold and Finlay to take up positions in order to prevent any incursion. He ordered Finlay to make sure that all the spires had indeed been cleared.

Cody and Hardy joined the men up front and spread the word for them to prepare to cross the street that formed the outer perimeter to the square. Mortar and Lewis gun units were brought up to clear the way. The buildings opposite were already hopeless skeletons, but the enemy second line defending them proved stubbornly entrenched.

Cody had to act fast before the momentum was lost. He decided on a flank attack from in front of the cathedral. Ordering Mowforth to spread out his men along with the mortar and Lewis teams, he ordered Smalby to move up with him to where Cobbold and Finlay were established.

The enemy didn't seem to have its third line anywhere nearby. Taking the risk to leave the cathedral lightly defended, together with Cobbold, Finlay and Smalby, Cody rushed the row of buildings from the side. The rubble made it dangerous going. Two men were felled by obstacles, but their colleagues kept going, repeatedly firing ahead of them and tossing their grenades in order to clear the way.

An hour later, the action had been deemed completed. Mowforth's men crossed the street and occupied the second line, and Cody turned the remainder in order to continue to move through the town. He ordered Jones to lead a team to scour all the buildings for enemy stragglers who might have been missed. Behind them, the other companies advanced once again in order to consolidate the ground that had been taken.

They reached within sight of the candle factory before the third enemy line showed itself in the dark. The shooting was so intense that Cody was left with no choice but to dig in and wait for the return of daylight. A photographer arrived from brigade to capture them taking up their positions at first light, so that the story could be relayed to the newspapers back home.

Throughout the night, the enemy contented itself with shelling up to the cathedral and square. Once it became clear that there would be no more initiatives that night, Colonel Wilkes sent a message to Cody to join him at his new headquarters next to the cathedral.

Cody found the colonel already with the other captains, including Quinn. They were debating the next move. Cody confirmed the enemy seemed to be well dug in. They should expect to incur heavy losses if they attempted a rush.

The colonel congratulated Cody for his flank attack and advance. Cody replied it had only been made possible by Quinn's action against the snipers. With so many raw recruits, it had been a miracle that C Company had managed to get so far.

"And no booby traps."

"Only the one," said Cody, referring to the flag incident earlier on.

He avoided going into detail. There was bound to be an inquiry.

"What about those accidents?"

Cody wondered how the colonel had heard of them and why he took an interest. There were much more serious challenges to address.

"That's what I meant, Colonel. We need to get my men out of here and into field training as soon as possible."

The colonel seemed annoyed by his response, but left the matter alone. He returned to the subject of the next move against the enemy.

"It has to be another flank attack," Cody warned. "Division should think of a new front to distract them."

Everyone agreed, but they did not know the breadth or depth of the enemy line. Colonel Wilkes undertook to make an approach to brigade right away.

It was getting light again. They dispersed, and Cody, Hardy, and Quinn made their way together to the new firing line.

Cody never heard the shot. Quinn fell to the ground. No sooner had Cody and Hardy bent over to attend to him than Cody felt a sharp pain in his leg. He heard the shot a fraction of a second later. He keeled over before struggling up again. When a third round caught his shoulder, he fell to the ground for good, knocking himself out in the process.

12

The medical board, which only sat twice a week, reluctantly awarded Cody a week's leave. He had already been laid up for two months.

"What's a few more days?" he said afterwards to his nurse.

She had looked after him since his arrival at the south-coast hospital, and in her last contribution to his recuperation she was busily sewing on his new wound stripe in time for Kate's arrival.

"Make good use of them, Captain," she said, smiling, as she bit off the last thread.

Despite their closeness, she had always refused to give her name. Such locking out of any deeper relationship had made seeing Kate and the girls more pressing.

Kate arrived in her brand new Stellite. Cody had eagerly waited outside for her the entire morning. As he stepped out onto the gravel to greet her, he felt overwhelmed returning to the real world.

"You're not going to be a burden on me, are you, Michael?"

It was a fine greeting. He was tempted to turn around. No-one had warned him about the extent to which he would feel so lost, bereaved of the close attention of the doctors and nurses, and the camaraderie of his fellow wounded for which even Kate could be no substitute. Her lack of interest in his situation, her wanting to get back to her own life as soon as possible, get done with the inconvenience of having to come and fetch him, for which she had been appallingly late, made it all so much worse.

The hospital had been short-staffed and encouraged family members to stay for long hours with the patients. Not once had Kate exploited the opportunity. Impatient and as inconsiderate as she had become, she only came twice during Cody's stay, and for only twenty minutes on each occasion. Yet she now had the car.

"I love the marble," she said, looking across to the flights of steps he had just descended.

She had remembered it everywhere inside as well. Cody had hated it. While struggling around on his crutches, he had constantly been afraid of injuring himself on one of the countless sharp edges.

"If only they had rounded those bloody edges!"

The Stellite sped away. It was Cody's first time. As they headed for the main road, Kate endlessly recounted her drives to London, what she had learned about car maintenance, and how easily she had mastered its handling. Then she described the fun she had had there, the plays, the visit to Karno's, the cinemas, and walking around the parks with Deborah. It was all she talked about as she hectically raced through the countryside and seemed to accelerate before every bend. There hadn't been a word left for the girls, or how they had been looked after.

"Oh, by the way," said Kate, whose long and undone hair was blowing violently around in the wind as she negotiated the last bend home, "I've signed the papers for the cottage."

By the time they finally stepped through the front door, after the two-hour journey, Cody had had more than enough. The feeling of let-down and abandon had only ballooned.

There were no children to greet them. He had even hoped they would have come to fetch him, but hadn't complained. This was becoming like one of his returns to the front, full of nasty surprises.

"Where are they?"

Kate explained, claiming that she had already told him during her last visit. She had packed them off to boarding school one-and-a-half hour's drive away.

"How could you?"

He stood there trying to think what to say next.

"Celia is only three, for heaven's sake!"

He was livid. She had lied. She should have consulted him. He no longer counted. It was as though he had become a ghost before his time.

He needed to see them right away.

"I must take them something."

"Out of the question! I gave them a hamper when I left them there."

Kate had become feral in his absence, too self-centred, so removed from her previous self. Cody thought about what the change would mean for the girls. He searched for positives. At least it would bring order to their lives. Regularity had never been one of Kate's strong points. But being sent away to school was cruel. It would make them feel distanced, cut off, unloved. It would damage them forever.

Still coming to terms with what she had done, he posed his belongings on the floor and flopped onto the settee. He asked her how often she had been to see them.

"We'll go tomorrow, Michael."

She disappeared into the kitchen to prepare a very late lunch. Cody spread his arms and tried desperately to reach out for familiar territory. Kate was humming away in the background. She had never done that before either. He felt even more disorientated.

He just sat there. He thought back to his long and complicated evacuation after being bowled over twice in the square, the small corner of France that he had saved for its denizens. There had been a succession of short journeys and fellow passengers of every kind, none of whom he had known. There had been the stretcher to the first aid post, the cart ride to the dressing station further away from town, the light railway to the clearing station, the mainline Red Cross train to the coastal base hospital where he stayed for a week, to the port, and finally the cold and windy voyage back home and one prolonged hospital stay.

Not that he had known what to expect, each of those environments had had something strangely predictable about them, something reassuring, a sense of direction. Now that he was home, everything felt different. He couldn't get his mind off how Kate, her hair for once let down, had been going on and on as she drove. He had watched her mouth move in a totally new way, for the very first time unlovable, a way which shocked and somehow revolted him. It was no longer accompanied by the reserve and ingrained domesticity that he had always known. This was no longer the demure woman he thought he had married. He feared it had been he who had set it off, her realisation that after all those years he nearly had no longer been there.

His thoughts switched to the army. Corporal Jones, now back at the front, had sent a message that the five widows were happily employed. A few days after that, from Major Hickman he had learned that Quinn had returned and been put in temporary command of C Company. Any glow of optimism had disappeared at once. What if Quinn ended up proving himself? When he had passed by at the hospital, the major had thought of nothing better to tell Cody than that he and Quinn had been shot by an enemy sniper who had held out in one spire.

"Why didn't you have it cleared?"

It had not been the occasion to put up a defence. What good would it have done?

"And what about all those accidents?"

Festering in bed after the major's visit, Cody had soon doubted that he would retain his command. The visit had surely had a purpose: to initiate a process. It had occurred during the early days. During the weeks that had followed, for want of any other explanation, Cody had suspected the hand of Quinn.

And now all this.

Kate had magnanimously proposed that they drive to the school first thing. It wouldn't be one of her usual late starts.

"Thank you!"

"And then to London. Deborah will have us."

Cody opened up his gramophone, that had been well appreciated at the hospital. He went upstairs to fetch a different case of discs.

"Oh, by the way," called out Kate from the kitchen, "she has promised us an Elgar concert."

When he came down again, Cody noticed two gold candlesticks on the mantelpiece. He went up to examine them. They were heavy for their size.

Kate walked in.

"Do you like them?"

They seemed an excellent find. He asked her where she had discovered them.

"London."

They didn't go to bed early. Instead, Cody got out an old bottle of whisky and played his discs repeatedly, while Kate, unfazed by the lack of her husband's attention, returned to a watercolour she was working on next door.

As he sipped away, Cody quietly summed up what he had come back to. His beloved girls had gone. With her newfound riches, Kate seemed to have launched herself into a new life, one of profligacy, one that had drifted away. At the front, Colonel Wilkes, Quinn, and Major Hickman it would seem, were conspiring against him, perhaps all the others too.

He thought of the anonymous nurse and his wounded neighbours. Worse times always followed good ones. He was now paying the price.

He got out Jones' letter that he had kept in his top pocket. The one place he might be welcomed, the widows' new home near the Quinn estate, was out of bounds. He cast the letter aside.

He had nothing left but to finish the whisky and play the rest of his discs. His motivation to do anything useful was rapidly seeping away. In the next room, Kate got frustrated with whatever she had been working on and quietly took the back stairs to go to bed without saying a word. Cody tried once more to reconcile the world he had returned to. He was tempted to see if she was painting out of character again. Nothing fit at all.

He stayed put. There was no point in making things worse. He thought of the pleasure of the revolving garden shed that he would one day afford. It had become a recurring daydream, being able to point it in the most benign direction possible, shut out the side winds.

Perhaps he was getting too old.

*

Things were a little better when they drove into town to pick up enough petrol cans for the journey. Despite the freezing cold, they had consensually lowered the roof in order to enjoy the fresh air, and Kate had kept her hair bunched up.

Besides the picnic basket, Kate had pre-loaded the boot with extra hats, gloves, and scarves so that they could do the same with the girls, and some local cheese to leave with them.

"Did you *have* to wear your uniform, Michael?" she asked as they set off again.

She could have said that earlier. It was only a small *contretemps*. She had just much more bitterly complained about the cost of the petrol. It had been a positive sign of financial sobriety.

"Why?"

"Oh, nothing, darling," she said. "Just makes me feel estranged."

He didn't understand, but said nothing. Perhaps she might have preferred a higher rank for turning up at the school. He wondered what to expect. The uniform, whichever it was, gave him identity and respectability. If they were going to go out in London afterwards, it seemed important. If nothing else, it would ward off any threat of white feathers. There had still been plenty of stories doing the rounds at the front.

"You look military even without it."

As they sped along the last stretch of the metalled coastal road, Cody warmed up to seeing the girls. He wondered if they had settled in. Was the headmistress a tyrant? Was the food up to what they had been accustomed to? Were they being treated fairly by their classmates? How had they taken to doing everything at a preordained time?

At least they had each other. He recalled arriving at his first day-school at five years old. It had been savage. Many of the children were screaming. One boy was running around trying to escape, chased by his parents. Within a couple of weeks, he and other boys had found what looked like a disassembled cage behind a shed. They had conspired to set it up to lock up their teacher. Unity of purpose had brought them together. Now he couldn't believe such thoughts started so early.

"Girls would never do that!" said Kate.

She was handling the car well for once, and there was no traffic to speak of. She talked of films she had seen in London, of the horrors of the newsreels from France that she had looked away from, of a distant cousin who had been killed in the Middle East. But her all too brief talk of the war only proved how little it really meant to her. In her mind, the arrival of the Americans would soon put an end to it all, and that was pretty well it. She had no notion of the cost in lives.

"You'll come home soon, darling," she said. "With my money you'll be able to choose what to do."

Cody had been thinking about staying on. The army would provide him with freedom from home, postings abroad. He had also toyed about taking up a civilian job in India. That he could never come to terms with was the idea of employment in England, even if there were to be any for the millions of servicemen suddenly become available. Kate's new comportment had only consolidated his determination.

He thought, though, about what Kate had just said. He remembered Barker and all his talk about printing. Could he ever muster the interest to set up shop to print Kate's works? Would that help to seal their future together, stop him wanting to flee, bring him, and her, back to a family fold? Perhaps he could set up in his future shed.

Kate started going on about London again. He wondered why on earth she had purchased the cottage.

The school turned out to be an unfriendly gothic building that stood on its own on a barren hill outside town. After the initial shock, it looked quite modest. They parked on the large, paved area in front, next to two ponies and traps and a run-down motorbike. There seemed to be grounds at the back. The coast behind them looked like a twenty-minute cross-country walk away. Looking upwards at the school, Cody noticed that all the windows were cracked open, somewhat harsh for such a chilly day. It wasn't the same as doing it at home. Even though he had always criticised the French for never doing so, he feared they would be greeted by coughs and sneezes.

"Don't be ridiculous, Michael."

No sooner had they entered the outsized hallway than all three girls came rushing down the wooden stairs. At first impression, they appeared to be happy. Once their torrent of stories about sports, adventures in the large estate attached to the school, and their new friends had waned, they let on about how much they missed home.

The musty surroundings were off-putting and reminded too much of old times. They started walking together towards the coast.

"Miss Sherriff makes us think of you," Elizabeth said to Kate.

"I'm like her?"

"No," said Elizabeth. "She never smiles."

Kate glanced at Cody. They both knew that Elizabeth was covering up a host of experiences that all three of them would remember forever but never talk of.

"You'll see," said Cody, straining himself to reassure. "When you come home, you will see us differently. It's part of growing up. You will discover how important home is. You will never take it for granted again."

Then he thought for a while about his own view of home.

"You may not know it now," said Kate as they turned around, without having descended the cliffs, to head back to the car, "but you will end up thanking Miss Sherriff."

They drove out onto the Downs to find a place where Cody could haul out his gramophone while they ate. Kate had made watercress and cucumber sandwiches, the girls' favourite apart from cheese. They were alone and together. It was turning out to be a special occasion. For the first time since hospital, Cody felt happy.

"Why do you always have that with you?" asked Mary.

He felt caught out. To an outsider it would almost seem an obsession. He found the answer just in time.

"It reminds me of home and you three," he said, smiling. "You should look for something like that in *your* life, Mary."

The girls excitedly talked about Christmas when they had returned home for a short while. They had all gone for a walk and finally spotted the white deer sitting on its own in a tiny clearing.

"What happened to the others?" Cody asked.

"Nowhere to be seen," confirmed Kate.

"I hope nothing has happened to them," Elizabeth said.

Cody wasn't sure if they could be hunted or put down as pests but said nothing. He was certain they wouldn't have lasted long in France, a land of inveterate hunters, especially in present times.

"Well, girls, I have to return to my own hunting," he said.

They knew enough to understand what he meant. The idle thought occurred to him he had his own white deer to contend with. His name was Quinn.

Their departure was tearful. Cody found it dreadful, but Kate, having been through the same when she was as young, took it in her stride.

"I got used to it," she said as they drove off. "But that first visit from my parents was the most difficult. I cried for weeks and got bullied for it."

It was a rare admission on her behalf, but it meant nothing to Cody. His family had always kept him and his siblings at home, if for no other reason than the lack of means. He only hoped that Kate was right when she spoke about the independence and self-responsibility it would instil in the girls. He feared it would go too far and end up making them impossible to marry off.

Saying goodbye to the girls had made Cody think about his departures from home to return to the front, and the most recent trauma of leaving hospital. Kate had to be right, it was an important experience, but that didn't make it pleasant.

Perhaps he should listen to Kate. Building up a professional life centred on home wouldn't be such a bad idea after all.

*

Deborah Harrington was delighted to see them, and not at all put out because Kate had omitted to warn her. They had even walked through the front door unannounced and surprised Deborah sitting there reading a newspaper. Her first action was to telephone to book tickets for a concert.

"That's what best friends are for!"

She took both by the hand and, after hearing about the girls, talked a little about when she and Kate had been to school together.

"Wonderful memories, darling."

Later on, she turned out to be far more interested than Kate in Cody's war experiences. Every minor detail intrigued her. The challenges her husband was facing maintaining the peace in India were small change by comparison.

Kate had read the newspaper while it had all gone on.

"As long as it doesn't snow, we'll go for a ride tomorrow," Deborah said. "We'll cycle around Wimbledon."

Then she remembered Cody's injury.

"I hope you're up to it, Michael."

He replied that he was. He had even used an exercise bicycle during the last weeks in hospital.

"I'll lend you Bucephalus," she said.

Cody tried to imagine what he was in for.

"David swears by him, but his chain keeps coming off."

For an early dinner, she took them to a small restaurant a mile away where they ate little better than rations, and then they drove into town. Kate told her about her husband's gramophone, that he had purchased after the last time. He had kept it with him at the front. Deborah was proud and delighted that she had been responsible.

"Cost just under three pounds," Cody boasted, avoiding saying how much he had paid for all the recordings.

"I'm trying to imagine you out there," Deborah said laughing, "playing that thing away and thinking of me while getting killed by men with spikes on their heads!"

"Surely it's dangerous?" asked Kate.

Cody insisted he had never been shot at while playing it. No doubt it was because the enemy was well known to like music.

The concert ended up being a lot more appreciable confined to the acoustics of an enclosed hall. They had seats behind the orchestra, facing the conductor who was quite distracting with his extraordinary energy and frantic movements. Kate and Deborah sat next to each other and insisted once too often on whispering to each other during the music, but such was Cody's regard for his wife's best friend that it didn't put him off. The music carried him back to the front, remembering those rare but satisfying occasions when everything came together, when he successfully conducted his company, one to two hundred men doing as they were supposed to in the face of the enemy.

Before long, his daydream abruptly ended. The antics of the conductor before him seemed more like those of the colonel, and more often than not, on the unpredictable front, the result was out of tune.

They drove straight back and decided on a final nightcap before turning in. The weather didn't look as though it would turn, so Deborah went into the hall to call some friends for the ride in the morning.

"It's something we should think of," whispered Kate once she was gone.

"Bicycles?"

"The telephone."

Cody caught himself instinctively frowning. This was ridiculous. Telephones were expensive, difficult to get, and not for pleasure.

The following morning, Cody was the first awake. He crept downstairs and picked up the newspaper lying on the sitting room floor. Before long, Deborah appeared fully dressed. She was surprised to find Cody sitting there.

"I swore I heard you sleeping."

Cody didn't understand why she had said that. Then he remembered a quip she had once made about how only the guilty made noises at night. He had retorted that it was nothing of the sort, but an appeal for attention instead.

"Michael, darling!" Deborah said. "You must buy a telephone so that I can speak more often with my best friend."

Cody frowned. This sounded like a conspiracy.

"Do you know how difficult that is?"

He also had reservations about the invasion it would represent, let alone the misuse of a utility. Besides, all the neighbours would call in to use it, and everything was guaranteed to be urgent. He dreaded the thought.

"We'll see," he said as he headed upstairs to get dressed and wake up Kate.

Just after breakfast, four of Deborah's friends arrived in identical Panama hats, and they set out together. Cody had none of the expected problems with Bucephalus and, with its classic tall frame inlaid with gold markings, it looked quite superior to the others.

As they rode towards the common, Kate pushed ahead, and Deborah slowed down to ride at the back. She wanted to ask Cody a little more about his injury. Cody described the retaking of the square and his failure to make sure the church spires had been cleared. Deborah was enthralled. By the time he had finished, it came to him he had said none of this to Kate.

"Last night you told me you had ordered someone to do it," Deborah said.

"It's part of the perils of having command," he said. "Any normal person ends up needing to do everything himself."

"But you didn't."

"That's what they teach us, to trust others. All too often, it's wishful thinking."

He talked about Quinn. She was shocked.

"It must be awful to put up with people like that. David has similar stories. I don't know how you men cope with it."

It preyed on Cody's mind that when he had mentioned Quinn's name Deborah had reacted as if it meant something. Just in case he had made a *faux pas* he changed the subject. He invited her to tell more about her husband in India.

A little later, still riding next to each other, Cody described his two months in hospital and what some of the other patients were in for. He related some of the funny stories they had to tell. It was the only time he had ever been confined more than a few days.

"The experience was unique. The environment was very special indeed."

Deborah talked of a friend who had gone over to France as a Red Cross nurse. She had come back with the same stories; despite all the suffering she had witnessed.

"This will change us," predicted Cody. "We will have become *blasé* over matters so grave. The question is what will happen to those who follow."

"Those?"

"Generations."

He asked Deborah about her friends. They were still up ahead with Kate, and getting along well, and Kate had pinched one of their hats. The two men among them seemed ripe for service.

"They're both doctors," she said. "I should have introduced you all better. I was so keen to set off. They talk like you about all the contrasts. One of them has spent time in France, over a year, I think."

118

They had lunch in a pub before riding back. One friend had selected it for its beer, but the thatched roof and low ceilings also made the place exceptionally welcoming. Kate was well away with all the company, very much playing the lead and being interesting. Cody said little, and every now and again noticed that Deborah was glancing at him. There were no barriers between them. He felt comfortable with his wife's best friend.

They returned home and had tea. Shortly after the others had left, with all the promises of repeating the fun occasion, Cody announced it was time to head back. Deborah and Kate hugged each other while Cody loaded up the car. Kate climbed in and started it up.

"Oh, I've got something to show you," Deborah said, grabbing Cody's arm.

She had always been very tactile. Cody continued to find it strange, and he never forgot it.

She led Cody back into the house.

"Take care of her, Michael, darling," she said as soon as they were out of sight.

It had been a ruse. But the way to every doorway Deborah encountered had always been an excuse to say something, finish a conversation, or start a new one. Without understanding why, Cody had always liked her for it.

This time, she looked concerned.

"That money won't do her any good at all," she warned. "I know her. Please be careful."

Cody looked perplexed. How on earth could he do anything being away all the time? She fingered his lapel almost playfully. He felt uncomfortable.

"Take care of that man Quinn, for a start," she said.

His mind froze. His face went cold. Quinn? A warning? And she didn't know him.

Or did she?

"*Captain* Quinn?" Deborah corrected herself. "The tall, blond-haired *Captain* Quinn."

Cody's jaw had already dropped. He desperately wanted to ask more.

"Just be careful, darling. Keep her in line."

The journey home passed in total silence. Cody remained dumbstruck by what Deborah had given away. He felt humiliated and betrayed. An uncontrollable storm had overtaken his mind. Quinn had somehow needled his way into Kate's life, perhaps into Deborah's as well. How on earth could it have happened? Had he come to the cottage, or had it been in London?

A telegram was waiting for him when they arrived. It ordered him to report to an officers' training course on the French coast right away.

"I want to see the girls again before I leave," he said, almost for want of finding something to say, to release himself from the imprisonment of his latest thoughts.

"We'll go to the school first thing," proposed Kate, almost as if she wanted done with it. "I'll leave you at the port on the way back."

As they approached the school, Kate announced she was in a mind to return to London straight afterwards. Cody had suspected it. She had loaded some cheese in the boot again.

They spent several hours with the girls, this time treating them to a restaurant in the nearby village where they ate surprisingly heartily. None of the girls had ever been a great eater.

"Are they feeding you enough?" Cody asked.

They just kept eating.

Any overnight snow had gone. The restaurant had a large garden that ran down to the river from where it was possible to join a country path running through a delightful meadow. Kate strode ahead with Mary and Celia, while Cody followed with Elizabeth.

He wanted to get to the heart of whatever she might be thinking. He was still worried that she might hide bad things about the school.

"I'm afraid next time you won't come back at all," she said. "I'm afraid we won't ever see you again, daddy."

Cody was alarmed. She had said nothing like it before. It must have come from classmates.

"Of course, I'll come back, Elizabeth. Most fathers come back."

She skipped once or twice and then tugged on a reed leaning across the path.

"Well, what about mummy's new friend?" she asked.

"New friend, Elizabeth?"

"The tall man with blond hair. Do you know who I mean?"

"No, Elizabeth."

"*He* brought us presents."

Saying nothing, Cody knelt down and hugged his daughter while the others continued on unawares. He was furious that Kate had refused that they bring presents. Suddenly, he looked forward more than ever to returning to the front, despite what might wait for him.

They didn't go inside when they returned to the school. But this time Cody spotted Kate slipping Elizabeth the package of cheese. She must have done the same before.

As the port neared, Cody imagined his three lonely girls waking up at night to feast of Kate's cheese. Kate had cleverly made their life of exclusion more bearable, no doubt uniting them in their sorrow. He wondered about the other girls in the dormitory. Would they be forced to share the cheese? Or would they deliberately use it in order to buy friends?

What on earth were they doing to their girls?

*

As he lined up to report to the landing officer, Cody's thoughts returned to Quinn. With Elizabeth's comment consolidating what Deborah had said, there was now no turning back. He had to confront the man who, in more ways than one, would do him harm.

13

Cody had expected to be processed by an army of attendants before being allowed to install himself. He looked down the long and sad wainscoted dormitory badly in need of a coat of paint. Halfway along the left-hand side was an amateur portrait of a woman who resembled the Empress Josephine. All twenty beds had identical folders propped against the pillows, fronted by a small card in French announcing that the bed maker's name was Marie. Cody picked one at the far right-hand side, closest to the large window, and scanned the deserted seashore outside.

Behind the long beach that disappeared into the horizon, each side there were shallow dunes, only fifteen feet high, backed by a wasteland of gorse that went back as far as he could see from his position, a few more benign bushes and timid trees nearer the chateau. It was all quite grand. He wondered to whom the chateau belonged, and how much its owners were being recompensed.

He unpacked his belongings and filled the small wooden cabinet by the side of the bed, stored his suitcase and gramophone under the bed, and then lay down to browse his folder. The first sheet gave the schedule of lectures and the names of the mostly senior officers who would present them. He looked down the list of names of those who would attend, and the regiments they came from, but recognised no-one. A second page was dedicated to dining arrangements. Attendees were asked to be punctual, as the two concurrent courses that week would take it in turns for their meals. It seemed like a missed opportunity.

The last sheet had just three typewritten lines advising visitors to carry their side arms whenever outside the building, and preferably to remain accompanied. The password of the day, it announced, was to be found posted downstairs in the foyer.

He picked up the card signed by Marie. Beside her name, there was a sketch of a woman in traditional costume. He embraced it. At least he wouldn't have to make his own bed.

The chateau had been a three-hour train ride from the port, during which Cody had buried himself in a Conan Doyle purchased just before boarding the ferry. The train had seemed like a village on the move, the journey littered with stops at tiny, isolated stations. Passengers had come and gone, focusing on themselves, never reaching out to make conversation. At one point, a frail woman and two young boys had boarded and sat opposite him and consumed slowly the lunch they had carried with them, saying nothing, endlessly peering at the passing scenery.

Waiting at the isolated station had been a charabanc assigned to the final fifteen-minute journey. But Cody had been the only passenger to alight. It had still been early.

"You seem to be the only one, Captain," the uniformed driver had concluded.

At last, an English voice. Cody had asked him how many he expected in all.

"About forty, sir. Two courses this time. Yours and a commanders' training course."

The details had been scant. The telegram had merely stated that Cody's week-long course concerned intelligence techniques and an update on enemy capabilities.

They had overtaken a family of *campagnards*, all dressed in black, walking along the side of the road. Cody had asked the driver if he had the latest news from the front.

"Poor weather in most places, sir," the driver had said. "It's given us three weeks of calm. The French and Canadians haven't been so fortunate."

Cody had noticed the 'us'. This was his first training course in France. He had expected that it would be conducted in splendid isolation.

"We get almost daily visits from the front," the driver had assured him. "They always talk about it."

They had soon got there. Cody had decided that he would rather have walked it in order to have enjoyed the countryside that he had forsaken earlier on.

After an inspection of his papers at the front gate, they had driven along a long, wooded driveway until the chateau had come into view. It was a grey building with plenty of windows with frames and shutters painted in light green. From behind, it had an unobstructed view directly out to sea. It was surrounded by large lawns and a kitchen garden, and further out on the right-hand side were tents dedicated to outdoor activities. Nearby, there was a large open field with several earth banks.

"For demonstrations and testing new equipment, Captain," the driver had explained.

Apart from the sentries at the gate, there had not been another soul around, outside or in. Entering by a large double front door, the driver had escorted Cody up two flights of stone steps to the empty dormitory close to the landing on the second floor.

"Remember to sign in at the desk, Captain," the driver had warned before taking his leave. "There'll be someone there in an hour."

There was time to scout the grounds with no obvious threat of precipitation. Cody descended the two flights into the large empty hallway that stank of boiled vegetables. Before going outside, he took a quick look at the notice boards. He scanned the list of regiments for the commanders' course. One instantly caught his eye. He checked the corresponding name.

His heart sank. His mood had been disrupted. Quinn's name was there. Suddenly, the week ahead had a different outlook. This was Colonel Wilkes' disruptive thinking. He imagined the worst. Change was in the air.

He looked away. He was furious at the colonel. Quinn was a newcomer, callow, an opportunist. He, Cody, had had his position for over two years already. He had successfully commanded his company through countless actions. He was respected by his men and colleagues. To add insult to injury, he had been the one officer in the entire battalion to have held out a hand to his replacement. The detestable Quinn was soiling his existence, bent on coveting his entire life.

He suspected Quinn had engineered the affair during his absence, another of those nasty surprises one always got when returning to the front. He had to escape, get outside, walk in order to subdue the maelstrom invading his mind, walk until he finally calmed down.

He climbed down the well-trodden path that led to the steep dunes and reached the beach below half running. At least he felt fit. A westerly wind was whipping up dry sand from the upper part of the large stretch in front of the retracted waterline. He could smell seaweed. He looked up at the chateau and noticed a line of cooks and servants leaning against a back wall looking out to sea and watching him at the same time. They waved, and he raised his hand in acknowledgement.

Forcing his way along the shoreline, he raised the lapels of his coat and tightened down his cap, skilfully bypassing driftwood and flotsam that looked as though had been there for years.

He wondered what would happen if he kept walking, off the estate, along the coast as far as possible. The place was wild and empty. From the beach, he could still not see the line of trees that he knew stood further back. The presence of the rough sea to his right was overwhelming.

He looked in vain for signs of a boundary. In his mind, he reached for freedom. He could happily disappear along this beach, claim that he had lost his senses. Everywhere was deserted. This had to be why he was expected to carry his sidearm.

He cursed Quinn. Life with Kate had looked perilous. Would he discover it had ended altogether next time? Would she write to him, her first and last letter to the front? Would he be compelled to find accommodation at an officer's club on his next return? Would he ever see the girls again? Kate could now afford a solicitor, he couldn't. What on earth had he done wrong for the world to fall in on him in such a way?

For a few dark minutes, he entertained returning to the front to end it all. He thought of the aftermath. He would die a hero, his body, or whatever was left of it, transported back to the village cemetery, his name inscribed on a memorial at the village crossroads, haunting Kate each time she passed.

He had to be wrong. Kate would quit for London. He would be interred where he had fallen.

He needed to be certain. He should wire the colonel. He should consult the padre. He should stand his ground and confront Quinn the interloper. Or would Quinn play games, pretend innocence, even somehow turn the tables? The man who had so rapidly sparked the dislike of his colleagues, who seemed to have even alienated his own brother-in-law, could yet turn out to be deviously resourceful.

Was he rushing headlong into paranoia? Had even the ever-reliable Deborah misread Quinn's intentions or been speaking figuratively? Had Elizabeth referred to someone else, an old friend of her mother's? And what if Cody had misread the colonel's intentions?

After two hours of pushing himself to his physical limit, enough to fracture once and for all the infernal circle of negative thoughts, Cody finally calmed down and became more objective. It had become dark. There hadn't been wire or sentries along the shore. What kind of place was this, so open to chance?

He thought about becoming an intelligence officer. He would regret the loss of command, all he enjoyed about coming to his men's support, sorting out their personal problems, anticipating ways to improve their performance, having the ability to decide their actions, and the permanently exciting challenge of living up to their expectations. He would instead enjoy wider contacts, even outside the brigade. It would lift the claustrophobia and destructive insomnia of the trenches. It would put him further away from danger, give him a greater chance of surviving an increasingly deadly war. He had long-lost count of the colleagues who had already disappeared for good. Perhaps Quinn had served him a favour after all.

Perhaps Quinn might pay the price himself.

The beach continued on for ever. The tide had started to return. He was approaching headland that jutted out to sea and would soon have to take a path higher up.

He turned around and headed back. His mind had become more positive. Why jeopardise his future? He wouldn't take the turn of events as humiliation. He wouldn't hold it against the colonel or Quinn. Why waste energy?

The lights of the chateau neared. His stride had become more determined, his shoulders straighter. His lungs felt in good shape. His career move was a blessing in disguise. Quinn didn't need to be his adversary. If something had indeed happened with Kate, well, sorting out the business would be conducted honourably, the best man allowed the takings. He would hold no grievances. If he had failed to address the rift between himself and his young wife, then he had brought it upon himself. He would look for someone better. Matters were bound to become more awkward now that she had her fortune. Quinn was better attuned to money than he. He had to maintain rights to see the girls.

He thought of Quinn in command of C Company. It would soon wear him down in turn. Whenever he returned to Kate, she would face yet another worn-out soldier, a far more complicated and troubled character than he. She wouldn't stand him for long. She might even be lured back into the arms of an older intelligence officer...

Cody allowed himself a chuckle.

By the time he reached the chateau, his mind had reverted. There was no way he would allow Quinn to get away with anything. He would pursue him, get into his mind, destroy him if needed. How careless of him for not spotting the predator from the start. How ashamed he felt having talked about his personal life to such a dangerous usurper. How naïve he had been.

There was at last someone at the front desk. Cody went over to announce himself. The elderly sergeant made no apology for not having been there earlier.

Upstairs in the dormitory, there were five new arrivals. It turned out that all had arrived on the same ferry as Cody but taken a later train. They introduced themselves, and Cody recommended the fine walk he had just taken along the shoreline.

"I had assumed you people would come from the front," Cody remarked as they each casually lay on their beds, their hands behind their heads as they engaged in conversation.

It turned out that they had all been newly conscripted. They were all very young, half his age. He was the only captain among them, one of a disappearing race of volunteers. They should have stood up, but he was glad they hadn't.

"You'll count the days," he warned them when they asked what to expect at the front. "You'll forget nothing at all, even if you thought you had."

He recounted his time in the trenches, the great camaraderie and respect, the constant fear, seeing friends and acquaintances getting killed by the dozens every month, the dreadful food, the infestations, the nightmares that were actually welcome because they meant one had finally fallen asleep, the endless marches to new positions, the pleasure of being relieved, but the danger of getting back behind the lines, the deafening and terrifying explosions, and the dreaded sight of the effects of silent gas clouds.

"And you'll never talk about it all when you get home," he ended. "They would never understand."

A batch of six more interrupted them. Their appearance instantly gave away where they had come from. Most had recently been promoted and were expecting the prospect of a welcome escape, albeit short. As each of them introduced himself, but related nothing at all about the front, Cody realised he was still the only man present who had ever had command of a company. No-one challenged him over it, believing that behind his convocation lay a story best not told.

While he listened to the others speak, Cody reminded himself that no-one had yet confirmed his reassignment. It had been entirely his assumption. He could still be wrong, just a combat officer widening his knowledge, still a commander.

The sound of a gong interrupted their conversation.

"Our turn," Cody announced after checking his watch.

Each of them straightened up their uniforms as they descended. The hall had at last become animated, the smell of cabbage at its zenith. In the dining room, they distributed themselves on benches and then rose when a major appeared and took the head table with a staff of three.

"Welcome, gentlemen," he said. "My name is Carter."

Major Carter, tall and middle-aged and with a very pale face, talked about his past. He had worked in intelligence back in London, in Egypt before that, and on the Western Front for two years at battalion and divisional levels. He assured them they would benefit from the course that he had personally prepared. During the week ahead, speakers would include intelligence officers from the front to explain their different experiences with the enemy and how to deal with them.

"As it happens," Carter said, "the other course this week includes instruction on new armaments, both our own and the enemy's, and so I thought it would interest you to spend half a day there as well."

It was in that positive atmosphere that they collectively sat down, and orderlies ferried in the food. Cody was bemused by the whole proceedings, so remote from what they would soon return to. He glanced towards Carter as he conversed with the officers sitting next to him. He wondered whether he was a man who had regretted his re-assignment.

"Eat up, Cody, sir!" the corporal in front of him said.

He held out his hand.

"Carpenter."

Carpenter was as young as the rest of them. He said that he was posted further north, but he had heard about the recapture of the town. After he noticed Cody's wound stripes, Cody told him about his getting shot. Carpenter then lifted his wrist to show off his own. For the last one, he had received a bayonet wound in the thigh.

"Caught by surprise," he said. "It pushed me into intelligence."

They ended up at the mess. It had English beer on draught and quite a lot of French wine.

"We'll start with the beer," proposed Carpenter.

The others were doing the same. The mutually agreed plan was to graduate to wine over the week. A sign on the counter rationed it to one bottle per person.

"A bit mean!" said Cody to the orderly who had also been the chauffeur who had fetched him.

"You wouldn't believe how bad it used to get here, Captain," he said.

"And who's Marie?" Carpenter asked.

"My wife."

"You live here?"

"Thought we'd escaped!" the orderly said regretfully. "Five years ago."

They went back to find a table.

"Tell me about your first wound, Carpenter," Cody asked.

"Gas, that one, Captain. Yellow Cross. Nasty. We all filed out of the trench, guiding each other by the shoulder. No-one washed us down. We were like a line of processionary caterpillars! Untouchables!"

Cody was confused. Carpenter explained he had first served in the Aegean.

"Those bloody pine trees!"

*

There was still no sign of Quinn, and Cody avoided going looking for him. The first day started at eight, after a copious English breakfast with a peculiar French taste. The first lecture concerned the collation and distribution of all forms of intelligence so that it got to each battalion in the field. There was brief talk on mapmaking and the arrival of new field units to supplement the principal work carried out in Southampton. They examined specimens of enemy maps in order to compare nomenclature and pick up on some of their better points and deficiencies. Cody felt he already had gained a good excuse to visit Lieutenant Barker.

The second and last talk of the morning concerned communication practices, cypher, and the latest trends in both. Despite the advances, it turned out that nearly all divisions were still employing the well-worn techniques of runners and pigeons. As for telephones, Cody told the class about how his battalion had been able to more rapidly bring down howitzers on already-located enemy trench mortars by having identified each of them with a single name instead of having to read out coordinates.

They kept together all day and saw little of anyone else. Each time they crossed the cabbage-smelling hall to the dining room, or took a smoking break outside, Cody kept a corner of his eye out for a tall man with blond hair. Quinn was mercifully nowhere to be seen.

The bonus session on new armaments was particularly interesting. They watched a demonstration of a captured *flammenwerfer* and another on firing tracer bullets.

"Could have done with those," Carpenter said.

He explained that when he had been wounded, the enemy had arrived with *flammenwerfers* to clear the trench. Had he and his colleagues been able to see where their rounds went, so many of them would have survived.

They were shown photographs of enemy pillboxes for housing machine gun crews, as well as an array of impressive strongpoints that had been overtaken. Major Carter, who was holding the session himself, reported that the enemy was increasingly resorting to delayed action mines whenever they abandoned a position. Sometimes they went off days later. It reminded Cody how lucky his battalion had so far been.

The subject that held Cody's greatest attention was more down to earth. It concerned ball ammunition. Although most of the talk was about muzzle velocity and penetration, Cody was particularly impressed by the reports of improvements in reliability. The rounds left far fewer traces, thus rendering equipment more reliable, promising a reduction in the number of jams his men experienced in the heat of battle. In the syndicate of four or five participants that rounded off the session, he made a point about how people too readily forsook the more relevant basics for highfalutin ideas.

"Whatever you say, Captain," one other sarcastically said.

Cody was in danger of being perceived a bore. Even though Carpenter came to his defence, it marked a turning point. Cody could see that most of the men around him were of a different way of thinking.

During the informal conversation that followed, they talked about heavier equipment. Major Carter told them about how one of the new Handley Page bombing machines had been forced to land in his lines and had stunned them with its size. The crew hadn't realised they were in friendly territory and had been about to set it alight. It was only because of the bayonets so rapidly closing in on them they had desisted. Cody admitted that he still hadn't got over his first sight of tanks, monsters among much smaller men. He added he had seen the bombers from afar and imagined how the major must have been equally impressed at close range.

Despite their reservations, Cody's fellow attendees let him speak. He talked about the gas clouds.

"Whether you like it," he told them, "the awe brought about by the physical presence of huge equipment is occulted by the near-invisible."

Major Carter agreed. He described a frightening incident where his entire trench had succumbed. The enemy could have walked in at that moment.

"The invisible is the worst," he said.

His comment made Cody think about Quinn. Where the hell was he?

14

It was the third day of training. Cody felt himself more than ever to be an outsider, distanced from his fellow attendees by what he had already lived, Carpenter included. Much as they were a lively and pleasant bunch, there was nothing in common. They came from a different generation, poorly adapted to reality, bombastic, too hopeful and inexperienced, unprepared to appreciate what he, ascetic and the *de facto* father of the class, had to say. Listening to their cackle made him feel claustrophobic. They were always there. Even in the trenches, one could be alone, see the sky, think in solitude.

At least he had tried.

They were at dinner, making the usual noise. Cody had to escape, restore his *amour propre*. His mind bursting from the cacophony of their schoolboy conversation, he made a *fuite à l'anglaise*. Intending to walk along the beach, he followed the same route he had taken on the first day.

It was pitch black. The steep and sandy path winding down to the water's edge was easy enough to locate and keep to. The wind was blustering, but this time headed away from land, from the direction of the front in fact.

He felt relieved. It was a pleasure to at last be alone. He thought of Kate. How he wanted her to be walking beside him, supporting him, bonding together even though she was as young as those he was fleeing, the shadows in their relationship become invisible in the dark.

He was grasping at straws. It was already too late for Kate.

Once he reached the beach, the gusty wind sweeping down the dunes freshened his face. It provided relief. The noise in his head subsided. He felt restored. He could hear the tide close by, much closer than before, pushing against the wind.

He followed the water's edge at a safe distance, strolling instead of striding in order to wipe his mind clean through calm. He reflected upon his upcoming return to the battalion. What would he discover there?

He thought back to the last lecture of the day, on cyphers, from a colonel whose name he had forgotten. He had been well chosen for the task. The only annoyance had been that he had kept asking "Do you understand?" as if that solved the problem. The colonel had lost an arm at the front, and it had evidently knocked him out of what he had so enjoyed, but he seemed to be holding his own, given the opportunity to explain what had been his passion for so long. There was hope for Cody yet.

He found himself confined to the rear of the beach to avoid the spray that curiously braved the wind. The ground started to become uneven. He brushed an obstacle, which he assumed to be a piece of flotsam. He decided to risk closer to the water.

Every now and again, long stretches of wet sand were littered with pebbles and gravel. How much the girls would have loved to have been there, on a strange and foreign shore, picking up trophies, uncovering new mysteries.

There was a sudden dip in the wind, lasting only a few seconds. He had been lured even closer to the water. The obstacles had gone, but his socks and face had become wet. The waves threatened more than ever. They helped to stir up new thoughts.

He tried to discern a little more about his immediate predicament, what differentiated him from his junior colleagues. Their carefree view of life and death seemed only to highlight his abstemiousness. Their minds seemed unladen. People who had so little took risks. More often than not, those would spell disaster, destroy progress, make men unequal through selective terrible experience, and in the end undermine stability. Only men like he held the truth, held the army together.

He thought back to when he had first come out to France. How unstable and ignorant he too had been in his ideas, too keen to prove himself. His face flushed when he remembered some of his stupidities.

He had to purge his thoughts. He stopped and turned towards the ocean and let out a scream. He resumed his walk. A gust of wind and spray returned his complexion to normal.

That morning, they had played out scenarios, but it had not gone down well. It had been the one time that he and Major Carter had communicated so closely, an all too brief, frustrated glance in each other's direction. Cody had had an inspiration. He laid out the scenario of Quinn's position, left on his own, envious to secure his place, and become suspicious of the enemy's withdrawal. Every single one of them had taken the bait and prescribed what Quinn had done.

"Now I will tell you what happened," Cody had said.

Major Carter had already lit up, his instinct telling him that Cody had come to his rescue. Blow by blow, Cody spelt out what had occurred after Quinn and his men had stepped out into no-man's-land. His audience had felt uncomfortable. He had described the aftermath, the murderous shelling and destruction, and the discovery that Quinn had been right after all.

By the end, Carter had been beaming. Cody had thrown at them the moral question of whether Quinn had been justified. A chaotic discussion had ensued. Cody had won. During his moment of hubris, he had wanted to announce that the culprit was there among them, following the second course, pretending to be a commander.

There was another gust of wind. Cody was revelling in the thought of Quinn being convoked to explain himself when he was abruptly halted.

He had heard a noise.

He stopped dead. He swore it came from behind. It sounded like one of the brief stumbles he had just made himself. He turned around and waited for a shout or flash of light. Perhaps there were sentries out. He frantically searched his mind for the password.

"Anyone there?"

He regretted his earlier scream.

The only sound was the crashing of the waves. He waited for a couple of minutes before deciding that it had been an illusion. He resumed walking. The wind returned in force, once again streaming down from the uninterrupted wasteland behind the dunes. The beach never seemed to end.

Twenty minutes later, he wondered if he had even reached Normandy, whether, if challenged, he would find himself unable to recall the password that seemed to recede to the back in his mind the further he got away. Perhaps another password was in force there.

He again had the impression that someone was behind him. He stopped a second time.

"Who's there?"

He scanned across the water to see if he could make out the shadow of a boat. It was far too dark. There were no traces of luminescence. He looked inland, increasingly higher up. The jutting headland had to be close by. He had lost his eyes altogether. His imagination took hold, just like at the front. He unbuttoned his overcoat and holster and pulled out his revolver.

It seemed so futile. The target would be the flash of a gun and it would already be too late.

He doubted it. Was someone playing games? What if he shot them? At least his stalker could not see him either. But he could certainly hear. He kept still. He wondered if the enemy sent spies into the region. Why be warned to carry arms?

He raised his revolver, pointing it towards where he imagined there to be a presence, like a macabre *séance* out in the open. His mind controlled his aim. He quietly paced out a large circle on the sand, dampening his socks again at the water's edge, his gun kept pointed towards the same inner position. He would need to dive as he fired. Running away would create noise, present a fatal target. He questioned where he was aiming. What if his stalker had moved sideways? What if there were several of them?

After coming full circle, he inched closer to the dunes. He needed to get out of the wind, give himself cover. He should have thought of that before. It would be like his longed-for revolving shed. He would hear better.

He waited, tempted to crouch, gun pointed out to sea, praying for a single sound. There was nothing but wind and the action of the waves.

He heard a footstep on gravel nearby. He had not been imagining.

"Who's there?" he shouted.

There was no answer.

"I have my gun drawn! *Je suis armé!*"

Again, nothing. The sea kept crashing. He had been on hundreds of night patrols in the past, knowing full well that the enemy was somewhere out there, maybe close by, most likely in front. But the lack of certainty in this case, the possibility that it was someone from his own side, on any side, made it impossibly difficult. There was no firing line. There were no companions to provide extra pairs of eyes, no friendly snipers, only the cover of the soft dune right behind him. Whoever was out there was a sadist, feasting on creating fear, bringing him to a humiliating submission, readying his prey to beg for mercy.

He had given himself away again. He manoeuvred sideways. His heart was beating out of control. Now he could hear nothing, even if it happened. He was one step from dropping to his knees, drawing his adversary in by subterfuge and then delivering the final upwards blow at close quarters.

"Quinn, is that you?"

He remembered about the password.

"The password, man! The password!"

But supposing he was wrong? Supposing it was a local? He couldn't risk shooting without cause. It would alert the sentries wherever they were. It would develop into a scandal.

He moved sideways again.

He had to return to safety. Ceasing altogether to care about noise, he scrambled up the side of the dune onto the small path that led back to the chateau. He encountered the full force of the wind. It would protect him. He sprinted as fast as he could. It would be a long time before he got there. How he would look stupid to anyone who shone a lamp.

Forcing his revolver back into its holster to avoid an accident, he kept sprinting. At least he had recovered, driven by fear.

The lights of the chateau came into distant view. They changed everything. He made one long dash, deciding to stay out there, conceal himself to see if he could spot the shadow of his opponent crossing the lawn. He stopped every now and again to listen out for his pursuer.

He finally reached thick bushes bordering the lawn. He crouched down and waited, trying to calm his breath, waiting for his heartbeat to subside to normal. He felt back in charge. This was what he was good at. His breath caught up. His pulse descended. He imagined how he would have looked had he been visible while escaping, scared and humiliated. Supposing the whole affair had been organised by Major Carter? Supposing the others were party to the spectacle?

He shook his head. He had no doubt at all. This was Quinn for certain. His field of view was now excellent. He was well-placed enough to see most of the back of the chateau that faced the sea. He continued to wait. How many shadows would he spot?

Nothing appeared. He felt relaxed. On the second floor of the chateau, through the small gaps in the closed shutters, he could see the lights going out.

He wondered if there were sentries within the perimeter of the chateau. Had there been patrols on the beach, after all? How would he make himself known when he emerged? Or might it have been *they* who had been playing their *jeux macabres*, as they did with all unsuspecting visitors? Would everyone hear about it at his expense during the morning session?

No, he decided for a second time, this was Quinn.

Something moved near the back of the chateau. His heart leapt. Its thumping resumed. He just made out a figure at the top of the dune about to cross the small stretch of lawn that separated it from the back door. He ran across in order to get closer.

Appearing around the corner of the chateau, he realised he was too late. The door had just closed. He waited another ten minutes, his back to the wall. The lights went out downstairs as well. Removing his shoes, he entered the door and crept up the cold stone steps to the dormitory. The edges of the steps were rounded. He felt safe. The door was left ajar. He made his way along the line of beds, gently brushing each of them to count his way to the end. He was home.

He removed his damp boots and socks and lay down otherwise fully clothed. His heart was still racing. His feet were now freezing. There were sounds of sleeping all around him. He waited for a telltale stir. It never came. Whoever his stalker had been had come from another room.

*

The orderly clapped his hands as he strode up and down the dormitory, throwing the large shutters open on his way. Cody had slept well after covering his feet. He sat up and instinctively looked down to the deserted beach outside in the growing light. He got up and removed his clothes in order to take a shower ahead of the others. No-one seemed to notice that he had already been dressed.

By the time they all descended for breakfast, twenty minutes later, Cody had decided to confront Quinn, try to delve directly into the mind of the sadist. He walked over to the reception desk.

"You have a Captain Quinn on the commanders' course?"

The old sergeant turned away and picked up a list lying on the desk behind him. Seeing something that appeared to confuse him, he reached for a logbook nearby.

"There *was* a Captain Quinn, Captain," he said after a few seconds. "Wait a minute…"

He disappeared into a back office and came out with a colleague, another sergeant.

"That's correct, sir," the colleague said. "Orders came for Captain Quinn to return to his battalion."

"Can I see them?"

"I'm sorry, Captain. The Captain took them with him."

"Did *you* receive them?"

"Yes, Captain. They came through at four o'clock."

Cody was frustrated and relieved at the same time. It gave him precious time. Quinn's departure left him with one less burden. He would be saddled instead with thinking about how their confrontation would take place once he got back to battalion. He wondered what could have been so important to have pulled Quinn away.

*

That night, Cody retired early to bed. All day he had been thinking off and on about Quinn. It had got to his nerves. For once, his colleagues had provided a useful distraction.

At the last minute, before falling asleep, he got dressed again and put his suspicions to the test. This time dropping his revolver into his overcoat pocket, he descended to the foyer and went outside to the back.

Glad that he had done so, and refreshed by the familiar wind, the sound coming from the waves and smells from the beach, he walked the same route as the night before. He stopped time and time again and listened.

At one point, the wind stirred some pebbles just by him and made him jump. A loose twig followed, noisily racing across the sand. A short while later, he thought he heard movement. He walked towards it, intent to find out once and for all. He encountered nothing. This, he decided, felt differently.

He walked for about a mile more before deciding to about turn. He got back to the dormitory just before lights out. He thought about challenging his colleagues in the morning, just in case, but then decided against it. It had been a very personal experience he was condemned to keep to himself.

The calm, brought about by nothing happening, caused him to fall asleep much faster than the night before.

He dreamed about confronting Quinn once and for all. There were two railway tracks back to the front, parallel and close to each other, one for each of them. Quinn was in the train ahead, to his left. Cody shouted to his engineer to go faster. They began closing in. Cody grabbed the revolver, again in his pocket. It suddenly turned dark. Perhaps they were in a tunnel. Cody would be obliged to fire blind. There were flashes. Quinn had evidently drawn his own pistol and was firing in all directions. It proved his guilt. Cody now knew that he was entitled to respond in kind.

The trains were racing alongside each other, taking it in turns to race ahead. Cody stood on the roof of a carriage. There was a flash. It came from almost in front of him. He fired back, three times, from his pocket, sweeping his gun from side to side in order to ensure a hit.

Both trains screeched to a halt. They were now in open countryside, still in the dark. They went on for what seemed miles, but eventually stopped at practically same time. Cody climbed down onto the side of the rails and hurried over. A stretcher party was carrying someone out onto the far side of the track. Cody climbed between the carriages and caught up. He pulled back the cover. The light from the carriage was enough to make out a face. There was no blond hair. The dead man being posed on the side of the track was Colonel Wilkes.

Cody climbed into the nearest carriage, determined to find Quinn. Passengers, looking as weird as the band of snipers, but dressed in civilian clothes, constantly stood up and made his way impossible. He got lost, couldn't remember if he had been going up or down the train. It went on and on, and Quinn was nowhere to be found.

Cody had just killed the colonel. They would come looking for him. He had to escape. He jumped back onto the side of the railway line. The men carrying the colonel saw the burn marks in Cody's coat, dropped their charge, and chased him. People appeared from nearby woods and spread out to obstruct his way.

They were closing in on him...

15

A staff car rapidly came to a halt just ahead of Cody. The rear door swung open.

"Cody, isn't it? The 10th?"

Major Hughes was from one of the sister battalions. He had arrived on the same train.

"We're neighbours. Climb in, Captain."

Cody was relieved. It had looked like his journey from the railhead was going to be a long walk. It was the very last thing he needed.

"Look as though you need reviving, Cody!"

The train had been packed full of troops. Cody had been one of the last to board and had been condemned to ride in the guard box.

"I had forgotten that they're open here," he admitted.

At one point, it had even started to snow.

Near the entrance to the rail yard, they passed a 12-inch naval gun mounted on an isolated railway truck. After agreeing that guns were making the greatest difference in the war, Major Hughes explained he was returning from escorting an officer whom he had defended in a court martial.

"Sad affair," he said, giving no details. "Why are some men so inclined to dig themselves into trouble?"

All Cody could think of was the waste of resources. Inquiries were bad enough, but at least they had a more direct bearing on conducting the war. If an individual had cracked, it was not worth making a great fuss over.

The state of the narrow country road became worse. The driver encountered problems negotiating the massive furrows caused by endless traffic to and from the front. The cold had hardened the ground, and the going was terrible.

Fifty minutes later, they arrived at 10th Battalion headquarters. Cody had talked about the chateau and the uncertainty as to his future.

"Best of luck with it all, Cody," Major Hughes sympathised, before heading on to his own battalion.

Relieved to be on solid ground at last, Cody got out his pipe to celebrate. His face lit up when he recognised some men and officers walking around. He had expected a totally new crew. Hardy ran up and saluted.

"Thank God you're back, Captain!"

Hardy explained he had remained with Smalby but assigned to the ranks more often than he would have liked. He was eager for a change.

"Had no time for stocktaking," he said.

That made Cody wonder for a moment what might have happened to the supply of provisions.

The new front lay quite a few miles into open country beyond the canal. Hughes had reported that the brigade had fared well over the last few days. Division attributed the success to the enemy diverting troops to counter an American initiative further south.

Cody went over to report to Colonel Wilkes. Wilkes turned out to be uncharacteristically cheerful. He didn't hesitate to confirm that Quinn had done an excellent job filling in for him. C Company had to be proud of its achievements. When Cody asked if he would resume command, Colonel Wilkes appeared surprised.

"You are resuming command from today," be barked in his raspy voice that Cody had been spared for so long. "You're manning the line, Captain!"

No homecoming was ever perfect.

"The commanders' course. Quinn. I had concerns," he stuttered.

It was not a virtuoso performance.

"Officers need to understand each other's tasks!" Wilkes said.

His suspicions unallayed, Cody left the tent more convinced than ever that his own days in charge of C Company were numbered. As he walked towards the trenches, he noticed a row of Lewis guns that had been set up on posts and pointed to the sky. This was new.

Hardy came running up with a spare gas mask.

"New rules, Captain. One hour a day."

He had seen that Cody had been distracted by the Lewis guns.

"Almost every night now, Captain. Sometimes several the same night."

Cody donned the mask and continued towards the front. The mud had hardened there too. He was halfway there when he heard the bugle. He passed men with their boots wrapped with canvas and straw to fight the cold. Everyone had donned their masks.

He reached the firing line determined to play the game with Quinn, pretend that nothing had happened back at the chateau. He would even congratulate him for recent successes. He needed to discover the lay of the land first.

He found Quinn with Lieutenants Finlay and Cobbold. Cobbold had removed his boots and was applying grease after violently rubbing his feet, not something he should have been doing during an exercise. The three of them appeared to be getting on well. They broke off and courteously shook hands with the new arrival. The ensuing exchange looked rather stupid and long-winded with everyone in their masks.

"You see how much we've gained, Captain?" boasted Cobbold, putting his boots on again.

They resumed discussing administrative affairs while Cody listened in order to catch up. Once the hour was up, and it became easier to converse, they shared their stories about the latest routing of the enemy. Mowforth and Smalby turned up and added their own bits to all that had occurred. It had apparently taken place after a hostile patrol that had soon turned into a fiasco for the enemy. The battalion had jumped at the opportunity.

As each of his interlocutors added a little more about the event, Cody felt increasingly uneasy. This had gone well for Quinn. After several minutes, he had heard enough. Unable to help himself, he cut them off. He asked Quinn to go over trench details before he took over. Quinn didn't reply.

"There's no map yet, Captain," warned Cobbold before taking off with his colleagues.

Cody looked at Quinn. The onetime intelligence officer seemed to have forgotten himself.

"We should rough one out together right away," Cody said.

"Of course," Quinn said coldly, with a hint of a sneer, as if he knew better. "We didn't need one yet."

He walked off, supposedly to get an old map and the wherewithal to mark it up, but he didn't come back.

It began to snow. After a fifteen-minute wait, Cody called back all four lieutenants.

"Let's get something down right away," he told them.

Against the rules, he had decided to deal with the issue there and then rather that head to the rear. Lieutenant Smalby left for brigade, presently a mile away, with a request for copies of the latest aerial photographs. Mowforth, Finlay, and Cobbold, meanwhile, roughed out the trenches and known enemy positions. Avoiding pointing the finger of blame at his replacement for the oversight, Cody wondered all the same what they all really thought of him. He knew he could never ask.

That night, after studying the revised map, and informing Quinn and the colonel, Cody sent Lieutenant Mowforth out to reconnoitre the enemy wire along as much of a hundred yards as he could. The platoon wore white. Working from right to left, they soon came across a sentry guarding a machine gun post behind an opening in the wire. Twenty yards on, they were spotted by a second sentry who opened fire.

They waited it out in a shell hole. The sporadic shooting lasted for a quarter of an hour, but only the sentry kept firing. One man had been hit at the first instance but had kept quiet, and as soon the shooting ended, he was helped back by two colleagues.

The patrol resumed for two more hours. When Mowforth scrambled back over the parapet, Cody was delighted. He congratulated him and reported that his man would survive his wounds.

"Well?"

"We covered all of it, Captain," Mowforth said. "Apart from the one sentry, all looked very quiet indeed."

Cody couldn't decide whether it had been an enemy ploy. When they arrived together at headquarters, the colonel and Quinn turned up to hear Mowforth's debriefing.

Cody marked up his map with each of threats that Mowforth singled out. Even before Mowforth had finished, the colonel had decided to chance it. After sending a message to brigade, and bringing the artillery liaison officer into the discussion, he ordered A and B companies to move up for a pre-dawn raid.

Cody and Mowforth re-joined the firing line. The news went down well. Everyone was keen for a fresh move. As Cody went along the front trench to speak to each of his lieutenants, men were shedding their greatcoats and padding and checking their rifles prior to inspection. Others joined them, emerging from where they had been stationed along the avenues and alleys. Mortar teams had moved up from their positions behind and were setting up at regular intervals.

Cody encountered Corporal Jones who had already started his inspection. Jones broke off from giving one of his men a dressing down.

"Rings a bell, Captain?" he whispered. "Bit last minute, isn't it?"

Cody chuckled and assured him that brigade was in on it and that there would be artillery backup.

"Good luck, Corporal!" he said before moving on.

Men from A Company started arriving with extra cases of bombs and ammunition and wire and other materiel for consolidation of any trenches gained.

At four-thirty, the mortar teams opened up, targeting the enemy trenches in front on both sides and to their rear. The artillery joined in with a creeping barrage.

The enemy kept deathly quiet. After thirty minutes, C Company jumped off and advanced in two waves each of two platoons wide, with the remaining platoons in similar formation behind them. One of the eighteen-pounder field guns started firing short and five of Cody's men ferrying materiel were wounded. Cody was up front, Hardy alongside as usual with a spare rifle. Finlay sent forward a messenger to report the loss. A second messenger had been sent back to get a warning through to the artillery.

Cody and Hardy pressed on. No more shells were landing short. It seemed a long way to the enemy line, and for a change there was little wire in the way. It was only towards the last stages that the line came into action. The response was weak, and few men were hit. When they finally landed inside the hostile trench, they saw that the mortars and artillery had done well. Those who had survived had remained hunkered down until the very last minute.

As C and D Companies invested the network of trenches, they soon rounded up ten officers and eighty men without a shot being exchanged. They immediately ferried back their wounded for attention in 10th Battalion first aid tents.

Cody ordered the captured trenches to be turned and stops placed as far as possible beyond in order to hinder any counterattack. The loss of Finlay's men meant that the right flank stop was short, and the enemy took advantage. Enemy troops retook some twenty yards with bombs before being beaten back with a vicious firefight settled by the arrival of Lewis guns.

Cody did the rounds of his men as they settled into their new positions. Morale seemed excellent. All his officers and NCOs were accounted for, and the enemy had left the trenches clean and free of booby traps.

The major came forward to report that A and B Companies had moved up to the old firing line. Battalion losses were looking like about twenty killed and thirty injured. The colonel had ordered C and D Companies to stay in place. Parties were on their way to lay wire as well as cables back to headquarters.

From the prisoners interrogated before they were sent back to Quinn, Cody fully learned of the success of the shelling. Two of their company commanders had been killed, along with some seventy troops dead or wounded.

By the time the sky lit up, it had become clear that the enemy was not about to retaliate. New maps had to be drawn.

The business of consolidating the new front took them all day. With the likelihood of an eventual response from the enemy, additional Lewis gun teams were deployed to occupy the line of freshly prepared loopholes.

Cody had spent several hours working on a new map by the time the colonel came forward and saw what he was up to.

"Let's talk about this, Cody," he said, beckoning him to follow back to the old line.

He led him through the communication trenches that were being hurriedly prepared by the rest of the battalion. Cody was convinced that he would get admonished for carrying a map in the trenches.

The major was waiting for them at headquarters.

"You shouldn't have to do that, Cody," Colonel Wilkes remarked once they had arrived. "Where are the bloody survey people?"

The major got up to go looking for Quinn. The colonel briskly reached out his arm to hold him back.

"Changes are speeding up," the colonel said. "We need someone more experienced than Quinn in intelligence."

Cody listened intently, determined not to give away his delight at Quinn's forthcoming demise.

"The map people should have already been here," the colonel said. "Quinn should have made certain of that."

Then came the punch line that Cody had come to least expect.

"Quinn has performed extraordinarily well in your absence, Cody," the colonel went on. "Hasn't he, Major?"

"Extraordinarily well," Major Hickman said. "And the men appreciate him."

Cody already felt sickened.

"I have been considering this, Cody," the colonel said. "You are the only officer in the battalion who stuck up for Quinn after his fiasco. Time has moved on and everyone now respects you for it, Quinn included."

It was untrue. Cody knew what was coming.

"I could substitute Talbot, Fuller or Cragg," the colonel said, "but I think you would be best."

"And Quinn?"

He already knew the answer. He wondered how many times they had rehearsed this.

"As Major Hickman said, Captain," said Colonel Wilkes, "C Company has accepted him. He is younger and fitter than you and has proved himself in action. But he doesn't have your experience. I need you with me. I need a better intelligence officer. This map business, for example, is something that I know you would never have stood for."

Cody saw through it all. Quinn had gone to work on them in his absence. It was a *fait accompli*. Why bother talking about the latest success? For all he knew, the entire battalion could already be in the know. Any resistance he put up would be met by sheer *schadenfreude*. All he could now do was to accept it all with grace and put all his efforts into the challenge of his new position.

"I want to keep Hardy," was all he could say.

The colonel and major both nodded. Cody hated them for their lack of courage. He felt deceived by his lieutenants who had not let on. Above all, more than ever, he detested Quinn himself. It was quite unlikely that someone of his own age who had been side-lined in such a manner would ever get any further promotion. The colonel and major had too easily been carried along. His journey had ended.

As soon as the battalion had been relieved the next day, Colonel Wilkes convoked his four captains and their lieutenants to announce the change. In fairness, he did a good job praising Cody, but Cody was in no doubt about what they all felt about it. To all extents and purposes this constituted a demotion, and every one of them would see it that way.

Cody looked across to Quinn. He saw the usual smugness on his face, his adversary trying as hard as he could to suppress the arrogant grin that had become his trademark. He looked away in disgust.

The group dispersed. Cody went over to the padre's tent to announce the change. Father Drake's reaction was to remain diplomatic over the affair. In the few minutes they were together, he even tried to be positive about it.

Taking on his new appointment with all the determination he could muster, Cody headed off to find the snipers and reassure Hardy. He tried once again to discern the pros and cons of his new situation. He would miss the men, but he would no longer be saddled with the torrent of administrative duties that had always bored him to tears, matters of uniforms or new conscripts, ammunition supplies, or the cheating that went on over food provisions. He had been forced to become a Jack-of-all-trades. The paperwork was endless and kept increasing. His mind could now focus on a single track, go deeper into detail. He would become more professional, a true specialist. Perhaps his situation had promise after all. The colonel had cunningly waited for him to have had a success as commander before announcing the transfer. Cody would outplay them all by remaining courteous and helpful for as long as he could. Any sign of bitterness would be swept under the carpet for good.

He walked past Quinn, lecturing three of his corporals in his habitually arrogant and patronising manner. How he hated the sound of his voice, his self-satisfaction. How he pitied the lieutenants for being so blind. Yet, at first glance, Mowforth, Smalby, Finlay, and Cobbold appeared to be treating their new commander with the same deference that he had enjoyed himself. It aggravated him no end.

He encountered Captains Talbot, Fuller, and Cragg. They were conferring over something while Talbot was carving again, but stopped as soon as he arrived. Cody knew he could say nothing. He had been deserted. To a man the battalion had about turned. He was on his own and had to make the best of it.

He continued in search of the snipers. He thought of Kate and her complaint about his uniform at the school. What would she think now? Did she have to know? Would she even care? Might Quinn tell her?

He encountered Corporal Jones headed to join his colleagues. The tall Jones looked at him straight in the eye. He was as serious as ever.

"I never expected it, Captain."

Cody could see he meant it. He patted him on the shoulder and replied that everyone needed to move on. He reminded Jones of his good work.

"It still leaves a horrible feeling indeed, Captain," Jones said in his pure Welsh accent.

"Keep me advised on the women," Cody said just to say something.

He saw he had a rare chance of being frank.

"How have things been under our friend?" he asked.

"I know he'll self-destruct in the end, Captain."

Cody wanted to smile. He told Jones to forget such thoughts.

"He may have got wind of my coming to see you about the women," Jones warned. "I can't be sure, but he's turned distinctly unfriendly towards me out of the blue."

Cody was alarmed. Other than the women themselves, the only person who could have said anything was Kate. But he couldn't say any of that to Jones.

"I have something else to tell you, Captain," said Jones. "Something I should have long ago."

"Yes?"

"I sent my son to watch your house in order to warn me of your return."

Cody laughed. He had suspected it all along.

"Thank you, Captain," said Jones, relieved. "There's one more thing, though."

"What is it, Corporal?"

"I nearly turned up several days too early."

"Early? How do you mean?"

"My son saw someone he assumed was you."

There followed a moment of silence.

"You mean...?"

"Yes, Captain. I didn't know how to tell you."

The padre appeared just behind Jones while Cody was still recovering from the news. Jones uncomfortably tipped his helmet and moved on.

"I was surprised," Father Drake finally admitted.

"Thank you, Father," Cody said. "There was a dark time a short while ago when I needed you badly, but it's now over."

"Glad to hear it," Drake said before moving on himself. "Don't hesitate. I have always appreciated you."

Cody continued searching for the snipers. His self-consciousness in front of the sea of faces all around him dissipated. Despite the bad news from Jones, he felt elated, his morale restored. He was certain he still had people who thought well of him. He was annoyed with himself for having lost so much confidence in himself, for thinking that his entire entourage had abandoned him. And a third confirmation of what Quinn had been up to at home had validated his suspicions for good. It hadn't been paranoia after all.

He finally located the snipers. They were seated around an open fire in a dark corner, the moving flames causing light to dance across their faces. Four of them were playing cards. Schemensky welcomed him, but no-one stood up. Ignoring it, Cody explained he intended to spend time with them once they were back in the line. He said that he had a lot to learn.

"But Captain Quinn said he would keep us," Schemensky protested. "He said that Colonel Wilkes had agreed."

"It's nothing against you, sir," the Scotsman said.

That sounded grotesquely obsequious. It also spelt trouble to come. Cody stormed off, saying nothing. He had been humiliated. What Quinn must have told them had to be nonsense. But that he had said anything at all was what Cody had feared. Quinn had alienated them in advance. This was a *coup monté* if there ever was one.

At headquarters, Cody learned the colonel had left for brigade. The major pleaded ignorance, but agreed that what Quinn had done was reprehensible.

"Have you spoken to him about it?" he asked. "This is between you two, isn't it?"

Cody looked at him in a way to show his disgust.

"According to the snipers, the colonel was party to all this, Major," he said. "Please advise him upon his return that I will not be taking over the sniper team until he had made the position clear."

He turned to leave.

"To them and Quinn!" he called out.

The major had looked uneasy, enough to give Cody satisfaction. But Cody was still angry enough to take the issue up to the brigadier if necessary. It would surely get him into trouble, but he had no choice than to stand his ground. The colonel had managed the changeover poorly indeed. It reflected on his authority. The brigadier needed to know.

Emerging from headquarters into the cold night air, Cody was struck by a sobering thought. Supposing the brigadier had changed sides as well?

Deciding he would seek Hardy in the morning, Cody retired to the hut, which served for all five captains. Talbot, Fuller, and Cragg had already turned in. After lying there for several hours, unable to sleep, and further aggravated when Quinn turned up in the early hours, he finally nodded off.

He dreamt himself lying at the bottom of a trench. It was rock-hard and uncomfortable. There was a strong, blinding moonlight from directly above. Around him were hostile soldiers in white suits and gas masks creeping around with their bayonets pointed to the ground. They were finishing off all those they came across. He was frantically trying to unholster his gun. One of them removed his mask. It was Quinn. Cody came to the realisation that the reason he could not get his side arm out was that he had his arms caught in endless barbed wire. It was everywhere.

When Cody woke up in the morning, both his right wrist and jaw were aching.

*

Three days later, the battalion was back again in the trenches. Cody had his tent close to headquarters and Hardy was with him. Colonel Wilkes had profusely apologised over the sniper affair and had reprimanded Quinn in front of Cody. Quinn had been ordered to tell the sniper team in person that Cody was taking them over.

"And make damn sure you speak the world of Cody and that it is in their interest to have him as their commander!"

The sullied Quinn had headed off to carry out his orders. He had turned around and appeared to sneer at Cody who had been following him at a distance, ready to arrive once he had spoken to the snipers.

Cody thought about the colonel's performance. He remained convinced it was put up. Whether he liked it, the colonel and Quinn had become bound in common cause. Their unholy union would remain an obstacle that required taking on with care.

Early the following morning, Cody woke up after yet another nightmare. Again, his jaw ached. Bad dreams seemed to be appearing thick and fast. This time he had dreamt that he and Quinn were running next to each other towards the enemy line. Both fell to the ground at the same time. Quinn, looking as immaculate as always, showed his intense disappointment when his scruffy colleague got up again.

They ran into a narrow tunnel. Quinn was ahead. Again, he looked well-dressed and sure of himself. Cody started praying that the roof would cave in.

The colonel appeared behind them. He ordered that they abandon the tunnel, as it had become too dangerous. Walking back towards the colonel, Quinn disagreed. The tunnel would lead to victory. He gave a speech that had nothing to do with anything.

Quinn's men and the snipers caught up with them, ignoring the colonel as they overtook him. Quinn and the colonel now stood beside each other arguing their cases. They were shouting over each other, a dialogue of the deaf as strong as there had ever been. Cody, remaining ahead, had to take position. The colonel was failing to make his case and was becoming emotional. Cody knew his superior was about to decide something he would regret forever. Quinn was the better man.

Somehow, Cody and Quinn landed up in a church spire. It turned out to be the cathedral. They were hunting for the sniper who had felled them both.

An enemy plane flew directly towards them and opened fire. The sniper had been there all the time. He shot at them from behind. Cody prayed Quinn would slip and fall. He got out his revolver to fire at the sniper. The man was tall and had blond hair.

It was Quinn.

16

A week had passed since the truculent snipers had been ordered to accept Cody's command. He remained convinced that even their superficial compliance was a charade, that behind it all Quinn's nefarious influence had not gone away.

Determined to win them over, Cody had spent his entire time with them. It had been hard and demoralising. Never had he experienced such difficulty in bringing men around. Their supercilious behaviour in front of the rest of the battalion did not change. Forever flaunting their ghillies, camouflaged faces, and hessian-covered rifles, their comportment remained feral, but Cody was determined to see the challenge through. He had no choice. This was a contest between himself and Quinn.

The battalion was encamped in close reserve, a mere half-a-mile behind the front line. Cody had been sufficiently wrapped up in the pursuit of his cause that he had lost touch with goings-on in his old company.

Father Drake turned up at his canvas hut and asked to talk. He seemed troubled. The laconic Hardy discretely took his leave.

"It's your old company," the padre said, lowering his voice. "Have you noticed anything?"

Cody told him of his preoccupation. The challenge to ween his snipers off the influence of their old commander was proving tough.

"So I heard."

Father Drake recounted his intermittent recent contacts with C Company. Changes were afoot that he couldn't fathom. Quinn was keeping his distance as usual, and the lieutenants were saying nothing, but some men seemed to be unhappy with whatever was going on, although no-one was letting on what it was about.

"I shouldn't be asking you this, Cody," he went on. "Are you able to find out what's happening?"

Cody had no time for this, but he knew it was important. He thought of Jones, his one sure ally, but said nothing.

"What's worrying you, Padre?"

"Perhaps nothing at all," said Father Drake as he stood up to leave. "But we know a little about Quinn. Find out what you can. See if anything troubling is happening. For the sake of morale."

Cody wasn't surprised one bit. With the support Quinn now enjoyed from higher up, his influence could spread to the entire battalion. It could spell awful times ahead. Cody had to help.

Apart from the bombing raids at night, the front had been quiet for days. Cody took a brief break to spend a few hours in town.

"Go, go!" urged the colonel, still in an unusually good mood and quite oblivious to the troubles that were brewing in C Company. "Try to gauge the morale there and get me something to read if you can find it."

Cody walked the distance alone, surprised at how little activity there was along the road. The town turned out to be the opposite, no doubt because of the break in the weather. The streets were inundated with sorry-looking men and women, almost always shoddily dressed in black, aimlessly wandering around as if they too needed to breathe fresh air. Cody examined them closely as he passed by. They were all in terrible shape, their clothes mostly torn and filthy. Some of them were fumbling around in the rubble just as he had seen so many times before. Yet again, the town appeared infested by a pale-faced *demi monde*, emerging from its dark cellars, scurrying around to keep itself busy.

He crossed the abandoned railway line and headed for the post office to send telegrams to Kate and the girls asking for news. Three days before had been his birthday, and for the first time they seemed to have forgotten.

On his way, he passed what remained of a bookshop. Books were lying around in the rubble, mostly damaged by rain and snow. He ventured inside and dug his hand into a pile in order to pull one out. It was a pocket-sized biography of a Napoleonic general of whom he had never heard. It would do for the colonel. His fastidiousness would be tempered by the challenge of reading French.

As he emerged after a long wait in the post office queue, he spotted his friend the priest across the small square. He waved and cried out. The priest stopped, saw him, and headed over, passing on his way two saplings that were miraculously still standing and looking healthy, the only traces of optimism around.

"You won't believe it," the priest said excitedly in French, once he was within hearing distance. "There'll be a play this afternoon."

"Theatre, Father?"

"The first in two-and-a-half years. Come!"

It was impossible to refuse. They passed another small square on the far side of which was a long wall with several tall posts in front of it.

"To teach us a lesson," said the priest, seeing that Cody had been distracted, but trying not to look himself. "They shot about thirty in all. Mostly young men. Three women."

Cody asked if he knew anything about the Napoleonic general in the colonel's book.

"Not really. He came from somewhere in Brittany. If I remember rightly, he was a rascal. But they all were then."

"Perfect!"

They arrived at an unpretentious theatre building, hidden in a backstreet behind. It was still intact and looked as though it could house about two hundred. The priest explained several people had volunteered to clean it up and scavenge enough chairs and benches to put on a spectacle. Cody asked which play they had chosen but recognised neither the author nor the title.

"Won't you come to watch, Captain? We would be honoured."

Ignoring the fact that he would not understand a word of what was being said, Cody accepted. He was keen to see how such a morose population would rise to the occasion. Perhaps there would be dancing and music.

The theatre had filled up well before time, and surplus audience was noisily standing in the aisles or leaning against the walls. Cody caught on that he was the only foreigner there. The priest insisted he sit at the front, embarrassingly expelling a young man who thought he had a better right to be there. Fortunately, his older neighbours were more accommodating.

The play began almost at once. The curtain rose to expose a dazzling stage enhanced by bright lights, illuminating garish costumes and scenery, all of which so contrasted with the sorry state of the audience. There turned out to be no music or dancing at all. The play, which seemed grim and appeared to be taking place in the Middle Ages, went on and on, with long unintelligible and melodramatic speeches by heavily made-up male and female actors putting on performances of a lifetime. Despite the unexpected distractions, Cody soon became lost and bored. The rest of the audience, however, remained enthralled, every now and again curiously breaking into a nervous laughter. A special and rather particular cocoon had been created in order to lock out reality.

During the only intermission, almost everyone rushed for the foyer or outside, as if desperate to escape the intensity of what they had been watching. Everyone spoke in order to make up for their hour of silence. Some began to smoke, but the odours emanating from their pipes or cigarettes were often dubious.

Glad to be rid of his hard seat, Cody allowed himself to be swept along, ending up outside in the street at the edge of the crowd. As he got out his pipe, he spotted the priest talking to a group of people who appeared better dressed than anyone around them. He headed over to join them.

"*Mesdames, Messieurs, le Capitaine Cody,*" the priest announced, stretching out his arm while mentioning that Cody had been responsible for capturing the square that had set off the relief of the town.

After a torrent of congratulations and appreciation directed at Cody, the priest introduced his entourage. They were evidently notables. They resorted to English and shook hands with Cody, but no-one said a word more about the action.

Cody asked them about the play, admitting that he had more than struggled.

"It's about how a new *seigneur* comes to town," one woman, dark, tall, with a serious face and in her fifties, told him.

Cody pictured the character she was referring to.

"And how he enslaves the local population with a system of indulgences."

"Indulgences?"

"He had them paying for anything they did wrong, as well as for the remission of the souls of their dead," said the bespectacled man standing next to her who might have been her husband. "They are told that their future happiness will only come from their sacrifice."

The man seemed quite erudite. Cody had forgotten how much the French took life so seriously.

"But people were laughing," he pointed out.

"Recent events," one other said. "It's why we chose it."

Cody understood that to mean the occupation. They asked him about his background and talked about visits to England before the war. He found them a strange contrast to their fellow citizens, not to mention most of their fellow countrymen he had so far encountered, even many of the chateau proprietors who had provided accommodation to officers. At least he was learning something.

A hand bell was rung from inside. They politely broke up and headed back, and Cody forged ahead to ungainly fight his way to his front seat before it was taken. He hoped to see everything in a better light in what was to follow.

It wasn't to be the case. Losing track of what was being spoken, he became bored again, but there was no way he could insult his hosts by leaving. His mind wandered. From a certain point of view, the war itself was a reversion to the Middle Ages. He tried to equate the gesticulating characters on the stage with individuals in the battalion, changing his mind as he went along. The *seigneur* was no doubt Colonel Wilkes. Or could he be Quinn? Cody studied the comportment of the troupe standing to the rear of the stage. What if they were his snipers? Were there parallels to be learned?

When the performance finally ended, Cody found and thanked the priest, and said goodbye to the small group he had met.

"Here! Captain!"

It was the erudite man. He handed over a well-worn paper-covered book in a large format. It was a copy of the play.

Walking back to camp, Cody resolved to corner Jones discretely at the first opportunity and ask him about what was going on. Since there were so many prying eyes around, it might take a few days to find the opportune occasion.

He was only a hundred yards off when bursts of gunfire and explosions broke out at the front. Ahead, he could make out men mustering to wait for orders. The enemy had raised two balloons, and low-flying planes appeared to be dropping bombs, although none of them were venturing as far as the camp.

A motor machine gun unit suddenly overtook him. He hadn't heard it coming. He began to run.

"They're trying something, Moose," Captain Fuller shouted as soon as Cody arrived. "We don't know what yet."

There was chaos. The cookers had just finished dispensing hot food and tea and were hurriedly dispersing. It seemed an odd time for the enemy to carry out any sort of manoeuvre. Without stopping off to get his helmet or mask, Cody ran to where his snipers would be assembling. He found them with Hardy. He asked them what they knew.

"Surprised as you are, Captain," the Scotsman said.

Schemensky joined them without saying where he had been. He repeated the same as the Scotsman. Cody looked over to the draughty and crowded iron shelter that was presently serving as battalion headquarters. An orderly emerged with instructions from the colonel to head up to the firing line. The battalion there was calling for snipers. Deciding to stay with his men, Cody ordered Hardy to fetch his gear.

It remained chaotic all the way. A and B Companies had just started a new communication trench that would take them all night and were presently lying low. Nearby, other parties who had been burying cable, and linesmen deployed to repair existing wires, were doing the same. Inside the existing trenches, men were hurrying in both directions, shells were causing damage on all sides, and the mass of explosions in front were getting noisier. Several times they tried asking for news from people heading for the rear, but no-one seemed to know what was going on. By the time they reached the firing line, it was nearly dark.

Cody found a captain and asked how they could help. After adjusting to the exaggerated appearance of Cody's snipers standing behind him, the captain shouted he was well enough off on his right flank but needed resources twenty yards along the left, near where there had just been an explosion. The enemy was pouring ordnance into his position. An 8-inch howitzer was causing a lot of trouble, there had been a few 77's as well, and the enemy were trench mortaring like never before.

"We just had a patrol out," he said. "Nearly went bad."

He said he had other things to attend to. His communications had just gone down, and it was too dark for flags, so now he had to resort to lamps.

"We think they're about to jump off," he warned as he left.

"Now?"

"I know. Makes no sense," he said. "They know bloody well that we will have just changed watch."

He stayed put long enough to explain that one of his sentries had spotted the projection from a *flammenwerfer* coming from the trench immediately in front of them, as though they were testing it before use. During the afternoon, the enemy had used dummies in order to attract sniper fire. He had deliberately held off, but they had been on tenterhooks ever since.

Cody mentioned the balloons. Before taking off for good, the captain said that an airship had been spotted heading north in the morning.

Cody knew what was in front. There was a large slag heap behind the enemy's position, and for several days there had been concern that the enemy was using it to conceal preparations. As soon as the latest disturbances had broken out, the artillery had pummelled the area just in case.

They took up position along the firing line where the captain had indicated. Although it had been pretty badly damaged, there was enough of a fire step left to make use of. As Cody waited below, his men started picking out targets and shooting, but there was no sign that the opposition was on the move.

"Here, Captain," shouted Schemensky.

Cody climbed up to look through a spare peephole. The shells and bombs kept falling. The exchange of fire from both sides intensified.

The captain returned and thanked them for coming forward.

"Know any more?" Cody asked.

"Your guys are still in reserve," the captain said. "I think it's a false alarm. They're just trying us out."

Cody reminded him that none of the latest reports had indicated any enemy activity further back. If the intention was a push, they hadn't built up for it. He agreed with the captain, but stayed with his men until matters blew over.

After another hour, the enemy quietened down altogether, and there was no sign of gas.

At four in the morning, doing his rounds prior to the stand to, the battalion major turned up on his rounds and said they could return.

"Cody, isn't it?"

Cody hadn't recognised Major Hughes in the dark.

"Thank you for coming forward," Hughes said before continuing along the trench. "We owe you!"

Once given the all-clear, they slowly trekked through the trenches and back to camp, thinking of nothing but sleep.

Cody thanked his men, and they dispersed. The colonel would be angry that he had risked going forward when he didn't have to, but at least he and his men had spent time together.

By the time Cody emerged from his tent, it was mid-morning. Hardy was preparing him a late breakfast. It was a hurried affair. Cody had to see the colonel to report on the town and hand him the book.

On his way over, Cody spotted the tall figure of Jones assiduously walking across, fifty yards away. He saw where he was headed and hurried to cut him off. He had chosen well. They were masked from view by what little remained of trees and bushes behind the camp.

Jones seemed delighted to see him. Cody asked how things were.

"I'm hearing rumours of strange goings-on in C Company," Cody told him. "What's our friend up to, Jones?"

He knew he could get away with such a question. Jones would never think that Cody had any intention of exploiting a situation for personal benefit.

"What sort of things, Captain?"

Cody admitted he didn't know. Changes in behaviour had been reported, and some men were troubled.

"I'll keep an eye out, Captain."

It didn't take long. The next day, a day before they were due to return to the front line, Jones sought Cody and took the risk of jumping inside his tent. It was dusk, but Cody was annoyed by the risk Jones was taking.

Cody put down the copy of the play. He had been struggling almost as much as when he had been watching, and soon appreciated the interruption.

"There is something odd going on, Captain," Jones confirmed. "I'm going to need a few more days to find out more, but it concerns our friend."

Cody asked him what he knew so far.

"He's putting some kind of pressure on certain men, starting with the lieutenants," Jones reported.

"Pressure?"

"He's holding them to something, and they are unhappy about it. But no-one is talking openly. I think they are afraid. It looks as though more and more men are becoming part of whatever is going on. I'll find out, Captain. It won't take long."

Cody thanked him, but warned him about taking risks and told him to remain circumspect. He said to avoid at all costs coming anywhere near his tent from then on. They would have to choose their next meeting place cautiously.

"Maybe a written message would be safer," said Jones.

"Maybe, Jones," said Cody.

"By the way, Jones," he said, waving his copy of the play. "I need some help with translation when there's time. Can you lend me Hopper?"

17

"Captain Cody, wake up, sir!"

It was Corporal Jones. Hardy was at his side and they both had their helmets on. It was dark outside. They were interrupted by the nearby explosion of a high velocity shell. The enemy had been pounding the lines all day long with their long-range guns.

"An officer from Wit trench," Jones said, dropping several papers and a half-eaten sausage onto Cody's table. "In a deep dugout. His colleagues got it."

Cody had fallen asleep while reading the play. Earlier on, he had been checking on the damage caused by a shell landing uncomfortably close to battalion headquarters. It had mercifully only destroyed a few dozen water tins and several bags of coal.

He got up, and Jones led him outside while explaining the luck his patrol had had. The enemy officer had been eating. The raiding party, led by Finlay, had arrived right on top his position and had to exchange fire at close quarters. It was Jones himself who had bagged him.

"The captain had me bring him over, sir."

Cody thanked him and instinctively saluted the bareheaded prisoner with what looked like a fencing scar on his right cheek. He was well-built and tall.

"Thank Captain Quinn on my behalf, Jones."

Jones and his two guards took off. This would be Cody's very first interrogation in his new position, and he intended to make the best of the peace offering from Quinn. He had Hardy fetch his rifle to guard the prisoner.

"Hauptmann Gerlich!" the prisoner announced, saluting, and clicking his heels in return, except that he was wearing gumboots that only provided a feeble thud. "12th Bavarian."

His English was perfect.

"Follow me, please, Hauptmann," Cody said, nodding to Hardy to follow.

Cody's instinct was that this was a fish he had to hold on to for as long as he could before handing him over to brigade. It would be a tussle, and he would have to get the colonel to play along. He led them the short distance to the small officers' mess cabin next to headquarters, this one better suited to holding and interrogating a prisoner, not that it had ever been so intended. Leaving Hardy outside, Cody pulled up two chairs either side of one of a few small trestle tables otherwise used for playing cards. He had to remain patient with the prisoner. There was no point in provoking a negative reaction from such a valuable asset.

He invited him to take a seat and formerly introduced himself.

"Where are you from, Hauptmann?" he asked.

The prisoner replied that his family lived in a small village just south of Munich. He had been at the front almost since the beginning of the war. Cody was about to tell him he had never visited Germany when he spotted a half-full wine bottle on the ground, behind a chair to one side. He got up and went over to fetch it and offered it to the prisoner.

"No glasses here I'm afraid, Hauptmann," he said, "but I'm certain this was opened within the last two days."

The prisoner grinned but refused, complaining that he had been captured before satisfying an empty stomach. Cody took a swig himself to show it was safe and placed the bottle on the table. The red wine was very sweet indeed, nothing he recognised, but he didn't glance at the label.

"How long have you been here, Hauptmann?"

The prisoner merely grinned.

"Frankly, it doesn't matter to me, Hauptmann," Cody said. "I was just making conversation."

"Between officers?"

"Yes, between officers."

Cody studied his face and posture. He appeared well-educated. His accent and grasp of English already suggested that he had spent time in England. Since he had clammed up, Cody decided to leave him alone for a while. If nothing else, he would eventually succumb to sampling the wine. On an empty stomach, it might help to open him up. Cody left the cabin, closing the flap after taking care to bring the oil lamp with him and asking Hardy to stay put outside.

Almost two hours later, it was still dark. There remained an hour-and-a-half until dawn. Cody got up from his bed, relit the oil lamp, rifled through the prisoner's papers spotting nothing of obvious interest, picked up the remaining sausage, and headed back to the cabin.

As he reached for the door, he smiled at the thought that he was totally in charge. Hardy, who seemed to still be alert, noticed.

"Good luck, Captain!" he whispered excitedly.

The prisoner was slouched over the table. Sure enough, the level of the wine had dropped, but only slightly.

"Hauptmann!"

The prisoner came to. There occurred that instant during which he remembered where he was. He sat up straight, corrected his collar, but didn't reply. His eye fixed on the sausage in Cody's hand.

Before Cody could say anything, an aggravated Father Drake brushed open the door. It was unusual for him to be up so early.

"Have you come across my altar wine, by any chance, Cody?"

He had just been tipped off that it had lubricated a card game the night before. It was Sunday morning, and it had been his very last bottle. His nearest source would be in town, if he was lucky.

Spotting the padre's dog collar, the prisoner politely stood up.

"You're Catholic, Hauptmann?" Father Drake asked.

The prisoner nodded. At last, some reaction.

"Did the captain tell you that his father is also a priest? A Protestant one?"

The prisoner stared at Cody and sat down again.

"May I, a little?"

"Be my guest, Hauptmann," said Father Drake, glancing at Cody to show that he was doing him a favour. "Just leave me a chalice's worth for later on."

The prisoner helped himself and handed over the bottle as Cody landed the remaining sausage on the table.

"Father, may I speak to you privately?"

Father Drake, who had been distracted by the level in the bottle, gave Cody a puzzled look. Cody was equally surprised. The battalion padre wasn't supposed to get involved with prisoners. Cody shrugged his shoulders and they both left.

While Cody was waiting outside on his own, he spotted the colonel returning from his morning round of the trenches. The colonel thanked him for the book and handed over a few coins.

"Excellent find, Cody," he said. "What on earth inspired you to give me that one?"

Before Cody could field a reply, the colonel added that it had been intended as a birthday present for the brigadier, but that he had read it first.

"Always pays to be one up one your superior!" he said.

He returned to business in hand.

"I understand Quinn has found you an officer."

Cody wasn't at all surprised that Quinn had volunteered the information. The colonel talked about an incident that had occurred the night before, a couple of miles up the line. He had just heard the report. Enemy storm troops had carried out a raid while the local commander was momentarily absent checking up on a wiring party. No Very lights could be fired, and the SOS had to be sent by lamp. A stretch of trench was overtaken, mostly with stick grenades, but, strangely, the enemy didn't stay to exploit the gain. They were there less than ten minutes before scarpering back to their lines.

"They only seemed to be interested in food," the colonel reported. "They helped themselves to any they could get their hands on."

Cody asked if he could be allowed to keep the prisoner for a while.

"You know what trouble that will cause us, Cody," the colonel warned. "Why?"

Cody explained he needed the opportunity given all that had been going on. The prisoner had already shown signs of being prepared to open up to the padre.

"Father Drake?"

He made a motion towards the cabin. Cody held out his arm.

"Let's see where it goes, Colonel. Please."

"Wants to confess," Colonel Wilkes said.

He wanted none of it. He thought for a couple of seconds more.

"Do what you have to, Cody," he said. "You delayed telling me about it, alright?"

Cody thanked him and the colonel walked off muttering something about interfering padres. Meanwhile, Corporal Jones appeared in the background. He was on his own.

"Did you see those beautiful golden rain rockets they have, Captain?" he called out.

Cody realised he could now get away with talking to him about the other business and approached him.

Jones spoke first.

"Learned anything yet, Captain?"

Cody shook his head.

"And you?"

Jones replied he was gradually uncovering snippets of information, but he wasn't yet sure what they added up to. Quinn was repeating what he might have done with the snipers, generating an inner circle within the company. It seemed to get larger, but Jones himself had not yet been approached, and all the men who appeared involved so far were relative strangers to him. It was too risky to get close to them.

"And the lieutenants?" Cody asked.

Jones wasn't as sure as he had been, but it seemed to him impossible for Quinn to go on without some connivance on their behalf.

"But what does it all mean, Jones?" Cody asked. "What does he give in return?"

"I don't know, Captain," Jones said, sounding frustrated. "But our friend seems to have a hold on anyone he brings into his circle. They follow him like flies."

Cody recalled the play he had watched in the town but kept it to himself.

"Let's assume he has created some sort of lien on them," he said. "What might it comprise, and how does he bring it about?"

"I can't imagine, Captain."

"Me neither, Corporal. Keep on it, but be careful."

The tall Jones saluted. Just as he left for the trenches, Cody remembered his play.

"Don't forget about Hopper," he called.

Jones replied he would send him at the first opportunity. Cody headed for where the open-air mass was due to be held. He intended to pull the padre aside straight afterwards.

The mass had taken much longer than usual. The padre's sermon seemed to have a lot to cover, no doubt spurred on after the pilfering of his wine, and that he had had to dilute it with water.

"I need some of your time, Father," Cody said after the gathering had dispersed. "Can we walk for a while?"

The padre suggested they cross the field behind. They would be well out of hearing and less likely to be seen. Once they were fifty yards off, Cody said he needed to talk about Quinn.

"Something is indeed going on in C Company, Father, but I have yet to get to the bottom of it."

"What have you found so far, Cody?"

"Quinn is generating some sort of hold on his men. It's something that goes way beyond normal command. Something no doubt similar to what he had done with the snipers."

Father Drake looked surprised.

"What did he do with the snipers?"

Cody found it strange that the padre had not caught on. He explained how he had completely transformed their behaviour soon after he had arrived. They had become very close together and begun to lock out outsiders.

"Some kind of cult, perhaps?"

He looked alarmed. This seemed beyond him.

"That's what I wanted to discuss with you, Father," Cody said.

Realising that he had fallen on the perfect way to attract the padre's attention, he discussed the play he had seen in town as it had been explained to him. Father Drake thought the story sounded familiar, something he might have seen in his younger days.

"An avaricious noble who takes over a community and enslaves his parishioners with a system of indulgences," Cody said.

"Ah, yes, that's it," Father Drake said, even citing the name of the play. "I saw it in French, in fact. The noble had an odd way of atoning for his feeling of guilt."

"Well, Father?"

"Better to be sure."

For a while, they continued walking in silence.

"You can find out more?" Father Drake eventually asked.

As they turned around to head back, Cody promised he would keep him informed.

"And what about your prisoner?"

"I have spoken to the colonel," Cody said. "He's allowing me slack, but wants nothing to do with it."

"So?"

"I think you should speak to him. But not yet."

"I'm on call, Captain, but remember that I might not be able to tell you everything," Father Drake said, before heading off for a round of the trenches to follow up on his sermon.

Cody went straight to see the prisoner.

"I asked to speak to the priest," Hauptmann Gerlich said.

"That depends, Hauptmann."

"Don't think for one minute I will tell you anything, Captain."

The prisoner stared at him disdainfully. He obviously felt that he had won the first point over talking to the padre. He intended to maintain his act of superiority.

Cody amused himself with the sudden thought of the similarities between the prisoner and Quinn. They appeared to be men of similar arrogance. Even Gerlich's facial expressions sometimes reflected Quinn's, particularly when he sneered. It gave him an idea. In dealing with the prisoner, he would imagine that he was speaking to Quinn. By working on him, he might even discover a way into Quinn's own mind. He had nothing to lose and perhaps plenty to gain.

He wondered the extent to which Hauptmann Gerlich himself might have been involved with his side's behaviour during its occupation of the town. He attempted to provoke his reaction. He recounted what he had heard there, the executions, the theft of materials and belongings, what happened to some women, and the destruction of precious orchards.

Hauptmann Gerlich said nothing. He even looked away.

"Of people you lined up and shot!" Cody said, keeping his voice subdued.

The prisoner wasn't about to fall for the bait.

"You should be proud of yourself," Cody said. "This town will never recover from what you have done to it. Women will never forget their shame. Children will grow up to discover the inexplicable things that happened to their parents. And you sit there with your pretence of innocence, your revolting arrogance and feeling of superiority."

He saw that he was still getting nowhere.

"I am glad that you are the first of your race that I have had the displeasure to speak to!"

Cody regretted it almost at once. It had sounded stupid and had given away his inexperience. The prisoner continued to look around, giving the impression that he was bored.

Cody got up. He would leave his prisoner to stew a little more on his own. Eventually, the man had to react.

Just as he was closing the door behind him, the prisoner called out.

"You English…"

Cody went back inside.

"British!"

"If you prefer, Captain!" the prisoner said. "You *British* are despicable. You are scum. You're cultureless and ignorant, pretentious snobs and drunkards. You plunder your colonies and send them to fight your wars. The workers in your towns and cities fester in slums. It's not for nothing that Marx, Engels, Dickens, and so many others found themselves grotesquely inspired by what they saw in your revolting country."

Cody did his best to conceal his satisfaction. He had single-handedly driven the prisoner off balance.

"You know nothing about us, Hauptmann," he taunted.

"I went to university there."

Cody smiled. He had been right.

"To Cambridge," Gerlich went on. "In the small villages and farming communities all around, people were only just surviving. They were well meaning, but ignorant. Worn away by alcohol, even worse than here. You will find no such contrast in our fatherland. Everyone is proud there and well-educated. Bismarck saw to that."

Cody didn't know where to take it. He knew nothing about Germany. He had always vaguely imagined it to be a never-never land inundated with Teutonic bombazine and Biedermeier, forests, castles, ultra-modern turbine halls, and a dominant officer class in charge. It was hardly material for an argument, but at least he had opened up a wound.

He tried once more to place Quinn in the prisoner's seat and said the first thing that came to his mind.

"Hauptmann," he said, "I know nothing about your country. I don't want to. I have seen how you behave in others."

He leaned towards the prisoner.

"You are not civilised as you pretend to be, Hauptman. You are savages, gorgons, men-beasts. You are machines only able to march to drumbeat."

The prisoner shot up, intending to land Cody a blow. Hardy stirred outside.

"How dare you!" Gerlich said, on the verge of failing to hold himself back.

His face was red, almost as much as the colonel's. Cody had never sparked such fury in anyone before. But despite the fun of it, he realised it was over. He called for Hardy to enter.

"Captain," the prisoner said. "You have no idea of what we are capable. You will soon change your mind."

"Take him to brigade," Cody ordered as he emerged from the cabin.

The prisoner just stood there.

"I will speak to the padre."

Cody told Hardy to stay put and went to see Colonel Wilkes.

"Well?"

Cody explained how he had managed to get to the wrong side of the prisoner. If nothing else, he had been destabilised enough for the right person to exploit the opportunity.

"I trust you don't do the same to your dear missus!" said the colonel.

It seemed rich, coming from him.

"Well, he's still asking for the padre," said Cody.

Hopper was waiting for him outside.

"You wanted something, Captain," he announced.

Cody led him back to his tent and handed over his copy of the play.

"Read it when you have time, Corporal," he said. "Tell me what happens in the end."

That night, before settling in, Cody looked across towards the front where both sides were intermittently sending up flares along miles of front. He noticed some of Jones' golden ones. Everyone was nervous.

He reflected on the interrogation. Even though amateurish and unproductive, it had given him pleasure to have so infuriated his prisoner. Hauptmann Gerlich's standing in for Quinn had given him a strange feeling of power. He would do better at the next opportunity.

He thought for a while more. The prisoner seemed to have let on that something was about to happen. Hopefully, Cody had prepared ground for progress. He would fetch the padre in the morning.

18

"Well, Father?"

The padre appeared disturbed by what he had just heard.

"You mentioned knowing a priest from the cathedral, Cody?"

Explaining no more, the padre requested that Cody enquire about any thefts they might have had.

"From the cathedral, Father?"

The padre nodded. Cody understood he should leave straight away in order to allow resumption of the interrogation. So as not to have to confront the colonel again, he asked the major for permission and a horse.

"Checking up on the prisoner's statement, sir," he said, without giving details.

He arrived just as it was getting light. The place looked morose. There was hardly anyone out in the streets. The resumed quiet at the front made the town doubly haunting. Rows of shattered houses and buildings seemed to serve for nothing. A dog crossed the road in front of him, a rare sight indeed, and it was starved. The bar from where the old man had once appeared had since been completely flattened. They had started to clear the streets nearby, but it didn't stop Cody repeatedly having to negotiate rubble strewn in his path.

He made his way to the cathedral, tied his horse to a bent iron railing just in front, and found the small door open. Inside, an old lady was making vast clouds of dust with her sweeping, without appearing to notice or care. Keeping his hand close to his mouth, Cody approached her and she stopped. With a few appropriate gestures, he described the priest and asked if he was to be found. The old lady disappeared, defiantly carrying her broom with her. After a few minutes of silence, Cody sat down in a pew and wondered what the prisoner had said.

The pew he had chosen was on the right of the central aisle. It occurred to him he always seemed to head for that side when he entered a church, or any large space for that matter, instinctively following an anti-clockwise motion. Sometimes he would even head as far right as possible, describing the widest circle he could. He wondered why. Were there lessons to be learned? Perhaps, as intelligence officer, he should catalogue enemy movements in order to detect such trends.

The silence lasted. He felt secure. The atmosphere reminded him of his father's own, much smaller, church. There was something very special and reassuring about places of worship, and even more so cathedrals, refuges from anarchy.

He became distracted by a lone side chapel nearby, across the aisle to his left. It was tiny, closely surrounded with stone, a refuge within a refuge.

The woman finally returned.

"*Il arrive, Monsieur! Il arrive!*"

She resumed her maniacal sweeping of the central aisle. Cody decided they gave her the task just to keep her busy. He pulled out his handkerchief and kept it firmly pressed against his face and half-closed his eyes. In front, a young boy in a cassock appeared and started lighting candles, presumably for the first mass of the day. Cody remembered volunteering the same for his father, when his elder brothers didn't get in first in order to have the rest of the morning free.

Five minutes later, the priest arrived. Recognising Cody once he dropped his handkerchief, he walked up to him with open arms. They shook hands and went to the front of the cathedral in order to escape the dust. The look on his face seemed to show what he thought of the old woman. He confirmed he was getting ready to celebrate mass.

Cody came straight to the point and asked him if anything had been stolen from the cathedral. The priest looked surprised.

"*D'où est-ce que vous auriez entendu cela?*" he asked.

Cody told him about the prisoner, an officer. The priest hesitated.

"Tell me," Cody said.

The priest was making it quite clear he didn't care to talk about it.

"For the sake of your parishioners, Father."

It was pretty feeble, but the priest's reluctance to say anything was incredulous. He made an excuse about wanting to stay neutral. Then he muttered something about Cody's father perhaps being a mitigating factor, but he felt uneasy.

"*Mon Père, s'il vous plaît!*"

The priest stared at him in a manner that almost copied Hauptmann Gerlich's expression earlier on. The irony was not lost on Cody.

Suddenly, the priest appeared to have reconsidered. No doubt he wanted to have done with it in time for his mass.

"*Des soldats anglais, Monsieur.*"

This was the last thing Cody expected. The priest hesitated before following on.

"*Il y avait un officier en charge, Monsieur. Il possédait une flasque.*"

The priest had evidently been afraid of retributions. Cody knew he needed to convince his friend that he could be counted on. He struck on the idea of telling him he was an intelligence officer. The priest would confuse that with the military police.

"*Un gendarme?*"

"*En quelque sorte, Mon Père.*"

The priest glanced at Cody's cuffs and opened up, although it still might have had more to do with getting back to work than moral duty. He described watching the theft take place and reporting it to the Germans when they retook the town.

Cody understood everything that he said. He asked him to describe in detail what had happened.

It had been British soldiers, five of them, the priest explained. He had reason to suspect they were still in the area and that's why he was afraid. Then he repeated the presence of the officer. He had seen him with his own eyes. He was definitely in charge.

Cody asked what they took. The priest led him over to the small side chapel that Cody had been looking at.

"*Nous en sommes spécialement fiers de ceci,*" he said.

Cody noticed that there were no candlesticks on the altar. The priest confirmed he saw the men helping themselves to the two candlesticks, as well as a small religious painting on the back wall.

"*Chandeliers?*" Cody asked.

"*En or, Monsieur! En or!*" the priest said.

When he described with his hands the distinctively flared collars of the candlesticks, Cody's uneasiness turned to horror. He wanted not to believe it. Knowing where this was heading, he asked the priest to describe the officer. First came the height, and then, inevitably, the blond hair.

"*Jeune,*" the priest said. "*Peut-être vingt-cinq ans.*"

After he mimicked the officer's sneer, there was no doubt at all. Cody couldn't escape the truth.

"*Et les autres? Est-ce qu'ils semblaient étranges?*"

"*En effet, Monsieur. Ils me semblaient tous bien étranges. Et l'officier ne s'arrêtait pas de renifler sa flasque.*"

As the priest described the painting, Cody was visualising Kate in front of the candlesticks on their mantelpiece at home. He felt unwell. He discreetly propped himself on the stone balustrade.

The priest's wandering distracted him. Cody sensed he was hesitating, but wanted to say more.

"*Quoi d'autre?*" he asked.

He repeated it twice more before the priest stuttered his answer. In the background, the first parishioners were arriving and taking their places. The priest became almost inaudible, trying to hide what he was saying. He whispered that, after the incident, all the men had left to guard the main door, except for the officer and one other.

"*Et puis?*"

The priest replied that the officer had removed his tunic and shirt, and the man who had remained had used a whip to flay him.

"*Quoi? Un fouet?*"

It had gone on for some time, the priest whispered, expelling any possibility that he had misread what was taking place. The officer had cried in pain. The echoes had filled the entire cathedral. The priest had been terrified of being spotted. In the end, after some minor first aid, the officer put his clothes back on and they took the whip away with them.

This sounded so bizarre that Cody asked him to restate what he had said. Once the priest had finished, there was no doubt in his mind that he had heard it correctly. Cody was dumbfounded. He could think of nothing else than to place his hands on the priest's shoulders in sympathy.

"*Merci, mon Père.*"

The priest was by now becoming more agitated than ever. Hoping that he would understand, Cody asked him to trust him and tell no-one. He should leave the matter to himself.

There was still quite a lot of mist when Cody rode back. In a field to his right, he could make out the shapes of two workhorses, similar to Shires, something like Percherons from what he could tell, although it was a bit far east for them. They appeared to have their bridles on. He assumed a farmer had begun to retrieve his battle-scarred field despite the risk of unexploded ordnance. He was bound to get stopped for it.

Cody stayed put for a while to take a better look, wishing he had a camera. Lying on the ground by a tree was what looked like an old cider press in pretty poor condition. He wondered why it had not been hauled away by the occupying troops. Perhaps it had been abandoned by them. Beside it lay a rusted bicycle, looking remarkably like Bucephalus. He imagined Kate and Deborah at his side in Panama hats, giggling at how he had looked perched on top of it.

The front remained deathly silent. From a pond nearby, he could hear bullfrogs. A woodpecker broke out in a rare tree just behind him. Spring, of sorts, wasn't so far away.

When he spotted two dead carcases lying just next to the pond, and what looked like a uniform splattered in mud, Cody forgot Kate and Deborah and moved on. The deceptively idyllic scene had concealed nasty realities. His mind went back to Quinn. It had always struck him how many people hid part of their true selves. He thought of himself, always trying to be likeable and able to impress others, hiding from view his weaker or more childish side. He reminded himself how he always felt drained the more he talked about himself. But this was small fare. What Quinn seemed to conceal was very peculiar indeed.

He forced his horse into a canter. He fumbled around in his mind to decide what to do with what he now knew. Quinn, and what had to be his snipers, appeared to have become engaged in theft and satanic rituals. It explained the whip in Quinn's wardrobe. Kate had been the unwitting receiver of stolen goods that Cody himself had seen and touched. It was all too much. Cody could not possibly tell anyone. All it could serve for would be to stoke his growing revulsion towards Quinn.

He wondered about the painting. Giving it to Kate, as well as the candlesticks, might have made her suspicious. Quinn must have held on to it or disposed of it otherwise. If Cody ever tracked it down to expose the affair, Quinn could always bring up the candlesticks. Being a receiver was condemned by the law.

Cody was cornered. He thought about his vastly adjusted image of the man he had long believed he had already sized up. This could only remain between them. He would have to lie to the padre, the very man, had he been a Catholic himself, to whom he would have had to confess. None of it bore thinking about.

He found the padre stoking his pipe replenished from his leather tobacco pouch that had softened with age. He was some distance from the hut, which still had the lone sentry in front of it who had replaced Hardy.

"I found out nothing," he lied.

Father Drake then confirmed that the prisoner knew British soldiers had stolen from the cathedral.

"Did he have any descriptions of them?" asked Cody.

The padre replied not, and Cody hid his relief. No mention of blond hair or a tall officer. No reference to furtive looks. The secret remained his for the time being.

"But I have to report it," the padre said.

"Let me deal with this, Father," Cody said. "Colonel Wilkes won't be able to do anything with the little information we have. I'll keep enquiring."

Father Drake reluctantly acquiesced and went off to attend to other matters. Cody wondered if he would eventually go into town himself to enquire. It wouldn't surprise him, as he already needed altar wine. Cody's lie would be exposed.

He went into the hut and sat opposite the prisoner. He was in a dilemma. It wasn't as if he could ask Kate to send him the candlesticks to hand them in. Quinn had cornered them both. There was only one conclusion. The way out was to find something else with which to corner Quinn.

Hauptmann Gerlich sensed Cody was troubled.

"You need me more than ever, Captain."

"Why is that, Hauptmann?"

"What I know could be a matter of your life or death."

"Hardly!"

"You have no idea, Captain," Gerlich said, arrogantly laughing.

"I don't steal from churches," Cody said. "Me, of all people."

"Oh, that!"

The prisoner must have been referring to something else. But it was too late. The man had long stuck in Cody's craw. He had to be escorted to brigade as soon as possible.

Cody left the hut and went to the colonel, reporting what the prisoner had just said when his arrogance had once again got the better of him. Something was undoubtedly about to happen. Someone more skilled needed to get their teeth into it.

Colonel Wilkes rushed a message to brigade, requesting a car and accompanying officer as soon as possible.

"By the way, Cody," he asked. "What was that business in town?"

Cody was already walking away. He pretended he hadn't heard.

Two hours later, Cody was standing outside the hut in the pouring rain. After haughtily bidding him goodbye, Hauptmann Gerlich was escorted to the waiting car. Cody knew he was glad to be getting attention from higher quarters. He had already caused the battalion to be about to be placed on alert. It was merely a matter of time before someone from brigade turned up looking for a tall officer with blond hair.

As soon as the car had left, Cody went to the firing line to distract his mind and seek out his crew.

Schemensky as usual was the first to speak. It had to have been he among those who had accompanied Quinn to the cathedral.

"As quiet as ever, Captain," Schemensky reported.

Cody warned them to keep a careful eye on what terrain they could see beyond the enemy line.

The weather had become useless for planes or balloons. That night, Colonel Wilkes, hesitating over the alert, sent out three patrols with instructions to observe but not engage. They were particularly to look out for any fresh gaps in the enemy wire. As had become usual, it was abundant, and would have to be in part cleared to allow any advance.

They came back with nothing. The alert was maintained all the same.

*

After several days, it was decided to hold back on the patrols. Using so many men out at night depleted the battalion's ability to defend itself in case of surprise.

Word came through that they were soon to be relieved. Every one of the 10th Battalion's officers and NCOs became convinced that something would break out before that happened. The weather, meanwhile, remained atrocious. The enemy showed no signs of being up to anything right up to the end.

Cody thought of the irony of the fact that the rest period the battalion was about to get was needed solely to compensate for the *angst* of the last few days. He recalled that the mere presence of Napoleon on a battlefield had been considered representing the equivalent of fifty thousand troops. Perhaps Hauptmann Gerlich had been very clever indeed.

Father Drake had continued to say nothing about the cathedral affair, and Cody had kept him at bay by being seen to go into town two more times, the first of them to fetch him wine.

"*Est-ce vous l'avez encore trouvé, mon Capitaine?*" the priest had nervously asked on each occasion.

Cody knew that such a task would not be difficult, especially if during interrogation the suspected officer was discovered to have telltale marks on his back. To buy time, he replied he believed that the officer in question had been killed.

The danger that Quinn might turn up in town was inadvertently eased by the colonel. Battalion effectives had been so depleted that it was decided temporally to reduce it from four companies to three. Because he was the junior commander, Quinn was assigned to command a burial party to clear up the corpses that hadn't been tended to for weeks.

In the muddy shell holes that littered the front out of the enemy's view, Quinn's ad hoc team found the remains of many who had obviously died waiting for rescue. Some of them appeared to have drowned in mud. Others, remaining alive with nothing to do, had spent their time pathetically tidying up and organising the surrounding ground they could reach with their arms, as if they were preparing their own battlefield gardens, and eventually their places to die. One of them had been pulled out in his last throes. When he had been carried back to behind the trenches, and his stretcher left on the ground waiting dispersal, he had sat up and continued the same with his remaining arm. Cody himself had watched the poor man, become insane, and his face now fully bandaged, pathetically preparing his own little territory.

"As close to a basket case as I've seen for a while, Captain," had said Hardy, who had been standing beside him as shocked as he.

Quinn's temporary posting earned him sympathy and respect from his colleagues, Cody included. For all that he might have been up to, not even Quinn deserved to have to deal with such dreadful business. He, and the men under his command, had coughed and retched their guts out for the entire time they were at it. Most of the corpses were those of men they had known. Father Drake had accompanied them. He knew full well that in the aftermath he would be called upon.

"They should never give that work to active troops," he said to Cody after the first day. "It's a specialist's work, and then some."

When the order to pull out finally came, Cody rushed to see the transport officer.

"Which route are we taking?"

The transport officer hadn't yet decided. He knew it would have to be a route march because of the number of troops, distance, and state of the roads. There were two choices, one of which passed north of the town. The transport bringing up the relief brigade would use that route because the town was still too encumbered with obstacles.

"I suggest we march the same route," said Cody.

"Why, Captain?"

"The enemy has only recently been in the town. They could have planted spies."

The transport officer replied Cody had a point. Cody was proud of what he had achieved. The tall Quinn, so recognisable in any troop movement, would remain out of sight.

"But what if we split the routes?" the transport officer then said, worrying about overloading the smaller road. "Anyone secretly counting wouldn't get their numbers right."

"The entire brigade's pulling out," Cody reminded him, becoming frustrated. "Whether it's half, the troops or double that, it still represents important numbers. Anyone knowing their job would recognise insignia, and it would be simple to come to the right conclusion."

"You're perfectly right, Cody."

Cody felt relieved. It had been close.

The transport officer ran into Cody a day later, after the order of march had been relayed to the company commanders, and the final relief was about to take place. So far nothing had been said of them, and the orders had stood.

"Good thing you convinced me over the northern road," he said.

"Why's that?"

"I've been under pressure," came the reply.

"Colonel Wilkes?"

"Captain Quinn, in fact. He was quite insistent."

"Did he say why?"

"Nothing at all. Sounded like a personal matter."

Cody realised he had saved the town one more time. If Jones' information had any truth to it, this time there might have been more than a small group of snipers helping themselves to the cathedral, and no doubt other places besides.

As he walked away, a thought came to him. He turned around.

"Did you mention my name, by any chance?" he called.

The transport officer looked surprised.

"Why yes, now that you mention it, Cody. Shouldn't I have?"

Cody headed for his tent, wondering what next lay in store for him. Quinn would certainly have registered his interference. The key question was whether it had made him suspicious.

19

Caroline Quinn, an attractive and energetic woman three years older than her much taller husband, hadn't been sure what to think. When her husband had last arrived on leave, and promptly disappeared for a day, for some trivial reason, she had gone upstairs to look through his bags.

Beneath his clothes in the first bag, and wrapped up in plenty of old French newspapers, she had discovered a fine religious painting of the Madonna and Child. Out of curiosity, she had rifled a little more and come across two gold candlesticks which were rather heavy. Assuming that these items were presents for her, she didn't search anymore and, with a certain embarrassment, put each item back as she had found it.

After her husband had said nothing before leaving again for the front, and following a few days believing that the objects, therefore, had been intended for their anniversary in a few months' time, she began to have doubts. These were religious items, quite outside any interest either he or she had ever had. She had first imagined a country overtaken by war, with its denizens desperate to sell off any belongings at all in order to raise money. Her husband might have simply taken advantage of the opportunity provided by a landlord or someone he knew. But these were objects that would more likely have come from a church. What on earth was going on?

Over the following weeks, she became increasingly suspicious. Supposing these were objects of plunder? Had he had others in the rest of his baggage? Had he been doing this before?

None of it made sense. The farm was doing extremely well. The estate was in the black by miles. The old general would not be around for much longer, and their inheritance promised to be significant. She began to suspect a dark side to her husband that she had yet to uncover. They had been married for a couple of years after a rapid romance. During all that time, she had seen him as the most charming and loving man she had ever met. It didn't seem possible that there could exist anything sinister about him at all. She felt more flummoxed than she had ever been.

She thought about her husband's relationship with his father. Before the war came along, it was the only thing in his life that she knew of that had been remotely testy. Given the old man's rather eccentric and forceful character, it wasn't as though she had ever expected a perfect calm, but to go from there to say that it might have left scars on his son was quite beyond anything she could ever imagine. No, her husband was the perfect man. He had always behaved impeccably towards her, and never talked badly about his father. The simple fact was that there was absolutely nothing to suspect. There had to be an acceptable explanation.

She had accordingly let the issue leave her mind.

Three weeks later, she had spent an informal half-an-hour with one of the five widows she had employed in one go. She had so far been more than satisfied with them all. They had continued to work hard, and she had even congratulated herself for taking them on.

In the course of their conversation, Caroline Quinn had asked about the children. According to the teacher at the village school, whom she knew well and often ran into in the village, those who attended school had mostly generated favourable reports regarding their behaviour and dedication. The widow had thanked Mrs Quinn once again for what she had done for them. They were all happy and together in their tied cottages, and the trauma of the tragedy that had beset them had been eased.

"We were so relieved when you changed your mind, Madam," she had said.

"But I never changed my mind!" had said Caroline Quinn. "What do you mean?"

The woman had described their first visit to the estate and being abruptly sent away by Quinn without even seeing him.

"It makes little sense," had said Caroline Quinn. "We were in great need of hands."

It was then that she had learned about the link between her husband and the five widows. She was devastated.

The two of them had been sitting opposite each other at a table, and she put her hands on the woman's.

"I can't understand," Caroline Quinn had said, plainly distressed. "I'm so sorry that this happened to you."

"It won't get us into trouble, Madam? I mean talking about it?"

"Of course not! This remains just between us."

That conversation had troubled Caroline Quinn for days. The only plausible explanation she could imagine was that her husband had been trying to hide something. She knew that if she ever talked to him about it, she would jeopardise the situation of the five widows. She had to keep the secret to herself.

She needed to put her mind at rest. She had to find out what had happened that had led to the death of the five men. How had the women known who to come to for employment so far away from where they had lived? Someone had to have helped them, tipped them off where to go. It could only have been someone from her husband's battalion.

She had gone back to the woman and learned about Corporal Jones and where he lived. But she had no idea how to exploit the information, as any enquiry she made would risk getting back to her husband. For the time being she had been stuck.

But the matter wouldn't go away. It was too serious. She had done something she would never have dreamed of before. She would go looking for any correspondence her husband might have hidden away.

She had looked high and low. His desk and cupboards yielded nothing. The bookshelves and books in them nothing either. The old suitcases and boxes in the attic only contained items from school and college. She tested the bottoms of cupboards in all the rooms. She looked for cavities in the walls. It all came to naught and, being who she was, that had made her even more suspicious.

In the middle of the night, she woke up with an idea. Her husband could be hiding things next door, in her father-in-law's half of the house. It could only be accessed by the front and back entrances. The old man was permanently there, but his cook and servant would take their weekly afternoon off that day. She had a few hours left to figure out how to conduct a search behind his back.

The old man was predictably delighted to see her. She was always so busy handling the estate on her own, but somehow often found the time to come around.

"Come in, Caroline! Come in!"

From the very first, he had taken to her attractive features, blond hair, and determined nature. He especially adored her company.

"Would you like something to drink, Caroline?"

She thought it wise not to appear pressed. In his present state, he was more likely to forget about the incident that way. She gladly accepted, and he slowly headed to the steps in the scullery leading to the cellar.

"No, wait a minute. I'll do it. What should I fetch?"

"Whatever you like, my dear. Take your time."

While he sat down on a chair in the scullery, she opened the narrow door, switched on the light, and clung onto the rope as she descended the steep and worn steps leading down to the musty cellar. There were cobwebs everywhere. She had to keep brushing them off her face and out of her hair. This was a world that she had only once ever visited, the first time she had met her father-in-law-to-be.

After two right-hand turns to the bottom of the steps, she arrived at a long and narrow room that housed racks of wine on both sides. There had to be a logic to the arrangement of the bottles. The labels were neatly facing upwards.

She saw geographical patterns. Halfway along, she found a Monbazillac that interrupted her thinking. It seemed perfect for the time of day.

Her father-in-law called down from the top of the steps.

"Have you found anything, my dear?"

"Not yet! I'm still looking!"

After tiptoeing over and placing the bottle on the last step, she looked around. There were two other rooms further along. Judging from the long sprouts coming around the corner of the first, someone must have forgotten potatoes there. She crept over and went inside. Besides several buckets of old potatoes, the shelves were covered in dust and old tools. There was nothing else to arouse interest.

The third room had a door. She gently tried to open it, but it was locked. The keyhole looked new. There were no keys hanging anywhere on the walls. If her husband was using this room, he would most likely have kept the key their side of the house.

She walked back and grabbed the bottle and headed back up the steps. Her father-in-law was still waiting for her at the top. He was delighted with her choice. As he slowly got up, she opened a drawer for the corkscrew.

"In that case, let's finish it, father!"

It was early afternoon. The servants would be back at six. If she was clever enough, the wine would put him to sleep. She therefore suggested that they drink in the most comfortable chairs in the long drawing room that led out to the glorious, shared garden at the back of the house.

"Tell me about the Second Boer War, father," she cleverly asked. "Why was it such a near disaster?"

The old general was quickly asleep. Leaving the front door ajar, Caroline Quinn hurried back to their half of the house. She went straight to her husband's study and rifled his desk once again. In the top drawer, she found several loose keys. In a rectangular leather box, she found two together, a large and small one. These looked more likely. Scooping the others up just in case, she would try them first.

On her way in, she went back to check on her father-in-law and then made for the cellar. She opened the box in front of the closed door. The larger key worked perfectly.

There was a light switch just inside. This room had been taken care of. Along the long and clean wooden shelves covered in newspaper were tidily arranged pieces of silver, a few decorative plates, quite a lot of jewellery in biscuit tins, a ceremonial sword and a couple of dark-brown glass bottles labelled with a chemical name she had never heard of, with a hip flask next to them. A series of framed drawings were leaning against the back wall. They looked odd. Several appeared as though they represented mediaeval torture scenes. But as she moved to take a closer look without touching them, something caught the corner of her eye. Closest to the door, as if it was the latest item to have arrived, was the painting of the Madonna and Child.

She now knew about what her husband had been up to. She fell into a state of shock. She became dismayed by the extent of his avarice. At first she was angry, angry at him, angry above all at having been deceived. She was angry at herself for not having caught on earlier. As she stood there gazing at what she had found, her wrath focused on the deceitful way that everything could be pinned on the old general. If ever the cache were discovered, all would be put down to his eccentricities. This was so wrong.

She remembered the two candlesticks. She hadn't seen them. She went up and down each shelf twice to be certain, stopping on the way to open one bottle and inhale what was inside, but being overcome by the potent smell that hit the back of her nose until she frantically sniffed outwards. To one end, she spotted a painted container she had at first passed off as one of the larger biscuit tins. It was heavy and had a single keyhole. She instinctively tried the remaining key from the leather box. It worked.

Inside, there was a small cloth bag with diamonds, and next to it a gold bar with no markings. Resting on top there was a pile of French share certificates and a few small bundles of envelopes. The lower bundles were tied with string. A few sitting on top were loose. They had been written in the same hand and addressed to a house in the village, but there was no named recipient. The postmarks were recent, and all from the same place that meant nothing to her.

One by one she opened them up. The handwriting was difficult, but she knew what the letters added up to. They were all signed 'K'. Tears ran down her face as she read each of them before carefully folding it up again. One of them had the only piece of potentially useful information. 'K' referred to sending her three girls away and purchasing a Stellite. Caroline Quinn knew what that meant. She had a Stellite too, recommended by her husband.

She couldn't take any more risk. Her head was spinning from the combination of wine and shock, and possibly what she had just sniffed. She placed the envelopes back as she had found them and locked the box. Taking one last look, she turned off the light and closed up, crept up the steps, and was soon back in the hallway. She peeped into the drawing room to see her father-in-law still in deep sleep.

Quietly letting herself out, she returned home to place the leather box and loose keys where she had found them. The residual sweet taste in her mouth reminded her of what she had drunk with her father-in-law. It had all been too much. She went upstairs to fall asleep herself.

She was woken up by the telephone by the bed. It was her father-in-law, apologising for falling asleep and hoping that she had let herself out without a problem.

"Of course, my dear," she said, tears returning to her eyes. "Thank you so much. We must do it again soon."

She thought about the address on the envelopes. She went downstairs to check the estate book. The house was on the list, which was no great surprise, but it was marked as unoccupied. Eventually, she would have to check it out.

In her Bradshaw, she looked up the place name on the postmark. It was a small village within reasonable reach. At the last census, there were almost five hundred residents. There couldn't be many of them with three daughters, a Stellite, and a first name beginning with K. It merited a visit.

20

The 10th Battalion stood in divisional reserve, seven miles to the rear. It was a region that comprised large stretches of farmland bordered by sprawling woods that separated them from the front. For reasons that no-one understood, unusually small areas had been allocated for each of the dozen camps occupied by the division. Concentration had mysteriously become the order of the day.

Although the camp emplacements were new, the shelters inside them were far from it. When the troops had first arrived, only a cursory first look determined that the mishmash of rather poor Armstrong canvasses, Nissen huts, and Y hutments had been scrounged up to the last minute to satisfy the need. Combined with the close billeting, this seemed a recipe for unrest.

And no-one felt safe. Although high velocity guns had not yet found their mark there, the short distance from the front increasingly invited visits from hostile airplanes. Lewis guns had been deployed, mounted and permanently pointed towards the sky.

The only blessing, it seemed, was that at last the days were getting longer. Escape to outdoor activities in surrounding fields had become more assured.

The 10th battalion's camp was no different to the others. Conditions soon provoked outward signs of frustration, especially after masses of conscripts arrived on the second day. Despite the daily training exercises, and football matches that followed, after little more than a week, most of the men wanted to return to action. The campsite being recent, cable and trench parties had to be organised in order to improve facilities. Royal Engineers arrived to command teams of volunteers supplied by each of the companies, and for once men were leaping over each other in order to take part. The colonel had caught on right away and it worried him. He added to the distractions by inviting a football team from one of the other brigades. It won by six goals to nil. The humiliating score was mercifully made up for with a five-mile trek to the divisional Pierrot troupe, always a favourite, putting on its show in a large winter-proof tent.

The following morning, in the spirit of relaxation and reflection, troops were marched six miles to an abandoned trench network that had been occupied by the enemy before the summer. Everything had already become overgrown. When an officer from division arrived to describe the last action there, men spread out and sat where they could to listen. It became an occasion that many of them would remember.

No sooner had the colonel and major recovered from so many sleepless nights at the front, than they devoted themselves to the backlog of inquiries and courts martial at brigade. In the first of them, a company in the 9th had had a machine gun snaffled during an enemy raid, and it had been deemed to warrant an inquiry. There had been several instances of desertion. As far as the 10th itself was concerned, a sentry had been found asleep by Major Hickman.

"We're closing in on ourselves," said Cody to the padre, after learning what the colonel and major were up to. "We're forgetting how to prosecute a war."

He had always found all the nit-picking over contentious past deeds and events a waste of time, something Quinn had also pointed out. He would rather inquiries concentrate on more serious issues likely to come, be more proactive. Most recently, for example, there had been the poor trench layout where they had received so many losses. Both forward and support companies had been far too close to each other, and had the enemy shelling been more accurate than he had, it could have put in peril a sizeable part of the battalion. And now there was the problem of the camps.

"What about those long-range guns, Father? How soon will it be before they find us?"

Father Drake agreed. Such a plethora of investigations took them nowhere. And it seemed to him to be getting worse with time. It was merciful, thought Cody, there had so far been complete silence over misdemeanours in the town they had recently left.

"Any more on Quinn?" Father Drake asked before taking off.

Cody shook his head. Jones hadn't reported. But times had changed for Cody. Since he now found himself with little to do, at last there was the opportunity for himself to keep an eye out for Quinn. He had already caught him discretely conversing with the snipers, Schemensky in particular. It had confirmed his suspicions. He needed to find out more.

He encountered Hopper. He hadn't yet started the play, but would now have more time.

"Thank you, Lieutenant. I hope you enjoy it at the same time."

The following morning, while the battalion was engaged in musketry practice due to be followed by a route march in the afternoon, Cody spotted Quinn disappearing on his own into the woods. It was the first such occasion. It could be what he had been waiting for. He decided to investigate.

After telling Hardy that he was going for a stroll, he took the opposite direction to the edge of the camp and skirted it all the way round to the side of the wood. If he entered at this point, he would stand a chance of creeping up on Quinn.

Realising at the last minute that this might be too risky, he headed to a high point on open land behind him and hid among bushes near the summit. He pulled out his field glasses and scanned the wood. There was a clearing inside, sufficiently wide to peer into. It had reportedly been created two years before, after a friendly airplane had crash landed and caught fire. If Quinn had arranged to meet someone, it would be a likely spot.

There was no sign of movement. Cody took the risk after all and moved in. He returned down the slope and entered the wood, taking increasing care not to step on anything that would make noise. He halted every minute to listen for movement. He gradually closed in on where he thought he had located the clearing and waited.

He waited for half-an-hour but heard or saw nothing. He had doubts. Deciding that he had been wasting his time, he backtracked by the same route he had entered, aiming again for the edge of the wood near the rise.

He started walking in open country away from the wood, having skirted the rise. The hour scheduled for the route march was approaching, and the men would have lunch in camp beforehand. As he hastened, he spotted Quinn about fifty yards ahead, walking in the same direction.

Cody darted back towards the wood to reappear at the other side of the camp, in reverse to the path Quinn had taken in the first place. Just before he reached the first trees, he looked around to make sure he hadn't been spotted. Quinn was continuing onwards. Cody stood there wondering why Quinn had not simply returned by the same route. He turned to enter the wood. He remembered nothing more.

He came to. It was getting dark. He felt a nasty bruise on the back of his head. He sat up and pushed himself over to lean against a nearby pine tree. His cap was still lying on the ground where his feet had been. He felt for blood. It had already dried.

He had to get back to camp before Hardy raised the alarm. He tried to lift himself up. He felt nauseous. His head was pounding. The wound was aching. He only just made it, precariously using the tree to maintain himself upright.

He moved forward, slowly bending down to pick up his cap. He felt stiff, but just about good enough to walk. He remembered his father's joke about not worrying about dying except for feeling awfully stiff and chuckled. He decided to copy Quinn and skirt the wood back to camp, keeping well out in the open despite the dark.

No sooner had he staggered forwards than he felt hands on his shoulders. The surprise made him jump. He was thrown to the ground. He looked upwards to see three shadows, faces impossible to discern in the dim light. They kicked him all over as he lay there, feebly trying to shield himself. He couldn't muster any strength to respond. One attacker produced a length of rope. They sat him upright and tied him up. They used one end to run across his open mouth so that he could not make a noise. After they nudged him back onto his side, he thought he heard them run off in the camp's direction.

He keeled himself over. They had gone. He tried to force the rope. His saliva was out of control, completely soaking the rope against his mouth. He'd always had that problem with pipes. He couldn't help thinking about Pavlov draining digestive juices from his dogs. There was nothing to do. He couldn't move. He could only think of Pavlov. He would be there all night, salivating until he dried out. He felt the cold. They would come back. One way or another, they were bound to come back.

It was still dark. He was still on his side. A full moon was high in an almost clear sky. It had become very cold indeed. At least there was no rain or snow. He had been awoken by movement nearby. His teeth were furiously chattering, out of control, biting into the already-soaked rope. But the juices had slowed.

He could hear guns up at the front. It felt strange being warmed by such a sound. Struggling to move his head, he looked around. There was nothing. He tried to move his torso, turn himself around again, lift himself up, but couldn't. His violent chattering waned. He fell back to sleep.

He woke up again. The moon had almost dropped out of sight. His mind felt rested. He had become used to the cold. He didn't care whether his aggressors returned. He thought back to what the French priest had told him. Several men had been with Quinn at the cathedral. At the time, Quinn only had his snipers. He knew they still conversed. The conclusion was inevitable. But what about C Company? How had Quinn dared risk exposing his deeds to others? How many had he been able to rope in?

There had to be a common cause, and it had to be pilfering. In their boredom and search for excitement, even the best could be lured by peer pressure. Being presently confined to camp, they would have become desperate. And had Quinn caught on to him? Had Father Drake finally gone to Colonel Wilkes, and the priest interrogated without him knowing?

Cody thought of Kate. Did she know about where the candlesticks had come from? She must have been suspicious. And what had happened to the painting? There were too many questions. His mind raced out of control, trying to flee the confinement rendered by such a vicious circle.

A conversation with a Belgian interpreter crossed his mind. It had been the year before. The man had escaped into neutral Holland from enemy-occupied Antwerp. There had been an electrified fence. Three of their party were shot by sentries right in front of it. He and the others used a rubber-covered board to keep the live wire off their backs. It had been a close-run thing. In their desperation to flee they had discovered an entire underworld ready to help them, sinister individuals pushing boundaries that conformists like himself could never dream of. And so it was with Quinn. He and his snipers, and whomever they had taken on since, had to be part of a clique intent on undermining the battalion and everything decent, abandoning one by one the rules and codes that held it together.

Cody thought about Quinn's growing catch beyond the snipers, increasing numbers among C Company and its lieutenants. He had won influence over Talbot, Fuller, and Cragg, even the colonel and the major. Cody had thought he had known them well. He had identified with them. Most of them had been together since the beginning. How on earth had Quinn been able to go to work so soon after arriving on the scene? How far could it all go?

He thought he heard a distant stir. He stopped thinking and waited. It was nothing. He tried to figure out Quinn's corrupted mind. He pictured an outcast to the rules of civil society, someone incapable of generalisation, unable to recognise truth or find patterns between truths, incapable of responding to any guiding light. He saw a visceral mind, obsessively focused on opportunities, on individual facts, unable to thread together all before him, blindly pursuing temptations as they occurred. Cody's father had often talked about such an underworld he had to contend with in his parish.

Cody needed to provoke Quinn to expose himself for what he really was. In his present state he couldn't imagine how. He would have to observe in order to figure it out.

Another hour had passed. It was now light, and there was a heavy frost again. He thought of his girls. Not for the first time he wondered whether he would ever see them again.

Suddenly, he heard movement in the bracken nearby.

"Hello?"

It was pointless because of the rope. He couldn't see. Someone was moving towards him. He forced himself around and tried to make out the face closing in. There was too much water in his eyes. The man bent down and spoke again. It was Quinn.

"Cody, what on earth are you doing here?"

"Help me!"

His cry was unintelligible.

"By God, you're tied up!"

He worked away at the rope.

"What happened, Cody? Who did this? Hardy warned us you had gone missing."

Cody was more focused on being freed. He became frantic. It slowed Quinn down.

"Hold on, for heaven's sake, dear chap! Hold on!"

Cody was finally freed. He threw off the loosened rope. Quinn lifted him to his feet and picked up his cap.

"Who did this, Cody?"

Cody was confused. He felt less present than his mind had led him to believe.

"Who did it, Cody?" Quinn repeated.

"I don't know," Cody stammered.

Quinn of all people! This was too much. He wanted to drop to the ground again.

"You've been hit!"

Cody feebly felt his head for a second time.

"Let's get you back right away, my friend."

Quinn held him up during the arduous twenty-minute walk back to camp. He had no choice.

"Lucky I came out for an early morning stroll," Quinn said. "I guess eventually someone would have found you."

Cody still tried to marry what he was hearing with all that he had been thinking.

"Take me to my hut. Let's not get anyone else involved."

"But we have to find out what happened, Cody. You can't stand for this. The battalion can't, for heaven's sake, man!"

Cody pleaded. He was too tired, weak, and confused to take it any further. No-one noticed their arrival. The sentries at the gate were distracted examining papers belonging to a lorry delivering provisions.

Hardy spotted them on their way and ran over to help. Once they entered the hut, they lowered Cody onto his camp bed. Quinn asked if there was anything else he could do. After Cody failed to reply, he quietly left.

"What happened, Captain?" Hardy asked. "I didn't know what to do."

Five minutes later, the medical officer arrived. He summarily examined Cody's head and asked him how he was.

"I fell."

The doctor cleaned up the wound and left.

Cody woke up. There was no-one else there, and it was still light outside. He realised his wristwatch had been smashed. He got up to open the flap. Across the yard, men were assembling for a cross-country run. It had to be early afternoon.

He still felt stiff and confused. Defying his state of mind and body, he went back inside and changed into running clothes. The exercise would loosen him up. But he would need superhuman determination to be part of it.

Hardy entered and saw what was happening.

"Are you insane, Captain?"

It was rare that he expressed such emotion, but his master's behaviour was beyond him. Cody persuaded him he was fine. He stumbled out to join the runners just as they set off, looking far less able than they to face any exercise. No-one seemed to notice. It would be a five-mile course, past the point where Quinn had found him.

As he struggled along, Cody thought about his aggressors. They had to be among them. There was no way they could try again during the run, just as long as he kept up with the rest.

Quinn caught up with him when they were half-a-mile out. He must have started out late. He didn't look surprised or make any comment about his state.

"May I join you?"

Cody said nothing but smiled. He had surprised himself with his running. He thought he was doing well. Quinn's presence would make no difference. They would force themselves too much to talk. Cody was still free to process his thoughts, come to some kind of conclusion whether his companion was playing a cynical game or being genuine. Had he got Quinn totally wrong, after all?

He kept up with Quinn. As they slowed down to pass through a gate, Cody spotted his snipers ahead of them. They had shed their camouflage. He felt he ought to catch them up. His physical state held him back.

They were about three-quarters of the way, and closing in on the camp, when Cody announced he had to rest. He wasn't alone. Some disused trenches were nearby. Several runners had accidentally stepped on human remains and were causing a stir. Quinn offered to stay with him. Cody insisted he keep running. He would only be stopping for a short while. Quinn refused.

Cody had to remain cautious, keeping Quinn at arm's length for as long as possible while recovering his bearings. Quinn couldn't be trusted despite his latest performance. Cody had to remain alert. Next time might be the last.

It struck him that he was shirking his duty. He had to say something, tempt the devil, put into action a sequence of events that would end up exposing Quinn once and for all.

But what?

Quinn unintentionally came to the rescue. He handed Cody a golden opportunity.

"Do you remember anything about what happened to you last night?" he asked.

"Nothing at all, Quinn."

"Do you suspect anyone? Even the slightest suspicion?"

"I do."

Quinn had not expected that. He looked at his fellow captain. Cody swore he saw the worry in his eyes.

"Can you tell me anything?"

"Not for the moment, Quinn."

"For heaven's sake, man! I'm here to help you!"

"Give me some time, Quinn."

"Can you give me an idea?"

Cody hesitated for effect.

"The cathedral where we were shot," he said.

"What about the cathedral?"

"There have been thefts."

"Thefts?"

"It may be us."

Quinn said nothing more.

"And there were strange goings-on in the cathedral, devilish ceremonies one might say."

It would surely pour yet more fire into Quinn's mind, a metaphorical *flammenwerfer*. Cody knew he had planted a mine. It was only a matter of time before it would somehow go off. This time he had to be ready for it. He even wondered whether he should let Hardy in on his secret.

21

It was Sunday and approaching midnight. The division's return to the front had been delayed, and according to the latest rumours there would be four more days to go.

Cody was walking back to his quarters. He had been listening to the colonel's endless difficulties in meting out justice at brigade and was keen to get some sleep. The ground was white with a fresh coating of powdery snow, hopefully the last of the season, and a bitterly cold easterly wind was trying to sweep it away.

A loud crack caused him to look across the field, beyond the wire to his left. Flames started leaping from the direction of an isolated ammunition dump. He sprinted back to headquarters to raise the alarm.

Within minutes, C Company was manning the Lewis guns, and Captains Talbot and Fuller were organising a fire party to ferry water from a nearby stream. Cody, Hardy, the colonel, and major all raced ahead to get a closer look. As they approached, they could make out that a wooden cabin next to the dump had gone up. The nearby munitions were piled up in boxes and crates under canvas. They represented a considerable amount of cordite.

As they ran, the colonel asked the others what they reckoned. Cody swore that he had heard nothing that had told of enemy action. Captain Fuller joined them just as they arrived. About fifty yards behind him followed the front end of the fire party, with the men staging themselves to pass along buckets. Hardy ran back to give a hand.

The colonel decided that the ammunition should be moved. Cody ran back to fetch a party to do just that. He found men from D Company mustered and waiting for orders and ordered them to follow him.

After a frantic twenty minutes, the fire had been completely extinguished, and the ammunition moved well out of reach. The colonel, Cody, Talbot, and Fuller, stayed back to examine the charred remains, poking around in the ashes illuminated by their torches. The ground all around was free of any traces of impact, and as far as they could see, there was no obvious point of ignition.

"It was a minor explosion," said Cody.

They were preparing to return when Quinn turned up. It was C Company's turn to provide guards for the camp, but that hadn't included the dump.

"Found anything?" Quinn asked.

No-one replied. Everyone was worn out.

"Leave a couple of sentries here, Quinn," the colonel said. "Perhaps we'll find something in daylight."

"I've already doubled the sentries around the camp, Colonel," Quinn told him. "This may be that risk of sabotage we were warned about."

The colonel's face dropped.

"Warned? Sabotage?"

Cody and the others were equally surprised.

"Cody?"

Cody should have been in the know. Pointedly staring at Quinn instead of his inquisitor, Cody replied it was the first he had heard of it.

Then it dawned on him what was coming.

"Of course you do, Cody," said Quinn. "I passed it on to you last night. Rumours of enemy attempts at infiltration."

There were too many people standing around. The colonel, who had become livid, ordered Cody and Quinn to join him back at headquarters before storming off. The rest of the party continued searching the debris with their torches.

"Look!"

Talbot thought he had found where the fire had started. After a lengthy examination the rest of them agreed. It was pretty obvious once it had been spotted, but there were no traces of an oil lamp or any other device that might have been responsible, and it was too cold and damp for any combustion to have been spontaneous.

Once they reached camp, everyone dispersed, and Quinn and Cody headed for headquarters. The colonel was still agitated when they arrived. The three of them waited in strained silence for the major. He turned up with Talbot, Fuller, and Cragg, surprised at their last-minute convocation.

"Cody!" Colonel Wilkes bellowed. "What's this about a warning?"

Cody sensed a show trial coming. This was typical of the colonel's churlishness. He should have known better with all his talk of justice. Cody swore that this he had not heard of any warning.

"Go and check!" the colonel said.

Cody left them waiting. He hurried the twenty yards to his hut. Hardy wasn't there. He lit the oil lamp. His table was empty. He pulled out the papers he kept in the satchel that served as his in-tray. One by one he placed them on the table, recognising each as he went. After about a dozen items, every one of which had surfaced during the previous twenty-four hours, he fell on a typed message he did not recognise at all. He drew it closer to the lamp. It had been addressed to Quinn, no doubt because he had been the previous intelligence officer. This was it. He froze.

Without checking the origin of the message, he walked back to headquarters with it in his hand. He found them all standing there in continued silence. The colonel still looked ready to explode. Apart from Quinn, the others appeared embarrassed by the theatrics of the occasion.

"Well, Captain?"

"Captain Quinn is right," Cody announced, handing over what he had found. "I suppose I received this message yesterday."

Colonel Wilkes snatched it from his hand.

"It's addressed to you, Quinn!"

Everyone looked at Quinn. Cody knew an answer would be at the ready. He feared Quinn would somehow rope Hardy into the affair.

"I gave it to you as soon as I received it, Cody. At five past seven."

Cody did not hide his cynicism over Quinn's too perfect memory.

"It's not recorded!" the major observed, looking over the colonel's shoulder.

"That's right, Major," Quinn said. "I was here when it arrived. There was no-one else. I took it directly to Cody."

Colonel Wilkes was beside himself. He abraded Quinn for bending the rules.

"We've got two days left. I will hold an inquiry tomorrow morning. Be there, all of you."

The company commanders had found themselves surprised by the announcement of the shortened stay. Cody felt relieved that the ugly session had ended, and that Hardy had not somehow become the scapegoat.

"We're going back to the same front line," Colonel Wilkes said with no further explanation.

"Should we alert the other camps?" asked Quinn.

For a moment, the colonel looked bewildered. Then he caught on.

"We're still not wired up to brigade or anywhere else," the major reminded him. "It's still a couple of days off."

The colonel thought for a while. To a man his entourage thought that had he been paying more attention to the battalion during the last few days, communications would have already been up.

"Cody, go to all the camps to warn them. Take my horse. Make sure a message gets to division."

Cody had discretely scanned the faces of his colleagues several times while the finale had played out. He had been literally saddled with the penance of calling on eleven camps. It would take him the best part of the night and hardly render him in form for the morning's inquiry. He swore he detected the usual air of self-satisfaction on Quinn's face. The others still appeared to display embarrassment that their colleague was being hung, drawn, and quartered in front of them, and that it would be pursued again in the morning. Yet Cody didn't have any illusions.

He would pay the price. He knew full well that, thanks to the colonel's style of management, of which brigade was conveniently oblivious, he himself would end up bereft of any moral support he once had.

Ten minutes later, an alerted Hardy appeared with the colonel's horse saddled up. Cody rode off through the gate and into the night with a map of the locations of the other camps in his overcoat pocket.

It wasn't long before he realised that his venture into the open countryside could lead to a trap. The entire affair had to be a setup. Quinn had initiated an endgame, with Cody's chances of survival in the balance, and he regretted not having, at the very least, brought Hardy along for protection. His nemesis had planned his move well. All the sentries on duty were his men. Quinn's lackeys could jump on him anywhere along the miles of open countryside ahead of him.

As the lights of the camp disappeared in the background, it occurred to Cody that Quinn had been even cleverer than he had at first thought. If he got seen to on the way, the inquiry would have to be called off, and questions regarding Quinn's handling of the message would become forgotten forever.

He wondered how Quinn had arranged for the message to be sent. He had to hand it to him.

He arrived at the first camp. It belonged to the same brigade at the 10th. A sentry escorted him on foot to the battalion commander, the colonel's horse in tow. Yes, the warning had come through, but they had not seen the fire which had been masked by an intervening wood.

The second camp, assigned to a battalion belonging to one of the other brigades, had not even received the warning. Cody assumed Quinn had cultivated an ally at brigade rather than division. He kicked himself for not having examined the top of the message.

In a casual conversation with the colonel at the third camp, Cody explained why Quinn had received the message instead of himself, and what it was leading to.

"I expect it's no coincidence that you are bringing this message in person, Captain," the colonel observed.

He was from the 3rd Battalion and remembered Quinn. They warmly shook hands.

He had visited ten camps already. There was still an hour to go before daylight. Cody had become convinced that anything Quinn had planned would occur after the last camp, somewhere along the last stretch home.

The colonel's horse seemed to still be enjoying the exercise in the windy and snow-covered countryside. Cody slowed down and leaned forward to pat its neck. He had just recalled a story from the aftermath of Waterloo that had concerned the aide-de-camp of Louis Davout, the head of the defeated French army. After coming to an agreement with the Allies, Davout had pulled back from Paris to Orleans. He sent his aide-de-camp across the entire country to warn his regional commanders of the agreement signed with the Allies. The aide-de-camp knew himself to be a marked man. A lieutenant-general, he was one of around thirty individuals held responsible for the so-called Violet Conspiracy that had supposedly led to Napoleon's hundred-day return. He was on borrowed time. He could be apprehended at any moment. The punishment would be exile or death.

Cody rode up to the last camp, counting the minutes. Troops were already assembling for an early exercise. The sentries directed him to their major. It was Major Hughes.

They greeted each other as old friends. Hughes was busy preparing for the morning's event. He explained they would conduct a mock dawn attack on a strong point they had prepared the day before. Cody recounted everything that had happened and passed on the warning. The major had received the message, but not heard about the fire. He sympathised with Cody's predicament. He knew Colonel Wilkes too well. Cody stood to have a hard time of it.

"And what about that Quinn fellow?" he asked.

Tempted as he was, Cody preferred to say nothing that would give away what he really thought. It was dangerous territory, even with someone as friendly as Hughes.

"The facts will speak for themselves, Major," he assured him.

"At least we'll have other things to think about in a couple of days," the major said.

Politely declining an offer to visit the strong point, Cody thanked the major and rode off at full speed.

The wind had not abated. Cody was finally on the last leg. He had been riding for four hours since setting out, and now wondered if his horse would last, let alone himself. He recalled spotting Elizabeth Thompson's grim *Remnants of an Army*, printed in one of Kate's magazines. It was now his turn, the dry heat of the Afghan desert replaced by the equally insufferable icy wastelands of northern France.

The terrain had at last become familiar. He had several small woods to pass, a low area with a small lake which would almost certainly still be frozen over. At the very least, he should be watchful for traces in the snow.

He thought of the irony of his predicament. After three years of nothing but confusion, uncertainty, and surprises at the front, for the very first time he knew what was about to happen. He felt serene. There were only two miles to go, yet he had become resigned to never seeing his camp again.

Through the dark, he spotted the shadow of a large barn on the left side. He had passed it before. This time there was flickering light inside, filtering through the sides of the boarded windows. Normally he would have ignored it, riding past without giving a thought. He did so until he spotted what looked like remnants of footprints in the snow, coming from the direction of the camp. He pulled up and dismounted, getting out the torch from his haversack to look more closely. These were indeed footprints. There were several of them.

He knew at once they concerned his destiny. Unable to resist, he led his horse across a swath of virgin snow and tied it to a tree close to the barn. Making his way towards the large door at the near end, he listened for sounds. Once he got close, he heard voices inside. He recalled the Belgian interpreter who had escaped to Holland. Cody was about to meet his own underworld, but these would be men he knew.

The door creaked and groaned as he opened it up, brutally announcing his arrival. Standing there in the dimly lit barn were seven figures. One by one he made out the faces of four of his snipers. Schemensky stood in front. Standing just behind them was the taller figure of Quinn. Lieutenants Smalby and Cobbold were standing beside him.

"We knew you'd come," Quinn said.

Quinn inhaled from the small flask that he held in his hand. Schemensky and his band stepped aside, and Cody and Quinn walked towards each other. Cody thought he recognised the smell of the solvent from the time he had visited Quinn.

"What have I done to you, Quinn?"

Cody wanted to open up his coat and finish what he should have done at the chateau, never mind the certain retribution from those around. But Quinn was unarmed. He was wearing his tunic and had removed his belt and holster.

Schemensky ordered the others to grab Cody. Four of them, including Smalby and Cobbold, rushed forward. They knocked Cody to the ground and punched and kicked him while Quinn looked on. It all felt familiar.

Cody looked up at his old lieutenants.

"Traitors!"

It went on for minutes. Cody doubled up to protect himself. Smalby and Cobbold shouted a stream of profanities and warned him he had long had it coming. While Cody suffered the repeated blows, it struck him that these men had so readily bonded together. He felt different, he always had. It was something he shared with Kate, and would no doubt be the same for the girls. Whereas the likes of Quinn had been brought up under the imposing shadow of his father, both Cody and Kate had had distant parents, ones that had rarely shared their emotions. It had left both of them handicapped in bonding with others.

"String him up!" Quinn ordered.

The four of them roughly removed Cody's overcoat and webbing and then tore off his tunic and shirt. They bound his hands and legs, and Schemensky threw a second rope over one of the overhead crossbeams. The end of the rope was tied around Cody's chest. They hauled him up so that he was just off the ground. Placing his flask back into his pocket, Quinn picked up his whip and menacingly positioned himself behind.

Cody was past caring. As the tail of the whip landed on his bare back, he tried desperately not to scream.

"This will teach you, holy boy!" said Quinn.

"Moose, isn't it?" Smalby taunted.

They all laughed. The lashing seemed to never end. Cody stopped counting. Quinn shouted how much he hated Cody and everything he stood for, his pathetic face and stupid mind, how he would teach him a lesson for good, bring him into line with the rest of his acolytes.

"I despise your bloody pedestal, Cody!" he screamed.

The others laughed at what they perceived to be an oblique reference to Cody's short height.

The whipping went on and on. Cody had become too weak to reply. The others looked on, enjoying the spectacle of the higher officer being humiliated. Quinn passed the whip to Cobbold. Each of them took it in turn to lash Cody as viciously as they could, one strike each.

"Traitors, all of you!" Cody whimpered.

He came to. He was on the ground. The first thing he heard was the Scotsman's voice. Cody's hands and legs were still bound. He had been dragged to the side of the barn and was bleeding across his left shoulder and upper arm, on top of what might be surging from his back. His back felt on fire. He looked across to where it had all happened. He counted four figures lying there taking a rest. One other was hanging from the same beam and was being whipped in turn. Through the blood pouring across his eyes, Cody tried but failed to make out who it was. He recognised Quinn's voice from the side, egging them on. He recognised the solvent again.

Cody woke up a second time. The lamps had been extinguished. There were traces of daylight coming through the gaps next to the doors and windows. The macabre ceremony was still going on. This time, it was Quinn's turn. Cody couldn't for the life if him imagine why grown men, struggling to stay alive in war, would engage in such an evil diversion. Quinn was both crying and shouting, urging them to hurt him more and pleading with Schemensky to lift his flask to his nose. It was a disgusting sight.

The men on the ground got up. The door behind him had opened and there was a rush of cold air. Cody only just managed to twist his head to see what was happening. He saw that two of them had returned with buckets of water, complaining that they had to break the ice. Quinn was released and, stripped to the waist, everyone washed themselves, helping each other. Some of them, Quinn in particular, were badly scarred. They had a first aid bag and took it in turns to dress each other's wounds.

Once they had finished, they walked over to Cody, untied him and repeated the same, but for much longer. Cody found it impossible to accept that these were men who had just been laying into him, but he was in no position to refuse.

They left the barn together, all fully dressed. No-one said anything. Cody, almost unable to stay upright, untied his horse and, hanging onto the rein, led her alongside. His greatcoat was buttoned up enough so that no-one could see the state of his clothes underneath.

Before they came into full view of the camp, Quinn had the common sense to shout out the password earlier than usual to his nervous sentries manning the wire ahead.

The troops were having breakfast. Cody felt he had to hit the sack. He first headed for the colonel's tent to report that his mission had been completed.

The colonel wasn't there. His orderly replied he had been called to brigade on an urgent matter. Cody went to the major's tent and learned that it was all about the front. Relieved that the inquiry had been delayed, Cody announced he was exhausted and would rest for the morning.

"You do look in a bad way, Cody!" the major said.

Cody replied it had been a hard ride. He lied he had brushed a few trees on the way and fallen twice.

He asked about the inquiry.

"My guess is that with what the enemy appears to be up to we won't see one for a while," came the reply.

On his way to his hut, Cody encountered Father Drake. He had returned from leave in Dublin during the night, but his route wouldn't have taken him past the barn. The padre observed the same thing as the major.

"Get some rest, Cody."

Hardy was already there. He was no fool, but Cody insisted on his story.

"Bloody 'ell, Captain! You ain't telling me nothing!"

Cody curtly warned him that for his own safety it was better that way. Hardy knew his master well enough not to pursue the issue.

At last, he was on his bed. His back was stinging, and he felt pain all over. Hardy went off to distract himself at headquarters. As Cody started to fall asleep, he tried to imagine how he could respond to Quinn's outrage. He could not possibly admit to anyone what had happened. It was too incredulous and humiliating to talk about. It was yet another thing about Quinn that could never be revealed because of his own involvement.

Cody had arrived at the realisation that Quinn and his venal band had to be taken care of before matters went any further.

And he would have to do it alone.

First thing the next morning, the colonel summoned Cody and the company commanders. He looked grim.

"I have bad news," he announced.

It was worse than bad. There was soon to be a reorganisation of the army in order to compensate for shortages. The number of battalions per brigade would be reduced from four to three. Since the 10th Battalion was the Regiment's Benjamin, it was certain to be one of the disbanded.

"I wanted you to know before you heard rumours. Believe it or not we're copying the enemy."

He explained that most of the battalion would be distributed among the others. Some, especially the officers, could expect to change regiment.

"The final order is expected within days."

Approaching the mess, they each tried to understand what the news implied. Comrade officers who had served together for years would never see each other again.

"It was going to happen eventually," said Talbot. "At the very end, I mean."

"Why us?" said Fuller. "We're one of the best."

Cragg agreed. Surely division would see sense and choose another battalion instead. Cody reminded them that plenty of others would share the same fate. The demise was due for one in four.

They sat down, intending to continue their discussion. As the others debated over what might happen to them, Cody glanced at Quinn, who like himself was saying little. It came to him that Quinn had more to lose. It was highly unlikely that he would find himself with any of his camarilla. It would throw him back to square one.

Cody smiled to himself. This was the army's unplanned way of destroying the evil that Quinn had created. The way things presently seemed headed, by the time he recreated another elsewhere the war might even have ended.

He changed his mind. What had he been thinking of? Quinn had already done too much damage. He should not be allowed the remotest chance to even try the same elsewhere. And there had also been Kate.

The writing was on the wall was indelible. There was no time to spare. Cody had to do something about his adversary soon indeed, and whatever he did had to be permanent.

22

There was now no doubt that the enemy had begun his build-up for an attack. Aerial reports repeatedly talked of fresh troops and artillery moving into the area and, until the latest bout of bad weather, hostile airplanes were being chased away throughout the day.

The 10th Battalion was back in the trenches. Cody was concerned about forward trench E.9.1. At a mere fifty yards from the enemy, it would soon become untenable in case of sustained attack. Gas was out of the question. Artillery support was not an option either. Such a small distance would barely contain half of any defensive fire, and friendly casualties would be inevitable.

Colonel Wilkes refused outright to consider pulling back. He saw the situation as an opportunity. He even became angry when Cody tried to insist. Cody suspected Wilkes was afraid to recommend any tactical retreat to high command.

It was true that, thanks to the colonel's efforts at brigade, the front line had never been so well equipped. Among the fresh armaments that had arrived were new 6-inch Newton mortars that could wreak havoc on the opposition. Cody let the matter go and headed for his tent in the rain. He intended to pore over his maps that he had left there in the dry. Whatever the colonel said or thought, the inescapable fact was that the battalion was dangerously entrenched. If the hostile surge was large and prolonged enough, the colonel's short-sightedness could force its early demise. Only the bad weather was preventing it happening.

A bout of thunder greeted his arrival. He had already figured out that a much safer line to hold would be two hundred yards to the rear, politically almost an impossibility. He sat down to pursue his heretical line of thought. The network of communication trenches in-between could easily be rendered unusable and booby-trapped while pulling back. And once the enemy launched his attack, there would be enough time and space for the artillery, stronger than ever, to retaliate without friendly losses. It seemed so obvious.

He thought of one argument that he had not yet deployed and was certain to be already preying on the colonel's mind. A pull-back would solve the problem of the shooting gallery that existed just behind the trenches. This was an exposed line of duck boards that made up the only approach from the rear. Unable to be dug any deeper in the present conditions, it was a sniper's and machine gunner's paradise from a small segment of the enemy line. Even under defensive fire and smoke, troops could not pass during the day without being decimated. Dozens of messengers had already been lost, dropping like flies, drowning in the surrounding mud before they could be rescued. If the enemy took the expected initiative in daylight, countless reinforcements rushing to the front line would be lost before they got there.

The persistent noise of the rain on the canvas failed to distract him. When, for a moment, he turned to a larger scale map, Cody spotted an opportunity that no-one had yet seen. It was a classic situation brought about by an advance, only days earlier, further along the front, and by a neighbouring division. A line extrapolated three miles westwards from the perilous E.9.1 landed on freshly occupied ground, with enemy-held territory in-between. The outline of E.9.1 fire trench was fairly straight. If the battalion were to withdraw and allow the enemy to take it, out-of-sight artillery could provide a lethal enfilade all the way along the trench. The artillery would be able to place spotters safely in the new front line to carry out their bracketing. The side scatter of any landing shells would be only a matter of yards, ten times less than in the direction of fire. Any enemy concentration would be rapidly obliterated without friendly losses. The plan would constitute a perfect trap.

Cody knew he had to be doubly sure of his facts, ready for the inevitable challenges from all those who had not had his idea, not to mention yet more vicious attacks over his defeatism. Explaining none of this to Hardy, the pair of them took off on foot to scout the area he had in mind for the artillery.

They got there in two hours. The rain hadn't stopped. Cody regretted not bringing along the artillery liaison officer, but that would have alerted the colonel too soon. With his long experience, he felt he knew enough to predict what would be said.

The ground turned out to be uneven, but it was sturdy and accessible by gravelled roads that led to the rear. The area comprised fields and a smatter of corpses that had yet to be cleared and stank atrociously.

"Look, Captain!"

Behind some trees, Hardy had spotted an extraordinarily large, damaged, and deserted chateau built in a sort of filigree style. It was too obvious a target for enemy artillery to be useful.

"This had to have been an estate," Cody observed.

It must have been a small paradise in its time. The thought oddly provided comfort for what was going through his mind.

The reserve camps there were further back, well out of sight. The nearest trenches that constituted the latest front line were five minutes' march further north on slightly higher ground. The artillery could install itself at night just before needed, well out of the enemy's sight. With the present weather preventing flying, the surprise could be total.

Cody continued to walk around with Hardy, looking for possible snags.

"Can you tell me what this is about, Captain?" Hardy said, adjusting the rifle slung on his shoulder, muzzle pointed downwards. "Perhaps I can help you."

"Not yet, Hardy. Too secret. Just keep a lookout."

On their way back, Cody tried hard to anticipate the questions that would come his way. Having such a volatile colonel had long taught him to be several steps ahead, and having to deal with another division added layers to the challenge. The new firing line would still find itself in the same grid reference as the old one. If the change of naming rules was adhered to, the trench would carry the same identification as its predecessor. To avoid any accident, everyone would have to be doubly reminded to provide map revision dates with their target coordinates. But that had become normal procedure. There could be no objection.

It irked him it looked dangerously simple. He was damned if he could spot a flaw. He decided to sit on his plan overnight to be surer, a tactic he had so often resorted to in his dealings with the colonel. After a bout of sleep, however interrupted, his mind would wake up with a different take. It would serve to secure his mind.

They got back just before dusk, soaked to the bone despite their capes, and exhausted by all the mud that had returned because of the recent thaw. The air had stilled, and even the drizzling had stopped.

No sooner had they reached the tent than they heard the gas alarm coming from the direction of B Company in reserve. Two men came running towards them waving their arms.

"Yellow Cross! Artillery!"

One of them admitted he had been smoking and had sounded the alarm when he had tasted burning in his mouth.

The shelling went on. There was nothing to do but gear up and sit it out with the tent flaps firmly closed.

As they listened, Hardy counted. He always did that.

"A hundred and five, Captain!"

Cody couldn't imagine how Hardy could claim to have heard all the impacts, but he let him have his say.

Once things had quietened and the all-clear given, they emerged to see medical orderlies rushing into the camp area just in front of the shooting gallery. Lieutenant Finlay passed by and reported that B Company had not properly washed down with their Vermorels. Several men were suffering from blisters after sitting on chairs. Hardy couldn't resist a rare chuckle.

"Bloody fools!" said Cody.

Captain Fuller was not the best at training his men, and he would most likely blame them instead. It was at times like this that they paid the price.

Cody headed for the front line to check on his snipers. The line was being held by Captain Talbot. Things were calmer on the way, and he had removed his gas mask long before he arrived.

Schemensky, who, like everyone else, seemed to have put aside the barn affair, was quick to explain that their predicament was absurd.

"Best steel loopholes we've ever had, Captain. But we're too bloody close to use them!"

The enemy gunsights were notoriously accurate.

Three hours before dawn, enemy storm troops invaded the left flank of the line. From his tent, Cody heard bugle calls and rushed outside to see the flare go up. His very first thought was that his enfilade plan had been too late. He ran over to headquarters. The colonel was precipitously calling brigade for reinforcements. With the full moon in place, and daylight on the way, the timing couldn't have been worse for the gallery.

Within an hour, lorries started ferrying in additional troops. As the reinforcements shuffled along the shooting gallery duckboards, scores of men were picked off and fell into the mud. Cody and the others watched in dismay from their position outside headquarters. It had become too light to do anything. There was no chance of rescue of those who had been incapacitated. The walking survivors were ordered to keep moving forward as fast as they could. The front had to be held at all costs.

The enemy opened up with gas to the rear again, this time with Blue Cross, aiming at the shooting gallery itself in order to increase the confusion. Everyone had box respirators and put on their masks, but some got caught out in the confusion and fell off the duckboards. First aid teams were rushing over with bicarbonate of soda to receive the injured. The drier ground on the near side of the shooting gallery became littered with men suffering burning throats, chests, and noses. Space began running out for the survivors to pass. It was becoming the Armageddon that Hauptmann Gerlich had predicted.

After two hours, all had changed. It became clear that the colonel's reaction had worked, and the attack been successfully held off. Reinforcements were continuing to cross the shooting gallery, but the lull up front permitted the going to become slower, and spaces allowed between the men. The enemy snipers seemed to have been done away with by the mortars. A contact aeroplane, the first of the day, flew over and dropped a red smoke bomb well behind the enemy line. The artillery followed up for ten minutes.

Cody went forward with the colonel to get a first-hand report of what had happened. Captain Talbot explained hostile troops had infiltrated the right side of the front trench and bombed their way along, but a Lewis gun team had pinned them down and, at the end, a direct overland attack by a platoon from D Company had put paid to them for good. The colonel went around congratulating both companies.

"They've tasted blood, Colonel," Talbot warned. "They'll be back."

The second attack came four hours later, despite the daylight. Jumping off from so close a distance meant that once again they were almost on top of A Company before sufficient fire power could be brought upon them. It was another close-run thing. The Newton mortars had once again churned away. Talbot had sent up his second SOS rocket, but there was nothing artillery could do but to send ordnance behind the enemy trenches in order to dissuade reinforcements. It must have eventually caused the attack to peter out.

Cody had stayed up front and joined in the sniping. He left his team in order to scout along the firing line. He saw how messy the fighting had been. Fresh bodies were lying everywhere.

When he returned to his men, they were sitting along the fire step talking. Above them, Schemensky was keeping an eye out with a periscope.

"We were picking them off like flies, Captain," the Scotsman reported from the far end.

Between them, they reckoned they had had well over thirty kills. Such a score had rarely happened in such a short time. Cody climbed up to steal a brief glance through one of the loopholes. The number of bodies out there was considerable. In places, they were lying on top of each other.

"We were alright once the enemy was on the move," said Schemensky, still at work with his periscope. "Their storm troopers masked their snipers."

But Cody saw that if the enemy ever found a way of getting enough troops moved forward in the first place, the firing line would stand no chance. He couldn't hold off any longer. No-one distracted him on his way back through the communication trenches and across the gallery. He had time to think. The enemy would certainly be tempted to try again, and after nightfall. Passing by his tent to fetch his maps, he headed straight for headquarters.

The reaction he got took him by surprise. Colonel Wilkes was at once excited and called for the major. The day's experience had shifted his mind. During the discussion that ensued, he asked Cody to repeat what he had said about being careful when calling for artillery.

Cody and the colonel followed up by riding together to brigade. They planned to request for the artillery move straight after dusk. For the first time, Cody felt the colonel was prepared to stand up to the brigadier.

"What do you think, Cody?" asked the colonel, looking upwards as they rode side by side.

It was cloudier than before and had got colder.

"Precipitation on the way," warned Cody.

That would keep enemy airplanes grounded.

It continued to go well after they arrived. Brigadier Lightfoot congratulated Cody and promptly admonished his own team for not having spotted the opportunity. He promised to clear the operation with division right away. There were adequate guns only two miles back, and so the move up could be rapid. Since the only need for accuracy concerned lateral alignment, that part could be sufficiently figured out in advance. The guns could be raining ordnance down on the enemy within an hour of moving out.

"Pull back from E.9.1 at twenty-two hundred," he ordered.

He had taken to speaking French time in anticipation of the forthcoming change everyone had been warned about.

On their way back, rain started tumbling down again. When they arrived, Colonel Wilkes kept Cody with him and summoned the major and four commanders. Talbot, Fuller, and Cragg turned up within minutes.

"Where's Quinn?"

Major Hickman reminded him he was due back from a forty-eight-hour leave during the day. The colonel pressed on, informing them he would personally fill Quinn in as soon as he arrived. Cody couldn't help wondering what Quinn had been doing.

Before they dispersed, a message from brigade confirmed that the operation had been agreed to and squared with the neighbouring division. Companies A and B were to deal with blocking off unneeded trenches. Quinn's C Company would man the old firing line, fitting it out with dummies and, at Z hour, pull-back through the remaining communication trench and across the shooting gallery to the new line. It would leapfrog over D Company, which would remain just forward of the shooting gallery until the last minute. Headquarters and everything around it would pack up and pull back straight after dusk.

Talbot suggested mining everything they abandoned, including the filled-in communication trenches. Concerned about having enough mines left in reserve, the colonel replied that the job would have to be covered by the artillery. Turning to Cody, he addressed the question of maps. The expected action could get out of hand at any point and become far greater and long-lasting than anyone had expected. Everything had to be prepared by the book. He wanted the new deployment to be covered with an appropriate trench map. There was little time to do it.

"How well do you know those people?" he asked Cody.

Cody simply replied that he had to take off right away. The nearest field unit was Barker's, and it was an hour's drive away. He requested a staff car. The colonel called brigade for one to be sent over right away.

The car turned up twenty minutes later. Cody was already waiting in his cape and cap. After providing directions to the driver and asking him to hurry, he settled down in order to mark the revisions on his map. The sliding around in the mud did not help, and the constant scuffing of the rear seat against his back gave him a distracting pain.

To Cody's relief, the field unit turned out to be easy to find despite the pouring rain. It occupied an isolated industrial building on the edge of the town where it was located, not far from a large camp. It was surrounded by a tall chain fence topped by looped wire. Sentries stood in front of a purpose-built wooden gate which fronted a small yard wide enough for a couple of lorries.

Cody had the driver pull up on the opposite side of the road. After sprinting across, he presented his credentials and orders to the sentries and asked for Lieutenant Barker.

After a couple of minutes, a delighted Barker emerged from the building in a cape and recognised Cody at once. He came through the gate and told the driver to stay parked where he was before leading Cody back to the building.

They entered a small meeting room near the entrance, removed their capes, and hung them to dry out. As Barker looked over Cody's orders, Cody apologised for not having provided any warning and explained that the changes were urgent. When Barker got up and left the office, Cody assumed he was clearing matters with his superior.

Barker soon returned.

"Follow me!"

Barker led him into the factory area at the back. He beckoned for a draughtsman sitting in a windowed cubicle to join them. Cody laid out his map on a table next to a printing machine and explained his changes.

"Why the urgency, Captain?" Barker enquired.

Cody hesitated. He noticed Barker wasn't stuttering this time.

"It helps if we understand," said Barker. "Don't forget that everything we do here is top secret as well."

Cody explained his plan and when it would take place. Barker went out to get a copy of the larger scale map and examined the two together.

"A good one," he said. "But are you sure the enemy hasn't already foreseen it?"

Cody told him that, independent of the weather, the enemy had already attempted to take the front line at significant cost, but still had plenty of reinforcements. There was little likelihood that he would back down now.

"They're invested."

Barker and the draughtsman went over Cody's changes one last time, considering what they now knew. It would be a standard one-pass correction to the existing map. Barker went off with the draughtsman to look up their stock in the adjoining warehouse. They returned and declared that Cody was in luck. Trench E.9.1 was there in blue, but had not been identified, so that must have been done on the last overprinting.

"How many, Captain?" he asked.

Cody replied fifty would do.

"You'll get me shot!"

He explained that the time required would be all preparation. Printing such a small quantity would be rapid. The draughtsman promised his modifications within the hour and disappeared. Barker made sure that a printing machine be held at the ready and for pre-printed maps to be brought to the pressroom. The maps would be overprinted in black to differentiate between blue used for friendly lines and red for the enemy's.

"The French use the colours the other way round," he pointed out in passing. "Expect us to follow suit fairly soon."

Cody winced at the thought of yet another change. Even simple ones always brought unforeseen confusion.

To pass the time, Barker invited Cody to a tour. The factory area was quite small, and the equipment, although old, only recently installed. Barker explained the lithographic process and how the limestones were prepared. There were several women among the operators, and all of them had been brought over from home. The warehouse in the next room was much larger, sprawling with racks of different maps waiting to be overprinted.

There was still time to go once they had finished. Barker invited Cody into a small canteen for tea. Two women in smocks were already there, whispering between themselves over a shared cigarette.

"How's my brother-in-law?" Barker asked.

After the last time, Cody had least expected such a question. Barker was equally surprised when Cody told him that Quinn had taken over his command.

"You mean…?"

They both realised that it was neither the place nor time to go any further.

"I shouldn't say this to you, Captain," Barker warned without hesitating, "but be careful of that man."

Cody asked him why.

"I've always had serious problems with him. He has strange ways indeed."

"What kind?"

Barker sighed, almost looking annoyed with himself for having raised the subject.

"It's complicated. *He's* complicated. He's a deeply troubled man. I don't know why my sister still thinks the world of him."

Cody came out with the details behind the five-widow story and asked Barker if that surprised him.

"It's completely in character."

Cody thanked him for being so candid.

A woman came to the open door to report that they would be ready in five minutes.

"We should make our way," said Barker.

Cody couldn't resist a last question.

"Just how complicated is your brother-in-law, Barker?" he asked. "How far does it go?"

"Take great care, Captain," Barker repeated.

He said nothing more. The look on his face was enough.

They started the print run. Pointing to the notation marked next to the new fire trench, Cody complained that getting used to the new nomenclature had been difficult.

"Wait until the colours change!" said Barker.

As the female operator fed the sheets into the machine, Cody asked more about the process. It was going through his mind that he could easily persuade Kate to part with some of her new money for such a machine, or rather a simpler version of it. Perhaps it would be a way of keeping them together, a working couple reproducing her art. He could get her to draw directly onto a lithographic stone. He already had the vision of converting their garden shed into a workshop. If it could still rotate with all that weight, all the better!

"What a brilliant idea!" said Barker, appearing to take the revolving idea seriously.

The draughtsman, who had re-joined them and noticed Cody's interest, saw that the operator was nearing the end of the run and about to shut the machine down. He took an extra sheet from the pallet, handed it to her, and asked her to hold off. Leaning over the stone, he worked on it a little.

"This is something we have to do whenever we have some unwanted ink on a print."

The next copy that came off had no trench markings at all. The draughtsman smiled as he passed it over.

"And we can do it the other way around, put ink back," he said.

Cody saw how easy it was. He asked if he could keep the sheet. Barker went to fetch a cardboard tube to keep it separate.

"You helped yourself, Captain," he warned. "Do you understand?"

Throughout the journey back, Cody couldn't help thinking about what Barker had said about his brother-in-law. It gave him the satisfaction of having not got Quinn properly measured earlier than he had, but it raised questions how far he might go in the future. What had already happened had been bad enough.

The rain was still pelting down. The driver had to slow down even more than before.

"Just get me home safe," Cody said after the driver had apologised.

As the staff car slid from side to side and his back got worse, he tried to study his original map. He thought about the companies and their rotas. C Company would be on the firing line that night, and for at least one more after it. It would be Quinn himself who would have to call in the artillery, and a direct telephone line was being laid down for that purpose.

Cody glanced towards the carton tube bouncing around next to him. It didn't take long for him to have a thought. He tried to shake it off his mind, but it wouldn't go away.

The driver announced their imminent arrival. Looking outside and trying to figure out how the driver had imagined that he was closing in on the camp in the blinding rain, Cody tried again to forget what had come to his mind. It was too evil. He tried desperately to push it away.

They finally pulled up close to the shooting gallery and Cody told the driver to return to brigade. Cody reached headquarters, having barely kept the maps dry under his cape. Keeping the carton tube to himself, he handed over the maps to the major for their distribution.

"Wait until the last minute, Major," he warned. "The ink still needs to dry fully."

Colonel Wilkes called him over. He wanted to see for himself where Cody had planned for the artillery to be sighted. They would be joined there by the brigadier and the artillery captain, as well as a liaison officer from the other division. Men would already be there, staking out the gun positions.

They took horses. On the road leading to the position, they were overtaken by the brigadier's staff car spraying up mud, but the rain soon washed them down.

They arrived ten minutes later. The artillery captain then went off to assure himself that each of the planned gun positions was correct. Twelve guns were expected. He made sure that the ground had been adequately levelled and markings properly aligned.

"By God, this better work, gentlemen!" said the brigadier, glancing at both Cody and the colonel, everyone keen to get out of the rain.

"This is almost too good to be true, Cody!" the colonel whispered as they continued to walk around. "Why hasn't the enemy caught onto this?"

The brigadier, alongside them, said nothing. Cody looked up. There was no chance of any planes for a while. It was indeed going far too well.

*

Cody woke up just after two o'clock. He had slept well, albeit for only a couple of hours. It was the first time for a while that he hadn't been woken up by a nightmare. He sat up and looked over at the roll lying on his worktable next to the oil lamp. He thought of Quinn, up there on the new front line, about to face an enemy brutally determined to get matters right one last time.

Did he really need to do anything to make sure that Quinn would be done for? He thought of the men, many of them once his own. Had they really deserved to become collateral in a private feud? Yet these were men who had deserted him. They counted Smalby, Cobbold, and untold others. They and the snipers had too readily gone over to a criminal madman. They had condemned themselves. There was only one man he needed to save, and that was Corporal Jones.

He thought about his father, the church, and all that he had ever been taught. It had been in direct contradiction to the evil presently trespassing his mind. How could things ever be reconciled?

It was too late. He was committed. He could have tried to expose Quinn for who he really was, but he would have failed. He would never have been believed. He would have been accused of resentment and jealousy. He had no choice. It was for the army's sake.

Quinn was certain to have gone to the firing line with his new map. Cody knew that side of him too well. He got up and lit the lamp. Removing the map from its tube, he opened it up and laid it flat on the table. He placed weights at each corner, one of them his revolver. He got out his fountain pen, poured a little black ink into an ashtray and then some water to dilute it down. Holding a proper copy in his left hand for style, he wrote in the trench name as carefully as he could. But instead of writing where he should have, he placed it next to the old trench, the trench only fifty yards from the enemy.

The paper was only slowly absorbent, so he used his blotter. After gently blowing the ink in order to ensure that it wouldn't set off, he rolled the map up, put it under his cape, and emerged from his tent.

He crossed over to the nearest avenue in order to head for the firing line. It was still raining. With no moon to help, he found his way from memory. The trenches leading off had already been abandoned and destroyed. All along there was deathly quiet, but he knew men were there.

He arrived in front of Quinn's tiny headquarters. The rain had subsided. Quinn wasn't there. Pulling aside the gas curtain, he soon spotted Quinn's copy of the map. He had done nothing to conceal it. Cody unrolled the one he had brought and folded it in the same way. Then he made the substitution.

As he forged his way on to the snipers for the last time, he thought about what he had just done. Supposing the enemy didn't attack after all? Supposing Quinn had a crisis of conscience and taken his map to the rear. Supposing he somehow caught on that his map differed from the rest?

Cody greeted the snipers. They greeted him back. He wondered what they were really thinking.

"Good luck!" he said.

As usual, Schemensky was the first to speak. He was rubbing his hands.

"Thank you, Captain. You think it'll be tonight?"

"I'm certain."

After ceremoniously shaking hands with each of them, Cody made his way back to headquarters. At least the mud in the trenches was passable this time.

He found the colonel squaring matters with Quinn. He had just asked to have two patrols out at the critical time instead of one. Cody noticed the colonel was about to open up his trench map. At all costs, Quinn shouldn't see it. He had to act fast.

"Who will lead them?" Cody asked.

It was an expected question. The intelligence officer, for one, would want to be certain that the best men had been chosen.

"I was thinking of Smalby," Quinn said.

Cody pictured the man who had beaten him up.

"How about Corporal Jones for the second," he said.

Quinn wasn't about to argue in front of the colonel.

"Excellent choice, Cody," he said before walking off.

Cody breathed a sigh of relief. Colonel Wilkes had forgotten about the map. It would make Quinn more reliant upon his own when the time came. He called out while Quinn was still within earshot.

"Send me Jones as soon as he returns."

It would be normal for him to ask for a first-hand report at such a delicate time and, given the situation, Quinn was bound to prefer to have sent a man of lower rank than one of his lieutenants.

Jones could yet be saved.

23

It hadn't taken long for Caroline Quinn to locate the Stellite. She drew up in front of the Cody cottage and knocked on the front door.

Kate opened. She was wearing a smock and her hands were covered in paint.

"Please excuse me," she said.

"My husband paints as well," announced Caroline Quinn.

Kate immediately sensed that this woman was a bit too sure of herself.

"Can I help you?"

Caroline Quinn introduced herself and asked to come in. Kate realised who she was. She hadn't expected her to look so attractive. She noticed the identical black car parked behind her own. It made her uneasy.

"A Stellite too!" was all she could say.

"May I come in?" Caroline Quinn repeated.

Kate stood aside and closed the door behind her. Caroline Quinn listened for the sound of the girls and then remembered that there had been mention of sending them away.

"I think you know who I am…"

"Kate. Call me Kate."

"Ah, yes, of course. Kate."

"Our husbands are serving together," said Kate.

"I know."

They looked at each other in silence. Caroline Quinn broke the ice.

"Can I see what you're working on, Kate?"

"You won't like it, Caroline!"

"You'd be surprised!"

Kate reluctantly led her into her studio. There was newspaper all over the floor. Caroline Quinn immediately fixed her eyes on the easel standing before her.

"I think one calls them flagellants, doesn't one?"

Caroline Quinn hadn't forgotten the drawings in the cellar. She made her protest by raising her nose a little and turning away. Kate, become irritated, led her into the sitting room in order to get her away. The very first thing Caroline Quinn noticed was the pair of candlesticks on the mantelpiece.

"I know very well where those came from, Kate," she announced.

She strode across and picked one up. Kate, taken unawares, immediately thought she intended to hit her. She rushed over to pick up the second one. They began to struggle. Caroline Quinn let out a scream. Kate thought she had gone insane. She managed to lift her candlestick up in the air and bring it down on Caroline Quinn's head. All went quiet as Caroline Quinn collapsed onto the stone floor. Kate looked at her in shock. The edge of the collar had gone straight through her skull and blood was already flooding the floor. Kate rushed over to pull away a small carpet in time.

As soon as it was dark, Kate quietly opened the front door and looked around outside. She had her coat and gloves on. It was cold but dry. Everywhere was quiet, and the moon was momentarily obscured by clouds. She opened the front gate and went back inside to drag Caroline Quinn's corpse to her car. Caroline Quinn's boot was empty except for two petrol cans. Kate gathered the body up and forced it inside, pushing it further in by forcing the boot door. She returned to close the front door and gate before reversing Caroline Quinn's Stellite and pulling out into the road.

She was risking nothing. Even if she were to be spotted and recognised, it would be too dark for anyone to read her number plate. She knew where to go, and Caroline Quinn would have brought enough petrol to do the journey.

There was no-one on the dark road. Five miles before she reached the Quinn estate, she turned off into an isolated country lane. Just as her map had shown, a small stream ran alongside the road. The bank became steeper. After a mile, she stopped the car, pulled Caroline Quinn's body out and placed it in the driving seat, removing the blood-stained sack covering her head, and pushed the car over the bank.

She had to get as far away as possible without being seen. She had brought a luminescent compass and set out across the field behind. After about five miles, she threw away the sack and, after another two, her gloves. It was only ten o'clock, and she had plenty of time.

She reached the port town before sunup. The first train would be in just over an hour. She decided to stroll along the front so as not to be seen near the station any longer than necessary.

One more time she went through all that she had done back at the cottage. Both candlesticks had been cleaned several times with bleach, as had the floor. She had wiped all the walls just in case, as well as anything Caroline Quinn had touched during her brief visit. She had put her smock on the fire before taking a hot bath, after which she had vacuumed the floors and disposed of the dust in the garden. She couldn't think of anything she had forgotten or overlooked.

By the time she had alighted at the local railway station, she had decided what to do to make the final stretch home. She didn't want to be seen on public transport or walking along the road.

"Good morning, Mrs Cody! On one of your walks again?"

It was the farmer who supplied the village's milk, the husband of her friend. He always made an early morning delivery to the depot in town, and he had seen her before on one of her long early morning outings.

"I've run out of energy and forgotten my gloves," said Kate, delighted to see him. "Can I borrow a ride?"

"Never thought I'd ever see you beat, Mrs Cody! Hop on!"

As they took off together, she jokingly pleaded with him never to tell anyone, especially his wife.

Back at the cottage, the smell of bleach hit her as soon as she opened the front door. She threw open the windows and the back door and proceeded to wash down several times with soap and water. Now that it had become daylight, she inspected the two candlesticks to make sure she had done a good job. She had thought of getting rid of them as well before remembering who had given them to her.

As her mind continued to calm down, she thought more and more about what had happened. It had not been her fault, only a ghastly misunderstanding that had caused her to defend herself. She thought of Deborah. If it ever came to the worst, she would ask her father for help. That's what friends were for.

That evening, she had calmed down enough to think about her husband. He had become so dull, doleful, and effete. What little had remained of his beguile had frittered away since the war. She believed that he had lost interest in her. Besides, he didn't have a penny to support her. There was no getting away from it. Her future lay with Quinn. They had so much more in common, and his lovemaking was infinitely more rewarding. He had already showed what he had felt about Caroline. He had instantly taken to the girls, openly regretting that he had no children himself.

And now she had become pregnant. It might even have added to her reaction to Caroline Quinn. Her life with her languid husband was finished for good. The taller and more handsome and exciting Quinn had swept her away. She couldn't wait to tell him the good news.

24

There were still several hours to go before daylight. At battalion headquarters, everyone quietly waited. Major Hickman returned from his rounds, and although he had nothing to report, no-one doubted for one minute that action was on its way.

Colonel Wilkes, on his own at his desk to one side, looked tired and dejected, whiling away the time thinking of the imminent disappearance of his battalion.

"We must make this count," was all he could say.

Everyone resolvedly agreed.

Quinn had both patrols out as planned. The artillery had reported many hours before that it was in position, and the direct telephone line proved to be working. For the umpteenth time, Cody looked at his broken wristwatch. Why had he continued to wear it? Time had always sought to bedevil him. It reminded him of the chime mechanism on his father's church, constantly losing minutes, being visited repeatedly by the costly maintenance man who took weeks to come, only to fail to solve the problem once and for all. He recalled the occasion, soon after the battalion's arrival and deployment in Flanders, when he had been blown off his feet by a shell. It had resulted in his first wound stripe. Once he had regained consciousness, he had seen the bodies of his men all around him. No-one had stirred. He couldn't hear anything. The clock on the nearby church had showed six. He assumed they had been lying there for twelve hours. It had only been minutes.

A runner arrived from the trenches. There was nothing to report. Fortunately, it was dark. Had he been shot on his way across the gallery he would have been sacrificed for nothing. The telegram and letter his family got would never have told the truth.

One hour later, a second runner brought the same message. The colonel, sorely wishing he could take the major's place, asked him to return and gauge things for himself. Delighted to be distracted, the major donned his overcoat, gas mask, and helmet, and headed off. Cody knew he would spend all the time there he could, once again engaging with the troops and recognising faces along the way. Without the heavy responsibilities of his superior officer, the major could afford to be more relaxed, even at times like this. He also kept a thick diary, something no-one else had time to do. Even if nothing were to break out that night, another visit to the trenches would fill a few more lines.

One hour later, the major returned. For once he had been brief.

"Patrols still out," he reported.

The extended quiet made them increasingly suspicious. There was always something to pay attention to, even on the most uneventful nights.

The telegraph suddenly broke into chatter and startled them all. It confirmed that the other battalions were experiencing nothing either. In the various headquarters along the front, minds had become aligned, and eyes and ears pointed towards the abyss ahead. One or two patrols further along on either side were reported to have already returned empty.

Cody asked the major if he knew who was leading Quinn's patrols.

"Lieutenant Smalby and Corporal Jones," came the reply.

Cody was relieved at hearing Jones' name. At least something was working to plan.

Twenty minutes later, everything changed. The telegraph jumped into action just as a third runner appeared with news from Quinn. Both patrols had returned. There was considerable movement behind the enemy firing line.

It was time to extract Jones. Cody passed the runner a handwritten note reminding Quinn to send Jones for debriefing right away. The colonel, who had been woken up, stood up and walked over.

"Well?"

They waited ten more minutes before the first hostile mortar shell exploded, soon followed by two more.

"Call it!" ordered the colonel.

An orderly let off the rocket just as Jones' exhausted blackened face appeared in the dark.

*

Quinn didn't need to be told. He immediately gave the order for the pull-back and his men were fast to react. Leaving the dummies behind, they hurriedly shuffled into the only remaining communication trench. There were explosions and sounds of ricocheting all around them. Quinn stood there at the corner, encouraging his men to move faster. He looked over to Schemensky who was still on the fire step reloading in record time. The others would do the same further down the line. These were his real heroes.

Since the communication trench had already been blocked off towards the rear, one by one the fleers climbed out and silently ran across open ground and through the gallery, stripped of all the paraphernalia likely to slow them down or create any noise. Minutes later, the first of them was sliding onto the fire steps of the new trench E.9.1. Mortar and Lewis gun teams were already in place and at the ready. Everyone hunkered down and waited for the rest of their colleagues.

By the time Quinn and the snipers arrived, back at the trench they had abandoned the assault was in full swing. The enemy appeared to be using all he had. Trench mortars, bombs, what sounded like rifle grenades, and now a fair dose of whiz-bangs and longer-range guns were going off at will.

"I can't believe they'd use the heavier stuff so close to their own line," said Schemensky who had sided up to Quinn with the rest of the snipers as soon as they had arrived.

"That's how they are," said Quinn, as if he really knew.

As they held their heads close to the trench wall, the massive waste of effort up ahead gave everyone a good feeling. They had got out just in time.

Quinn looked at Schemensky. Both had been thinking that the colonel had left it a little fine.

"Are you sure it wasn't our intelligence officer?" Schemensky asked. "It was *his* plan."

Quinn sniggered. He didn't think Cody was capable of it.

The bombardment abruptly ended. With their heads still down, none of them could see what was going on, but they could smell the cordite. The first wave of infantry had to be arriving. Several of Quinn's men stood up to look.

A minute later, the flashes all along the line proved that the trench was being turned. Quinn could imagine what was now going through the enemy's mind as his dummies were being torn apart in fury. Any minute now would come their big surprise. He revelled in the power at his fingertips. Lieutenant Finlay, who was nearby, asked if they could open fire. He was not alone in thinking that the enemy had to remain pinned down before he got new ideas.

Quinn gave the order. Every single arm let loose. Even the orderlies joined in. Once again, the new mortars seemed to do an excellent job.

Quinn leaned against the side of the trench with one hand on his receiver and the other holding his map. Schemensky was up on the firing ledge with a periscope, giving a blow-by-blow account of the little he could make out in the dark. Hostile troops appeared to be still pouring into the old fire trench.

Quinn decided it was time. He lifted the receiver and gave his call sign, glancing at his map one last time.

"Open fire on E.9.1!" he shouted. "Repeat, E.9.1!"

The surrounding men looked across, startled by how much he sounded excited.

There was absolute silence from the other end. For one frightening second, Quinn feared that the line had been cut. He repeated his message.

"Captain," came the reply, sounding inappropriately calm. "That's your own position."

Quinn was taken aback. He pulled the map towards him and shouted for Schemensky to bend down to shine his torch. No, he had been right.

"E.9.1!" he bellowed into the mouthpiece.

"Captain," came the reply. "We're not aligned on E.9.1."

Quinn started to shake. His company was in danger. The guns had to open fire. How could this be?

"*I* was responsible for the new referencing system!" he said. "If I tell you E.9.1, I damn well know what I mean!"

"But Captain…"

"Get your guns aligned for heaven's sake man, or you will have the blood of an entire company on your hands!" Quinn screamed.

It was only a minor adjustment made on the hoof. The guns opened up in sequence for the spotters to do their business.

Everyone realised they had become the target. The first flashes blinded them. The ground shook as they had never experienced before. The hail of shrapnel did the rest.

The survivors of C Company deserted their posts. Quinn, dazed and confused, drew his revolver and shouted for them to stay in place, but almost everyone ignored him. Within minutes, only the lieutenants, Cody's snipers, and a few diehards who had been among the earlier adherents to Quinn's cabal, were left. E.9.1, and almost everyone else left inside it, had ceased to exist.

Jones had been waiting outside headquarters, but no-one had yet called him in. As soon as the explosions began much closer than expected, he rushed inside and requested to be allowed to re-join his unit.

"Go!" the major said.

Cody caught on too late to call him back, but Jones didn't get as far as the trenches. Too many men were escaping in the opposite direction. He tried in vain to force his way through.

Finally, it appeared that the last of the fleeing survivors had dispersed. The entrance to the trenches was now his. He rushed to the first corner and made out the lone, tall and unmistakable shadow of Quinn swaggering towards him. Quinn was about to keel over. Jones ran forward to grab him. He felt his captain's smouldering uniform, but not his arm on the other side. Quinn continued to stagger towards headquarters with the equally tall Jones propping him up. Between the explosions behind them, Jones heard nothing but screams and cries for help.

"The Company! Schemensky!" Quinn said.

He was almost unintelligible.

They were all lined up outside headquarters, leaving only the telegraph operator at his post inside. Father Drake and the medical officer had joined them, fully prepared for the order to evacuate. They stood there mesmerised. The macabre scene before them was telling them little except that a dreadful mistake had occurred. The colonel and major remained as speechless as any. The friendly shells kept landing on the wrong trench, and too close for comfort. Behind, the enemy had become totally silent.

"Colonel, we have to warn Artillery," Cody said.

Colonel Wilkes looked to be in a trance.

"Colonel!"

"Yes, yes," he said, almost unable to take his eyes off the nearby inferno.

Cody rushed inside and picked up the telephone.

"We told him!" the captain on the other end wailed after shouting orders to men around him. "We told him!"

Within seconds, the shooting had ceased. It seemed like an eternity while the guns were being realigned. Cody re-joined the others as they pointlessly looked through their field glasses for enemy movement. There were no flares or explosions to help them.

"Please God!" the colonel said. "Please God!"

The padre, who had dropped his bags on the ground, looked as though he was reciting a prayer to himself. The medical officer had run forward to attend to the wounded arrivals. The artillery resumed. Explosions at last took place further back where they should have. Everyone glanced at each other in the dark. Their relief was palpable.

Colonel Wilkes, finally restored to normal, ordered the reserve companies forward. As the men ran into the trenches, illuminated by the light from the explosions ahead of them, two tall figures could be made out approaching them. It was Jones and Quinn.

Everyone rushed forward to assist. Despite his terrible state, Quinn was still trying to swagger in Jones' arms. He looked pathetic. Cody instinctively retreated into the headquarters hut behind him, refusing to believe that Quinn had survived.

Breaking free from Jones, Quinn stumbled past the others and staggered inside, leaning against the doorpost to keep himself upright. The oil lamp just below him told all. His face was completely blackened. His uniform was partly missing and smoking in several places. His right arm had been blown off just below the shoulder, leaving behind shreds of his tunic. His eyes were fixed on Cody.

Cody became distracted by something in Quinn's remaining hand, crushed against the revolver he was grasping. It looked like a smouldering remnant of his map. Quinn stood there for two or three long seconds before collapsing forwards, narrowly missing the telegraph desk on his way down. Jones rushed in to catch him, but was too late. The medical officer arrived right behind him, pushed him aside, and knelt.

He looked up at Cody.

"He's gone."

As the others moved in to pick Quinn up, Cody leaned over and removed what remained in Quinn's hand. Behind him, the others were staring at Quinn's back. It had become completely exposed.

"He's been lashed!" the major said.

"Get him out of here!" said the colonel.

No-one searched to explain what had happened. The inquiry would come later.

*

The second bombardment had been such a success that the remaining companies could follow through with little effort. The front found itself pushed back half-a-mile further than the original E.9.1.

Two hours after daylight, once the new status quo had been consolidated, the congratulations flooded in. Colonel Wilkes put an end all his woes and joined the euphoria.

"Perhaps they'll now think twice," he told everyone.

He turned to Cody who stood among his euphoric entourage.

"You'll get a mention for this, Captain. And I wouldn't be surprised a DSO and promotion."

*

Before the day was out, Cody learned he was lined up to become major. He would be joining another battalion, yet to be specified. There was talk of Ireland.

He thought of Kate. He wanted to get a message back to her. Perhaps she would now be less ashamed of him wearing his uniform at home. Perhaps this too would help to keep them together.

His mind turned to the candlesticks. Should he tell her about Quinn? There was no point making a tricky situation worse. Kate had never mentioned Quinn. She would eventually find out. With luck, her grieving would be done with before his next leave.

He thought of Barker. His father-in-law's entire inheritance would go to his sister. They would never know that they had him to thank.

He thought about Deborah. Would she ever suspect anything if she found out about Quinn's death? Would she say something?

He thought about Corporal Jones. The good man had been saved but would never know that it was due to him.

Finally, he thought of his girls. They were all he wanted to live for.

Father Drake walked into the tent. He had an unopened bottle of altar wine, and for once two decent glasses.

"I heard the good news."

He added he must be looking forward to being gazetted.

"Napoleon used to decorate his men on the battlefield," Cody said.

He told him about the possibility of Ireland. The padre laughed.

"God help us! A *faux* Fenian. I'll warn them!"

Cody beckoned him to sit down. Pushing aside the bottle for a while, they talked about all the casualties from the night before. Half of C Company had ceased to exist. The snipers had gone.

They talked about the battalion. It was due to leave the front line that night and march back to the railhead to be disbanded.

"We'll make it a memorable march," said Cody.

Not once did either of them mention Quinn. It was as if he had never existed. As the padre opened the tent door, Quinn's body was being ferried past. He looked back at Cody.

"*Qualis vita, finis ita,*" he said.

Once the padre had left, Cody stared at the unopened bottle. He slid it in front of him and hesitated. How he would have liked to have shared the truth. War brought people so close to and far from each other at the same time.

He went outside. The front had become silent. Men were still carrying stretchers up from the trenches, but their charges were mangled corpses. Working parties were putting back into shape the network so badly damaged by Quinn's order.

Corporal Hopper turned up. He returned the play.

"I'm glad you survived," Cody said.

Hopper recounted what he had read.

"Not my kind of thing, Captain," he admitted in passing.

"I'm sorry about that. Tell me what happens."

"The *seigneur* dies."

Cody said that he didn't remember that from what he had seen, but by then everything had confused him.

"You're right, Captain," Hopper said. "It's obscure. It takes place off-scene, as if no-one isn't absolutely certain that it had happened."

"How does he die?"

"Fell on his sword, so they say."

"Why?"

"Well, Captain, first there is a hint that it might not have been suicide after all. But the townspeople decide among themselves that it is the convenient version to hold to."

"And?"

"It's a matter of atonement for what he has done."

He handed over the play and took off, looking relieved that he was done with it.

Jones walked past and saluted. Hardy arrived. He had a newspaper under his arm.

"I want to stay with you, Captain!"

They went back inside together, opened the bottle and poured themselves a full glass before sitting down.

"Nice glasses!" remarked Hardy.

"I'll see what I can do," said Cody.

Hardy thanked him and read his paper. As Cody slowly sipped away, he summed up the situation to himself. He felt no remorse. He had done the right thing for the world and stopped the gangrene. Home life had been rescued, and the battalion allowed to die in peace.

25

Eighteen months later

It was a beautiful late summer's day, typical for the Midi. The steamer sailed out of Marseille harbour, destined for its first stop at Alexandria.

Cody's tour of duty in Ireland had lasted a year. The ever-faithful Hardy had stayed with him for almost half of that before deciding to return to civilian life and re-join his family. There had been the occasional contact with Jones and the padre, but no-one else from the 10th Battalion.

Cody was headed for a new life in India, as an estate manager for a maharajah, as it turned out only three hundred miles from where Deborah's husband had been serving. But Deborah never knew that. She had cut off all ties at the same time as Kate.

Cody's wife and country had spurned him. No-one seemed to have had any use for a veteran like himself. He had tried in vain to contact his former colleague captains, and even the colonel and major. None of them had replied. Each had no doubt been coming to terms with their loss of such an intense experience that had left them, like Cody, feeling deeply bereaved. They, too, had no doubt found themselves wrapped up in the difficulties of resuming normal life. It had become everyone for himself.

It had been Kate who had sparked off Cody feeling himself to be an outcast. He had called home on his way to Ireland but had never got further than the doorstep. No doubt still waiting for a sign from Quinn, Kate hadn't hesitated in announcing that she wanted a separation, right away.

"Is it someone else?" he asked.

Kate had immediately replied that there was no-one. But it had sounded too defensive. Little did she yet know that she would find herself waiting longer than she could imagine for her beau.

"And the girls?"

"They're *not* going to Ireland!" she had said.

That was the last time they spoke. She had refused him entry. She had already packed a trunk with his belongings and dragged it down the stairs to remain outside the front door. From that day on, their contact had been through her London solicitor. Nothing had come of Cody's appeals for the right to see his girls. Nothing came of her thinly disguised pleas to stage an *in-flagrante-delicto* to facilitate a divorce.

Casting aside his sorrows, which had taken up his entire time in Ireland, Cody had decided to escape. One day his girls would come and find him.

"Captain Cody?"

"Major, actually."

"The gentleman at the far table is inviting you to join him."

The waiter was vaguely pointing aft, so as not to appear rude. Cody looked across and spotted a bearded man waving at him. He had a smart-looking woman and two young boys at his side. Cody walked across, waiter in tow, wondering who on earth it was.

"Captain!"

The beard had fooled him, but the voice hadn't one bit. It was none other than Hauptmann Gerlich. Gerlich stood up and clicked his heels, and then they shook hands as old friends. Cody couldn't help noticing that Gerlich's benign new face hid most of his scar, not to mention tempered the facial expressions that had once resembled Quinn's.

"This is my wife, Elvira, and those are my twin boys, Steffen and Max. Please, won't you join us?"

The waiter walked back to fetch what Cody had left behind. Gerlich talked about his time as a prisoner of war. By chance, he had been sent to a camp just outside Cambridge.

"I had walked there so many times before. I knew what lay beyond the wire. And you, Cody?"

Cody talked about the last months of the war, his promotion, and his time in Ireland. His marriage and any possibility of soon seeing his girls had evaporated, and, through an advertisement in the London Times calling for an ex-officer, he had found employment in India. He wasn't at all sure what to expect, but the estate he was to look after was greater than the size of Wales.

Gerlich announced he was escaping Germany. The place was falling apart, he said. He was an engineer by training and hoped to find a position in Namibia.

"My employer is looking for an engineer," Cody recalled.

The London recruiting agency had even asked him if he knew anyone.

"*Ach*, but being German I don't think I would be let in," regretted Gerlich.

"Well, the estate is supposed to be independent of British control," assured Cody.

"But not the ports!"

Cody was excited by the idea all the same. He promised to enquire.

For the rest of the voyage, they were both more than happy to stick together. Frau Gerlich, who had auburn hair and was in her mid-thirties, turned out to be delightful and entertaining, and the twins, who were ten, remained polite and permanently well-behaved. Cody enjoyed everyone's dry sense of humour. Frau

Gerlich came across as such a pleasant and homely person that Cody couldn't help thinking how preferable a partner she would have been to Kate.

Once, when they found themselves alone, he congratulated Gerlich on his choice.

"She suffered terribly during the war. It's another reason we're leaving."

Inevitably, they spent many hours ruminating over their recent past. Gerlich had completely dropped the arrogance he had shown at the front. Cody refrained from mentioning the fact that Gerlich's comments had led to the destruction of so many of his compatriots. For his part, Gerlich could not possibly know in what way it had also led to the demise of Quinn and his henchmen.

They talked about Ireland, a neutral subject. For most of his stay, Cody had found himself as acting colonel in a small-town barracks. He had seen only one action of note, when he had stumbled on a rebel convoy in the countryside. No-one had been killed, and the rebels had escaped after abandoning their arms and vehicles.

"It's becoming more serious now," observed Gerlich, spotting the headlines of an English newspaper lying on the next table.

Cody mentioned Major Hughes. He had left for Ireland at the same time, and they had met up. It had been he who had been only too happy to tip Cody off about the India job mention.

"Wished we had served together," he had said.

They talked about lost friends and acquaintances, not only those who had died.

"You must have been constantly thinking about them while you were a prisoner," Cody said.

"*Ach*, you can't imagine, Major," said Gerlich. "And more and more as time went by. They say that any human being needs to bring closure to a drama in his life, to discover why it took place, to find out what happened to others, and what became of them."

"But of course, Hauptmann Gerlich!"

"I now know it's not just about tragic events. It's about everything. When I discovered that I still had savings at home, I hired an old policeman and gave him a list of the men I remembered, the ones that kept coming back to my mind."

"And then?"

"And then nothing! One by one he located them, either their grave, their sanatorium, or their home. Look, I have the list here! I keep staring at it."

He pulled it out of his coat pocket, as though it had been at the ready. It took up several pages. Frau Gerlich, who was with them at that point, rolled her eyes.

"I won't ever do anything with this," he admitted. "It's just a question of tying up loose ends in the mind."

"At least you now know," said Cody.

"*Exakt, herr Major!* At least I now know! No loose ends dangling around, as you would say."

The Gerlich's left to return to their cabin. The newspaper was still lying there on the next table, so Cody stopped the waiter from removing it and helped himself. An article halfway down the second page caught his eye.

'STILL NO CLUE ON SOUTH-COAST MURDER.'

It mentioned a widow called Mrs Quinn and where she had lived. She had been found in her car a year and a half ago, and the police had decided that she had been murdered and were making a last appeal for information. There was a picture of her.

Cody was deeply shocked. He had never heard of the incident. It couldn't have reached the Irish press, and nothing had come from Jones. He thought at once of Mrs Quinn's brother and wanted to send him a belated telegram of condolence. He wondered about the future of the farm. He thought of the five widows and what might become of them.

He went out onto the deck and stood at the side rail. The sun was setting, and it was calm and warm. He wondered who on earth might have done it. Had Quinn's pastime caught up with him? There was no mention of robbery. Barker must have returned to civilian life. The old general must have asked him to join the farm. Cody thought of Corporal Jones. The telegraph office had already closed. He would send him and Barker messages in the morning.

*

It was early morning. The steamer had arrived in the bay of Alexandria during the night, and the engines were silent. Swallows were swooping overhead, but across the water all seemed quiet. The Gerlich family had packed and were huddled together on deck, everyone in their best clothes. Cody had received a note to join them to say goodbye. He still thought it strange that the very last war acquaintance he would likely meet had once been his enemy.

There were a few minutes to go. Gerlich was recalling his last time on a boat.

"Can you imagine how it was when I returned from internment? Everything was upside down."

"I suppose I was lucky to get a sort of halfway house in Ireland," Cody said.

"Halfway house!" Gerlich said as if he had enjoyed the expression, but he said nothing more.

Cody wanted to talk about Barker's sister, but it would mean nothing to Gerlich, and he had not seen much of Quinn either. A loudhailer called for departing passengers to muster. Cody shook hands with them all. He thanked Gerlich for his therapeutic company.

"And yours, Major!"

As everyone waved goodbye, Cody couldn't imagine the journey they were letting themselves in for. He even wondered whether he had heard the truth about what they were up to. At least he had left them his future address.

*

It was weeks later that Cody finally arrived in the small town far from anywhere that would become his place of work. It lay hundreds of miles from the coast. The immediate countryside was fairly flat, with a higher plateau nearby, and there were forests all around. From the very beginning, the almost misty scenery, colours, and smells had seemed very special and alluring.

It was late afternoon, but still scorching hot. Cody was the only white man in sight, but at least most people he encountered were of his own height. The pony and trap that had greeted him at the railhead fifty miles away took him straight to the palace. It stood next to a temple and an open rose garden. The palace was vast in relation to its surroundings and stood a little way back from the busy main road, but it had seen better times and badly needed repair and a fresh coat of paint. Parked on the bare ground in front was a large, covered Rolls-Royce.

Cody tipped the trap driver whom he assumed was in the employ of the estate. In the background, in the main street beyond the railings, he could hear music. He wondered if he would get used to such cacophony. As he gazed at the creeper-infested balconies in front of him, two servants descended the twenty steps to take his bags.

A third man emerged just behind them. He was impeccably dressed in white and appeared handsome. It had to be the maharajah himself. He seemed much younger than Cody had expected, in his early thirties, and as skinny and short as most of his compatriots. He was evidently relieved at the sight of his new employee.

"Welcome, Major!"

He sounded as though he too had been educated in England.

"You can't imagine how happy I am to see you at last!"

The first thing Cody learned was that his predecessor, an Englishman who had hailed from the India Civil Service, had been fatally mauled by a tiger four months before. His business affairs for the estate were in a mess and would take months to set right.

"You'll need to travel a lot, Major," the maharajah warned. "And avoid the malarial areas at all costs."

That, Cody learned, had provoked the demise of his predecessor's predecessor. The maharajah introduced his private secretary who would accompany Cody to his bungalow, half-a-mile north along the main street from the palace. It would be he who would introduce him to the rest of the establishment and his job in the morning.

"And keep your guard with you at all times!"

The maharajah was pointing to a stuffed tiger head hanging on the wall next to a bear and a bison.

"Join me for dinner tomorrow night, will you?"

The small bungalow came with a servant who slept under a mosquito net on the back porch. He spoke a smattering of English, enough for Cody to understand what he would be eating for that night, a choice between chicken and eggs.

"My name is Ahmed, Dewan sir!"

Cody wasn't sure what protocol allowed for. He certainly wasn't a dewan. For the time being, 'sir' would have to do.

Before he started unpacking, Cody set up his gramophone, which had arrived in advance with his main luggage, wound it up and played a disc. It was Elgar again.

Ahmed screwed up his face.

"Don't you like it, Ahmed?" Cody asked.

Ahmed was reluctant to speak his mind. He appeared shocked. Cody's predecessor had had no such contraption.

"I tell you what, Ahmed," Cody said to keep the peace, "I'll only play it when it suits you. How's that?"

"On Fridays would be fine, sir," said Ahmed, looking quite meek, hoping that Cody would not catch on to his ploy.

Cody decided not to object. He would give it time. Nobody could hold out against delightful music for long. He dreaded having to be subjected to the local noise he had heard earlier on. It sounded made in hell.

His bedroom turned out to be unbearably stifling, even with the shutters wide open, so during the night he pulled out some cushions and set up a net next to the servant.

Breakfast was fad, which suited him to the ground, and the coffee was excellent. The servant had no doubt been well trained. The bungalow came with a bicycle, and at a quarter to nine Cody peddled his way to his office, which he knew lay next to the palace. The street was already swarming with people, street sellers, and every kind of non-motorised vehicle known to man. There were stalls selling meat and fish, and elephants seemed to be all over the place. So far, it looked as though the maharajah had the only car in town.

Just before he arrived, beyond the rows of dwellings to his right, there was open land. Cody realised that there was a lake with mango groves close by.

The maharajah's secretary was waiting for him. He was seated at the large table in front of what would become Cody's desk. While they drank tea, the secretary described the small town. It had five thousand residents, a balance of Hindus and Muslims.

"The maharajah has had second thoughts. He will be joining us in a while."

"No British here?" asked Cody.

"No British, sir!" confirmed the secretary with a chuckle. "There is a liaison officer who comes from time to time from Waltair. He drives around in a lorry. You will meet him in a few weeks."

"Is the maharajah married?"

For an instant, Cody feared he might have gone too far.

"There's a maharani, Major, and two young daughters. They're presently visiting her family in Madras."

He explained the maharajah had received his title the year before. There had been a memorable ceremony with fireworks to celebrate, and a gun salute by the palace guard of forty. Some British officials had attended.

"It came as part of the birthday list," he said.

Cody was wondering whose birthday list was being referred to, as the estate was supposedly independent, when the maharajah strode in and asked Cody if he had slept well.

"I'll get used to it, sir!"

When he explained where he had slept, the maharajah laughed,

"I'm afraid you've just missed the monsoon season," he said.

Saying nothing about how Cody should behave towards his servant, he unfolded a map he had brought with him and laid it out on the table.

"That's where you will find the nearest white face."

The town he was pointing to was a hundred miles away. Oddly enough, he said, the town where they were had the remnants of a Christian cemetery. It dated back fifty years, to the time when the British troops last occupied the region. The graves were swept down once a year.

"We remain gloriously independent now," the maharajah said. "The malaria was too much for them!"

Cody decided once and for all not to ask about the birthday list. In the end, the three of them spent the entire day together, during which Cody furiously took notes. Late morning, they drove ten miles to a village along a rough road that entered the forest. People stopped all the way to watch the Rolls driven by the maharajah himself.

As they sat down in the local administrative office, the maharajah explained, with rather more insight than might have his secretary, the structure of his organisation and the process for collecting local taxes that needed constant engagement. An employee brought them food for a working lunch.

When they got back later in the afternoon, the maharajah summarised Cody's responsibilities and introduced him to the most important outstanding business that had to be attended to. By the time he and the maharajah were to have dinner together, Cody was quite exhausted. The persistent heat wasn't helping.

"You'll find life here very relaxed," the maharajah said as he poured Cody an Irish whiskey, thinking it would make him feel less disorientated. "Normally, I wouldn't have come to see you for days, to let you settle in first. But my finances are in a bad way. I need you to get things back on track as soon as possible. You'll discover that I'm owed several lakhs."

He mentioned that Cody's main adjutant would be the chief accountant. He was a local, and he had just joined the estate's service after attending college in Waltair.

"I know his family well," the maharajah assured him.

It prompted Cody to ask when he would meet his team. The maharajah promised he would come in person in the morning to make it happen.

"They are all good people as well, Major," he said. "But you must be constantly behind them. That's why I asked for a military man."

Cody was hungry enough to appreciate the curry that the servants brought in.

"I'm afraid the food here is not exciting," the maharajah said. "Your Ahmed won't help much either."

They paused talking business in order to eat. The maharajah talked about his pastimes. He rarely ventured outside the estate, he admitted, but his passion within it was tiger hunting. He promised Cody that as soon he had settled in, he would take him along.

"We'll go out for a week or two," he said. "Have you ever ridden an elephant?"

The maharajah explained he had a stable with veterinary staff, as well as someone in charge of all the elephants on the estate. But Cody was almost asleep by then. His shirt was clinging to his body despite the late hour. He wasn't yet sure if he would ever get used to the heat.

*

Cody had slept once again on the porch that night. Ahmed, who had snored most of the time, had happily accepted to move to the bed inside. It had allowed him to prepare breakfast without waking up Cody.

It was half-past nine. Cody cycled to the office, making note that it was already too hot, and that in future he would try leaving before eight instead. The chaotic scene on the way in now seemed a little more familiar and less shocking.

The maharajah had not yet arrived, so Cody decided he would introduce himself to his staff. He entered the large office, which was one floor down from his own. Everyone stood up in unison. They were all male and dressed in trousers and open white shirts.

"Good morning, everybody!"

"Good morning, Major!"

They all sat down again, and he went around shaking hands, asking people's names and what they did. He caught on that one of them appeared to consider himself his factotum and insisted on following him around, and so he asked him to lead the way and write everyone's name down. The man took to his task with envy.

There were twenty employees and every one of them could speak good English. One or two mentioned Cody had five similar offices around the estate, and that those were where they expected him to travel most. The factotum fetched a map to show him.

From what he was being told by each person he met, Cody had the impression that he was being introduced to his team in reverse order of seniority. As he made his way from one desk to the next, he saw they were encircling a small glass cubicle in the centre of the office, stalking a tiger as it were. Inside, he spotted a man whose dark head of hair was being illuminated by a ray of light coming from a small hole in the roof. It seemed odd.

"Don't we get rain here?" he asked the factotum, pointing to the hole.

"It will get repaired in time, Major, sir," said the person whose desk they happened to be approaching.

Cody thought back to what the maharajah had warned him about chasing people. The buckets still on the floor confirmed that there must have been problems during the monsoon. He assumed that he would have to remind them of any promise several times at least before anything happened.

Every now and again, the man in the cubicle sneaked a glance in Cody's direction. After almost a quarter of an hour of trying to avoid an accidental meeting of eyes, and the maharajah having still not arrived, they finally led Cody into the cubicle. It was even hotter than the rest of the office.

"And this is your chief accountant," the factotum said. "He is your right-hand man."

As the factotum took off to fetch a fan to cool them both down, the chief accountant obligingly got up from behind his desk. He abandoned his spot of light, and Cody could see that he was sweating as much as himself. He was unusually tall. Cody noticed he seemed to swagger as he skirted the desk. As he offered his wet hand, he couldn't help noticing the man's prominent square jaw.

But it was his soft and arrogant-sounding voice that sealed it. It was identical to Quinn's.

Printed in Great Britain
by Amazon

18490473R00139